A Powerfu

F

By John C Hardinge

1116 27 August 1942

Tanaka's intervention force of heavy cruisers *Myoko, Nachi, Haguro* and *Mikuma*, light cruiser *Kitikami* and destroyers *Yugumo, Makigumo* and *Kazagumo* had assembled at Rabual. Their mission was to try and crush the American landings with a night attack. Privately Tanaka considered this a very dangerous assignment. The beachhead was well protected and even at 25 knots was eight hours steaming away. That meant that they would be returning to Rabaul in daylight, within range of U.S carriers. Even considering they had been promised air support on the return leg, it seemed a dicey affair.

0252 28 August 1942

Tanaka had started encountering enemy ships almost an hour ago near Laruma Point and had changed his formation to line ahead and hugged the coast as much as possible, slowing down to 12 knots in an effort to reduce his wake as much as possible. It had apparently paid off as so far there had been no sign that he had been detected by the enemy. He was now passing the village of Torokina and would have no choice but to leave the shoreline and sail out into Empress Augusta Bay. He had little doubt that would mean detection; however, all his ships were closed up for action and a solid phalanx of enemy ships was starting to show in the region of Gazelle Bay, eight to ten thousand yards away.

0316 28 August 1942

Sure enough, Tanaka's force was detected at 0257. However, Tanaka had been able to make use of the confusion caused by his appearance amongst the allied to ships to wreak a little bit of havoc. Most allied ships had come to life fairly quickly after the alarm had been raised, however, one cruiser remained stationary almost from the start. Hamstrung slightly by his line ahead formation, his ships each reached a launch point, firing as they came with their forward armament, turned broadside on launch and retreated after a 150-degree battle turn. All had now completed their attacks and were now heading out of Empress Augusta Bay, having placed 64 torpedoes in the water after them.

Whilst his lead ships, the light cruiser *Kitikami* and his flagship *Mikuma* had not taken any damage at all, those ships further down the line had reported hits from 8-inch shells. However, hits had also been obtained on the surprise enemy and the stationary ship, as well as the other nearest it, had taken multiple torpedo hits.

0320 28 August 1942

Rear Admiral Lee's force, consisting of the battleships *North Carolina* and *Pacifica*, carriers *Langley* and *Australasia*, three light cruisers and seven destroyers, was cruising off Torokina, 20 miles to sea. He quickly heard about the attack via radio from the USS Quincy. Realizing the Japanese were likely to be heading back the way they came very soon, his first priority was to close the coast to increase their own radar coverage and assist the forces in Empress Augusta Bay and also cut off any possible escape for the Japanese force.

0338 28 August 1942

Both battleships had picked up the enemy force coming out of Empress Augusta Bay, what was seemingly the second to rear ship faintly visible at the distance of 10,000 yards as it was afire. Lee had detached the two carriers. Australasia could launch a night strike with her ASV equipped aircraft at a later stage but right at the moment he did not want any noise or lights. It was time to string a little trap of their own. Once the range dropped down to 9,000 yards both battleships were going to commence firing, *North Carolina* at the first target, *Pacifica* at the second. Once they opened up, all five of his destroyers would fire their own torpedo loads, as would the light cruisers *San Juan, Launceston* and *Hobart*, targeting the middle of the enemy line.

0352 28 August 1942

With the second enemy salvo slamming into *Mikuma* at less than 9,000 yards, two 14-inch shells had hit the bridge, blowing part of it over the side of the heavy cruiser. Hit again repeatedly in the next few minutes, the ship had rapidly become a barely navigable wreck. The light cruiser *Kitikami*, hit multiple times by 16-inch shells, had sunk in less than 10 minutes. Other ships had also suffered, most particularly the heavy cruiser *Nachi*, which had taken a torpedo that had blown part of her bow off and been hit multiple times by 6 inch and 5 inch shells, starting numerous fires that had caused her Captain to dump the vulnerable long lance torpedoes.

With Tanaka dead aboard Mikuma and the Task Force leaderless, it seemed that the whole Japanese force may be overwhelmed, however, what saved what remained of the Task Force can be attributed to Captain Mori Tomoichi, who ordered Myoko and his own Haguro to launch their remaining twelve torpedoes. It was this that finally caused the allies to sheer off when one found a home in *HMAS Pacifica*. Under fire by *USS North Carolina*, the Japanese finally disconnected with the allied fleet at 0413, leaving the struggling destroyer *Yagumo*, restricted to 14 knots and the crippled *Nachi* behind. The *Mikuma*, hit multiple times by shells ranging from 16 inch and 14 inch to 6 and 5 inch was already a sinking, immobile wreck.

0506 28 August 1942

Lt Commander Peter Reynolds nine ASV equipped Swordfish, accompanied by six Defiants had detected the two ships at 0442, making slow headway. The first Swordfish had descended, dropping flares over the two ships. The Defiants attacked first, scattering 20lb incendiaries all over the heavy cruiser, gaining six hits from 48 bombs and starting fires that nicely illuminated the ship. The remaining eight Swordfish attacked directly, not bothering with a hammer and anvil against the crippled cruiser. Hit by three torpedoes, she had gone down quickly.

0608 28 August 1942

Despite the damage inflicted on the Japanese, dawn brought a tale of woe to the allied forces around Bougainville, thought Rear Admiral Lee. *HMAS Pacifica* was on her way back to Tulagi for temporary repairs. Thankfully hit on the thickest part of the anti-torpedo bulge, she was none the less severely hurt on the incredible power of the Japanese torpedo. Other ships were not so fortunate. The heavy cruiser *USS Chicago*, hit three times by Japanese torpedoes, had slowly capsized and sank. The *Vincennes*, hit twice near the stern had suffered a similar fate only six minutes ago. The destroyer *Blue,* hit once, had broken in half and sunk, as had the thankfully empty transport *Ramsay*, hit by a torpedo at the end of its run.

In regards to damaged ships, the destroyer *Wilson* had her bow detached by a Japanese torpedo and, like *Pacifica*, was on her way to Tulagi. Joining her were the heavy cruisers *USS Quincy* and *Astoria*, both suffering from 5 inch and 8-inch shell hits.

0616 28 August 1942

The dawn had finally arrived, much to Captain Mori Tomoichi fears. His force, pushing at almost 30 knots, now consisted of only two heavy cruisers and three destroyers. He was only half way back to Rabaul. Thankfully all five modern ships had no propulsion damage, although at least two of the destroyers had taken hits. It was air attack that he now feared, although he had radioed Rabaul in regards to his situation and they had promised strong air support.

1024 28 August 1942

By the time the allies had completed search and rescue operations and sorted out the priority in regards to their own damaged ships, it was not until 0650 that they started preparations for a counter strike. This was immediately put on hold only 12 minutes later by the radar picket destroyer Blue radioing a detection of an incoming hostile raid.

Both carriers moved their CAP out to meet the oncoming raid, soon revealed when intercepted some 28 miles out to be six J1N Irvings, escorted by three A6M's. Upon detection, the force immediately turned tail and fled and no kills were obtained. By the time these various delays had occurred, a small strike from each carrier did not depart until 0758 and were delayed again in a protracted operation to sink the destroyer *Yagumo*, which, even lamed, was missed eleven times in a row by dive bombers making deliberate attacks until finally struck by three out of the next five, finishing her off.

With early morning reconnaissance showing that they would have to pursue the Japanese fleet to perhaps within 40 nautical miles of Rabaul to attack, it was decided to call off any further strikes and concentrate on today's main mission, hitting the main Japanese troop concentration at Arawa and the Japanese forces advancing through Panguna to follow the Jaba River (with its many native huts) to the landing area.

1604 29 August 1942

Although the air strikes had failed completely and largely gutted much of the Rabual air wing, thought Yamamoto, at least the surface force had secured a victory, sinking one battleship and four cruisers, as well as destroyers and three or four transports, even if at some cost.

The problem he had as these attacks needed to be followed up, yet he had little to follow up with, at least immediately. It would now be up to the troops on both Bougainville and Buka, the northernmost island, to hold on until he could intervene.

It would take perhaps another two to three weeks and he could sail a fleet from Japan of four carriers, *Kaga, Hiyo, Junyo* and *Shoho*, possibly even the escort carrier *Taiyo*. If he combined that with the transfer of some of his anti-shipping forces from Malaya, he may be able to break the allies.

2225 31 August 1942

Rear Admiral Charles Lockwood, USN, commanding all allied submarines in the South West

Pacific area, looked over the data provided by the second test. It was as conclusive as the first, but in a different way. Lockwood had ordered a net test at Frenchman's Bay, near Albany on 20 June 1942. Using the *USS Skipjack*, a full load of torpedoes was fired and, for comparison, the old Dutch Submarine *K9*, now RAN manned, fired six as well. Whereas the RAN torpedoes ran true, the Mark 14's ran an average of 11 ft deeper than set. Only one torpedo of the entire batch ran at the actual setting it was set at, all other running deep to some degree.

Today's test had been at West Cape, near Albany as well. The objective this time was to test the exploders on the torpedoes and the high straight cliffs offered the perfect vantage point. This required live warheads, and the results were again startling. Of the fifteen torpedoes fired, only five had properly exploded. Some other had exploded prematurely, other had hit but not exploded. More data would be obtained when divers recovered some of the unexploded fish, but the conclusions were all too obvious. The old *K9* had again participated, firing six fish, five of which functioned perfectly.

He owed it to his men to push this to the highest level, having gotten nowhere with Bu Ord. In fact, with Admiral King's support, eventually changes were made, however, it was not until February/March 1943 the first of the new torpedoes, renamed Mark 14A were sent to war. "After thirteen months of war, the three major defects of the Mark 14 torpedo had at last been isolated, always over the stubborn opposition of the Bureau of Ordnance. The fourth defect, a tendency to run circular, was never fixed, although thankfully this was not a common occurrence. The Mark 15 carried by destroyers had collars to prevent circular runs, but the Mark 14 was never given this feature.

1314 5 September 1942

Major General Vandegrift was pleased. His marines had advanced down the Jaba River and had captured Panguna on the 4th. His forces had been contacted by and joined by Forsyth's 9th Independent Company, which had provided him with some lovely detailed maps of the main Japanese dispositions on the island. The main Japanese concentrations were at the capital Arawa and around the half-constructed airfield at Kieta. He was now less than four miles from both. He had enjoyed almost complete air superiority, the Japanese air activity now being restricted to small raid of 3-4 aircraft, although one such raid had sunk a US destroyer two days ago. The bulk of the transports had been withdrawn and the focus of naval activity would soon shift to the East Coast to support the drive on Arawa.

1708 6 September 1942

The carrier landing trials of the F4U, conducted on the two newest USN carriers, *CV Lafayette* and *CVE Sangamon*, had not been a startling success. Pilots spoke disparaging of the aircraft's landing characteristics and the issues were even more magnified on the much smaller *Sangamon*.

The aircraft had a tendency to be overly "springy", bouncing badly on landing and the other main problem on landing was visibility. The cockpit, placed well to the rear and the long heavy nose made for poor landing visibility and a tendency to dip in the nose during landing. The landing gear issues were largely solved during early 1943, and the planes great characteristics, in particular it's great speed, made it a war winner. However, it always remained a difficult aircraft for a beginner and a hard aircraft to handle at low speeds.

It had failed it's carrier qualification trials, at least initially, however, with 180 already manufactured and production continuing, it was released to the Marine Corps on the 22 September for deployment, where it's landing characteristics would be less of an issue from land based bases.

0605 9 September 1942

The Task Force slipped out of Norfolk on the first leg of a long journey to the Pacific, consisting of *BB South Dakota, BB Washington, CV Lafayette, CL Cleveland*, two new *Gleaves Class* DD's, a Benson Class DD and three old "four stackers".

As Admiral King, who had turned up in the early hours to wish their commanders well personally, thought, he hoped they would do well. The Pacific would have a lull in reinforcements now until early 1943, with new ships coming on line in the next two months earmarked for Operation Torch in early November. With the British battling to hold the Afrika Corps in North Africa, it was badly needed to divert the Germans and their Italian allies' attention. It was also hoped Operation Thunderball, scheduled for mid-October, would also put a crimp in the German's plans. The units of B-24's were building up in North Africa now and the lengthening of airfields in Crete was well underway. With the Russians seemingly just hanging on in Stalingrad, every avenue to hurt the enemy must be explored.

1535 16 September 1942

Vandegrift's marines had reached the beach at Arawa on the 14th, his units then surviving a howling Banzai change by more than 800 Japanese that very night, which had flung the Americans back out of their newly won positions, only to retake then against the weakened Japanese by day on the 15th. His men had now dug in and had effectively cut the island in half, with the bulk of the Japanese troops trapped in the Southern part of the island. At this stage follow up landings had been prepared for the 22nd, using the Americal Division to land on Torau Bay, near the Southeast tip of the island, trapping the bulk of the Japanese between both forces. He was near the airfield at Kieta, but considering the Japanese would be unlikely to complete it within the next two weeks, he had halted and dug in. If they wanted to do more work on it for its soon to be new owners, he was fine with that.

1850 18 September 1942

Vice Admiral Nishizō Tsukahara had been recalled to take command of this mission from his previous post as Commander of the 11th Air Fleet. He had four carriers to commit to try and break the U.S hold on Bougainville, as well as the battleships *Kirishima* and *Hiei* and would pick up a heavy cruiser division at Truk. After refuelling there, he would strike at the U.S fleet around Bougainville. With all the remaining operational carriers of the IJN under his command, he could not afford to lose.

2343 21 September 1942

He had driven up from Point Cook and spent the day at Fred David's house In Kew. David was the chief designer for Commonwealth Aircraft Corporation and they had discussed the projects they currently had on the table ahead of Wednesday's aviation conference, chaired by Keith Park. For Heinkel, it was all about aircraft manufacture at present, not new designs, although their He 100 had had to be remodelled to accommodate the new Merlin 61, which was being retrofitted to some machines. CAC were modelling up a new long-range land-based escort fighter, but this was also in its infancy.

1202 23 September 1942

Vice Admiral Nishizō Tsukahara's Task Force had made its way to Truk without incident. At this stage they planned to depart at 1830 tomorrow to intervene at Bougainville. Tsukahara well recognised the need for caution, as he controlled all the IJN's seaboard air power, however, a victory needed to obtained.

1418 23 September 1942

Major General Alexander Patch's 23rd Infantry Division, also known as the Americal Division, had landed in Southern Bougainville yesterday to only scattered resistance and had quickly established a beachhead, which tomorrow they would attempt to advance out of. Well supported by air power and naval gunfire, they had taken limited casualties so far. Now it was a matter of closing the trap on the Japanese the bulk of whom were now isolated in the Southern part of the island.

1808 24 September 1942

Keith Park had expounded at length upon the RAAF and it's need for aircraft, giving detailed figures as to the number of aircraft in service and needed., broken down by type. It was quite illuminating and would be a challenge for all three major Australasian manufacturers. It read as follows:

Fighters:
Bell P39 18(Salvaged from USAAF write offs)
Brewster Buffalo 12(Ex Dutch East Indies)
CAC Boomerang 165(62 more to be manufactured to complete production run)
Curtis P40 93(234 more to come via Lend Lease)
Hawker Demon 44(Obsolete)
Hawker Hurricane 2(Ex Dutch East Indies)
Hencall He 112 168
Hencall He 100 442(Currently in production-numbers count RAN machines)
Hencall He 119 57(Currently in production)

Republic P43 61
TOTAL 972 NEED 1500

There were also 388 CAC Wirraways, trainers and not really fighters but pressed into use as such on occasions.

Bombers/Patrol:
Avro Anson 536
Blackburn Skua 18
Bolton Paul Defiant 32
CAC Woomera 2(unused prototypes)
Consolidated Catalina 68
Dornier Do 24 6(ex Dutch East Indies)
Douglas A20 39(12 ex Dutch East Indies)
Fairy Swordfish 98
Grumman Avenger 0(200 ordered)
Hencall He 70 34
Hencall He 111 63
Hencall He 211 16(in production)
Lockheed Hudson 142
North American A36 0(200 ordered)
North American B25 24
Supermarine Seagull 28(Obsolete)
Vickers Vildebeest 33(Obsolete)
Vickers Wellington 46
Vultee Vengeance 24(276 more to come under Lend Lease)
Westland Wapiti 29(Obsolete)

TOTAL 1243 NEED 1800

As Park had stressed, they were still short on their aircraft needs, with many of the types currently in service, particularly those in Australasia, obsolete types, particularly the Anson. More need to be done, but some of the shortfall would clearly have to be made up by purchasing and/or lead lease. Thankfully, over 900 aircraft were expected to flow over the next three months, half by purchase, half by lend lease. Meanwhile, production would concentrate on the Wirraway as an advanced trainer, the He 100 and 119 as fighters and He 211 as a bomber.

TRANSPORTS
Airspeed Oxford 262
De Havilland Dragon 101
Douglas DC 2 9
Junkers Ju 52 5
Wackett Garnet 6

TOTAL 371 NEED 800

With a desperate need for transports, manufacture of Boomerangs would cease and license production of the C47 transport would start, using the same engine, the twin Wasp.

2149 24 September 1942

Halsey had the report from the *USS Drum* in his hand. The submarine, whilst out of position and unable to attack had reported three enemy carriers plus at least one battleship having left Truk two hours ago. That would put them in a position to intervene, most probably on the morning of the 27th September, perhaps late on the 26th. It would be too late for the *Lafayette* group, not expected at Tonga until the 3rd October. He would have to fight the battle with his existing assets.

In the meantime he issued an alert to all air units in the Solomons and also New Guinea, in case they diverted to Rabaul. He would contact Kenney to see if extra search assets could be re-tasked or rebased to Tulagi to assist the Catalinas there. He had set a meeting of all senior staff for tomorrow 0700 to discuss the situation.

1646 25 September 1942

In fact the conference aboard *Ranger* did not commence until 1400, by the time the *Yorktown* and Spruance, as well as other ships under replenishment at Tulagi, had been recalled to the combat zone at Bougainville. How Halsey wished he had more access to air assets, however, *Lafayette* was too far way, the small Australasian carrier *Christchurch* was under refit and *Melbourne* and *Sydney* were at Fremantle, preparing for an aircraft ferry mission to Timor.

By consensus, he had agreed with Ray Spruance that they should combine their Task Groups to try and maximise their air defence. They would also withdraw today the support ships back to Tulagi. It would create some hardships and logistical problems for U.S troops on the island, but many of the main transports were due to leave today anyway. Only the supply ships were due to stay on station. What was not unloaded before 1900 was to leave with the ships. Although the covering force had lost the *Pacifica* damaged, as well as two U.S heavy cruisers sunk and two damaged, two were still left that could be kept on station.

The *Australasia* and *Langley* would stay as a "slow" group and he had added the small carrier *HMAS Albatross* as well, as she had been a Tulagi on an aircraft ferry mission.

In the finish he was left with a force of:

Fast Group(Halsey)(all USN ships)
CV Ranger, Yorktown
BB North Carolina
CA Pensacola, Salt Lake City, Northampton, Chester, Portland, New Orleans, San Francisco
CLAA San Diego, San Juan
16 DD

Slow Group(Collins)
CV Australasia
CVE Langley, Albatross
CA Dunedin
CL Launceston, Hobart,
CLAA Tromp, Jacob Van Heemskirk
12 DD(5 US)

He had kept little at Tulagi, just the seaplane carrier *Curtis*, the Australasian monitor *Gorgon* and cruiser/minelayer *Adelaide*, five DD's and six Australasian corvettes.

1125 17 April 2014(flash forward)

Maree Drake Brockman contemplated the border changes since pre World War 2, first looking at the pre 1939 map with the Colonial Empires on it and now at today's map. Substantial changes for sure, with the collapse of the old imperial systems and the growth of regional security and cooperation, with the exception of certain rogue states such as North Korea and Manchuria and crisis like the current in Ukraine. Australasia's biggest trading partner today was Japan, strange to ay after the events of World War 2, even though her strongest strategic alliance was still with the U.S.

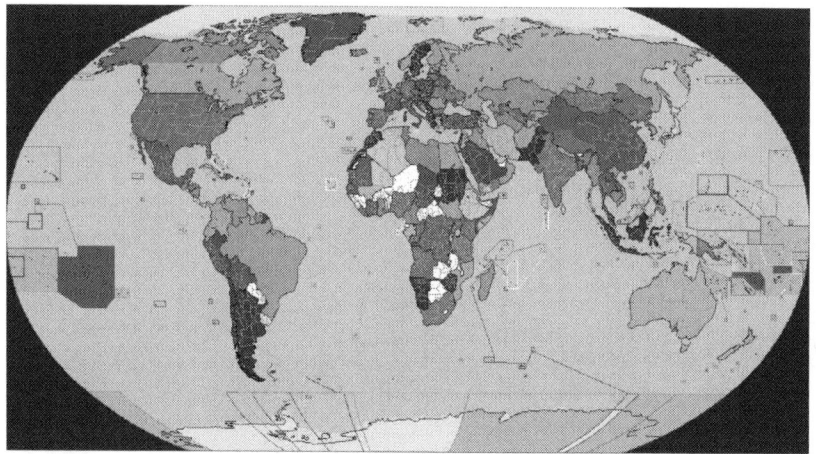

1908 26 September 1942

He would be in a position to put planes in the air at first light, thought Tsukahara. He was worried about the composition of his air crews, a "them and us" type arrangements with veteran crews aboard the *Kaga* and *Shoho*, however, the two new carriers *Hiyo* and *Junyo* were mostly green pilots leavened with just a few experienced hands.

Rabaul had been reinforced with 36 G4M's and 14 A6M's of the Genzen air group to assist in the operation. As he was well aware from previous encounters, it would all depend on the first spot in the morning. He had some sort of advantage there. Although it had required the expenditure of two precious high-altitude recon aircraft, both of which had been intercepted before a third had gotten through, it seemed the enemy fleet was still off the South West Coast of Bougainville. They seemingly had five carriers in two groups, far more than he had expected.

0452 27 September 1942

With Spruance urging caution, Haley had withdrawn the fleet to where it could still be within easy range of Bougainville yet at the same time enjoy more air support from both Guadalcanal and New Georgia. Currently they were steaming an almost triangular course between Shortland and Vella Lavella Islands, with Choisuel being the apex of the triangle. With an extensive array of Australasian coast watchers on Choisel, it should provide extra insurance of early warning, along with radar and air patrols.

By withdrawing he had placed himself well within the air envelope of even the shorter land-based fighters from Guadalcanal. Between it and Munta Point he could boast three squadrons of P-39's, two of Wildcats, one of Kittyhawks, one of P-43's and one of He 119's, over 100 fighters, in addition to bombers to the tune of two B-17 and three B-26 squadrons. Tulagi had been reinforced with a second squadron of Catalinas, some of whom were unaccountably on patrol already. Come dawn they would be supplemented with patrols from pairs of B-17's.

1136 27 September 1942

With the first Japanese search plane, a G4M being shot down by a flight of three P39's before it could deliver a full contact report, it was not until a huge H8K "Emily" Flying Boat that fought off three P40's whilst radioing a contact report back to Rabaul that the two allied fleets was finally spotted, two groups thirty miles apart. By the time this information reached Tsukahara in was three minutes past midday. He immediately gave orders to prepare a large strike. Operating 180 miles Northeast North of Torau Bay, he was currently perhaps 230 miles from the allied ships and would use the intervening time to close the range. There could be only one strike today. By 1309, he had also been found and spotted by U.S heavy bombers, who attacked without scoring any hits, but delayed his strike preparation.

1452 27 September 1942

Vice Admiral Tsukahara, normally a patient man, had almost lost it with the newly formed CarDiv 2, berating both carriers CO's. Whilst the well drilled crews of *Kaga* and *Shoho* had a strike containing 23 A6M's, 29 B5N's and 27 D3A's away at 1405, it had taken until 1449 for the tardy CarDiv2 to put up 26 A6M's, 12 B5N's and 23 D3A's. Tsukahara, well aware he had been spotted had been frantic to get the aircraft off the carriers. Thankfully, that, at least, had occurred. As it was, it would be near sunset before the stragglers would return.

1504 27 September 1942

The Genzen Air Group, reinforced with local forces from Rabaul, had a strike aloft for an hour as they headed South in search of the U.S heavy ships. Consisting of 51 G4M's and 23 A6M's, it was a formidable force that should reach the target area in the next 45 minutes to an hour. Lt Commander Harima hoped they would have better results than previously, when they had been harshly dealt with and caused no damage of note.

1508 27 September 1942

The smooth operation of the trained allied carrier crews had resulted in the decks being cleared off all carriers by 1448, the two large carriers putting up a huge strike of 55 Dauntless and 28 Avengers, escorted by 26 Wildcats. It was followed by a smaller strike of lower performance aircraft from the smaller carriers, 24 Swordfish, 12 Devastators and nine Defiants, escorted by nine He 100's and 9 Wildcats.

Halsey had ordered the two Task Forces to close up and they were now steaming only eight miles apart. A maximum effort was being undertaken by the two land bases to station as many aircraft over the two Task Forces as possible for CAP, so much so that a strike on either airfield would have dire consequences.

1539 27 September 1942

It had been the first strike from *Kaga* and *Shoho*, containing 23 A6M's, 29 B5N's and 27 D3A's that had arrived first. Alerted by coast watchers and sighted by radar 39 miles out, it had been intercepted by CAP 18 miles from the allied ships. Fully thirty Wildcats and six He 100's made the interception and the Japanese were forced to fight their way through.

In a running battle later joined by 12 more Wildcats, three more He 100's and three He 112's, the Japanese strike was gradually worn down, losing 10 A6M's, seven B5N's and ten D3A's for the loss of eleven Wildcats, a He 112 and three He 100's before arriving over the allied ships.

However, whilst the allied fighters had expected more support from land-based planes, when they battled their way back to the ships, nothing but empty skies greeted them. Losing five more strike aircraft to a large AA barrage, the mostly veterans of Car Div 1, ably led by Mitsuo Fuchida on what would be his final combat mission, conducted a perfect hammer and anvil attack on Spruance's *Yorktown*. Hit by three torpedoes and then three bombs, she was badly crippled, left stationary and burning. *Ranger*, targeted by only the last six dive bombers and only five torpedo bombers, escaped unscathed.

1554 27 September 1942

In fact, the allied land-based fighters had been drawn off by the appearance of the Genzen air group from Rabaul, which was intercepted at 1538 22 miles out. It's 50 G4M's (one having to turn back due to engine troubles) and 23 A6M's encountered a wall of allied fighters, 12 He 119's, 22 P39's and 14 Wildcats. Whilst the Wildcats and 10 P39's held off the Zeros, losing six fighters in exchange for eight Zeros, the He 119's, with their four 20mm cannon and the remaining 12 P39's, with one 37mm cannon and six machine guns, had a field day with the Japanese bombers, shooting down 22 for the loss of a single P39 and a single He 119 damaged so badly it had to ditch. Fighting their way through to the allied ships, they attacked the first targets available, Collins "slow group". There they ran into six He 100 and a He 112, which, although low on ammunition, downed another five bombers and one Zero in quick time for the loss of a single He 100.

However, the remaining 23 G4M's although badly rattled, conducted an attack on both the USS Langley and the HMAS Albatross, scoring one torpedo hit on each, losing another two aircraft to AA and another to fighters, as well as another A6M, on their retreat. Although cut to pieces, they had achieved a result.

1558 27 September 1942

If Vice Admiral Tsukahara had been briefly buoyed by reports of the damage inflicted by both his carriers and the land-based strike from Rabaul, it was a brief moment only, for the size of the strike that had appeared over his ships was huge, estimated at over a hundred aircraft. His CAP was only 32 A6M's, nine of those launching very late and would struggle to gain height enough to intercept any dive bombers.

1614 27 September 1942

The 55 Dauntless, led by Lt Commander Oscar Pedersen of the Yorktown, escorted by 17 Wildcats made their attack runs first. Twenty-three Zeros engaged the allied aircraft, however, a good ten of these were novice pilots and in exchange for shooting down six Wildcats and five Dauntless, lost eleven of their number before the remaining U.S planes were cleared through. Losing only two aircraft to AA fire with another two forced to break off with damage, that left a frighteningly high number to attack the Japanese ships(46).

By the time they had finished their attacks, Kaga had been hit once, Hiyo three times and Junyo fully four times, the last two carriers with serious fires and damage. It was then the turn of the torpedo bombers. Engaged firstly by nine Zeros, but with five again novice pilots, they lost two of the nine defending Wildcats and three Avengers in exchange for five Zeros. Japanese AA fire was very effective, forcing two Avengers to break off and shooting three more down, however, that still left 20 aircraft. These hit both the Junyo and the Hiyo once each, six aircraft concentrating on the so far unmolested Shoho missing, continuing the light carrier charmed life. As Pederson turned away, he could be confident that two carriers at least were badly damaged or possibly finished. Either way, they promised to be sitting ducks for the second strike.

1626 27 September 1942

The second Japanese strike had caught the allies somewhat on the hop. With three carriers damaged and the land based planes in retreat and much of the CAP trying to land on, the response to the Japanese raid was nowhere near as vigorous as to the two previous raids.

The only land based fighters still over the ships were the long range He 119's and it was these planes, ten in total that intercepted the Japanese 14 miles out. Even with the inexperience of the Japanese pilots, they were badly outnumbered and lost three machines in exchange for four Zeros and only a single D3A.

Arriving over the Task Force, the 23 A6M's, 12 B5N's and 22 D3A's were again intercepted by 18 Wildcats and four He 100's. Losing seven Zeros, three B5N's and four D3A's in exchange for a He 100 and three Wildcats, the inexperienced Japanese pilots were advantaged by the allies low ammunition stocks.

Led ably by the experienced Lt Commander Fukhodome, the B5N's scored yet another torpedo hit on *Yorktown*, by Fukhodome himself, losing two planes to AA including their leader. A lone plane, attacking the almost stationary *Albatross*, scored a hit as well, boring in to 700 yards before release.

The D3A's concentrating on *Langley* and *Australasia*, hit the former, damaged and lamed twice and the later once, losing two aircraft to AA fire, before a final three aircraft hit the also crippled and stationary *Yorktown* one final time.

1656 27 September 1942

The second strike, much slower with the Swordfish in company, consisting of 24 Swordfish, 12 Devastators and nine Defiants, escorted by nine He 100's and nine Wildcats had arrived over the Japanese ships at 1632. The CAP was weak, consisting of only 13 Zeros at high level and a feeble two at low. Seven were shot down in exchange for two Swordfish, two Wildcats and a He 100, clearing many aircraft through to attack what was already a scene of destruction. Both *Junyo* and *Hiyo*, listing and on fire, were finished, leaving only two fully mobile carriers, one already hit. Six Swordfish each went to *Hiyo* and *Junyo*, hitting *Hiyo* twice, causing her to turn turtle within 15 minutes. *Junyo*, hit once, was clearly finished as well, if she had not been before. The remaining twelve Swordfish conducted a hammer and anvil attack on *Shoho*, hitting her aft with a torpedo and immediately slowing the previously lucky light carrier. They lost only one Swordfish to AA fire. In what would be their final combat operation of the Pacific war (*Langley* being the only USN ship to maintain a complement of them), the twelve Devastators attacked the lamed light carrier. They lost one of their number but scored three hits, two of which exploded, tearing open the hull of the light carrier and dooming her. Finally, the nine Defiants landed a 250lb bomb smack in the centre of the *Kaga*. By the time sunset had arrived, only one carrier remained afloat, the *Kaga*.

1922 27 September 1942

Halsey's fleet was withdrawing under the cover of darkness. He had lost three carriers, with *Yorktown* too badly damaged to save, as was the escort carrier *Langley*, swept by uncontrollable fires. The small *Albatross*, not built for that sort of damage had been abandoned and scuttled after getting to a 22-degree list. Only on *Langley* had casualties been truly severe and Ray Spruance had survived on *Yorktown*.

He had also lost the destroyer *Worden*, torpedoed by a Japanese submarine sniffing around the Task Force, although it had been dispatched later. The damaged *Australasia* would require some months of yard work, although she had been able to land her aircraft on. Only the *Ranger* remained undamaged, but badly overloaded with refugees from *Yorktown* and *Langley*. They had pushed some aircraft over the side after landing, a waste to be sure but they had little other option. They included all the remaining Devastators, a cruel end to an aircraft that had finally scored a success.

None the less, he had badly damaged the Japanese. For the moment that would have to do. He could not stay on station with a solitary carrier. The landings would have to be abandoned of sea support, at least for the moment.

1945 27 September 1942

Vice Admiral Tsukahara had turned the badly damaged *Kaga* and the rest of his Task Force around, heading back to Truk. They may have bloodied the Americans, but they had not won the decisive victory necessary to sweep them from the area. The Genzan air group had been gutted, as had his own. Three carriers out of four lost, with planes that could not make it to Rabaul also lost, as none could land back on *Kaga*, who had two large holes in her flight deck. Some of the more inexperienced pilots had butchered their ditching's as well, with 23 men killed attempting to ditch, although 61 had been recovered. Some pilots had tried for Rabaul. He hoped they had made it.

2004 27 September 1942

Lt Commander Harima had arrived back in Rabaul. After departing with 51 G4M's and 23 A6M's they had returned with a miserable 21 G4M's and 13 A6M's. Their ranks had been decimated and many of those aircraft that had arrived back were damaged and would be unserviceable for a period of time. They had achieved results, but not in proportion to their losses.

1019 30 September 1942

It was a grim outlook, thought Yamamoto. Whilst they had almost completely captured their operational objectives, falling short only in the Southern Solomons and Timor, the cost had been prohibitive. His main concern now was naval air power, the decisive instrument so far in Japan's expansion and most certainly the decisive instrument in maintaining those possessions. It came in two forms, land based and carrier based. Both were ruined. His specialist anti shipping forces of G4M's and G3M's, needed to keep the Americans at bay, had been decimated.

His carrier-based forces now consisted of the escort carrier *Taiyo*. The light carriers *Ryuho* and *Nisshin* would complete in October and November, but their air compliments would both be less than 30. *Kaga* would not be ready again until likely April next year. Nothing else could be expected until late in 1943.

His surface forces had also suffered. With the conversions of the *Ise Class* he had effectively lost five battleships, with only two replacements of his pre-war ten. Heavy cruisers had also suffered badly. He would have to use light units to maintain his forces until he could regroup.

1543 3 October 1942

Lafayette had only docked at Tonga for few hours and she received orders to make all possible haste to Tulagi. She would be back at sea on the morning of the 5th with her two battleship companions and the light cruiser *Cleveland*, as well as four destroyers, making for Tulagi.

1212 4 October 1942

Australasia inched into the dry dock, joining *Pacifica* next door. Both the battleship and the carrier would be in the Sydney dry docks for some time, both not destined to re-join the fleet until mid-1943. She had replaced the light carrier *Christchurch*, which had just finished a refit. The two heaviest ships in the RAN were out of action and would be for some time.

1915 4 October 1942

There could be no thought of a Timor operation at the moment, mused Yamamoto. His last operational carrier, the small escort carrier *Taiyo* had been hit by a single submarine torpedo near Truk. Thankfully not badly damaged, she would be nonoperational for two months. Any plans he may have had would have to wait until December.

0801 10 October 1942

Major General Vandegrift had halted all offensive operations over a week ago and his marines were just holding on, strung out in defensive positions. Only small patrols were the order of the day, no large unit actions. Patch's American Division was similarly restricted and he knew small groups of Japanese had been slipping through his lines to the North of the island, where the Japanese had run a convoy through relatively unmolested a couple of days ago, losing two transports, but only after they had delivered their cargo. He had no option but to wait and hold on. He had been given a date of the 15th for the fleet's return. All they could do until then was hold on and conserve their most precious assets, food and ammo.

1716 13 October 1942

The campaign in Northern New Guinea was going as well as could be expected, thought Lt General Freyberg. Naturally Kreuger's HQ staff had thought it could go faster, but every last strongpoint had to be winkled out and the Japanese had shown themselves willing to hold on to the last man. Kreuger had visited two weeks ago and was well aware of the issues in campaigning in such dense, wet jungle, with its many gullies, gorges and cliffs and, in the interior, mountains.

His forces had captured Mubo in late August and his two prongs were placing real pressure on the Japanese, firstly directly on Salamaia from Wau, where his forces had fought a bitterly contested advance to Pilimung. His coastal forces had also advanced, repelling all counter attacks, including a spectacular 1500-man attack at Lababia Ridge, in late September. The ridge's only defenders were one Company of the 6th Brigade and two field guns. The Australasians relied on well-established and linked defensive positions, featuring extensive, cleared free-fire zones. By these assets and their determination, the Company had defeated the Japanese envelopment tactics and wiped out 1000 of the 1500 attackers.

Bobdubi, the last village before Salamaia had been captured a week ago and his coastal forces had pushed North past Salusto and trapped the Japanese to the South of Salamaia in a small coastal beach strip. His plan was to now annihilate that force before conducting a final push on Salamaia itself.

1502 15 October 1942

Major General Alexander Patch was sure pleased to see the fleet back. Now consisting of fully four 16 inch gunned battleships, any requests for shore bombardment were likely to be met promptly.
Halsey had detailed a two specific shore bombardment groups and a night group that would operate once he was resupplied again and his advance to support Vandegrift was underway on the 18th, consisting of:

East
BB Indiana, South Dakota
CA Pensacola
4 DD

West
BB Washington, North Carolina
CA Salt Lake City
3 DD

Night Group(Australasian)
BM Gorgon
CVE Noumea(With seven night capable Swordfish)
3 DD

Two carriers were now back on station and provision of any air support was well taken care of.

0703 24 October 1942

The long line of ships had departed on what would be the United States first major amphibious operation in the European Theatre of War. The massive fleet, consisting of three battleships(one modern), six escort carriers, three heavy cruisers, four light cruisers and scores of destroyers and transports would hit North Africa on 8th November in conjunction with British Forces.

It had not come a moment too soon, with the 8th Army clearly about to be attacked by Rommel at El Alamein. This would go a long way toward taking the pressure off a situation with the Germans seemingly pressing everywhere, the Russians just holding on in Stalingrad. Two days after the attack had gone in, Operation Thunderball would be launched. B24's and UK bombers, staging through Crete, would be launching a major raid on the oil production facilities at Ploesti.

1219 25 October 1942

Chiang Kai-shek was confident now that he had stabilised things in Burma. He had received enough equipment now to equip one complete and one partial armoured division. His Stuart light tanks had been supplemented by 50 Sherman's and he fleshed out his second division with armoured cars and a few T26's. The British had also been reinforced. If they could hold the initial Japanese attacks with his better infantry divisions, the cream of which were in Burma, he could then use his two armoured divisions to counterattack and hopefully split the Japanese front open in conjunction with the British. If he could drive them back to the Thai border, they may lose their reluctant Thai allies, which would change the whole situation. If Thailand rebelled, the front could conceivably be reduced to the Isthmus of Kra yet again, allowing the Japanese to be easily bottled up. That would allow him to use his better divisions in China and perhaps finally deal with Mao and his vermin.

Rough world map October 1942

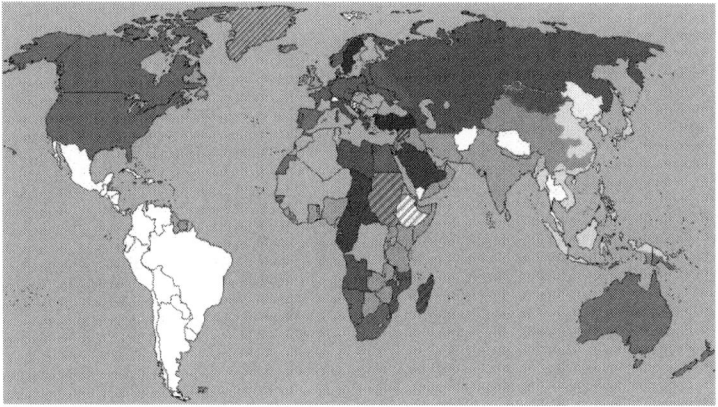

1906 26 October 1942

I-21 had watched the American forces come steadily closer. The carrier was steaming into exactly the launch set up that he desired and at 1910 he ordered a full spread from his forward tubes at the carrier, hoping to fire again at the battleship behind her.

As he continued to watch, she started to turn slightly away, complicating the solution. He was finally rewarded with one clear hit on the carrier and two on the battleship from torpedoes that had continued on the run. He was never able to report this, the *I-21* being dispatched after a 50-minute hunt by one of the four destroyers escorting.

0513 27 October 1942

It made depressing reading, thought Halsey. Japanese submarine activity had become increasingly active around the islands, this submarine being the third dispatched in the last three weeks. This time it had come at a cost. Both the *Ranger* and *North Carolina*, who had limped back to Tulagi, would require extensive repair, probably in the U.S. In actual fact, neither ships would be ready again until April 1943 and this brief 1942 sojourn would be all the *Ranger* would see of the Pacific until after wars end, the rest of her service being in the Atlantic.

0818 1 November 1942

Vandegrift's marines and the Americal Division had been grinding the Japanese forces trapped between them, compressing the Japanese into a strong point around Mounts Kongara and Nasio, having cleared all the coastal areas of the island. They had captured the airfield at Kieta on the 24th. Forsyth's 9th Independent Company had attacked along the beach at night, and captured intact the bulk of the Japanese construction equipment whilst his main force overrun the nearby town and the strip itself. They had done some work on the strip itself using this equipment in the intervening week, but the imminent arrival today of Seabees would speed the process up.

1715 1 November 1942

Colonel Mushai Yammamori's command, compressed into the interior highlands of Southern Bougainville was nearing the end of its resources. Not supplied for nigh on three weeks, it had been attacked constantly and was low on both ammunition and food. All his heavy weapons had also gone. They were also burdened with a large amount of wounded and sick men. Cut off from all beach areas and with the allies having total air superiority, they were bombed and shelled by day and even by night, his men getting no rest at all. There was now one option only. Tomorrow night his forces would charge the enemy positions, attempting to break through, cross the Jaba River lowlands and try and joining up with Japanese forces in the North of the island.

2035 1 November 1942

Rear Admiral Rear Admiral Norman Scott's force had intercepted the Japanese convoy, almost certainly another troop reinforcement convoy for Northern Bougainville or Buka 15 nautical miles North of Buka. He now had the lead two Japanese ships dialled in radar for his first salvo. The Japanese were coming right towards him in line ahead, their nine-ship formation effectively letting him cross their T with his two heavy cruisers and six destroyers.

2059 1 November 1942

The two ships at the head of the Japanese line, the light cruiser *Kiso* and the destroyer *Kasumi*, were smothered with 8-inch shellfire from both heavy cruisers, *Portland* and *Pensacola*, as well as their attendant destroyers. However, their trained night fighting abilities caused them to make use of their favoured weapon, the torpedo. The destroyers, packed with troops, none the less, turned into the American ships, targeting the two heaviest, the cruisers *Portland* and *Pensacola*.

The *Pensacola*, hit by three torpedoes, turned turtle and sank. The *Portland*, hit once, was left staggering back to the South, badly lamed. In the follow up clash between the destroyers, the U.S destroyer *Nicholas* was badly damaged.

For the Japanese, the destroyer *Natsagumo*, hit repeatedly by the modern U.S destroyers *Fletcher, Nicholas* and *Radford*, amongst the first of the *Fletcher Class* to arrive in the Pacific, sank in the early hours of the day. She joined the first two ships with mortal damage and sank quickly with very heavy loss of life. The light cruiser *Kiso* had floundered before daybreak, taking the body of Admiral Mikawa with her. It had been a very costly interception by the U.S Navy, but it had prevented the landing of more troops and the casualties amongst the troop compliment of the three sunken ships was heavy indeed.

0656 3 November 1942

Vasily Chuikov's forces in Stalingrad had been gradually pushed back into a thin strip on the East Bank of the city. Worse still ice starting to form on the river would soon make resupply not possible. He could not hold on for much longer against the sheer weight of metal facing him. He was not supposed to believe, but he hoped to God relief came soon.

1146 3 November 1942

Vandegrift's marines had been subjected to a massive night-time assault by Japanese troops, attempting to break through his lines and escape to the North. It had been a hard-fought battle, full of small unit actions all along the line. He had little in the way of artillery support, although what he had received from his own guns and the monitor *Gorgon* offshore had been useful.

In the end it had come down mainly to automatic weapons, and when these failed, pistols, bayonets entrenching tools and even fists. It had cost over 450 casualties, but his line had mostly held and very few Japanese had escaped. There were mounds of enemy dead, with only 22 taken alive. It had been a costly operation, but the Southern half of the island had been secured.

1914 5 November 1942

Rommel's last attempt to break through using the Italian of the Ariete and Trento Divisions had been a failure. He had held off counterattacks from the British and Canadian forces and his line still held, but logistically he was finished. Short of fuel and ammunition, but particularly fuel, he had little option but to retreat in an attempt to shorten his supply lines. Little enough was getting through by sea as it was, however, the extra distance required to transport it to his current location could reduce that to virtually nil. Panzer

Army Africa would start it's retreat tomorrow, a retreat that would become more urgent as the events in French North Africa became apparent.

1607 9 November 1942

Vice Admiral Chūichi Hara boarded the battleship *Hiei* at Rabaul. Heavy cruisers had bombarded the airfield on Bougainville on the nights of the 1st and the 4th, seemingly with little real effect, as on each occasion it appeared to be drawing much closer to being finished. Intelligence had estimated that it was only days from becoming operational, so his Task Force, consisting of the *Hiei* and *Kirishima*, heavy cruisers *Takao* and *Maya*, light cruiser *Oi* and seven destroyers had been detailed to conduct such a bombardment tonight.

Perhaps that would set the Americans back on their heels. With their own airstrip on the island of Buka being raced to completion, it was important that they got in first, before the US could transfer aircraft to the island.

2233 9 November 1942

Willis Augustus "Ching" Lee had his Task Force cruising 20 miles East of Buka passage. With the Japanese having attempted to bombard the airfield twice at night within the last nine days, he wanted to be fully on guard against a third attempt. If they succeeded in getting in to bombard the airfield, he wanted to make sure that he could cut the corner on any retreat by steaming direct to mission point. If they got in to do the bombardment, they would not get out again.

Despite the loss of the North Carolina, his force still consisted of *BB Washington*(flag), *BB Indiana*, *BB South Dakota*, *CA Salt Lake City*, *CLAA San Juan*, *CLAA San Diego* and 11 DD. Eight nautical miles to the Northeast he had placed the tiny carrier *Noumea* with its night capable aircraft, escorted by two light cruisers and five destroyers.

2358 9 November 1942

Vice Admiral Chūichi Hara was in good spirits. His force had run into an enemy cruiser, escorted by two light ships and had sank all three of them at limited cost, the heavy cruiser *Maya* having taken two heavy calibre hits that had started fires and the destroyer *Wakabe* having also taken a few small calibre shell hits. He was now withdrawing after successfully bombarding the airstrip. It had been a successful night's work and he was 5 nautical miles South of Mission Point.

0018 10 November 1942

A Japanese course change to seaward had changed Lee's original plans and his battleships were now on course to directly pass the Japanese line on an inverted parallel course, less than 12,000 yards distance. His three battleships had targeting solutions on the first three ships in the enemy force, not known to Lee at the time, but what would later prove to be the *Oi, Hiei* and *Maya*. Carefully waiting until ready, he ordered his destroyers to fire star shell and commenced firing at 0023.

0029 10 November 1942

Vice Admiral Chūichi Hara was horrified at the destruction that had already befallen his command. The light cruiser *Oi*, hit by multiple 16-inch shell hits was a blazing, out of control wreck, heavy cruiser *Maya* rearmost turrets had both been blown over the side and she was a smoking wreck as well. *Hiei* had been hit multiple time from stem to stern and had staggered out of line, on fire.

He had immediately ordered his own units to return fire and hits were now being obtained on the Americans, but it appeared he was fighting four battleships. A he watched with at least some satisfaction; he could see *Kirishima's* guns score heavily on one U.S battleship.

0038 10 November 1942

Rear Admiral Lee had his own problems. In a battle that had started so well, he had initially wondered what the hell the *Indiana* was doing. She had left his line, blocking the line of firstly the *South Dakota* and secondly the *Washington* and as she started to make a long, slow graceful circle out towards the Japanese formation. Hit by 14inch gunfire from the *Kirishima*, her helm had jammed and she was heading out towards the Japanese formation, making her the main target of most of the Japanese torpedo attacks and shellfire.

He battle turned his line to keep parallel to the Japanese, continuing to engage and pound their line in the hope that their offensive efforts would be distracted from her. It was a forlorn hope as Captain Merrill reported firstly two torpedo hits on his ship and then four minutes later two more. The destroyer *Cushing* had also taken a hit.

0104 10 November 1942

Captain Iwabuchi Sanji's *Kirishima*, ablaze and with two of her turrets and much of her secondary armament knocked out had escaped the Americans, at least for now. His battered battleship still had many uncontrolled fires and with damage and flooding in her engine room and damage near the bow was restricted to a crawling 10 knots. He was accompanied by only the cruiser *Takao*, itself only lightly damaged and five of his seven destroyers, having lost the *Tokitsukazi* and *Amatsukazi*, while the destroyer *Wakabe* as badly damaged as his battleship. He had been forced to leave the *Hiei*, battered to pieces and immobile and the *Maya* and *Oi*, both sunk or sinking.

0246 10 November 1942

Rear Admiral Lee had only lost two ships in the engagement and suffered minimal damage to others, aside from the cruiser *Salt Lake City*, which had suffered heavily from both 14 inch and 8-inch hits and her had bridge and upper works demolished.

What had shocked him was that one of those ships had been the *Indiana*. What had been the decisive factor was that the two groups of torpedo hits, each of two fish, had impacted relatively close together, close together at both the stern and bow. The bow had detached and the stern hit had torn an enormous hole in her starboard engineering spaces, shutting down much of her electrical power and pumps. The battleship had rolled over and sank 12 minutes ago, joining the destroyer *Cushing* on the bottom.

0303 10 November 1942

The biplanes had come out of the darkness, one dropping flares and four attacking. His crews, alert and all too prepared had downed one but another had hit the cruiser *Takao* with a torpedo, slowing her to 15 knots, which outpaced his battleship none the less. With flooding barely under control, he was only making eight knots and Captain Sanji feared what the dawn would bring for the crippled *Kirishima*.

0818 10 November 1942

The carrier had been a hive of activity since 0430 and she had launched two strikes aimed at the struggling Japanese battleship. Commander William Matheson had personally led the first, launching at 0602, consisting of 18 Dauntless, six Avengers and 12 Wildcats. They had found the struggling ship at 0703, 28 miles off the North Coast of Buka.

She had been escorted by six Zeros, but the Wildcats had swept these aside, shooting down four in exchange for a single loss. The Avengers had placed a torpedo into the crippled battleship. It would have been a second but a Jap destroyer had taken the missile instead, breaking her back. The dive bombers had lost one of their number to flak, but had hit the crippled battleship four times with 1000 lb bombs and the heavy cruiser once.

He had hung around to watch the second strike, which arrived just in time to see the battleship sink. Concentrating on the heavy cruiser, the 12 Dauntless hit her twice more with 1000lb bombs. Three Zeros, newly arrived, tried to break up the torpedo strike but all three were downed by Wildcats after shooting down a solitary Avenger. The nine torpedo planes delivered the coup de grace, hitting the cruiser three times.

A follow up strike later in the day would also sink the limping destroyer *Wakabe* at a cost of two Dauntless shot down by intervening Zeros. Only three destroyers would make it back to Rabaul. Vice Admiral Hara, after 36 hours at sea, would eventually be amongst a group that made it to shore at Buka.

0909 10 November 1942

Rear Admiral Collins was not happy. The Monitor Gorgon and the two corvettes *Ballarat* and *Geelong* had run headlong into the Japanese force and all three had been sunk, the last two smaller ships by gunfire.

The old *Gorgon*, hit twice by torpedoes, had quickly turned turtle. Survivors had indicated she had hit the Japs that had sunk her. From all reports, the Japs concerned were probably on the bottom of the Solomon Sea themselves. Losses had been heavy, over 300 men, however, it appeared to be a day of heavy losses.

1614 10 November 1942

Queen Marie of Greece, invited to watch with her husband King Paul, had watched the survivors of the raid come back to Crete. many planes were missing and many had been shot up, one B24 landing with a good section of wing missing.

They consisted of USAAF B24's and RAF Wellingtons and Halifax's. despite losses and injury's, they spoke of hitting the target hard. It just seemed like such a massive waste of life, the whole thing. She had head similar sentiments from her sister in Australasia, but as Alice had written, what choice did they have. As it was Crete was the only part of Greece that was free.

1619 11 November 1942

Chief Engineer Marcu Alexandru had surveyed the damage. It was extensive but would be unlikely to cut into oil production by more than 0-5%. However, if they wished to scale up production any further it would be at this stage, impossible.

He hoped the allies would not be back. With three Luftwaffe, two Royal Bulgarian Air Force and one Romanian squadron of fighters, as well as heavy AA defences, the allied bombers had paid a stiff price, near sixty bombers.

1808 11 November 1942

Eisenhower was happy with the results of Operation Torch. Algiers, Oran and Casablanca had all been captured and the bulk of the Vichy forces had surrendered, some actually welcoming the allies.
In many cases they had resisted, however, it had been a largely unequal battle. The incomplete French battleship *Jean Bart* had been badly damaged by the *USS Massachusetts* and one cruiser and 11 destroyers had been sunk by allied naval forces at minimal cost. With Rommel in retreat, things were looking up in Africa.

1435 20 November 1942

Major General Stepan Ioniscu's First Romanian Armoured Division had been smashed, swept aside by the furious tide of Russian T34's and men. It's old Pz35 and Pz38 tanks had not been able to make an impact of the Russian advance and a belated Cavalry charge yesterday against the Russians that had been slaughtered brought back memories of what he had been told about the Poland campaign by German officers. The casual bravery of his soldiers had not been enough to hold the Russians and they had broken through on all fronts. For the 6th Army, still battling to take Stalingrad, it would represent a disaster.

1111 22 November 1942

Vandegrift's marines and Patch's Americal Division had started their offensive on the 20th November and had pushed the Japanese back, capturing the villages of Torokina in the West and Mabin in the East, respectively. Things were going well and casualties had not been as heavy as expected, resistance being relatively light. It would be even better when they had constructed an operational airfield, but that was still 1-2 weeks away, the airfield itself being badly damaged by the Japanese shelling but the loss of so much equipment being the overriding factor.

More had since arrived and construction was again underway, however, photo recon by Australasian P-43's indicated that Japanese efforts on the Buka airfield was complete, so that would soon be another issue that needed dealing with. Halsey's naval forces had promised a strike within the next two days.

0906 24 November 1942

Captain Meji Hori surveyed the damage. It was almost complete. Thankfully only six A6M's had arrived on the 23rd. All had been destroyed. Impacted with seemingly hundreds of craters, some massive, the airfield at Buka would be out of action for at least three weeks, further hampering their effort to prepare and fortify the island.

1249 26 November 1942

Major General Edwin Harding's 32nd Infantry Division had slogged through the swamps and jungles of West New Guinea for five months and had finally captured Kokonao two weeks ago. His division was desperately in need of a withdrawal, prolonged exposure to the jungle leaving many men with sickness. He had been promised relief by the middle of December. After then, the advance could be undertaken to capture Nabire, which would close off the West Papua Peninsula, trapping the Japanese troops in New Guinea.

1016 28 November 1942

Admiral Theodor Krancke looked over the scene of destruction at Toulon. Such a waste, so many fine ships destroyed. Three battleships, a seaplane carrier, seven cruisers, thirty destroyers and eleven escorts, all scuttled. Most would never see the sea again.

1203 30 November 1942

Vandegrift's marines and Patch's Americal Division had continued their remorseless advance up Bougainville, compressing the remaining Japanese into the Northern third of the island. The Japs appeared to have given up on further reinforcing the island and they had captured Asilima on the West Coast and Wakunai on the East within the last three days. The main enemy now would be the terrain, the interior of the island comprising the Emperor Range, dominated by the 9000 feet Mount Balbi.

1318 1 December 1942

The airfield at Kieta was finally operational and had received its first occupants, two squadrons of Marine F4U's, that had replaced the P-39's in the island chain two weeks ago. They had been joined by a squadron of B26's and two flights of RAAF He 100-D4's optimized for ground attack.

1416 2 December 1942

Yamamoto had attended the commissioning ceremony for the *Nisshin*. With the *Ryuho* and the repaired *Taiyo*, he again had three small carriers, four once the escort carrier *Chuyo* commissioned later this month. However, the losses of the 10 November still burned deep in his mind and he had restricted operations in the Solomons to destroyer Divisions only. It looked more and more like a withdrawal from Bougainville would have to be attempted. Thankfully the small passage between it and Buka would make a major operation unnecessary.

The navy had continued to take losses, two destroyers being lost to US submarines in supplying the Aleutians in November, the destroyer *Hayashio* off New Guinea to U.S medium bombers, the armed merchant cruiser *Hokuku Maru* in the Indian ocean to RN light forces and the destroyer *Takanami* two nights ago in a minefield in Buka Passage. It was all taking a toll and his capacity for offensive operations was minimal.

1619 6 December 1942

It was perhaps the largest Task Force ever put together by the RAN, thought newly promoted Vice Admiral John Collins. Consisting of the new Amphibious Carrier *Brisbane*, four infantry landing ships, *Kanimbla, Manoora, Westralia* and *Monowai*, six new "River" Class escort destroyers and four old R and S Class frigates.

The covering force would consist of three carriers, *Christchurch, Melbourne* and *Sydney*, newly equipped with Avenger torpedo bombers and A36 dive bombers, one heavy cruiser, six light cruisers(including *USS Phoenix*) and ten(three U.S) destroyers. The destination was Port Moresby, and, eventually Lae. It was intended to launch an amphibious assault on the town on 28 December, with landings to the East and West of the town by 4th Division.

The following day, the U.S 503rd Parachute Infantry Regiment, together with four gun crews from the Australasian 4th Field Regiment—who had received a crash course in the use of parachutes—and their cut-down "baby 25 pounder" artillery pieces, were to make a parachute drop at Nadzab, just west of Lae. Once airborne forces secured Nadzab Airfield, a brigade of the 11th Infantry Division, a militia formation, under Major General Drake-Brockman, could be flown in, to cut off any possible Japanese retreat and secure the allied rear. The whole operation would be proceeded by an extensive series of raids on both Rabaul and Lae, reducing the effectiveness of both bases and blunting their ability to strike back.

0918 18 December 1942

It had taken almost three weeks of heavy fighting on Bougainville, but the Japanese had finally been cleared from the mountain areas and had been compressed into the last coastal plain area of the island. Major General Alexander patch could finally see the end in sight, with his forces having captured Dios just today and the marines having captured Puto two days ago. The Japanese, bombed strafed and shelled, appeared to be at the end of their tether and were slowly being driven back into the narrow Bonis Peninsula, the strip of land bordering Buka passage, although resistance had now stiffened considerably.

1212 18 December 1942

Lt Commander Richard Lake's *Albacore* watched the two-ship convoy come steadily towards him, one large and one smaller destroyer. Releasing a four fish spread, he was heartened to see two hit and the target explode in a mass of flame, rapidly breaking up.

The light cruiser *Yura*, carrying 380 troops for Madang had gone down rapidly 18 nautical miles from the small New Guinea port. Destroyer *Hokaze* did her best to rescue what survivors there were as the submarine, out of torpedoes, slunk away.

1538 18 December 1942

The *Hokaze*, packed with survivors from the *Yura* was only six nautical miles from shore when hit by two torpedoes from *HMAS King Brown*. Breaking up rapidly, she sank in less than 12 minutes. The loss of life from both sinking's was large, less than 100 men from a total compliment and troop carriage of more than 750 from both vessels. The battalion of troops to reinforce Madang had been annihilated.

Bougainville map

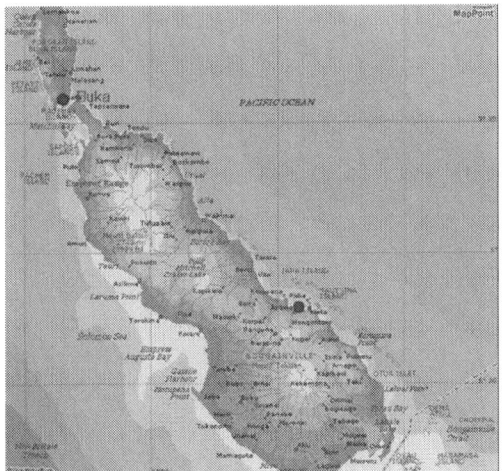

9 June 2013(flash forward)

Crown Princess Maree Drake-Brockman was studying the Korean War and Australasia's involvement. Her mother and father were in Sweden for Princess Madeline's wedding and would be staying in Denmark afterwards with Crown Prince Frederick and that other Australasian Princess, Crown Princess Mary of Denmark. In the meantime, she was eking out some studying time before mid-year exams.

She went over the causal facts of the war, Kim Il-sung's invasion of the South, the retreat, Bradley's landings at Inchon, the advance to near the Yalu, followed by Zhu De's Manchuria's intervention with soviet tacit support and the eventual brokered peace deal. Maybe they should have gone all the way at the time. God knows two of the world biggest pariah states were Manchuria and North Korea.

1112 19 December 1942

Yamamoto had determined that he would try and evacuate the remaining men on Bougainville across Buka passage onto Buka Island and had set a date for the operation, on the nights of the 25th and 26th. Hopefully the allies would be fat and lazy after a Christmas meal. In the meantime, his troops would withdraw into the Bonis Peninsula in preparation. It would require the commitment of destroyers to get it done, but considering the short distance involved, should present no great logistical issue.

1022 20 December 1942

It was large raid, 26 B17's and 22 B26's, escorted by 26 F4U's, 12 Wildcats and eleven He 119's, designed to flatten Rabaul and destroy as many aircraft on the ground as possible plus be the first step in the neutralisation of the base. It would also mark the first real combat debut of the Corsair. Following on from the raid, hopefully when most of the CAP were grounded was a scheduled attack of six 40mm cannon armed He 100's, designed to strafe anything left on the strip.

1108 20 December 1942

The big bombers warmed up on the strip, in all 20 He 211's, making their first large scale raid, with the 20 escorted by eight RAAF Kittyhawks and 22 USAAF P-39's. Much like the raid concurrently happening at Rabaul, it would be followed by a squadron of low-level Boomerangs, each with a 250 lb bombs and eight 20lb incendiaries. It would be a busy day for the Japs, though Squadron Leader Greg Waldon as he gunned his He 211 out for final take off from Port Moresby on their way to Lae.

1514 20 December 1942

Lt. Commander Tadashi Nakajima looked out forlornly at what had been Rabaul air bases. It was a mess, destroyed buildings on the two main strips, three of the four runways cratered. At least fifteen aircraft destroyed on the ground in the first bombing, with another four fighters that had just landed destroyed on the second pass.

They had lost eleven A6M's defending the base, bringing down six enemy fighters and two of the notoriously difficult to kill bombers, with AA bringing down one twin engine fighter and a bomber. The AA emplacements themselves around the airfield had also been a prime target, with many destroyed, as had been the primary fuel dump.

1518 20 December 1942

Ensign Toshi Gobi looked over the ruins of Lae. It was an airstrip nowhere near the size of Rabaul, containing 24 A6M Zeros and five Nakajima J1N Irvings. The raid by 20 or so enemy heavy bombers of a new type had destroyed two Shotai's of Zeros on the ground as well as two Irvings. Seven Zeros had also been lost in combat in exchange for three fighters and two of the new bombers(one mainly due to AA).

After the raid, another had developed, however, thankfully the Zeros were still aloft and they had shot down two of the attackers, RAAF Boomerangs, in exchange for two Irvings caught on the ground and destroyed with incendiaries.

1117 26 December 1942

The early morning recon from the P-43 Lancer was now in Halsey's hands aboard the *South Dakota*. The Japanese were withdrawing off the island, having completed a partial evacuation last night under cover of darkness. No doubt the planned a full withdrawal over the next one of two nights. He thought about how he may be able to put a crimp in those plans. He had little in the way of night capable aircraft, but a squadron of PT boats had arrived at Tulagi two weeks ago. With them, and perhaps the involvement of the cruiser minelayer *Adelaide*, they could perhaps interdict this last traffic off Bougainville.

The campaign would be over very soon and the next one beginning. Even before the Japanese withdrawal, he had received orders to report to Pearl on the 8th January for conference, no doubt to discuss future operations.

2046 26 December 1942

Whilst *HMAS Adelaide*, laid mines at the Western entrance of Machin Bay, the other two ships in her flotilla, the old *Clemson Class* destroyers *Pruitt* and *Preble* laid mines at Eastern entrance to Buka Passage. In the finish, it was the U.S destroyers that bagged a victory, the modern Japanese destroyer *Teruzuki* running directly into the minefield and sinking with heavy loss of life at 2313. The three old ships were proving that they could still be useful.

0732 27 December 1942

The loss of the destroyer *Teruzuki* to a mine had been compounded by the loss of her sister ship *Atkizuki*, driven into another minefield trying to avoid U.S PT boats. The small coaster *Mono Maru* had also been sunk by said PT boats. It was small comfort that they had destroyed one.

One large barge had also been sunk by aircraft that had arrived at night and, whilst the destroyers had departed at 0430, deeming it too dangerous to stay any longer, daybreak brought air attacks from the air wings of the Lafayette. The aircraft attacked two barges currently in transit, turning them over, killing over 200 troops and then bombed and strafed those now of Buka, as well as two barges left on Bougainville.

For the 432 Japanese troops left on Bougainville, there was no escape. Engaged by U.S troops late in the day, they fought as usual to the last, however, this time 66 prisoners were taken, only five Japanese, the rest Korean's "recruited" into the IJA to serve as construction labourers. By 1845 on the 27th, the battle for Bougainville was over.

1106 28 December 1942

Major General George Vasey's 4th Division had secured a substantial beachhead already east of Lae, on "Red Beach" and "Yellow Beach", near Malahang and was already beginning an attempt to encircle Japanese forces in the town.

The ships near the beachhead had been attacked by Japanese bombers, some ten aircraft escorted by twelve fighters from Rabaul at 1025, but had been met by 18 fighters from the carriers and had been driven off with no damage to the defenders. Six of the bombers had been shot down and five escorting fighters in exchange for four of the Navy's He 100's.

This same morning, the U.S 503rd Parachute Infantry Regiment had made an only lightly opposed parachute drop at Nadzab, just west of Lae. The airborne forces secured Nadzab Airfield, cutting off any Japanese retreat to the West.

1405 31 December 1942

It was smiling all round at the ships commissioning. Secret smiles from many of the USN senior admirals. They knew that this was only the first of many to come in 1943. With only one fleet carrier in addition to this newly commissioned ship, *USS Essex*, but twelve escort carriers now in commission, the USN had already surpassed the IJN. Six Fleet carriers, ten light carriers and over twenty escort carriers were expected in 1943, not even counting the many cruisers, destroyers and other escorts, all of which promised to deluge the IJN in steel.

1808 1 January 1943

The 4th Division faced formidable natural barriers to capture the actual township of Lae in the form of rivers swollen by recent rain. They came to a halt at the Busu River, which could not be bridged for two reasons, the 4th lacked heavy bridging equipment and on-site engineers, and the far bank was occupied by Japanese soldiers. However, today a three-hour continuous attack had secured a bridgehead after fierce fighting.

Breaking into the town the following day, the area had been secured by the 3rd January. Salamaua had been captured by 3rd Division troops on the same day. What enemy troops that had escaped had retreated into the Huon Peninsula, a mountainous area near Lae. They would need to be eliminated from there and after linking up with U.S troops at Nadzab, the next advance would be to Madang, then Wewak.

1906 3 January 1943

Vice Admiral John Collins had been happy with the Lae operation. The Japanese air presence from Rabaul had been very subdued, probably as a result of the base being attacked at least once every day for the last two weeks. Only two attacks in the last week had gotten through to the ships, each involving only a handful of aircraft that had done little damage. The fleet would be heading back to Sydney, there to await further orders.

1816 5 January 1943

General Shojiro Iida's campaign had kicked off after monsoon season on the 14th December 1942, so far too little effect. Vicious fighting had failed to penetrate more than eight miles on the Mandalay front, bringing him to within six miles of the town, but the layered Chinese defences, constructed over the intervening six months had largely blunted his drive.

To the North his much weaker forces had made some progress towards Lashio, advancing twenty miles, but against an enemy that was clearly not broken. Likewise, to the South his troops had advanced towards the port of Akyab, gaining some ground, but at a large cost. It appeared this would not be a repeat of 1942, the enemy appearing much better equipped.

His other major problem was the activities of enemy irregular troops behind his lines, these so called Chindits. They had been destroying communication and logistical hubs, particularly railways in this country with so few roads, hampering supply to his troops.

0555 8 January 1943

General Joseph Stilwell had carefully husbanded his resources, placing his best three divisions in reserve near Mandalay, the 100th actually in the city, the 200th, an armoured formation on the left flank and the 300th, a semi mechanized division with some tanks, to the right. He had also carefully gathered his artillery and, now the Japanese had expanded much of their effort over the last month for only minimal gains, it was time to launch an offensive of his own.

He hoped to pincer the town and then use his existing forces, including the elite 100th, probably the best Chinese division with the 200th, to crush the trapped Japanese forces. Orde Wingate's Chindits had plans to establish certain blocks and demolitions to stop assistance from Japanese forces to the South as well. In five minutes, his artillery would open up and hopefully the Japanese would get to find what it was like to be on the other end of the lash for a change.

1912 8 January 1943

General Walter Krueger had delivered his thoughts on the strengths and planned operations for the South Pacific Area. It was clear from the discussions that a strategy of "island hopping" across the Pacific, bypassing strategically unimportant islands and enemy strong points was to be the tactic of choice.

In areas where there were large land masses and large concentrations of troops, such as New Guinea and, eventually, hopefully the Philippines and/or Formosa, a more conventional approach would be used.

Aircraft carriers and amphibious assault capability would be the order of the day. For the South West Pacific area, the immediate priorities would be Buka and a clearance of the North Coast of New Guinea. It did not appear at this stage that Rabaul would be invaded.

For Nimitz's command, the two immediate points now that Torch had finished and Bougainville captured would be Tarawa, scheduled for June/July 1943. In the meantime, amphibious assets would be retained to assist with New Guinea and Buka operations and a campaign would be undertaken to retake the Aleutian Islands, starting with Adak on 12 April 1942, followed by a simultaneous joint Canadian/US operation on Kiska and Attu in late May 1943.

1535 18 January 1943

Lt General Renya Mutaguchi's 18th Infantry Division was typical of many Japanese formations in Burma. It had lost 3000 men transferred to Bougainville and had another 580 dead and over 2400 sick with malaria and other tropical diseases, yet no replacements had arrived.

Attacked by the 200th Chinese Division, liberally equipped with both tanks and heavy weapons, it had given away, threatening the flank of the Japanese 33rd Division. The Chinese 300th Division also, equipped with armour had also broken through and not only had the 18th Infantry taken heavy casualties from this attack, over 800 men had been cut off and decimated by the advancing Chinese.

Shocked by the élan of the attacks and their firepower, the Japanese Southern Coast advance on Akyab had been thrown into confusion and units had been redeployed to meet the new threat, not an easy task in a jungle country with few in the way of roads. Arriving piecemeal, many smaller units had been destroyed and the Japanese had so far been thrown back to Meiktila. The Chinese had also made gains in Shan State, being only six miles from Monghsu, mainly due to diversion of Japanese forces to the central front.

The advance of the Chinese forces was slowing, which was just as well, as all Japanese forces in Burma were engaged currently aside from some garrison troops in Rangoon and politically unreliable Thai troops in the Eastern Shan states.

1014 23 January 1943

The *Gato Class* submarine USS *Guardfish*, under Lt Commander Thomas Klakring, had had a good patrol so far. two ships sunk, plus a Japanese destroyer on the 13th. Now another Nip tin can was on her way to Davy Jones. There were increased Japanese naval movements in his patrol area, which encompassed New Britain and New Ireland and he had reported this back to Pearl, no heavy ships, but extensive merchant traffic and lots of destroyers.

0907 25 January 1943

Yamamoto had taken the decision to abandon Buka. Attempts to complete the airfield had been routinely defeated by allied naval gunfire and aircraft from the fully operational allied airbase on Bougainville, only 70 nautical miles away.

At the same time, he was not prepared to give up on the Northern Coast of New Guinea, so important in sustaining the viability of Rabaul. He was in the process of stockpiling ships at Rabaul in anticipation of a dual operation on commencing the night of the 3rd February. Firstly, a loading and withdrawal from Buka, secondly, the transportation of 8,000 troops to Wewak and Madang to help secure their positions there. The troops would come from Rabaul, however, aircraft would need to be flown in from Truk and possibly Batavia to bolster Rabaul's weakened air compliment to provide air cover for the operation. It was hoped that two forces in play would weaken the allied air response.

0806 3 February 1943

The month-long Chinese offensive had petered out. Although much time was left until monsoon season, only a limited offensive operation in the North of Burma in April would be conducted by the Chinese during the remainder of the dry season. Both sides, logistically and manpower wise exhausted, paused to take breath.

The combined British, Indian and Chinese offensive had driven the Japanese back to a line of Kyaukpyu on the coast (captured by Indian troops two days ago) to Malun to Tatkon (100 miles from Mandalay) to Kunhing in Shan State.

Stillwell planned a much more limited offensive in April, using troops that could be made available by the straightening of his line with the gains made in January. His forces were less than 30 miles from Kengtung, an area of Burma garrisoned and allocated to Thailand. He was eager to test the Thai troops resolve to fight for their Japanese allies. As it was, over half of Burma now lay in allied hands, including the air base at near Heho.

0909 3 February 1943

At both FRUMEL in Melbourne and FRUPAC in Hawaii, it was obvious to all and sundry that the Japanese were planning to run a major operation, specifically a convoy, out of Rabaul. There were only two possible destinations, either Buka in the Solomons or the North Coast of New Guinea and a build-up of air and naval forces had been confirmed by air reconnaissance.

In the Melbourne headquarters of FRUMEL, Lieutenant Rudolph J. (Rudi) Fabian had sat down all night with captured intercepts with the Australasian Japanese language expert and cryptographer Athanasius Treweek, but was no closer to putting the final piece in the puzzle. None the less, all commands had been notified on 31st January. Hopefully the necessary deployments to stop the Japanese had been made.

1234 3 February 1943

Things were sure in a flap at Port Moresby, thought Lieutenant Richard "Dick" Bong. Two RAAF squadrons of P40's had all been moved to Lae in the last week and two flights of RAAF A36's had gone to Milne Bay to supplement the two squadron of Boomerangs and Hudsons already there. An extra six more P38's had joined his 39th Fighter Squadron in Port Moresby. Port Moresby's air fields were packed with aircraft, including a number of new arrivals in the last week. Bong was staggered by the amount of planes on the eight airfields, which numbered:

3 Mile:
89th Bombardment Squadron USAAF (A-20's)
8th Fighter Squadron USAAF (P40's)
80th Fighter Squadron USAAF (P39's)

7 Mile:
8th Bombardment Squadron USAAF (mix B25 and A24's)
63rd Bombardment Squadron USAAF (B17's)
64th Bombardment Squadron USAAF (B17's)
65th Bombardment Squadron USAAF (B17's)

5 Mile:
22nd Troop Carrier Squadron USAAF (C47's)
320th Bombardment Squadron USAAF (B24's)
321st Bombardment Squadron USAAF (B24's)
No 22 Squadron RAAF (A20's)
No 30 Squadron RAAF (He 119's)

12 Mile:
No 75 Squadron RAAF (He 100's)
No 100 Squadron RAAF (He 211's)
No 101 Squadron RAAF (He 211's)

14 Mile:
13th Bombardment Squadron USAAF (B25's)
7th Fighter Squadron USAAF (P40's)
9th Fighter Squadron USAAF (P40's)
39th Fighter Squadron USAAF (P38's)
No 2 Photo Reconnaissance Unit RAAF (P43's)

17 Mile:
90th Bombardment Squadron USAAF (B25's)
71st Bombardment Squadron USAAF (B25's)
405th Bombardment Squadron USAAF (B25's)
35th Fighter Squadron USAAF (P39's)

30 Mile:
40th Fighter Squadron USAAF (P39's)
41th Fighter Squadron USAAF (P39's)
No 12 Squadron RAAF (Ansons)

Fishermans:
No 42 Squadron RAAF (Catalinas)
No 49 Squadron RAAF (Wirraways)

It was an aerial armada in the true sense of the word. His P38 squadron, the first in the South Pacific (the only other use so far in the Pacific had been in the Aleutians) had seen some combat, but hopefully he would have a chance to add to his score, currently standing at two.

1408 3 February 1943

Yamamoto's plan for the next few days operations were simple enough. It had involved the transfer of 43 aircraft from Truk, 30 from his carrier air groups on board Taiyo and 18 from Batavia, mostly fighters that had reinvigorated his sadly depleted air strength at Rabaul, before then at less than 70 aircraft. The convoy to Madang/Wewak would consist of nine transports, escorted by the light cruiser *Nagara* and a whole division of eight destroyers.

The evacuation of Buka would be undertaken solely by destroyers and frigates over the space of three nights from two ports, Buka in the South and Hanahan in the North East. He had assembled a force of 8 *Momi* and *Wakataki* second line destroyers, two frigates and two fleet destroyers for the task.

1615 3 February 1943

Rommel, newly arrived in Tunisia after a long retreat all the way from El Alamein, had little long-term hope for his command. They had a strong natural defence in Tunisia, true, buttressed by the Atlas Mountains, but the very lack of supply would be sure to kill them in the end. It was a viscous cycle, they needed more men to defend the front lines against advances from virtually all points of the compass, but the more men and equipment they brought in, the more food, water, ammunition and sundry supplies needed to be brought in by via an air and sea that the enemy had mastery over.

1808 3 February 1943

Lt Commander Peter Minchoni's PT Boat Squadron, now made up to a full 14 Boats, had been based out of Milne Bay for some time, but had received orders to move up to Lae, as a "forward base", three days ago. They had been followed by a six boat Australasian MGB squadron.

Having grown used to what comfort there was at Milne, the conditions at Lae were basic at best. However, there was clearly action in the wind and their transfer was likely temporary as their tender, *HMAS Abbekirk*, remained at Milne.

2226 3 February 1943

Yamamoto feared the tide of the war had already changed. The navy's losses, likely to be increased in this current operation, were unsustainable. He feared their remaining assets would be frittered away withdrawing and reinforcing outposts whilst the allies advanced across the Pacific regaining lost territories. This is what he had feared pre-war, but what else could he do?

After this operation he planned to use his forces defensively only, building the navy back up so it could at least attempt to fight a decisive battle once one of the four key areas of the Empire were threatened, namely the Dutch East Indies (specifically Java and Sumatra), Formosa, the Philippines or Borneo. Losses so far were huge and consisted of:

BB Kongo, Fuso, Hiei, Haruna, Kirishima
CV Akagi, Shokaku, Zuikaku, Soryu, Hiryu, Junyo, Hiyo
CVL Hosho, Zuiho, Shoho, Ryujo
CVE Unyo
AV Chitose, Chiyoda, Kimikawa Maru, Kimakawa Maru, Mizuho
CA Nachi, Mikuma, Mogami, Suzuya, Atago, Kako, Aoba, Furataka, Takao, Kinusaga, Maya
CL Jintsu, Sendai, Tenryu, Tatsuta, Yasoshima, Ioshima, Kitikami, Oi, Kiso, Yura

plus he had lost many mine layers, frigates and minesweepers and an incredible 37 destroyers, as well as seven of the 12 armed merchant cruisers he had commissioned and a number of fleet oilers. He feared this operation would be the cause of the loss of more of his precious destroyers. He had commissioned a design study into a cheap and easily built escort destroyer design and hoped to have it finalised very soon.

2237 3 February 1943

Admiral Royle, as the uniformed head of the Australasian navy, viewed the report he had prepared for Defence Minister Peter Fraser. He looked down the current strength of the navy and its losses since 1939.

BB Pacifica(under repair)
BM Nil Losses: *Gorgon*
CV Australasia(under repair)
CVL *Christchurch* Losses: *Melbourne(1), Wellington*
CVE *Sydney(2), Melbourne(2), Brisbane(2)*{Landing ship carrier}, *Noumea*(very small) Losses: *Zealandia, Albatross*
CA: *Auckland, Dunedin* Losses: *Perth*
CL: *Launceston, Hobart, Darwin* Losses: *Brisbane(1), Sydney(1), Suva*
CM: *Adelaide*
DD(*Tribal Class*): *Wik, Wiri, Nasoqo, Kurnei, Alawa, Warramunga, Tagalag, Koko, Palawan, Maori* Losses: *Ravu, Miwa*
DD(old): *Vampire, Stuart, Valhalla, Attack* Losses: *Waterhen, Vendetta, Voyager*
DDAA(*Clemson Class*) *Barnes, Albany, Clifton* Losses: *Richmond*
Destroyer Escorts: *Waikato, Tamar, Clutha, Darling, Todd, Waimbula, Derwent, Murray, Hawkesbury*
Sloops: *Swan, Warrego* Losses: *Yarra, Parramatta*
Frigates: *Tasmania, Success, Stalwart, Swordsman* Losses: *Tattoo*
Submarines: *Oberon, Otway, Taipan, King Brown, Death Adder, Brown Snake, Copperhead, Tiger Snake, K8, R35* Losses: *Otama, K9*

Corvettes/Minesweepers: 44 Losses: *Armidale, Geelong, Ballarat, Bathurst*
Assault Ships: *Monowai, Kanimbla, Manoora, Westralia*
Hospital ships: *Oranje, Wanganella, Manunda, Maunganui*
Sub Depot Ships: 2
PT Boat Depot Ships: 1
Oilers: 4

In addition, the navy had operational control over two Dutch AA cruisers and three submarines and one Portuguese destroyer and two sloops. Construction had been scaled back to only provide ships likely to complete before the end of 1944, so was now mainly only light attack craft and submarines.

Under construction were the AA cruiser *Hamilton*, six *Bathurst Class* corvettes(with a final two ordered), six *Snake Class* submarines and an increased number of MGB's, with some MTB's. The only other project the navy was looking at was a conversion of two more ships as MGB tenders. One vessel being looked at was the 7,800-ton *Green Seas*, a pre-war grain carrier that had been the RAN's only MAC ship conversion.

2348 3 February 1943

As the night wore steadily on, Nimitz reviewed the losses so far sustained by the USN in the war. It was in carriers that they had been most heavily hit. The losses sustained were serious, but his main consolation was he knew the Japanese had suffered just as badly. By the end of 1943 he knew these losses would be made good, whereas the same may not be said for the Japanese. His losses so far were:

BB Indiana, West Virginia, Oklahoma, Arizona, Utah(gunnery training ship only)
CV Yorktown, Enterprise, Hornet, Wasp, Lexington, Saratoga
CVE Langley
ML Ogala
CA Houston, Chicago, Vincennes, Portland
CL Nashville, Atlanta, Juneau, Raleigh
DD 25
DE 2
AO 2
MS 7
Gunboat 4
APD 3

He was sure there would be more. It promised to be a long war, a war of attrition or so it seemed.

0002 4 February 1943

It would be a busy day from tomorrow, or make that today, thought Rear Admiral Charles Mason, USN, Commander Solomons Air Forces. The island chain had five active strips, not counting the seaplane bases at Tulagi. They were, in order from North to South, Torokina and Kieta, both on Bougainville, Borokina, on Vella Lavella, Munda on New Georgia and finally Henderson on Guadalcanal.

Squadrons in residence comprised:
Kieta:
VMF 123 - Wildcats
VMF 211 - Wildcats
VMF 223 - Wildcats
VMSB 131 - Vindicators/Avengers

Torokina:
VMF 121 - F4U
VMF 122 - F4U
VMSB 233 - Dauntless
VMSB 234 - Dauntless

Vella Lavella:
No 2 Squadron RAAF - He 100's
No 76 Squadron RAAF - He 119's
No 16 Squadron RAAF - Ansons
No 1 RAAF Photo Recon Unit - P43's

Munda:
69th Bombardment Squadron USAAF - B26
70th Bombardment Squadron USAAF - B26
75th Bombardment Squadron USAAF - B25
67th Pursuit Squadron USAAF - P39's

Henderson:
VMI 253- C47's
VMSB 141 - Dauntless
VMSB 144 - Dauntless
VMF 224 - F4U
64th Bombardment Squadron USAAF - B17's

0633 4 February 1943

Captain Taro Onoshi's first mission to Buka had been successful so far. His high-speed force had arrived at Buka just before midnight, and, conscious of the need for speed of loading, had departed right on 0200. They were now 100 nautical miles to the North of Buka, having increased speed to 24 knots and had still not to his knowledge been detected by allied aircraft. The first night of what would be a three- or four-night operation had gone well.

1534 4 February 1943

It was not a sighting of ships that had alerted Rear Admiral Charles Mason, the allied air commander in the Solomons to the activities of the Japanese, it was the photo recon aircraft's images of Buka. The Japanese were preparing to pull out, with troops crowded around the dockyard area. He remained unaware that some had already done so.

The only place a relief force could come from was Rabaul and he immediately ordered full air coverage over both the island and to the North, first recon flights to leave at 0330. With a large tropical storm over New Britain that would not blow over for a day or more, he needed to see what ships the Japanese were using and spot them before they disappeared back under the storm front, the edge of which was some 80-100 nautical miles from Buka.

2030 4 February 1943

The weather gods had been kind so far, but they would need to be thought Captain Tawara Yoshioki aboard the light cruiser *Nagara*. Although they had been unmolested for 24 hours under the storm front, it was scheduled to blow away tomorrow and who knows what that may bring. The convoy, traveling at the crawling speed of 7 knots, was still off Commodore Bay in Northern New Britain. It was like they had deliberately assembled the most plodding, useless bunch of ships that could be put to sea, although in all fairness, they were probably all that was available at Rabual.

1635 5 February 1943

Captain Tawara Yoshioki's reinforcement force were still off Rottock Bay near the tip of New Britain when spotted by the enemy flying boat, which, even though pursued by the A6M's would almost certainly have gotten a sighting report off. Although probably too late in the day to be attacked now, he fully expected tomorrow to be a trial of combat for his slow-moving command. By daylight he expected to be West of Umboi Island, but that would still put him ninety to a hundred nautical miles from Madang and slightly further to Wewak, a long way for force traveling at a miserable 7 knots.

He had been well covered by fighters from Rabaul, but, as the distance widened between the convoy and the air base at Rabaul, that coverage would be harder and harder to keep up in numbers, fighters being able to stay over the convoy for reduced periods of time.

0704 5 February 1943

Captain Taro Onoshi's second, and final, mission to Buka had involved much more in the ways of delay. There were more soldiers than the previous trip and he had not been able to depart until 0314, being further delayed by an attack by U.S PT boats at 0358. This had been successfully driven off with little damage, sinking one U.S boat, however, it had delayed his force.

It had not taken long past fist light at 0638 for his force to pick up a "snooper", which now arrogantly circled too high for his escorting A6M's to intercept. Worse still it was a beautifully fine and clear day, perfect for visibility. With one, possibly two more missions to the North of the island scheduled for the next two days he had to keep his motley force of old destroyers intact.

0805 5 February 1943

Captain Tawara Yoshioki on board the *Nagara* watched as the three allied P-40's disappeared. They had fought a brief battle with the A6M's shooting one down. He was now spotted, without a doubt and would have to last the day. He was only 80 nautical miles or less from Lae, so he expected the allied air response would be swift.

0812 5 February 1943

Rear Admiral Charles Mason's Solomons Air Command had been well prepared for combat operations on this day, consequently, the preparation of strikes from the units under his command was prompt, the first strike leaving Torokina at 0822, consisting of 21 F4U's escorting 20 Dauntless. A strike from Kieta consisting of eight Vindicators and seven Avengers, escorted by 29 Wildcats had proceeded it by eight minutes. F4U's from Henderson had been moved up to fly CAP over the two Northern Airfields.

From Munda, 24 B26's and nine B25's met their Australasian escort of 11 He 119's and 12 He 100's over Vella Lavella. Lastly, from Henderson 10 B17's launched at 1002, picking up four P-43's forty minutes later. One hundred and fifty-five aircraft were heading North for the attack on the convoy of destroyers evacuating troops from Buka.

0839 5 February 1943

Port Moresby was also a hive of activity, Lt General Kenney actually being on site at the Port Moresby headquarters. He watched with approval as the officers came up with a general strike plan, realising full well that today was the only day they would have to attack the enemy convoy.

Whilst the two RAAF P-40 squadrons based at Lae provided rotating top cover for the base, Port Moresby fighters would "stage through" Lae on their way to the convoy, picking their bomb groups back up and escorting them through the target. Logistically it would be difficult, but doable. They planned to hit the convoy with a series of "rolling raids", spaced out over the course of the day. These were later revealed to be:

Raid 1:
35 B25's, 26 P39's
Raid 2:
29 B17's, 9 P40's, 12 P39's
Raid 3(Milne Bay)
6 A36's, 8 Hudsons, 12 Boomerangs
Raid 4:
10 US A-20's, 11 RAAF A20's, 21 B24's, 19 P40's
Raid 5:
12 B25's, 15 P38's

Raid 6:
19 He 211's, 9 He 100's, 11 He 119's
Raid 7:
12 Ansons, 3 P43's

The air forces had been practicing skip bombing and masthead bombing, thought Kenney, well there was no better practice than real missions.

0906 5 February 1943

Captain Joe Foss's VMF 121 "Green Knights" were part of the first raid to hit the Japanese evacuation fleet on its way back to Rabaul. The first strike consisted of 21 F4U's and 20 Dauntless. The Japanese fighter cover was large, with 18 Zeros but also 11 of a new type of fighter that Foss had not seen before. It looked not dissimilar to the Australasian He 100. During the course of the combat, Foss had almost learned the hard way that the new Japanese fighter did not conform to the performance standards of the Zero and that he could no longer go into a dive and escape as they had from lighter Japanese fighters.

The F4U's had battled hard against the defending Japanese fighters, losing three and also four Dauntless to the Japanese fighters in exchange for seven Zeros and three of the new type. Thankfully, many of the Japanese pilots looked to be novices. The remaining 16 Dauntless had pressed the attack, but the small destroyers made for difficult targets, although one hit was scored, breaking the back of a destroyer with a 1000lb bomb.

0927 5 February 1943

Kieta's raid developed quickly after the one from Torokina, gain running into the Japanese CAP, somewhat reduced at 11 Zeros and eight of the new type of fighter. Consisting of eight Vindicators and seven Avengers, with a heavy escort of 32 Wildcats, the 11 Zeros engaged the 16 Wildcats escorting the Vindicators, losing four of their number in exchange for two Wildcats. The Vindicators, unworried by the fighters, missed their nimble targets, their targeted destroyer evading all bombs aimed at her.

The Avengers, escorted by 16 Wildcats were engaged the eight new Japanese fighters and lost three Wildcats and an Avenger in exchange for two of the new fighters. However, all the remaining six aircraft missed their torpedo attacks in what was an unsuccessful raid.

1034 5 February 1943

Squadron Leader Edgar "Cobber" Kain lead his squadron of He 100's and their accompanying He 119's into action against the depleted escort of seven Zeros and six Japanese aircraft of a new type. They exchanged two He 100 and a He 119 for three Zeros and two of the new type, their numbers alone allowing the US bombers clearance through to their targets.

The 24 B26's and nine B25's from the USAAF scored two hits, with one of the B-25's pilots, having mastered skip bombing in practice, putting this to good use, placing a 500lb bomb neatly into a Japanese destroyer. Another was hit and stopped by a torpedo from a B26, before catching another from a B-26, causing the ship to sink in less than five minutes.

1037 5 February 1943

Captain Taro Onoshi's command had lost three destroyers, all unfortunately crowded with troops and the losses at sea had been heavy. With minimal fighter cover left, he had radioed Rabaul for reinforcements that he had been assured were on the way. The *Namikaze* had already sunk, as had the smaller *Sarawabe*. Her sister ship, the *Asagao* was being abandoned and would be scuttled. When he arrived back at Rabaul at 1523, it was minus three destroyers and near 1000 men.

1102 5 February 1943

The first USAAF raid would be the biggest of the day, fully 35 B25's escorted by 26 P39's. Major Alwyn Shaw, their strike leader, had decided to use, mast top bombing, a technique that they had some practice in. It involved the bombers approaching the target at low altitude, 200 to 500 feet, at about 250 to 275 miles per hour, and then dropping down to mast height, 10 to 15 feet at about 500-600 yards from the target. They would release their bombs at around 300 yards, aiming directly at the side of the ship.

They encountered a seemingly strong on-site escort of 15 Zeros and eight Ki 43 Oscars. The Japanese escort was largely ineffective against the P-39's, losing eight Zeros and four Oscars for the shooting down of four P39's and one B25, with two more bombers damaged. The allied bombers were largely left to their own devices, with only a few Oscars with their puny offensive armament breaking through, which was to prove devastating to the convoy. The B-25's largely roamed at will, losing one aircraft to AA with another damaged.

However, fully 30 B-25's were able to make runs on the ships and achieved six hits. The 6,500-ton *Oigawa Maru*, hit once and then stopped, was quickly hit twice more and was left sinking. The 2.700-ton *Aiyo Maru* was hit once and left almost immobilized, damaged severely. The destroyer *Arashio* was also badly lamed by a 500lb bomb which landed on her bridge, destroying not only her command staff but killing the commander of the Japanese XVIII Army – Lieutenant General Hatazō Adachit.

1140 5 February 1943

Captain Tawara Yoshioki on board the *Nagara* worried that the first raid may only be a taste of more to come, radioing Madang for any further air support they may be able to offer. With the *Aiyo Maru* barely making steerage, they were sitting ducks and he had to recover survivors from the *Oigawa Maru*. It was only 38 minutes after the first strike, whilst just starting search and rescue that a second raid arrived, consisting of almost as many aircraft as the first. Worse still his depleted CAP had received no reinforcements and now consisted of only eleven aircraft, seven Zeros and four Oscars.

1155 5 February 1943

The second U.S raid, consisting of 29 B-17's, nine P-40's and 12 P-39's encountered a badly weakened CAP of only seven Zeros and four Oscars. Destroying four Zeros and three Oscars on exchange for two P40's, the B17's were left unmolested and went about their business with no threat aside from the Japanese AA defences, which were light. Suffering only one B-17 damaged, the remaining 28 aircraft hit four ships.

In addition to finishing off the crippled and immobile *Aiyo Maru*, they also hit the destroyer *Shikinami* twice, leaving her sinking, damaged the largest ship in the convoy, the 10000 ton ex French liner *Teiko Maru*, with two hits plus also damaged the 6000 ton *Kyokuseo Maru*, slowing her to five knots and setting her on fire with a hit. The appearance of seven more Oscars near the end of the attack did little to help the Japanese, two being shot down by the heavily armed bombers in exchange for damage to one more B-17.

1216 5 February 1943

The Milne Bay raid appeared not long after the second force, consisting of less attacking aircraft this time, only eight Hudsons and six A36's, escorted by 12 Boomerangs. Intercepted by a CAP of four Zeros and six Oscars, the generally superior Japanese fighters this time had some success, downing two Hudsons and two Boomerangs in exchange for a single Oscar and a single Zero.

Although the Hudson attack caused no damage, the escort had completely missed the higher flying A36's whilst attacking the lower altitude Hudsons. This had unfortunate consequences for the smallest ship in the convoy, the 950-ton *Kembu Maru*. Hit twice by 500lb bombs by the dive bombers, she was to sink very rapidly indeed.

1318 5 February 1943

By the time the next US raid had appeared over the convoy, Captain Tawara Yoshioki was at least heartened to see 15 more A6M's arrive to replace some of the aircraft from his depleted CAP, giving him 15 A6M's and 4 Ki-43's as CAP. The US raid was again huge, however, consisting of 21 A20's, 21 B24's, escorted by 19 P-40's. Losing four P-40's and one A-20 to the Japanese fighters, they succeeded in bringing down eight A6M's and two Ki 43's in exchange. With the enemy bombers again only partially hindered, Captain Yoshioki knew his command was again going to have its head in the oven and so it was to prove.

The B-24's concentrated on the *Teiko Maru*, hitting her three times, which was more than enough to doom the liner, packed with troops. They also hit the damaged destroyer *Arashio*, finishing her off. The RAAF and ASAAF A20's, eschewed mast height bombing in favour of skip bombing, also achieving some success, hitting the big 8,100-ton navy transport *Nojima* three times, leaving her sinking.

Only four of his nine transports were left, in addition he had lost two of his eight destroyers and men were in the water everywhere.

1404 5 February 1943

Captain Richard Bong pulled his P38 into a tight turn, hoping to use his height and superior speed to come down on the Zero. His 15 P-38's were tangling with a smaller CAP than they had anticipated, only seven Zeros and three Oscars. By the end of the combat they had downed four Zeros and two Oscars in exchange for a single P38. The 12 B-25's they were escorting lost one plane to AA fire but hit the 7000-ton *Teiyo Maru* twice, disabling her so badly she would have to be scuttled and also hit the flagship, the light cruiser *Nagara*, causing superstructure damage and knocking out a gun turret.

1445 5 February 1943

The next Australasian raid came hard enough on the heels of the last one that the Japanese CAP still had not been replaced by another reinforcement group of fighters from Rabaul, and therefore consisted of only three A6M's and one Ki-43.

As Flight Lieutenant Richard Bennett moved the intercept with his He 100's, that left 19 He 211 four engine bombers and 11 He 119's cleared through. The He 211's hit the already damaged *Kyokusei Maru*, lumbering along at five knots, twice more, leaving her sinking and also hit the much smaller 2,800 *Teimei Maru* twice, sinking her rapidly. The He 119's, with no enemy fighters to attack, used their six 20mm cannons to good effect on the destroyers, scoring a spectacular success when the destroyer *Arashio's* long lance torpedoes detonated, breaking the destroyer in half. The destroyer *Asagumo* was also badly riddled with cannon fire. Only one transport, the *Sanei Maru*, remained afloat. The Australasian's lost one He100 and one He 211 in exchange for reducing the CAP to a single Zero.

1522 5 February 1943

With the last of the allied air raids having left Port Moresby, Lt General Kenney had asked about a follow up second strike to try and hit the enemy again, it being vital to stop the transmission of troops to Northern New Guinea. Too late in the day to refuel and stage fighters through Lae, he had made the decision to send another raid with the remaining B-17's and B-25's from the first two raids without fighter cover. He calculated that they would barely be back before dark, but it was deemed to be worth the risk.

1555 5 February 1943

The Australasians ran into a newly reinforced CAP, 13 Zeros having arrived over the remnants of the Japanese fleet, still conducting rescue operations. The strike, small only and consisting of 12 Ansons and three P43's, did not gain any hits, losing a P-43 and four Ansons in exchange for three Zeros.

1654 5 February 1943

Captain Tawara Yoshioki's ships had finally completed rescue operations and had again resumed course for Madang. It had been a disaster. If his original nine transports, only the *Sinai Maru* remained, along with the damaged light cruiser *Nagara* and the destroyers *Asagumo* (also damaged), *Shirayuki, Yukikaze, Uranami* and *Nowaki*. All were drastically overcrowded, full of men from the sunken ships. The only good news was that he was not far from Long Island and less than 60 nautical miles from Madang. He no longer intended to go to Wewak. Madang would have to do.

1731 5 February 1943

Major Alwyn Shaw's B-25's were flying their second mission of the day. Their force and the B-17's with them consisted of 26 B-25's and the same number of B-17's, escorted by only two RAAF He 119 long range fighters. Over the Japanese ships they were met by 11 Zeros and, for the first time, suffered some significant losses, two B-17's and four B-25's in exchange for five Japanese fighters. However, with 55 enemy aircraft, there was only so much the Japanese fighters could so. Many were unimpeded on their attack runs and hits were again suffered, with six bombs finding their way into ships.

The 3,800-ton *Sanai Maru*, so far untouched was the primary target. Hit three times, she sank slowly over the next 45 minutes. The light cruiser *Nagara*, hit again by a 500lb bomb, was slowed to 16 knots by engine room damage. The destroyer *Nowaki*, hit twice, was left sinking. It was the final airstrike of the day and for some Japanese soldiers, up to the third time they had been sunk in the same day.

2213 5 February 1943

Captain Tawara Yoshioki's ships had finally reached Madang. He was not to know that only the loss of all his transports had sped his force up enough that they had also avoided interception by a combined PT/MGB force as well.

Even as it was, the losses had been disastrous. They had lost all nine transport and four of his eight destroyers. This light cruiser *Nagara* was badly damaged, as was the destroyer *Asagumo* and they still had to run back to Rabaul the following day. He did not want to be caught in the harbour at daylight, for the only local air cover was six Zeros, two of those unserviceable. Of the 8,000 troops he had embarked, only 2.480 had made it to Madang, most with little equipment.

2314 5 February 1943

It had been a disastrous day, thought Yamamoto. He had lost three destroyers evacuating the South of Buka and had still to withdraw troops from the North. His reinforcement convoy to Rabaul had all nine transports and four of the eight destroyers sunk, with damage to other ships.

He had sent a small raid to Lae, hoping to suppress the base. It consisted of only eight unescorted G4M's, all escorts being tied up. This had also failed, losing seven of the eight bombers for no significant damage. He had lost fully 80 aircraft for the day, decimating the newly reinforced air wing at Rabaul, now back to less than 50 serviceable aircraft, not all front-line types. He would have to put off the withdrawal from Northern Buka a few days, perhaps using some of the ships currently at Madang to replace those lost.

"I went in and hit this troop ship. What I saw looked like little sticks, maybe a foot long or something like that, or splinters flying up off the deck of ship; they'd fly all around ... and twist crazily in the air and fall out in the water. Then I realized what I was watching were human beings. I was watching hundreds of those Japanese just blown off the deck by the cannons. They just splintered around the air like sticks in a whirlwind and they'd fall in the water."

1744 25 April 2014(flash forward)

She had finished her speech, to be delivered to the Victorian Vietnamese Community on ANZAC Day. With her father on Bougainville for ANZAC day commemorations, she had done the dawn service at the Shrine this morning and this speech would finish up a tiring day. She had brought her mother for moral support and glanced over her speech yet again. Like all royal speeches, it could not be seen as too political.

"It is a great pleasure for my mother and myself to be here and take part in commemorating ANZAC day and Australasia's involvement in the Vietnam War and the significant events that have followed it.

The ceremonial lighting of the candle by us this evening reminds us that for centuries people burned candles as part of ceremonies and religious rituals, at times of celebration and also of mourning. Candles are burned to remember loved ones and of past events, but they are also burnt as a symbol of healing and the bringing of new hope.

Tonight our candles burn in commemoration of Australasia's military involvement in the Vietnam War, which was Australasia's longest involvement in any war. We also recognise the many positive circumstances that have followed from it.

It is the focus on these matters that has brought us together tonight as Australasians. This evening we reflect that over 215,000 Australasian's were born in Vietnam and now live here as Australasians and Vietnamese is the sixth most common language spoken in our country, with citizens spread out over all twelve states.

We also reflect that the second and third generations of Vietnamese Australasians born here are now adding their contributions to business, life and culture. The distinctive Vietnamese 'hard work' ethic and industrious vitality have enriched our way of life. The Vietnamese influence is now as essential an ingredient to our multi-cultural community as fish sauce and lemongrass are to the Vietnamese cuisine now enjoyed by so many Australasians.

Yet, all this peaceful, harmonious activity had its genesis just fifty years ago with a small military beginning in what turned out to be a terrible war.

It was during July and August 1962 that the Australasian Army Training Team arrived in South Vietnam. This group of military advisers, led by Colonel Ted Serong, was the vanguard of the Australasian involvement in the Vietnam War. Soon it would lead to far greater support from every branch of our armed services.

From that small beginning, the arrival of just 30 men, our national commitment to the war would grow until almost 80,000 Australasian, soldiers, sailors, airmen and civilians would serve in Vietnam.

The Australasian commitment and support for South Vietnam from the early 1960's was in keeping with the policies of other nations, particularly the United States, in answering requests at that time by the government in South Vietnam for security assistance.

That Australasian involvement would only end eleven years later when my Great Grandmother the Queen issued a proclamation to that effect on 11 January 1973. And the last combat troops, a platoon of Diggers guarding the Australasian embassy in Saigon, would not leave until June of that year, almost eleven years after the first arrivals.

Seven hundred and twenty-nine Australasians died as a result of the war and over 3,800 were wounded. As we know, some who served in Vietnam are still suffering from the conflict, remaining scarred from the dreadful results of that war, even to this day. The war also became the cause of one of the greatest social and political dissents in Australasia since the conscription referendums of the First World War. Many draft resisters, conscientious objectors and protesters were fined or jailed, while our soldiers on their return home sometimes met a hostile reception, a response that today borders on the unbelievable.

Such response is all the more extraordinary because, as was the case with other armed conflicts that involved Australasia, our troops who served in Vietnam did so with extraordinary bravery and did our country great honour. They fought with exemplary gallantry, often in terrible conditions. Yet it was an unpopular war, without a doubt, fought, like so many modern wars, often by irregulars. Whilst its unpopularity was perfectly understandable, the question may be asked, what if we had not responded strongly in South Korea against North Korean and Manchurian aggression? If we had not taken a strong stance on East Indonesia and Timor? Those three countries, with which we have friendly political and trade relations, may not exist today.

Today, we recognise those service men and women as heroes and we now list battles such as Long Tan alongside Lone Pine and The Nek of Gallipoli fame; alongside Tobruk and New Guinea of the Second World War; and alongside Korea, in our national roll call of military valour.

And today we also remember with equal honour the Vietnamese soldiers from the Republic of Vietnam who fought side by side with the Australasians in many battles. We remember the Vietnamese people's bravery and the great sacrifices they made for their country and for their democratic values. We remember the intense suffering of soldiers and civilians alike. We also recall how Australasian men and women worked tirelessly to help maintain order and to provide protection and support for local Vietnamese communities, many of whom would not have survived had it not been for that protection.

But now, by the flickering light of the candles, we should also pause to recall what happened next, what happened after the war.

Before 1975, the numbers of Vietnamese coming to Australasia were low. In the census of 1976, the names of only 1,482 Vietnamese born citizens were recorded. This small number included some orphans from the war, Vietnamese wives of Australasian servicemen and just a few students who had come here for a tertiary education. All that changed in 1976 when the first boat arrived in Australasia carrying Vietnamese refugees who had by-passed formal immigration procedures. They were desperate to find a new home as they fled terrible suffering and privation in their motherland. Within three years, a further 58 refugee boats had arrived.

By 1981, the Vietnamese-born population in Australasia was over 55,000. In 1982, the Australasian and Vietnamese governments agreed on an orderly migration programme, emphasising family reunion, and two thirds of arrivals over the next few years were women.

And so within a few more years the Vietnamese-born population of Australasia would again double and we had a new generation of Australasian-Vietnamese. Many Vietnamese set up their own businesses, working hard to put their children through school and university. Today they have grown up to be among our leaders in nearly all walks of life.

It was that "hard work" ethic that created Vietnamese small businesses that have gradually transformed whole areas of Melbourne that I see myself every day like in suburbs like Richmond and Springvale into bustling, vibrant retail shops and restaurants that so suit a student like myself. And the same work ethic applied to areas in which those with a Vietnamese background were engaged, be it study, management, the professions and the like. Their positive contributions to our community have been far reaching.

So tonight, as we commemorate the Australasia's involvement in South Vietnam during the Vietnam War, we gaze at the candles we have lit together. We remember the past and the gallant sacrifices made at that time and we thank all those who served. We mourn for the dead.

But as we gaze together at the candle's flame we look forward, all of us as Australasian's, with fresh hope to the future. A future of peace and harmony, living and working together in this wonderful place, this place which is our homeland."

0722 6 February 1943

Captain Tawara Yoshioki's ships were back to sea and already 60 nautical miles back to Rabaul. He already had orders to use three of his undamaged destroyers in the evacuation of Northern Buka, scheduled now for the night of the 8th. He hoped it would go better than the Madang operation, where the town and airfield had even been shelled by what he presumed was an enemy submarine during the night, a shell hitting the pier and killing 12 of the long-suffering soldiers he had rescued.

0710 9 February 1943

It was not until after 0700 in the morning the Japanese evacuation from Hanahan Bay was discovered, the light cruiser *Kino*, eight destroyers and three frigates packed with the last of the troops from Buka. Loading had taken a long time and when discovered they were 52 miles due West of the Northern tip of Buka.

Again, the first strike was Dauntless escorted by F4U's, arriving over the Japanese ships at 0902. But by the time it had arrived over the Japanese fleet were almost into the channel between New Britain and New Ireland and well within the air envelope of Rabual, reduced in strength though that may have been. The 19 F-4U's battled the eight Ki-61 Tonys and 12 Zeros, losing three aircraft as well as three more dive bombers in exchange for three Tonys and seven Zeros. The Dauntless obtained only one hit, on the light cruiser *Kino*, their attack being badly broken up by the escort. However, this hit in the boiler room by a 1000lb bomb badly damaged the light cruiser and she was forced to struggle on alone, behind the rest of the Japanese forces.

The second attack, at 0938, consisted of seven Vindicators and four Avengers, escorted by 25 Wildcats and quickly found the struggling cruiser, escorted by five Tonys and three Zeros. The numerous Wildcats easily held off the Japanese fighters, shooting down all the Zeros and two Tonys in exchange for three of their own. The Vindicators, in their swansong as a U.S Navy aircraft, hit the cruiser twice with 500lb bombs, bringing her to a halt. Hit again by a torpedo from the Avengers, she sank rapidly, three bomb hits and a torpedo hit being far too much for the old ship.

By not stopping for damaged ships, Captain Taro Onoshi had assured the rest of his command a safe passage back to Rabaul, tying up soon after noon. For the more than 1000 men on the *Kino*, it was more problematic, just over 200 being saved.

1158 17 February 1943

Captain Felix Stump was a proud man. Captain of the *USS Lexington(2)*, just commissioned this morning. She was the second *Essex Class* now in commission, joining the *USS Independence*, with the Princeton to be commissioned within a week. The U.S Navy was starting to get back on its feet, it's offensive firepower already being restored. In addition to the fleet and light carriers starting to arrive, here were now twelve escort carriers in commission, quite excluding those that had gone to the RN.

0906 23 February 1943

Lt General Freyberg's amphibious landing at Finschhaven had been a complete success so far. Conducted by elements of 2nd Division led by 8th Independent Company. About 200 Japanese defending the area had been killed and casualties were light. Japanese air operations were low, only a small amount of strafing from a couple of Shotai's of Zeros. The capture of the Huon Peninsula would be the final operations in New Guinea for 2nd and 3rd Divisions, with 3rd pushing up from the South to isolate, trap and annihilate Jap forces in the region.

To the West, 4th Division had advanced along the coast, led by 5th and 6th Independent Companies. They had advanced up the Markham and Ramu Valleys. Apart from a small engagement around Kaiapit, where they had captured the village and killed over 200 Japanese, the Australasians were barely resisted as they advanced and they had arrived in

Dumpu yesterday.

From here they faced the mountains of the Finisterre Range, dominated by the 5000 ft high Shaggy Ridge. This was of vital strategic importance for both the Japanese and the Australasians. For the Japanese, it provided a strong obstacle to the Australasian advance north towards the coast, while also offering them the ground along which they could launch their own offensive in order to recapture the territory they had lost earlier. For the Australasians, the Japanese positions on the high ground signalled threat and their commander, Vasey, had already signalled to Freyberg that he would have to launch an offensive in order to capture this ground.

1156 1 March 1943

Lt General Robert Eichelberger had arrived to take command of US forces in Western New Guinea at the start of 1943 and was now pleased that they had at last achieved the objectives set. It had been a hard slog for both the 32nd and the 41st Divisions, but they had finally closed the door on Japanese expansion out of Western New Guinea, capturing Nabire in a set piece battle that cost 538 combat casualties and eliminated up to 2000 Japanese.

They had dug in troops along the network of rivers to the West, trapping the Japanese forces to the West in Vogelkop Peninsula in West Papua. The forces to the East, aside from some scattered survivors, were now almost non-existent aside from the garrison at Hollandia, a significant force over 250miles to the East.

New Guinea map showing remaining Japanese holdings in the North and far West

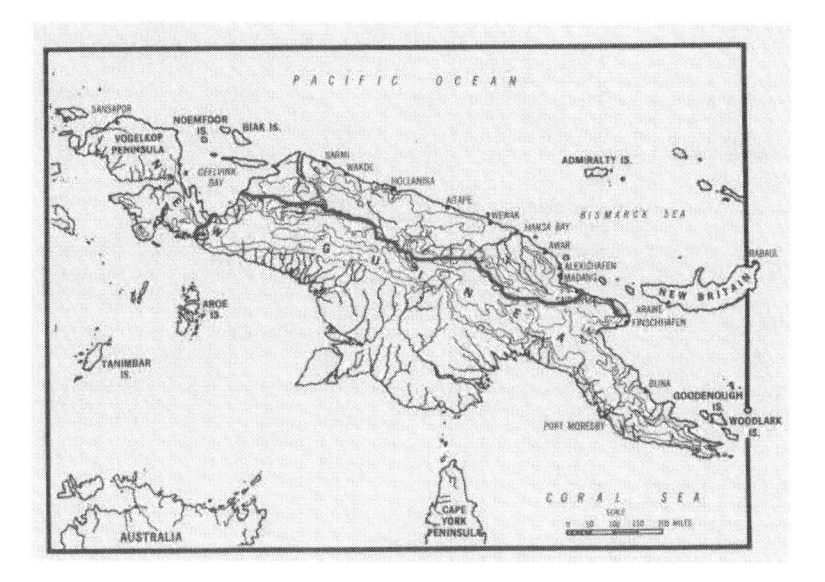

0908 9 March 1943

The situation of the German and Italian troops in North Africa was scarcely less desperate. As Rommel boarded the Ju 52, he hoped to avoid a situation like had occurred to the 6th Army at Stalingrad, surrendered over a month ago. He could not afford; indeed, Germany could not afford a similar loss of men here. The Italian navy was taking a terrible pounding to try and keep his forces supplied and he doubted their ability to lift more than a fraction of the troops in Tunisia off if needed. He needed to make Hitler see sense. To try and withdraw now whilst there may be still time. It would be the last time he saw Africa.

1506 20 March 1943

The 7,180-ton armed merchant cruiser *Noshiro Maru* and the 3,400-ton tramp steamer *Anji Maru* both slipped beneath the waves, the former under the hammer blows of three torpedo hits from the *USS Pollack*. What impressed Commander David Fairfield, however, was the torpedoes. They were a new batch embarked for this war patrol.

Of six fired, five had been hits. Even better, his patrol area Southeast of Jaluit Atoll in the Marshall Islands was proving very productive.

1643 22 March 1943

General Stilwell had moved most of his forces into position, including the 200th Division. Other forces he had been able to assemble from the drastic shortening of his line that the offensive in January had been able to provide. This would not be as big as the January operation and was focused on gains only in the North, the Shan States. He hoped it would take his forces all the way to the Thai border. Due to start on April Fool's day, he hoped that the date was not appropriate.

Burma map showing Japan/Thailand and UK/Chinese front lines

1255 27 March 1943

Rear Admiral McMorris was more than happy. The Japanese convoy, intercepted 180 miles West of Kiska, had consisted of one heavy cruiser, two light cruiser and four destroyers, as well as four transports. His own command had consisted of the heavy cruiser *Salt Lake City*, the light cruiser *Richmond* and four destroyers.

It had been the old light cruiser *Richmond* that had been the hero of the six and a half hour gunnery and torpedo battle, all in poor visibility at relatively long ranges, hitting the enemy heavy cruiser at least four times and causing her and the whole Japanese reinforcement convoy to turn back. One of his own destroyers had been damaged by two eight-inch shell hits but he had taken no other damage. With invasions scheduled for the 12th April, it was important that the Japanese had been turned back and that had been achieved.

0705 1 April 1943

Major General Vasey's 4th Division had managed to capture John's Knoll, the first key feature on the way to capture Shaggy Ridge. They planned to halt here until later in the month, having beaten off two Japanese counter attacks. With 2nd and 3rd Division, being withdrawn back to the mainland, having cleared the Huon Peninsula of Japanese in a bloody final campaign. The 6th Division was being moved into the fight, its arrival signalled by another amphibious "hook" to land forces at Alexishafen, cutting off Madang. When that occurred, 4th Division would attack the main Japanese stronghold at Shaggy Ridge.

1809 5 April 1943

Lt General Robert Eichelberger's U.S Forces had made rapid gains against only scattered resistance, using barges made locally to ferry troops forward. He had advanced all the way to the large lake and river system at Danau Rombebai. He had been halted here as he encountered the Japanese in force for the first time. His forces had also made some gains to the West, also against only scattered resistance.

1910 7 April 1943

It was a large naval gathering that had arrived at Dutch Harbour. The battleships *Pennsylvania, Idaho* and *Nevada*, the escort carrier *Nassau*, heavy cruisers *San Fransisco, Salt Lake City* and *Wichita*, light cruisers *Richmond, Detroit* and *Santa Fe*, 28 destroyers, 11 submarines and many support ships and transports. The 7th Infantry Division would assault Adak on the 12th.

0432 12 April 1943

General Joseph Stilwell's offensive in the Shan States had petered out, lasting only twelve days. It had achieved less than he had hoped for, but some gains none the less. The British had also launched a spoiling attack on the coast that had been more successful than anticipated, gaining 16 miles when nothing like that had been expected.

What was interesting was the rapid withdrawal of Thai units when encountered near Kentung, briefly throwing Japanese units into confusion. It boded well for a 1943-44 campaign, but with the monsoon season now only three weeks or so away, he had ordered his forces to dig in and guard his existing gains. The allies precious supply line and the Burma Road had been safeguarded.

0450 12 April 1943

Lt General Shojiri Iieda's forces had contained and turned back the Chinese and British attacks, still holding the vital oilfields in central Burma. He had lost ground in the flanks, however, and one thing was clear. With the tide seemingly turning he could not rely on Thai troops, who seemed reluctant to fight, nor could he rely on the Indian national Army. Although their troops had fought well, the turn in the tide had slowed the flow of troops to Bose's forces. Perhaps Tokyo would get off its ass and send him a larger share of troops and supplies. Burma was truly the last frontier for the army's replacement, supplies and all logistics.

Burma pre monsoon front lines in red (post 1942 monsoon season in green)

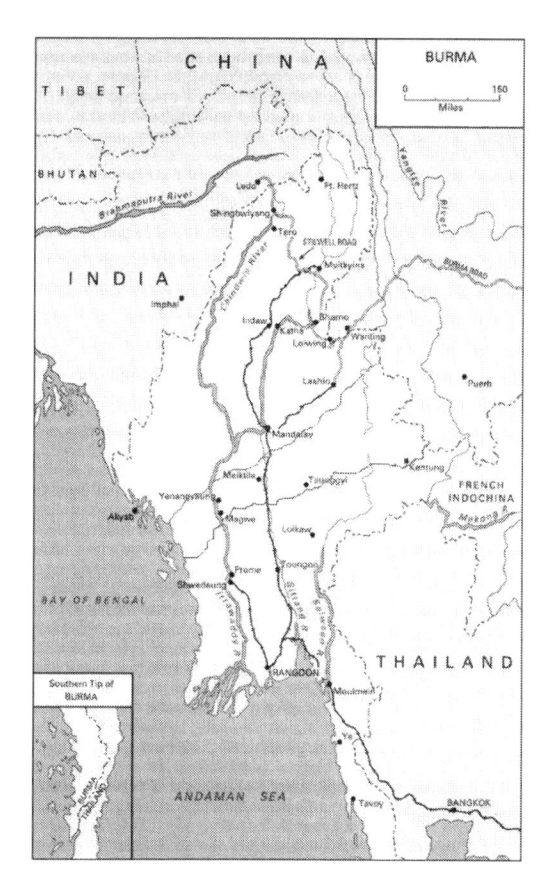

1123 12 April 1943

Major General Charles Harrison Corlett's 7th Infantry Division had stormed ashore to very scattered opposition, no more than 80 Japanese being located at the landing beach. They had rapidly gained a foothold, killing said Japs in exchange for only nine killed and 14 wounded. His forces had naval gunfire capability and lavish air support whilst his opponents, supposedly numbering 2000 to 4000, had nothing, so he hoped to make this a quick campaign.

1816 26 April 1943

The 7th Infantry Division had beaten off a major Japanese counter attack, killing over 500 and had secured the high ground and the down slopes of both Mount Reed to the South and Mount Moffatt to the North. They now had viability on the Japanese remaining forces, compressed into the lowlands near Kuluk Bay.

The main enemy had proven to be the weather, with far more hypothermia cases than killed and/or wounded. The Japanese main base at Kuluk Bay had been subject to a relentless air and naval bombardment for two weeks now. On the 29th, he would launch a final push to capture it.

1605 27 April 1943

Major General George Wootten's 6th Infantry Division had secured a substantial beachhead at Alexishafen already, effectively cutting of any retreat for the Japanese forces at Madang. The landings, easily covered from Lae now large airfield, had been pre-empted by a large strike on the small Japanese airfield at Madang, destroying at least 13 aircraft on the ground.

So far Japanese resistance had been light, the only garrison at the town consisting of a company of Japanese naval infantry which had been swept aside during the course of the day. He had suffered over 60 casualties, however, as the Japanese had continued to fight to the last.

0912 28 April 1943

Commander Warren Ebert had hit the seaplane carrier broadside on with three torpedoes from *USS Scamp*. As he watched through the periscope, the *Kunikawa Maru* rapidly capsized, taking her cargo with her.

0705 29 April 1943

Major-General Vasey's 4th Division had resumed its attack on Shaggy Ridge, using his three Independent Companies as "fire brigades to lead the attack". With the landings by the 6th at Alexishafen, if he could take Shaggy Ridge, they could sweep down and annihilate the remaining Japs in Madang.

0706 30 April 1943

Major General Julian Smith's 2nd Marine Division was ready to go from its base in American Samoa. It had just received its orders. Tarawa on the 9th of June. It promised to be a difficult campaign, the first real strike back in the Central Pacific, but he was looking forward to the challenge.

1716 2 May 1943

Adak had been officially secured. Not before a massive charge by the remaining Japanese. His attack on the 29th had rapidly gained ground, cutting the Japanese forces in two pockets near Adak Station on the 30th. This had been followed by a charge by the remaining Japanese that night under cover of darkness that had resulted in a number of hand to hand battles that had eventually been won by the superior firepower, training and numbers of his men. Mopping up operations on the 1st and 2nd had secured the island.

Captured documents had revealed the Japanese garrison as 3,866. He had captured 72. Every other Japanese now lay dead. He had lost 636 killed and 1901 wounded or injured, as well as 2024 cases of hypothermia.

0716 3 May 1943

The five big ships, with their escort of eight destroyers, were on their way to Pearl. The *USS Essex, Lexington(2), Independence, Princeton* and the battleships *North Carolina*, newly repaired, and *Massachusetts*. The last three carriers had their shakedown cruisers truncated by about three weeks; however, they were need for the Tarawa operation and would also get two weeks on exercises with the more experienced air crews on *Lafayette*. All four carriers embarked the F6F Hellcat, the new fighter. With the battleship *South Dakota* in the Atlantic, it would restore the U.S Pacific Fleet to five carriers and three modern battleships, ready for a renewal of offensive operations.

0709 5 May 1943

Yamamoto pondered a series of seemingly insoluble problems. He had resisted the temptation to dilute his carrier air groups by transferring them to land bases, however, that had allowed the allies to conduct operations around New Guinea with ease against the paltry air defences he had in place.

However, he at least had some good news. The *Kaga* had been repaired and her air group restored. The escort carriers, originally built for escort command, he had kept with the fleet. It was tough on escort command, but he badly needed even their limited capacity. He had eleven carriers or carrier conversions underway, but none could be expected before perhaps late October/early November. In the meantime, aside from the *Kaga*, he had the light carriers *Ryuho* and *Nisshin* and the escort carriers *Taiyo* and *Chuyo*.

0330 8 May 1943

Lt General Brian Horrock's 9th British Corps was ready for the final assault on Tunis and Bizerte. The Germans and their Italian allies had been squeezed into a narrow strip of coastal land covering both towns. Very little in the way of supplies was getting through. Admiral Cunningham, Eisenhower's Naval Task Force commander, had issued Nelsonian orders to the RN and USN ships under his command: "Sink, burn, capture, destroy. Let nothing pass". It had been taken to heart and the Italian navy had paid very dearly in a largely fruitless attempt to resupply their troops.

0616 8 May 1943

The allied air forces in the Solomons had started a campaign of offensive mine-laying, led by two squadrons of B-24's based on Bougainville. They had struck pay dirt this morning, three Japanese destroyers running into a newly laid field between New Britain and New Ireland. The destroyer *Koroshio* and *Oyashio* had both sunk after touching mines, the *Koroshio* touching two and sinking in less than 15 minutes. Whilst the *Michishio* had rescued most of the crews, two valuable modern destroyers had been lost.

1446 12 May 1943

Colonel General Hans-Jürgen von Arnim's command had been split into small pockets, only holding some coastal positions on Cape Bon. It was over. Although slightly over 1000 troops would escape over the next four nights, the last troops not surrendering until the morning of the 17th May, more than 240,000 German and Italian troops had been captured. It had been the worst disaster of the war for the Axis, topping even Stalingrad.

1756 13 May 1943

It had taken a fortnight of intense battle and over 900 casualties, but Shaggy Ridge had been taken. The 4th could now advance on Bogadjim, thought Vasey, to support the 6th in its final assault on Madang. Elements of the 6th were already advancing up the coast to Awar against virtually no opposition. Elimination of the trapped Japanese at Madang could open the way to Wewak.

1202 16 May 1943

The six escort carriers had arrived at Pearl yesterday and the "swapping over" of the aircraft that they had ferried had started. The *Lafayette* would pick up their Hellcats, exchanging most of her Wildcat compliment back to the escort carriers. She would have a two week work up with the new fighters prior to the Tarawa operation.

0907 19 May 1943

Vice Admiral Collins was happier to have the two largest ships in the RAN back in operation. Both *Australasia* and *Pacifica* had completed trials after repairs and were now fully operational again. It was just as well as General Kreuger was planning an operation in July to land elements of 12th Militia Division at Kaimana in West Papua as an operation to get behind the Japanese forces and at the same time provide some support to the flank of Timor, still held by Australasian forces.

New Guinea Map as of 19.5.1943. Blue dots (or similar!) are allied air bases

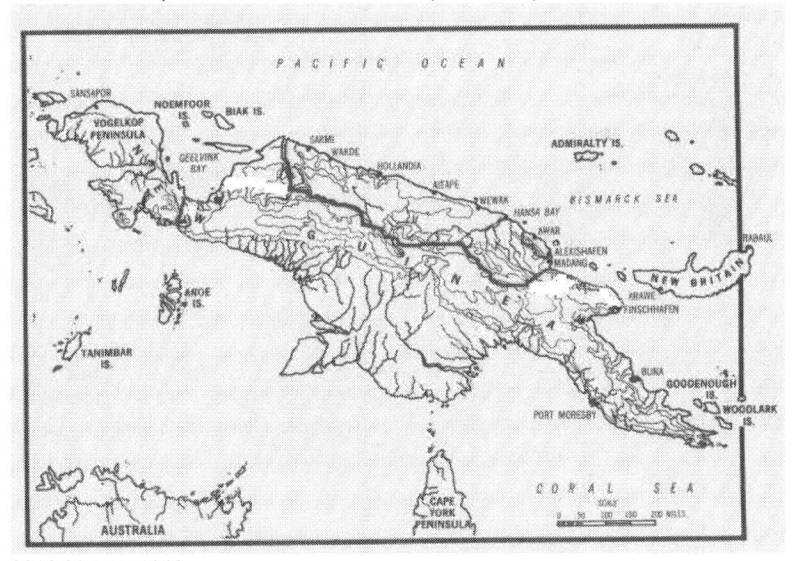

2210 22 May 1943

Keith Park reviewed how things had changed since the last aircraft review board figures in September 1942. Lend Lease had started to really roll, making up so many of the Air Forces previous shortcomings. Older types had started to be phased out, although many still remained on active squadron service. Numbers by type now read:

Fighters:

Bell P39 19(Salvaged from USAAF write offs)
Bolton Paul Defiant 31
Brewster Buffalo 12(Ex Dutch East Indies)
CAC Boomerang 202
Curtis P40 334
Hawker Hurricane 2(Ex Dutch East Indies)
Hencall He 112 156
Hencall He 100 538(Currently in production-numbers count RAN machines)
Hencall He 119 127(Currently in production)
Republic P43 56
Supermarine Spitfire 22(ex Portuguese)
TOTAL 1489 NEED 1500

Bombers/Patrol:
Avro Anson 508
Blackburn Skua 18
Consolidated Catalina 68
Douglas A20 55(12 ex Dutch East Indies)
Fairy Swordfish 94
Grumman Avenger 193
Hencall He 70 32
Hencall He 111 59
Hencall He 211 88(in production)
Lockheed Hudson 125
North American A36 189
North American B25 23
Vickers Vildebeest 30(Obsolete)
Vickers Wellington 43
Vultee Vengeance 291

TOTAL 1818 NEED 1825

Transports:

Airspeed Oxford 276
De Havilland Dragon 94
Douglas DC 2 8
Douglas C47 56(in production)
Junkers Ju 52 5
Wackett Garnet 6

TOTAL 445 NEED 800

Things had much improved, with only transports being in shortfall. With more P40's expected, some of the fighter types held in smaller numbers could be retired. It was planned to withdraw the He 70 and convert the four engine bombers to a transport role. An order for 75 Lockheed Ventura's would soon be fulfilled and the US had promised 20 Martin Mariners for patrol work.

1806 26 May 1943

The meeting at the out of the way villa was completely confidential, needed to be completely confidential for both parties that were involved. Count Gian Galeazzo Ciano's audience with the King had been brief, but he had made it quite clear what needed to be done.

The King would talk to Badaglio and sound him out. Within a few weeks perhaps they could get Italy out of this war, which had cost it a fortune in both lives, territory and economic ruin. The result of the war was clear to all those that were realists. It was now time to make sure they finished on the right side.

1906 28 May 1943

The operation had gone to plan, made easier by the remoteness of the location. Almost 12,000 Chinese POW's had been repatriated to China after a series of secret negotiations with Chungking. The Regent Pridi Banomyong could see the way the wind was blowing with Japan already on the defensive in Burma and having lost the Yenangyaung oilfields. Thailand was as yet only occupied by Japanese garrison troops, not any Japanese field armies.

He did not share the Prime Minister Plaek Phibunsongkharam's pro Japanese leanings. With the Indian National Army on the wane, he could see the allies shattering the front in the 1943-44 campaigning season. If that happened, Thailand would need to make a choice. Surrendering his units where they were encountered and allowing the allies in may collapse the front lines rapidly.

The Prime Minister's star was waning at a much faster rate than he thought. With the allies starting to bomb Bangkok, public confidence was sagging. His frequent absence from Bangkok had led morale to plummet, while a sudden proclamation that the capital and its inhabitants be immediately moved north to Phetchabun, a mountain village essentially, was greeted with universal discontent. And it wasn't only the public. The kingdom's ruling elite were becoming increasingly weary of Phibun, whose intimidation and demotion of dissenters within the government served to further unite his opponents, who were gathering around Pridi. Even the Japanese were becoming disaffected with Phibun. That a military scheme lay behind Phibun's attempt to relocate the seat of government certainly wasn't lost on the Japanese. Remote, with the nearest rail connection being a half-day's drive away, Phetchabun's main asset was its suitability as a mountainous fortress; moreover, the site was located in a region where the majority of the Thai army was based, an army that Pridi Banomyong was starting to make inroads into. If the allies moved rapidly into Thailand in 1943-44, the opportunity to take power and remove Thailand from this ruinous war would present itself.

2007 3 June 1943

Vasey's Division, the 4th, in conjunction with George Wootten's 6th, had Madang completely surrounded, the Japanese having withdrawn into the town itself. Elements of 6th Division had advanced up the coast all the way to Hansa Bay, only 50 miles from Wewak, before stopping. Eliminating Madang would clear the way for both Divisions to be deployed further up the coast.

1806 7 June 1943

It had taken four days of vicious hand to hand fighting to capture both the town and the airfield. Madang had fallen, at a cost of almost 1000 casualties. The use of almost 30 Sentinal tanks, half of them flamethrowers, had been essential in the final assault. Over 4000 Japanese lay dead amongst the ruins of the town, only 156 prisoners being taken, some of those Korean and Chinese cooks and porters. The road to Wewak was open.

1643 8 June 1943

Admiral Yamamoto can hardly believe the conversation as he hung up the phone. The battleship *Mutsu* had been moored at the flagship buoy midway between Hashirajima and the Suo-Oshima islands about two miles SW of Hashirajima. She was hosting 113 flying cadets and 40 instructors of the Tsuchiura Naval Air Group who are aboard for a familiarization tour.

Captain Tsuruoka's *Yamashiro* was moored about 1,100 yards Southwest of *Mutsu*. DesRon 11's flagship, light cruiser *Agano* and several of the squadron's newly commissioned destroyers are moored more distantly south of Hashirajima.

After lunch, *Mutsu's* deck crew had prepared to move to mooring buoy No. 2 because *Nagato* was expected to return at about 1300 from Kure after being dry-docked. There was heavy fog and visibility was down to 500 yards. *Mutsu's* magazines had contained a full load of ammunition including 16.1-inch Type 3 "Sanshikidan" incendiary shells designed as anti-aircraft rounds. Each shell weighs 2,064-lbs. and contains 1,200 sub-munitions. Each turret magazine contains 240 shells (120 per gun), including 50 "sanshiki-dans."

At 1213, *Mutsu's* No. 3 turret's magazine had exploded. Vice Admiral Shimizu, Commander of the First Fleet, a few miles away aboard *Nagato* had seen a brilliant white explosion. Shortly thereafter, he received a coded message from *Yamashiro's* Captain Tsuruoka. It says: "*Mutsu* blew up!"

Mutsu had broken in two. The 535-ft forward section collapsed to starboard, sinking quickly and laying on the pagoda mast on the floor of the bay. The 147-ft stern section upends, but remains floating. *Yamashiro* immediately launched two of her Vedette boats. Her crew had rescued 353 survivors of the 1,474 crew members aboard *Mutsu*. Only 13 of the visiting flying cadets/instructors are among the survivors. The navy can ill-afford the loss of 140 instructors and pilot trainees, particularly after the heavy losses sustained recently during the reinforcement of the 11th Air Fleet at Rabaul. *Mutsu's* stern was still bobbing in Hiroshima Bay.

The final list of those lost aboard *Mutsu* totalled 1,121 men including her skipper, Captain Miyoshi. It is a nightmare, thought Yamamoto, losing a valuable battleship for nothing. Later investigation put the blame on a disaffected crew member, who had effectively suicided the whole ship. The navy had been reduced to four operational battleships.

1904 8 June 1943

It had been a long day. A virtual all-day Defence Council meeting at the Palace. The three key figures in the government, Prime Minister John Curtin, treasurer James Scullin and Deputy Prime Minister and Defence Minister Peter Fraser sat reviewing the day's events.

Blamey had been in attendance and had reported on the needs of the army. It was decided that with the immediate threat to Australasia abated, that the army strength be held at its current composition of six Divisions, 1st, 2nd, 3rd, 4th, 6th and 7th and 12 Independent Companies, as well as two armoured Brigades. The Militia would be downsized from six Divisions to five to release some manpower back into manufacturing, agriculture and other essential industries. In regards to the disposition of forces, 1st Division were available for active operations, 2nd and 3rd refitting and resting after extended operations in New Guinea, 4th and 6th in action in New Guinea and 7th holding Timor. Discussion had also been had on the US offer of Lend Lease tanks, up to 450 Grant Medium tanks. It had been decided to decline this offer, as the army possessed nigh on 240 Sentinel tanks of similar utility and manufacture still continued, as well as over 500 carriers and armoured cars. With most of the warfare the army faced being jungle warfare, mass employment of tanks was not practical and therefore the army had not expanded their mechanised forces beyond the two Brigades, nor were likely to do so in the foreseeable future.

Park had reported on the air force and news had been good. Of his target of 165 operation squadrons, they had 150 fully manned and equipped. His major shortfall was in transport aircraft, although replacement of older types was always a priority. Lend lease had helped close the gap greatly, as had the governments purchase of 500 aircraft in the last quarter of 1942.

Royle had reported on the navy, whose next major operation would be an amphibious landing in July in West Papua. 1943 had seen no major naval battles and the navy had concentrated on rebuilding. Construction programs were winding down into greater building of smaller craft, even a destroyer's two-year build time perhaps too long to see action in the current war. Royle had talked about the desirability of more carriers and the government had tasked itself to investigate the possibility via the USN or RN.

Scullin had addressed the gathering on the economic implications for the country. Australasia was holding up surprisingly well, considering the crippling debts incurred during the first war. Australasia was actually almost in credit with the US in regards to lend lease, the value of Reciprocal Aid from not far from that of Lend-Lease, no doubt helped by the extensive amount of US troops in the country. Unemployment was non-existent.

The country as a whole was performing better than in the Great War.

Curtin though ahead. He had an election just on the horizon, perhaps two, perhaps three months away. As he had discussed with his colleagues, it would be important to win that so that his government could finish the job. He would have a tough opponent in the Fadden/Menzies led Liberal/Country Party Coalition.

2101 29 April 2014(flash forward)

King John had a long day. It had been the opening of the Kiribati parliament and he had presided over it, delivering the local government's speech. Kiribati, in common with all of Australasia's external territories that fell outside the twelve states, was a representative democracy with a parliamentary system in an associated state relationship with Australasia. The government exercised Executive power, with the Chief Minister as head of government. Legislative power was vested in both the government and the Parliament of Kiribati. There was a multi-party system. The Judiciary was independent of the executive and the legislature. The head of state was himself, represented by a local governor. The islands were self-governing in "free association" with Australasia. Australasia retained responsibility for external affairs and defence. Kiribati nationals were citizens of Australasia and could receive Australasian government services, but the reverse was not true; Australasian citizens were not Kiribati nationals (with the exception of his own family). Australasian residents needed to apply for a visa if visiting as more than a tourist and there were restrictions on land ownership outside of the islands.

This system had worked well through the Pacific Islands independence movements of the 1960's, 1970s and 1980's and was in place in all Australasian External Territories aside from tiny Pitcairn, Cocos Island and Christmas Islands, which were listed as External Dependencies instead. For all other external territories, namely Kiribati, Cook Islands, Tokelau, Niue, Norfolk Island, Nauru, Tuvalu and Samoa.

They were of course different to the twelve states, in the same way the foundation member states were different to the later three joining states. The external territories contributed three members to the House of Representatives, but no senators. The original nine states contributed ten senators each, with later joiners Northern Territory, New Caledonia and Bougainville contributing four each. The House of Representatives were, of course, decided on electorates of approximately 80000-90000 voters, being population based.

0616 9 June 1943

Rear Admiral Keiji Shibazaki looked at the long lines of ships on the horizon near Tarawa. They were obviously not friendly and he doubted the ability of his island's four 8-inch guns to inflict that much damage to this sort of ship concentration. He had limited air support and less than 5000 men. All they could do was sell their lives dearly.

0816 9 June 1943

The first wave of air strikes had gone in and now the three ponderous battleships moved in to engage the Japanese gun battery, *Colorado* leading *Maryland* with *Tennessee* in the rear. They had ample stocks of shells and the battleships had been instructed to soften up the island for a full day before landings commenced tomorrow.

1012 9 June 1943

Fred David had been impressed by the first flight of the new machine at Point Cook. He had designed her from the ground up and it was the mating of the new Griffon 61 engine with its two-stage supercharger that had given her the power that he thought the new fighter needed. The test pilot, Jim Schofield, had only moved her through a series of basic manoeuvres but the plane looked very capable indeed, being both longer ranged, with a higher rate of climb and faster than the He 100, if slightly less manoeuvrable and livelier on landing. The plane had almost touched 450mph in level flight, a large speed advantage over the He 100 at 416 mph, although this would be less when this was also re engined to the Griffon 61, currently also under development.

Fred David and CAC had decided to call her the CAC Cockatoo, if she made series production. CAC had the capability but shortages of the Griffin and the need for further testing would likely delay any production until 1944.

CAC-15 Cockatoo

0835 10 June 1943

Rear Admiral Keiji Shibazaki's forces on Tarawa had suffered a day's constant air and naval bombardment that had again commenced at first light. Now, two and a half hours later, it had stopped and he could see the US assault barges making their way in. Only two of his 8-inch guns were still operational and one of those had its rangefinder damaged and would be firing over open sights. He had placed his men, or those that remained to him, in forward positions, thinking if he did not stop them on the beaches the game was up.

1904 10 June 1943

It had been a bloody day for Colonel David Shoup's 2nd Marines. The Japanese had extensive fortifications, all close to the beach and had poured a withering fire into the

Marines upon their landing. Of the tanks that had gotten ashore, two had been lost due to emplaced magnetic mines and two to a Japanese artillery piece that had still not been knocked out. Others had been lost on the treacherous soft ground, becoming bogged.

By nightfall, over 5000 marines had been landed, but in some cases, progress had not been made beyond the high seawall of the initial landings and in no cases was a penetration over 800 yards achieved. Casualties were heavy, in the region of 1500 men. Shoup had been wounded himself but would continue to inspire his men in a manner that eventually would earn him his country's highest decoration.

1859 10 June 1943

Rear Admiral Keiji Shibazaki's forces on Tarawa had held firm and he had taken the opportunity to move his Southern Forces to the Northern Beaches during the night, as well as his only armour, six light tanks. His ability to communicate with his men had been hampered by the cutting of all telephone lines by the bombardment. Casualties from the pre-invasion bombardment had been horrible and today two heavy shells had hit the field hospital at the airport, killing most of the occupants. His 8-inch guns were both now silent.

2017 11 June 1943

With heavy gunfire and air support Shoup's marines had broken the back of the Japanese resistance, gaining a substantial footing on the island that had allowed the landing of the rest of the troops and tanks and supplies. It had been a hard grind, however, and his troops had even come under fire from behind when a group of Japanese had swum out and taken up positions on an old shipwreck located off the landing beaches.

0445 13 June 1943

Shoup's marines had started at general offensive at 1100 across the southern coast of the island. By late afternoon they had reached the eastern end of the airfield and had formed a continuous line with the forces that landed on beach Red 3 two days earlier.

By the evening the remaining Japanese forces were either pushed back into the tiny amount of land to the east of the airstrip, or operating in several isolated pockets near the western edge of the airstrip. That night the Japanese forces had formed up for a counterattack, which started at about 2015. This had only met with some limited success at high cost.

0500 13 June 1943

Rear Admiral Keiji Shibazaki prepared to lead his men on a final charge. There were less than 600 Japanese left fighting on the island, now split into three separate pockets. It was time to die fighting with his men.

1016 14 June 1943

The island had been fully secured by the marines, but at some cost, thought Colonel Shoup. 882 killed, 1876 wounded. An expensive campaign. It would cost another 26 killed and 61 wounded to clear out the smaller islands on the atoll of Japanese, this not being completed until the morning of June 20th.

0606 15 June 1943

It was a powerful force that had appeared off both Attu and Kiska on the morning of the 15th of June. It consisted of two separate Task Forces, one under Vice Admiral Kincaid, the other under Vice Admiral Thomas "Fuzzy" Theobald. These consisted of:

Attu:
BB Mississippi, New Mexico, Idaho
CVE Nassau, Breton
CA Salt Lake City
CL Richmond, Santa Fe, Detroit
9 DD's
Landing the U.S 7th Infantry Division

Kiska:
BB Pennsylvania, Nevada
CVE Prince William, Long Island
CA San Francisco, Wichita
CL Concord, Columbia
10 DD's
Canadian CA Frobisher
Landing the 6th Canadian Infantry Division

0812 16 June 1943

Colonel Yasuyo Yamasaki's forces on Attu had not contested the American's beach assault. With no naval cover, no fighter cover and no heavy weapons aside from machine guns and light mortars, it seemed a pointless exercise. He had only arrived at Attu by submarine in April, with orders to hold the island "anticipating no assistance". To that end, he had dug in his troops, less than 3000, on the slopes either side of Jarmin Pass, to protect the only town on the island and Chichagol Harbour.

0939 16 June 1943

Major General Potts 6th Canadian Division had gone ashore yesterday in a heavy sea mist that had made it hard to coordinate any activities at all. Japanese resistance was no far almost non-existent in all three landing locations, less than 20 being killed, although he had lost 24men himself to various booby traps. He had concentrated on getting his men and equipment ashore. With intelligence reporting 5000 Japanese on the island it promised to be a grinding campaign in the sub-zero temperatures. God knows what this place was like in winter and Potts certainly did not want to know.

The landings had largely gone off without a hitch, although a U.S destroyer had struck a sea mine and sunk. His plan was to move forward and get into a position for an assault on the harbour at Kiska, the only place with significant concentrations of Japanese. The ground near Kiska Harbour was relatively flat, offering less in the way of natural defences than Attu. If the mist cleared tomorrow, he hoped for major air and naval support and had plans for an air drop by the 1st Special Services Force, a joint Canadian/American force trained in cold weather warfare and jump capable.

Locations of Kiska Landings

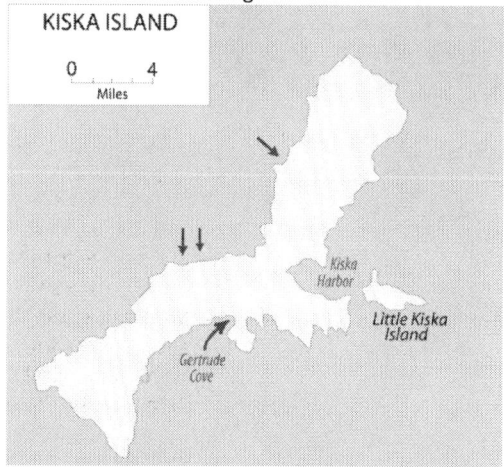

1635 16 June 1943

Yamamoto had pondered for some hours on the landings in the Aleutians. Unlike the landings on Tarawa, they were likely to be a protracted affair for the Americans and so gave his fleet an opportunity to intervene, if he wished to do so. Three of his five operational carriers were out of the equation, *Ryuho* and *Chuyo* ferrying aircraft to Truk. *Taiyo* was dry docked for a refit, as was the *Yamashiro* and the *Nagato*. That left him only the *Yamato* and *Musashi* and two carriers *Kaga* and *Nisshin*, as well as two heavy cruisers.

In the finish he decided that he could not let the Americans continue to dominate operations and must attempt to intervene. At 0505 on the 18th, he sailed with *CV Kaga, CVL Nisshin, BB Yamato, and Musashi, CA Tone* and *Chikuma, CL Oyodo* and 10 destroyers, with himself aboard *Musashi*. He also ordered all available submarines to patrol the area, not many would be available but it would all help.

0645 24 June 1943

The high speed of the enemy formation had stopped Commander Oliver Kirk of the *USS Lapon* getting into any sort of an attack position. He was patrolling near the entrance of the main harbour in the Kuriles, Paramushiro, and the presence of two of the monster battleships, so rarely seen, as well as a large carrier, putting out to sea and heading North would surely be of interest to Pearl.

717 25 June 1943

Major General Potts 6th Canadian's pressed the Japanese back to a perimeter ranging from a half mile to a mile from the shorelines and harbour at Kiska. It had been a brutal, uncompromising battle that had caused its share of casualties. Some days had been fought in clear skies, if cold weather, other in misty, creeping cold.

Naval gunfire support and air support had been the key, as had the landing of 10 Ram tanks that had done their own part in assisting to push the Japanese back, destroying six Japanese Type 95 tanks that had attempted to intervene with only one loss of their own. Now he had been told to expect enemy naval intervention and the task force had left Kiska last night. For the moment at least, it was back to going it alone.

1414 25 June 1943

Major General Charles Harrison Corlett's 7th U.S Infantry Division had compressed the Japanese back into a thin strip of land around Chicagol Harbour, capturing the heights above the town and both sides of Jarmin pass just yesterday. The Japanese had fought a stubbornly defensive fight, using an extensive network of tunnels and entrenchments to guard the heights. It had been an expensive landing so far, with over 300 killed and 800 wounded. More had had to be evacuated with cold related issues. His 30 T16 tanks had helped to secure the heights, but had proven inadequate when two Japanese light tanks had appeared and knocked out five. They had also gradually been lost due to mechanical reliability and he now had only four "runners". At least the Japs appeared to be out of both tanks and heavy weapons.

The fleet was still in the vicinity but he had been told the Japanese intended to intervene with their own navy and that he could expect no further support from this afternoon for "a few days", whatever that meant.

US T-16 tanks in their only combat appearance on Attu

1906 25 June 1943

Vice Admiral Kincaid had steamed slowly away from Attu. He had made a number of decisions in light of the likelihood of the Japanese putting in an appearance either tomorrow or the 27th. Firstly, he had withdrawn the Attu support ships back to Kiska, with the convoy leaving at 1825 today, leaving five destroyers to guard the combined transports and support ships. Secondly, he had combined his two forces, giving him total of:

Attu:

BB Mississippi, New Mexico, Idaho, Pennsylvania, Nevada
CVE Nassau, Breton, Prince William, Long Island
CA Salt Lake City, San Francisco, Wichita, Frobisher
CL Richmond, Santa Fe, Detroit, Concord, Columbia
13 DD's

At least combining his two air groups would give him enough aircraft for some sort of CAP, however, the amount of serviceable aircraft on the four small carriers amounted to only 42 Wildcats and 31 Avengers, although the island was in the range of long range aircraft such as P-38's and B-24's from Umnak.

2354 25 June 1943

Commodore Louis Junoit, RCN, had found himself in the unusual situation of being the commander of the residual naval forces at Kiska consisting of the RCN armed merchant cruisers *Prince Alistair, Princess Patricia* and *Prince Alexander*, five USN destroyers, two destroyer minesweepers, a couple of RCN frigates, in addition to normal transports and support vessels.

He hoped to God the Japanese did not break through, as his three 6,000-ton armed merchant cruisers with an armament of only four 6 inchers and four 4 inchers were not likely to stop them. Probably would not even stop them laughing if their battleships broke through.

0610 26 June 1943

With rare fine weather forecast for a couple of days things were very busy at Amchitka Air Force Base. The base and the island were only 50 miles from Kiska. Operational since March 1943, the airfield had been a constant source of irritation to the Japanese garrison at Kiska and with the invasion happening it's resources and been more than doubled.

It was now home to:
18th and 54th Fighter Squadron(P-38's)
344th Fighter Squadron (P-40's)
21st, 36th and 404th Bombardment Squadrons (B-24's)
73rd Bombardment Squadron(B-26's)

With the Jap Fleet possibly at large, they may find the next couple of days full of action, thought Captain Richard Browning of the 18th Fighter Squadron as he climbed into his P-38.

0654 26 June 1943

In 1941 or 1942 it would have been a disaster; however, the Kido Butai was no longer the force it had once been. Aware from radio reports from the Japanese defender he could do little to help that the allied naval forces had been withdrawn from Kiska, he had launched a strike from 160 Nautical miles to the South of Kiska pre-dawn. Retaining enough aircraft for a anti shipping strike on the allied fleet, he had launched 18 B5N's, nine D4Y's and 12 A6M's at the allied shipping at Kiska.

Appearing over the island and the allied ships at 0632, just as daylight broke, they were met by six P-38 Lightning's that had just started a dawn CAP over the fleet. Confident, the Japanese detached a Shotai of Zeros to pursue three B-24's engaged on an early morning bombing mission in support of allied troops, whilst the remaining Zeros engaged the twin tailed U.S fighters.

It had been far from the success that they had hoped for. The Zeros attacking the B-24's had finally brought down one damaged bomber in exchange for two of their own, the U.S bombers sticking together to concentrate their defensive fire. Of the nine Zeros that engaged the P-38's five had been lost in exchange for a single P38, with another P-38 breaking through and downing two B5N's.

The Japanese bombers had also had limited success, losing a B5N to AA fire, they had managed to torpedo the Canadian armed merchant cruiser *Prince Alistair*, leaving the ship slowly sinking. The dive bombers had targeted two ships engaged in fire support, the destroyer *Phelps* and the gunboat *Charleston*. After a series of misses, they finally hit the *Charleston*, leaving the 2,400-ton ship badly damaged.

Worse still, on the return leg they had been "bounced" by another two P-38's, losing another two B5N's. Unbeknownst to the Japanese a third P-38 had tracked them on their way back to the Japanese fleet, gaining a visual sighting at 0801, until driven off by three Zeros launched from *Nisshin*; both battleships and the *Kaga* having picked up the approach on their air search radar, newly installed within the last two months on all three ships.

0728 26 June 1943

The report in from a float plane from the heavy cruiser *Tone* had finally located the enemy force, identified as four carriers, ten heavy cruisers, four light cruisers and 13 destroyers. Yamamoto at once gave the order for a strike to be launched. He was 155 nautical miles from the American fleet, the main U.S formation being approximately 20 miles due South of the island of Agattu, itself located Southeast of Attu. Although his pilots may have been green, the decks crews of *Kaga* were not and by 0838 had a strike fully airborne, consisting of 20 B5N's, nine D4Y's and 15 A6M's.

0809 26 June 1943

Kincaid had finally received the report he had been after, the location of the Japanese fleet. With five battleships, he was confident he could take them in a surface engagement, but wanted to get as many licks in as possible with his carrier aircraft.

His four escort carriers all carried 12 Wildcats and nine Avengers, although three Wildcats and six Avengers had so far been lost on operations. He was fully prepared to launch a strike since early this morning, so wasted no time in organising a strike himself. The presence of a Japanese floatplane a half hour ago required that this be completed with all urgency and by 0916 he had 27 Avengers and 24 Wildcats aloft.

A land-based strike was also in the process of being prepared. He needed to put his slow battleships in between the landings at Kiska and the Japanese, so would reverse course to East Southeast after launch. He had retained a potentially strong CAP, up to 18 Wildcats.

0922 26 June 1943

Kincaid's air search radar picked up the Japanese strike at 0922, only a few minutes after his own planes had moved out. He rapidly launched his remaining ten Wildcats, giving him a CAP strength of 19 Wildcats, nine of which hovered over the Task Force whilst the ten actually aloft went out to intercept the Japanese formation, doing so 17 nautical miles out.

In a short dogfight they removed six Zeros and a Kate from the Japanese formation in exchange for two of their own in a running battle back to the U.S Task Force. There they encountered nine more Wildcats, six of which broke through to the Japanese bombers. Three attacked the B5N's, each gaining one success. The other three attacked the D4Y's and were surprised to find an aircraft faster than themselves, only managing to shoot down one for the loss of a Wildcat to the dive bombers gunner.

Losing a D4Y to AA fire, the dive bombers were the first to attack, but had limited success, failing to score any hits, the Wildcats at least breaking up their formation and making aiming difficult. The remaining B5N's, attacking through heavy AA, lost another of their number. In another uncoordinated attack, they would have achieved no success at all except their commander, Lt Commander Shimanoga of the *Kaga*, waiting in line as the last to attack, bored through the AA like the Pearl Harbour veteran he was to hit the escort carrier *Nassau* port side with a "fish". Having lost seven Kates, two Judys and fully nine Zeros, the Japanese formation retreated. The U.S had lost only four Wildcats.

1038 26 June 1943

The American strike had arrived over the Japanese fleet at 1022, just as a counter strike from the Japanese, consisting of the airplanes from this morning's strike had finished forming up. The strike that had been launched on the U.S fleet was still in the process of recovery, with many waved off as the Americans had been detected on radar. The unexpected size of the US strike, fully 27 Avengers and 24 Wildcats influenced the Japanese to commit as many aircraft as possible to fleet defence, with the 12 plane CAP being supplemented by three A6M's from the outgoing strike and two from the strike waiting to land, even though the last two possessed low ammunition stocks.

Only three of the Zeros broke through to the Avengers, the three that revered course from the raid. These shot down two of the torpedo planes before the Wildcats could intervene, at a loss of one of their own. In a wild melee between the escort fighters, six Zeros were downed in exchange for two Wildcats, the inexperience of the Japanese pilots being a telling factor. Two more Avengers were lost to heavy AA fire, but 10 attacked the *Kaga* and another 12 attacked the *Musashi*. Both took one hit, the *Kaga* being slowed to 24 knots and developing a two-degree list. The *Musashi*, hit on the heaviest part of her underwater protection, took on board 800 tons of water but her combat power was largely unaffected. As Lieutenant Richard Richardson flew back to the *Nassau*, his home carrier, he could report that they had hit both a battleship and a carrier. Little did he know what he was flying back to.

1105 26 June 1943

The appearance of 32 B-24's, escorted by 10 P-38's, had been the final pointer to Yamamoto that it was time to reverse course once he had recovered his last strike. He had only 10 A6M's left to fend them off with and this proved wholly inadequate.

His fighters shot down two P38's and one B24's in exchange for five Zeros, whilst AA brought down another bomber. Bombed repeatedly by the remaining 30 B-24, he considered himself lucky that they had stayed at high altitude and gotten only two damaging hits, one near miss that caused plates to be sprung on board *Nisshin* and two hits to *Yamato*, one of which the armour of number 1 turret had shrugged off and the second that had detonated on the rear 6.1 inch turret, knocking it out. At 1122 he reversed course to the South, signalling his strike aircraft of their anticipated new position. Perhaps the clouds coming up from the South may prove useful rather than a distraction.

1131 26 June 1943

Vice Admiral Kincaid was still somewhat in a state of shock as to what had happened to his command. It had been a disastrous morning. Firstly, the *Nassau*, hit by one torpedo, had violently exploded only 22 minutes later, sinking at 1012, with the fires apparently reaching her avgas storage. As the fleet had been involved in rescue, the escort carrier *Breton* had been hit down her length by three torpedoes, far too much for her merchant hull to take. She had quickly capsized and sank, less than 30 minutes after taking her torpedo hit at 1051.

Within one morning he had lost two carriers. The successful reported sinking of the offending Japanese submarine less than two minutes ago was some small consolation. Worse still, radar reported another hostile strike inbound, less than 50 miles away.

1154 26 June 1943

The second Japanese strike on the U.S force had caught the ships at least in a state of if not chaos, at least unpreparedness. Unfortunately for the Japanese, with part of their escort left behind to intervene in the last US strike, the 13 B5N's and eight D4Y's were only escorted by four Zeros.

This was to prove completely inadequate against the 10 Wildcats that were aloft, who quickly shot down three Zeros in exchange for one of their own and then started taking a toll of the bombers. Two D4Y's and five Kates were splashed in exchange for a badly damaged Wildcat, with a D4Y being shot down by AA.

Scattered and under pressure, none of the Japanese aircrew scored hits, aside from three D4Y's that picked the old light cruiser *Concord*, on the edge of the formation, as their target. One gained a solid hit with a 500lb bomb near the rear turret of the old light cruiser, demolishing it and causing heavy casualties.

1224 26 June 1943

The second strike from Amchatka, consisting of nine torpedo armed B-26's and eight P-

40's encountered seven defending Japanese Zeros. Losing three P-40's and a B-26's for two Zeros, the bombers had their formation largely broken up by the remaining Japanese fighters, generally more experienced pilots that were largely left from the slaughter of most of the other Japanese A6M's. They were not able to report any hits but did signal back that the Japanese fleet was in retreat. When Yamamoto had recovered the last of his strike aircraft at 1326, he headed directly away from Kiska, disappearing under low clouds at 1416.

For the first time since Pearl Harbour, the IJN had achieved some sort of a victory, sinking two carriers and an armed merchant cruiser and damaging two other ships. The irony of it was that Yamamoto remained unaware of this, crediting only one carrier, one merchant ship and one destroyer damaged.

0909 5 July 1943

Major General Corlett's 7th U.S Infantry Division had finally done it. They had secured the island of Attu, eliminating the last 300 Japanese on the island late yesterday and a few stragglers at first light. Yesterday, driven back to the beach, the last Japanese had come out of their holes to carry the fight to the US troops. It had been an expensive 21 days, costing 616 killed and 1300 wounded. The Japanese force had fought to the last, being effectively wiped out. It was a bloody business that made one sick to the stomach at times.

1314 6 July 1943

Hauptmann Werner Kuntz urged the huge Ferdinand forward, hoping the break through the Ivan's for the Mark IV's to exploit the breach. After months of building the Heavy Tank Battalion had penetrated the first defences. Operaion Zitadelle was well underway.

0018 10 July 1943

The persistent rapping of his batman gradually woke General Alfredo Guzzoni. He looked over at last night's girl, Carla, he thought. Moving out into sitting room he let the man in. He looked at the transmission. Large scale allied parachute landings all over Sicily. It could only be a prelude to a full invasion.

1214 11 July 1943

It had taken 27 days of bitter fighting, but Major General Potts 6th Canadian Division had finally secured Kiska. The Japanese defenders had gradually pulled back, fighting all the way, in many cases having to be quite literally blasted out of their holes.

Casualties had been very high, 1,112 killed and over 2,500 wounded, plus cold related illnesses. Japanese casualties had been almost total and in the region of 5000, possibly more. On the final day they had fought all the way down to the shoreline, the last 40 men engaging the Canadians behind sea rocks on what passed for a beach. He was proud of his men but the victory had come at a fearful cost.

2234 12 July 1943

Major Alexi Dankin relaxed next to his T34. It had been an exhausting day and, in all fairness, they had probably had the worst of it. Never the less, they had blunted the German offensive badly enough to bring it to a halt. The area around the village of Prokhorovka was littered with burnt out destroyed tanks, resembling a strange pattern of armoured pillboxes, although many would never fight again. Hopefully Fritz had had enough. One could not take too many more days like this.

2224 19 July 1943

Mussolini had begged Hitler to make a separate peace with Stalin and send German troops to the west to guard against an expected Allied invasion of Italy. The allies had already landed in Sicily and established a firm grip. He feared his army was on the brink of collapse.

He was on his private train, returning from a meeting with Hitler that day. He could no longer stand that fool's boasting. His expected offensive in Russia had little to show for it, but Hitler still seemed to think the Russian were on their last legs.

His mood darkened further when he received to pieces of news, firstly the allies had bombed Rome for the first time. Secondly, he had received a missive from Ciano - the Fascist Grand Council, not active since 1940 had called a meeting for the 24th.

1624 25 July 1943

Mussolini could hardly believe that events had moved with such speed. He was in the back of a locked van on his way to prison. At yesterday's meeting, Grandi had moved a resolution asking the king to resume his full constitutional powers, in effect, a vote of no confidence, he supposed, in Mussolini. This motion carried by a 19–7 margin. Despite this sharp rebuke, he had showed up for work the next day as usual. He had viewed the Grand Council as merely an advisory body and did not think the vote would have any substantive effect. That afternoon, he was summoned to the royal palace by the King. When he had tried to tell the King about the meeting, Victor Emmanuel cut him off and told him that he was being replaced by Marshal Badoglio. After Mussolini left the palace, he had been arrested on the King's orders.

1910 30 July 1943

Yamamoto pondered the operation. The Aleutians venture had been a failure or at best a break even. The *Yamato* and *Nisshin* would not be ready again before end August, *Musashi* not until September, *Kaga* not until October, plus his air groups would need to be rebuilt- again.

The islands had been lost, as expected and attrition continued to gnaw at his command, the destroyer *Niizuki* being torpedoed on the way back. He had lost another destroyer to a submarine off the home islands three days ago and two more also on the 27th. Grounded near Cape Gloucester on New Britain by a navigation error, both *Ariake* and *Mikazuki* had been pounded to bits by allied aircraft, Rabaul's reduced fighter compliment being swept aside.

Tarawa had also been lost and he feared it would only be the first of many amphibious operations in the Central Pacific. Reinforcing island garrisons would have to be a navy operation, the army had flatly refused to commit more troops to island operations, worried about their own reverses in Burma.

2314 30 July 1943

General Walter Kreuger contemplated his upcoming operations. With luck the campaign in New Guinea would not survive 1943. The U.S 41st Infantry Division had pushed up the North Coast against light resistance, capturing the villages of Sarmi and Wakde. The unit, exhausted more by the terrain and the tropical diseases it brought, would now go static. He expected its withdrawal within two months.

Tomorrow his next operation, using the invasion fleet he had assembled in Exmouth, would move to take both the Tanimbar Islands and land forces in Western Papua at Kaimana, hoping to again cut off Japanese forces. With them hopefully bottled up in the Vogelkop Peninsula, he then would conduct the final landings of the campaign, at Hollandia and Aitape on the North Coast in late September, isolating Wewak, the last Japanese stronghold.

New Guinea map 30 July 1943

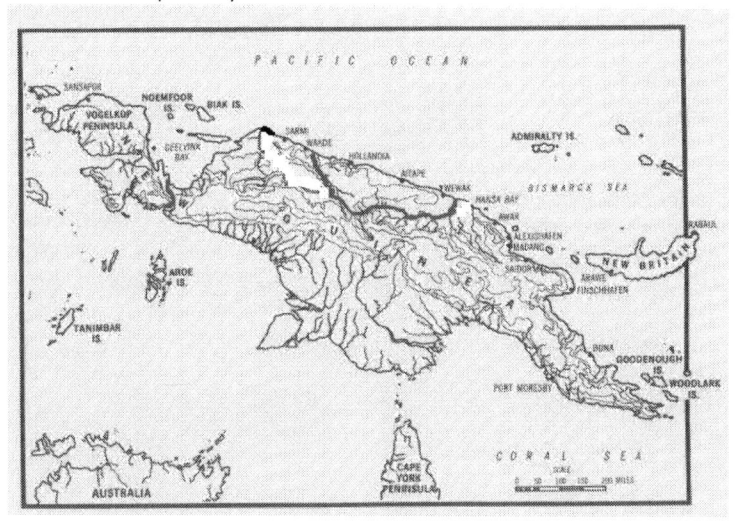

0818 31 July 1943

As July was brought to a close, Nimitz had fixed a date and location for the latest operation, Kwajalein, in the Marshall Islands, set for 12th September. He wondered if the Japanese would try and contest these landings like they had at Kiska. Kiska had been an expensive operation, both in terms of men and materials, but with it out of the way at least he could concentrate on the Central pacific theatre and downscale his Alaskan air assets to enough to regularly raid the Kuriles.

0657 1 August 1943

It had been a large force that had sailed from Exmouth under the command of the RAN Admiral John Collins, thought Captain Williard Merrill, USN. Truth be told his *USS Boise* and her sister ship *Phoenix*, based generally out of Sydney since the start of the war were more used to operating with RAN units than USN ones. He knew full well that many of his young crew had formed attachments and had "home port sweethearts", including his own XO.

His light cruiser was part of the covering force, for the West Papua operation, who's overall composition consisted of:

Covering Force:
CV Australasia
CVL Melbourne, Sydney
BB Pacifica
CA Auckland
CL Darwin, Boise, Phoenix
CLAA Jacob Van Heemskirk, Tromp
8 Tribal Class DD

Invasion Force
CVE Brisbane
Assault ships *Manoora, Monowai, Kanimbla, Westralia*
9 River Class DE's

Support Force:
2 AO's
1 Hospital Ship
1 DD(Portuguese)
2 Sloops(Portuguese)

Mine Warfare Force:
CM Adelaide
DD Stuart
8 *Bathurst Class* minesweepers

Tanimla Island Force:
1 Transport
CVE Noumea
1DD
4 FF

0716 3 August 1943

General Giuseppe Castellano woke in his Lisbon hotel room. He was, of course, traveling under a pseudonym, bringing his wife, son and daughter as cover. They were unaware of his real mission, as outlined by both the King and Badoglio. He was here for meeting with the British and Americans, set for tomorrow, in an attempt to remove Italy from this disastrous war.

1218 8 August 1943

Collins had been happy with the landings at both Kaimana and the Taminbar Islands. Kaimana's purpose was to trap and outflank the Japanese in West Papua and he had quickly put slightly over 5000 men ashore with limited opposition, the town being garrisoned by just over 150 Japanese.

The Tamimbar Islands landing had been designed purely from the start as a ground capturing exercise to that US Sea bees could construct an airstrips to support the Australasian air forces on Timor.
Timor itself had struck with many of its bombers at the two airfields at Ambon, closest to the landings, destroying 15-20 Japanese aircraft on the ground. However, for the first time since the landing began, radar had detected incoming hostiles, a fair-sized group of aircraft 46 miles out.

1346 8 August 1943

Ensign Kenji Mori's unit had suffered appalling casualties. His ten Ki 43 had escorted 16 Nakajima Ki-49's on an attack on the fleet in West Papua, but had been met by three He 119's and nine He 100's, 16 miles from the target and had lost five of their number and two bombers in exchange for two allied fighters.

Over the target they had encountered another swarm of Australasian fighters, twenty more He 100's that had shot down all the Ki 43's except himself and Warrant Officer Keno. With most of the Australasian fighters unengaged and another ten fighters of a type he had not seen before also joining the fray, the bombers had been massacred, only three surviving the carnage. No hits had been obtained.

1453 8 August 1943

Vice Admiral Collins force had broken up their second raid of the day, this one consisting of nine Lily's escorted by eight Ki 43's. For the second time they had been very roughly dealt with, only three aircraft surviving. His A-36's he had pressed into service as fighters and they had performed more than adequately in the role. During the course of the day he had lost only four He 100's and one A-36 in exchange for over thirty Jap aircraft. Hopefully those sorts of losses would take their enthusiasm away.

1619 8 August 1943

Commodore de Righi's small Tanimblar Island occupation force had also been the target of a Japanese raid. He had gotten his six hundred troops ashore with little incident on the 6th, where they had quickly overwhelmed the 60 or so defending Japanese and were spreading out over the island, encountering another pocket of 20 or so Japanese today. At 1536 he had picked up a small Japanese raid inbound. His force had a top cover of two He 119's from Timor and he rapidly launched his only fighters from his tiny carrier, three He 112's.

In the finish the raid had been revealed to be six Ki 48 Lilys and 5 Ki 30 Anns, escorted by six Ki-43 Oscars. The He 119's had knocked down two Ki 43's in exchange for one damaged and his He 112's had taken care of another plus one of the Lily twin engine bombers in exchange for one of their own. AA had shot down another.

It had not been enough to save his force from some damage, the transport *Canard* being hit by a 250lb bomb that had left her damaged, but survivable and the old frigate *Tasmania* being left sinking after a 500lb bomb hit. He had requested more air cover from Timor, his small carrier's two He 112 and five Swordfish not being sufficient.

1834 18 August 1943

The Tanimblar islands had been secured and de Righi's ships were heading back to Fremantle, the *Tasmania* the only loss. Securing the islands had cost 26 Killed and 61 wounded, in exchange for 196 known Japanese killed and three captured. He had lost an additional 44 aboard *Tasmania*, the old ship having broken up rapidly. The Japanese had attacked again, but after being seen off by six He 119's from Timor, losing eight aircraft, they had not tried again. Sea bees were due to arrive within two weeks and airfield construction would start.

1114 30 August 1943

General Castellano had briefed both the King and Badoglio about the Allied response to his proposals in Lisbon and the request for a meeting to be held in Sicily, which had fallen on the 17th August to allied forces. A Sicily meeting had been suggested by the British ambassador to the Vatican.

The meeting was set for the 1st-2nd, hopefully they would get what they wanted. His main concern was the inability of the Italian army to supress the large amount of Germans in the country, with more seemingly arriving every day.

1806 3 September 1943

There was much disagreement on the 1st September, with some declaring their inability to defend Italy against the occupying Germans. Badoglio appeared before the King, who decided to accept the armistice conditions.

A confirmation telegram was sent to the Allies on the 1st. The message, however, was intercepted by the German armed forces, which had long since begun to suspect that Italy was seeking a separate armistice. The Germans contacted Badoglio, who repeatedly confirmed the unwavering loyalty of Italy to its German ally. His reassurances were doubted by the Germans, and the Wehrmacht started to devise an effective plan to take control of Italy as soon as the Italian government had switched allegiance to the Allies.

On September 2, Castellano set off again to Cassibile in Sicily with an order to confirm the acceptance of the Allied conditions. He had no written authorisation from the head of the Italian Government, Badoglio, who wanted to dissociate himself as much as possible from the upcoming defeat of his country.

The signing ceremony began at 2:00 p.m. on September 3 on board *HMS Nelson*.

Castellano and Bedell Smith signed the accepted text on behalf of respectively Badoglio and Eisenhower. A bombing mission on Rome by five hundred airplanes was stopped at the last moment: it had been Eisenhower's deterrent to accelerate the procedure of the armistice. Harold McMillan, the British government's representative minister at the Allied Staff, informed Churchill that the armistice had been signed "without amendments of any kind".

On the 3rd of September the allies landed at Salerno. On the 8th the armistice was made public, the allies' landings at Salerno and Taranto on the 9th. Earlier that same morning the units of the Italian Fleet that could escape put to sea, bound for Malta and internment. On the 10th, the allies landed troops on Rhodes and other islands of the Dodecanese, forestalling a planned German attempt. The weakest link of the Axis had been eliminated, now becoming an "associate power" of the allies.

1235 11 September 1943

It had taken more than a month's hard fighting by Brigadier Potts 53rd Brigade, grinding the trapped Japanese between his own Brigade and elements of the U.S 41st Infantry Division. It had been bitter, bloody fighting, costing 467 dead and almost 1000 wounded, with similar casualties amongst U.S troops, but in the finish perhaps 6000 Japanese lay dead.

His units had also moved North, blocking the remaining Japanese in West Papua in the Vogelkop Peninsula. It would be the last operation in Southern New Guinea, only amphibious operations on the Northern Coast being later.

0708 12 September 1943

For Major General Charles Dodson Barrett and his 3rd Marine Division, this was his baptism of fire. Both himself and the Division as a whole wanted to prove themselves the equal of their combat blooded brothers in the 1st and 2nd.

They had gone ashore at the islands of Kwajalein and Roi-Namur in the Marshall's at 0645, having captured many of the outlying small islands yesterday. They were supported by two U.S carrier air groups, a close support group of seven escort carriers and nine older battleships and a covering force of five Fleet and three Light carriers, with four fast battleships.

2206 12 September 1943

Captain Masashi Kiyoki, commanding the 6th Base Unit, knew he had no hope the moment the Americans appeared. He had no air support and had been told not to expect any, no coastal artillery, he had no received any mines despite repeated request for them and his predecessor had constructed little in the way of fortifications.

He had considered his only hope was to stop the Americans on the beaches. It was a tactic that had caused some casualties, but had failed dismally. He had lost over 4,000 men on the first day, fully half his force, inflicting painful but not crippling losses on the enemy. Over half his troops had no combat experience and no training.

1602 14 September 1943

The Marshall's campaign had been quick and, he surmised compared to Tarawa, relatively bloodless, except for those involved in it, he supposed, thought Major General Barrett. His 3rd Marines had acquitted themselves well, with Japanese casualties in excess of 8,000 and the islands cleared. His own forces had taken less than 400 dead and approximately 1,500 wounded, indicating that the fighting, whilst brief enough, had been bloody. Despite the Japanese being under equipped and with no support, less than 250 were captured, half of those Koreans.

1904 17 September 1943

John Curtin had given his last pre-election speech, starting it like another Australasian Prime Minister did in 1972 "men and women of Australasia, It's time...." He had concentrated carefully on his governments sound war record, the sound state of the country's finances, the oppositions own internal infighting and his own party's sound credentials in looking after the disadvantaged in society. He had even gone back to Scullin's glory years and Labor's sound management since the 1920's-the fact that Scullin still had his hand on the economic tiler now was a sound electoral boon.

He had introduced Widows Pensions, sadly so in need now, child allowance and maternity allowances. The pension had been extended to cover aboriginals, who had also been given the vote universally for the first time, their voting participation only being covered by State laws previously.

He had also introduced laws to control monopolies in certain industries, both for public protection and to stop war profiteering. These had, of course, been opposed by the media, in particular the Sydney Morning Herald. Earlier in the week, after his press conference outburst against 'Rags' Henderson, general manager of the Sydney Morning Herald, Ross Gollan, then the SMH political rep, had summoned up his dignity and office patriotism. "Mr Prime Minister," he said, "if you speak like that about Mr Henderson, I will be forced to withdraw from this conference and take the other members of the SMH with me". "Mr Gollan," said Curtin, "you are at liberty to withdraw from my conference any time you like, and take your staff with you. But I tell you this, Mr Gollan. If you and your staff withdraw, neither you nor your staff will ever come to one of my conferences again". Gollan had stayed.

As he now relaxed with Peter Fraser, Frank Forde and Scullin, he knew he had to win this one. His health was not what it had once been, but he needed to see it through. He thought he should be alright, the opposition was practically moribund, wracked with its own internal infighting.

0912 24 September 1943

It was a huge fleet, now designated the 3rd Fleet, that sailed under newly raised full Admiral William Halsey from Pearl. They had received a very short stopover and would not now be back for some time. Their first task was a raid on New Guinea's North coast, hitting Rabaul and then Hollandia/Wewak, in support of the operation to seize these remaining strongholds on the North Coast scheduled for a weeks' time. They were then going to conduct a raid on the Marianas to remove any Japanese offensive capability there.

His forces now consisted of *CV's Lafayette, Essex, Lexington(2), Yorktown(2) and Enterprise(2), CVL's Princeton, Independence, Belleau Wood and Cowpens, BB's Washington, South Dakota, Massachusetts, North Carolina* and *Alabama*, plus numerous cruisers and destroyers, a huge force. *Lafayette* had also been the first carrier equipped with a brand-new plane, the Curtis Helldiver.

1643 25 September 1943

It was pandemonium at Princes Park. "Captain Blood" Jack Dyer for Richmond had marked in the forward pocket and kicked the winning goal, taking Richmond from one point behind to five points in front. Forty seconds later the siren had signalled the end to the 1943 Grand Final, Richmond defeating Essendon 86 to 81. Although not herself a supporter of either team, it had been a great, if brutal game, with a king hit on Richmond forward pocket Max Oppy provoking a massive all in brawl just before half time.

It had been a hectic week for Queen Alice. Secretly she had been pleased when Curtin had won a second term. He had done everything to deserve it and she certainly would have voted for him, if indeed she had been allowed to do so. Curtin's Labor Party had won 58 of the 95 seats as against the Liberal Party's 16 and the Country Party's seven, with two independents and two undecideds as yet. It had been a crushing landslide and she had been delighted to see the relief he had visibly shown when he had called on her yesterday so she could commission a new mandate for him. With the war proceeding positively, she was glad to see him continue on.

1235 27 September 1943

Admiral Royle had just come from the commissioning of *HMAS Hamilton*, the last major unit to be built by the RAN. A small 4,400-ton AA cruiser, she had commissioned just this morning. Tomorrow Halsey would strike Rabaul, then the New Guinea North coast over the 29th and 30th, before landing operations commenced on 1st October at Hollandia and Aitape, hopefully cutting off Wewak and isolating the last of the Japanese in New Guinea. He had committed a large part of the navy to the operation. With the manufacturing and agricultural sectors crying out for manpower, the end of operations in New Guinea by the end of 1943 was a target.

It would allow the RAN to curtail further growth, with the only new construction being landing craft and MGB's/MTB's. The end of land operations in New Guinea, when it did occur, would allow for a downsizing in the army. Only the RAAF was planned to grow as an offensive force. With the end of operations against Italy, the RN was already making rumblings about substantial transfers to the East, some of which would require Australasian support in terms of basing, dry docking, provision of ammunition and supplies.

The navy' strength was now:
BB Pacifica
CV Australasia

CVL Christchurch
CVE Sydney(2), Melbourne(2), Brisbane(2){Landing ship carrier}, Noumea(very small)
CA: Auckland, Dunedin
CL: Launceston, Hobart, Darwin, Hamilton
CM: Adelaide
DD(Tribal Class): Wik, Wiri, Nasoqo, Kurnei, Alawa, Warramunga, Tagalag, Koko, Palawan, Maori
DD(old): Vampire, Stuart, Valhalla, Attack
DDAA(Clemson Class) Barnes, Albany, Clifton
Destroyer Escorts: Waikato, Tamar, Clutha, Darling, Todd, Waimbula, Derwent, Murray, Hawkesbury
Sloops: Swan, Warrego
Frigates: Success, Stalwart, Swordsman
Submarines: Otway, Taipan, King Brown, Death Adder, Brown Snake, Copperhead, Tiger Snake, Black Snake, Dugite
Corvettes/Minesweepers: 49
Assault Ships: Monowai, Kanimbla, Manoora, Westralia
Hospital ships: Oranje, Wanganella, Manunda, Maunganui
Sub Depot Ships: 2
PT Boat Depot Ships: 3
Oilers: 4

In addition, the navy had operational control over two Dutch AA cruisers and three submarines and one Portuguese destroyer and two sloops. Under construction were the final three *Bathurst Class* corvettes, four *Snake Class* submarines plus MGB's and Landing Craft.

With the allied navies pushed to the limit, lend lease transfers were at a minimum, but the navy had acquired three ships. *HMS Archer*, a *Long Island Class* Escort Carrier, had been laid up by the RN in the Clyde on 18th August as possibly not being worth repair due to engine problems and had been decommissioned. The RN had agreed to transfer her to the RAN if the cost of repairs, which may take up to four months, had been paid. She would be escorted out by the also previously decommissioned *Newmarket*, an old *Clemson Class*. With new construction now coming out almost fortnightly in the form of the *Casablanca Class*, the USN had agreed to release the *Long Island* after she had completed one more aircraft ferry mission, giving the RAN both ships in the class.

2115 27 September 1943

It had not taken them long to start pulling his command apart thought Admiral Cunningham. Still, he should be happy with a job well done. It had been the RN that had won the Mediterranean campaign, he had no doubt of that.

Now he was to be downsized. Battleship *Valiant*, aircraft carriers *Illustrious*, *Formidable* and *Unicorn* escorted by Seventeenth Destroyer Flotilla, were to sail to Gibraltar on the 30th, thence to the United Kingdom. There they were to meet *HMS Renown* and *Queen Elizabeth* and attendant units, including at least two escort carriers. After "tropicalisation" refits, they would be on their way to the Far East.

1844 28 September 1943

There had been time when Rabaul, with its great natural harbour and forward position, had been the lynchpin of the Japanese defences in the South East Pacific. This was reflected in the still large troops garrison, the five airfields, the many facilities from field hospitals to offices and the almost 300 AA guns that dotted the harbour, town and surrounds.

However, with the contraction of the Japanese presence in Northern New Guinea and the loss of the Northern Solomons, particularly Bougainville, it had come under, if not daily, at least weekly raids from allied aircraft, including a day of massive raids comprising over 200 bombers from the Solomons and over 120 from New Guinea on 2nd September that had devastated much infrastructure that had not been repaired.

Halsey's aircraft had roamed at will, bombing and strafing and although they had lost fifteen aircraft to Japanese fighters and AA, had shot down over 30 defending fighters whilst so doing. They had also sunk the destroyer *Hagikaze*, the mine layer *Hoko*, *Patrol boat No 42* and the seaplane carriers *Sanuki* and *Sagawa Maru*, as well as a fleet oiler and four merchant ships.

The Japanese had counter attacked, sending 15 G3M's and eight G4M's escorted by three Zeros and eight Ki 61, this force constituting the remainder of Rabaul's air strength. Intercepted by almost 40 Hellcats, they had never seen the U.S Fleet, shooting down five Hellcats in exchange for 18 of the 23 bombers and the loss of eight of the 11 fighters. Their only success had been discovering the destroyer *Peary* prosecuting a submarine contact 15 miles West of the U.S task force, which a G3M had torpedoed, sinking her and allowing *I-45* to escape. As Halsey pondered the results, he considered it a good day.

1418 1 October 1943

Halsey's 3rd Fleet had struck at both Wewak and Hollandia, destroying both smaller airfields and hitting Japanese troop concentrations and AA sites on the 31st. His fleet had remained on site as the Australasian Fleet arrived later on the 31st, landings at both Aitape and Hollandia commencing on the morning of the 1st, landing elements of the Australasian 1st Division. Hollandia would also be engaged by a further advance of the U.S 41st Infantry Division, also scheduled to start this morning.

So far things had gone well, with little in the way of opposition and a solid beachhead had been established at both locations. Halsey's 3rd Fleet would depart on the 3rd, leaving the Australasian units to manage everyday support for the operations.

1216 26 October 1943

Lt General Leslie Morshead had taken over from Freyberg as GOC, New Guinea and his four active divisions had compressed the Japanese down to a perimeter around one town only, Wewak. 1st Division had taken only a week of fighting to burst out of both bridgeheads at Aitape and Hollandia, ably assisted by the U.S 41st Infantry Division, which would now be withdrawn for a well-earned rest.

Both 4th and 6th Division had fought their way to positions directly to the South and East, respectively, of Wewak, with 1st Division to the West. The last Japanese bastion in Northern New Guinea was completely surrounded.

Japanese positions in New Guinea 25 October 1943

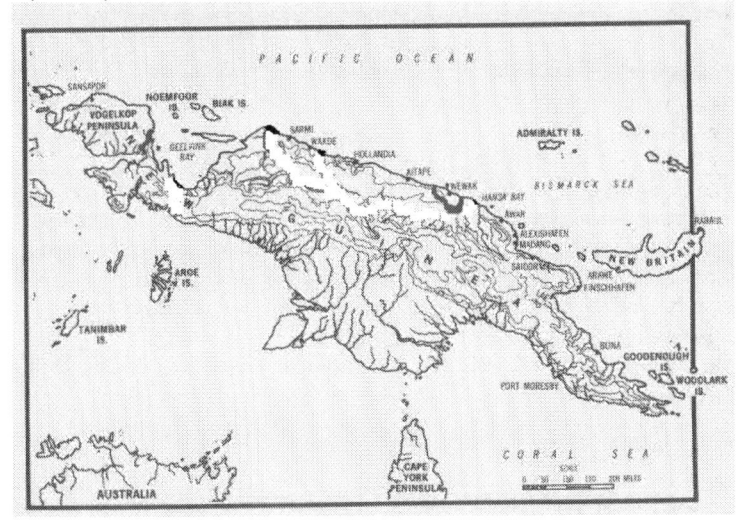

2019 26 October 1943

The evacuation of the beleaguered garrison at Wewak had become a military necessity. The army's cries for action could no longer be ignored and Yamamoto knew he would have to endanger more of his precious smaller escorts and destroyers to make it happen. He still did not have the fleet units for a proper engagement, but he was hoping that this may change very rapidly.

On the night of the 28th he hoped to start evacuating troops from Wewak, having assembled destroyers at Rabaul to complete the task. He had decided to fly down to Rabaul personally on the 31st to inspect whether it was worth continued use as a fleet base. The allies had been steadily pushing his forces back and would probably attempt a landing in the Marianas, which they had just raided, or the Caroline Islands, with its great base at Truk.

Despite more attrition of his smaller units and escorts to submarines mainly, a destroyer, two minesweepers and three escorts in the last eight weeks, he had been steadily rebuilding his fleet strength, in particular his carrier strength. With *Yamato* and *Musashi* both repaired, along with *Kaga*, he now had:

CV Kaga
BB Yamato, Musashi, Nagato, Yamashiro
CVL Nisshin, Ryuho
CVE Taiyo, Chuyo

In addition, the escort carriers *Kaiyo* and *Eikyo*, conversions of the liners *Brazil* and *Argentina Maru*, were expected in November, as was escort carrier *Shinyo*, a conversion of the German liner *Scharnhorst*. The two *Ise Class* battleship conversions were also on the cusp, he was going to the recommissioning of *Hyuga* tomorrow, with *Ise* barely days away.

The fleet carrier *Taiho* was due in February next year, two *Unryu Class* in May/June, another in August, as was the new battleship *Shinano*. He had decided that the next American landings, if conducted after middle December, must be contested.

0932 30 October 1943

The operation on the 29th and 30th had caught the allies on the hop and 4000 of the almost 8000 Japanese at Wewak had been evacuated by the ten destroyers and the light cruisers *Noshiro* and *Agano*. It was planned to do another run tonight, spend the 31st at Wewak and leave that night arriving back on the morning of the 1st November, ready to greet Yamamoto, who would have arrived the previous day. Rear Admiral Kaju Sugiura's plans of a second mission had hit a snag 11 minutes ago when the alarm had been sounded. Now the reason was clear. Waves of U.S carrier aircraft were filling the lagoon.

0938 30 October 1943

The Japanese run to Wewak and back had been noticed by allied reconnaissance but no assets had been in the area to deploy immediately. However, Captain Winston Meredith's *Lafayette* had been at Efate and had been rapidly moved up on the 29th to Tulagi after completing a rapid refuelling, with the light cruisers *St Louis* and *Santa Fe* with five destroyers.

She had closed Rabaul on the night of the 29th and launched at 0746 a large strike of 29 Helldivers and 27 Avengers, escorted by 21 Hellcats in an effort to knock out the Japanese light forces tasked with Wewak's evacuation. It would be followed by a raid of 12 Australasian A36's from Milne Bay, escorted by 10 He 100's early that afternoon and 23 U.S B-24's escorted by 21 Corsairs from Bougainville an hour before dusk.

1106 30 October 1943

Rear Admiral Kaju Sugiura looked around the scenes of devastation in Rabaul. The large American raid had concentrated on the ships in the harbour, not the airfields as was usually the case. Twenty two A6M's had been launched to oppose it, as well as five Ki 61's, however, these had largely been swept aside, 14 A6M's and two Ki-61's being lost for only five U.S aircraft shot down, with another two, possibly three brought down by AA fire.

For the ships he so desperately needed for the Wewak operation, it had been a sad story. The light cruiser *Agano* had been torpedoed twice and had sunk slowly. His other light cruiser, *Noshiro*, had been damaged by a 500lb bomb hit. Destroyer *Hatsuzake* had been torpedoed and sunk, as had the older destroyer *Oite*. The destroyers *Fujinami* and *Hayanami* had both been hit by 500lb bombs, *Hayanami* twice, and were both badly damaged. Their sister *Tamanami* had also been bombed, but her hit in the engine room had resulted in a loss of all power and she had rolled over to port and sunk. Of his two light cruisers and ten destroyers, only five destroyers remained.

2236 30 October 1943

It had been a bad day for Rabaul and Rear Admiral Kaju Sugiura. He had tried to strike back at the U.S carrier arrogantly cruising 165 nautical miles from Rabaul in the Solomon Sea but had only been able to muster 10 G4M's, although he had allocated eight Ki 61 with the best of his pilots. They had encountered a cloud of twenty or so U.S fighters and had lost five bombers and four fighters in exchange for four US machines. The five bombers that had attacked had gained a crumb of consolation when all their torpedoes had missed the wildly manoeuvring huge US carrier but one, continuing on, had hit and broken the back of a U.S destroyer.

However, that afternoon, the harbour had been attacked again by RAAF dive bombers. His puny CAP of nine A6M's and three Ki 61 had lost five more aircraft in exchange for one He 100 and one dive bomber shot down by AA. They had hit the destroyer *Onami* three times with 500lb bombs, slowly sinking her.

A follow up raid near nightfall by USAAF B-24's had shattered many of the dock facilities and the oil storage tanks. He had called off the Wewak operation. Yamamoto would be flying into a scene of chaos tomorrow.

0906 31 October 1943

Lieutenant Frank Barber's entire P-38 squadron, 17 machines in all, including even the reserve, had taken to the sky. It was a curious mission, they had been selected from two P-38 squadrons, only experience pilots based on Bougainville. He had been informed that they were intercepting an "important high officer" with no specific name given and that the three bombers would be the priority targets, the escorts were of no consequence.

The P-38's had presumably been selected as they had the range to "loiter" over the area North of Rabaul. They would be followed most of the way by twelve Australasian He 119's, which would make a "tip and run" attack on Rabaul to keep the Japanese distracted.

1119 31 October 1943

Yamamoto had been brought out of his musings by the sudden, violent evasive manoeuvres of the G4M. The pilot almost simultaneously shouting that they were under attack by enemy fighters. The bomber twisted and dived sharply and he was flung against the side of the aircraft, cracking his head.

As he struggled upwards, he could see smoke pouring out of the left engine. He looked at Ugaki, who returned a worried face. As he started to speak back to his chief of staff, he was startled to feel a kick like a mule and a red stain appear on Ugaki's pressed white uniform. He felt weak and as he looked down, sinking to the floor of the rapidly descending aircraft he could see blood seeping from two holes in the chest of his own uniform. Two minutes later the G4M hit New Ireland's West Coast near the Kamdata River. Japan had lost its best Admiral and his chief of staff, search parties not finding the crash site for three days. Yamamoto had been thrown clear but had died rapidly from blood loss.

1202 31 October 1943

It had been a difficult mission, but they had done it well. Intercepting three Bettys and 6 Zeros over Western New Ireland, Lieutenant Frank Barbers P-38, had poured fire into the middle Betty, despite its pilots best evasive efforts. She had turned over onto her back and crashed into the jungle. It had been rapidly followed by the leading aircraft.

The third had stayed aloft longer, it's pilot clearly an expert and its gunners managing to shoot down it's attacking P38. The end was inevitable, however, and the plane had crashed heavily on the beach of nearby Duke of York Island. The escort fighters had been vastly experienced pilots and in all three P-38's had been lost in exchange for all the bombers and three Zeros. It did not seem like a great exchange, but Barber remained unaware that he had effectively killed the uniformed head of the Imperial Japanese Navy.

1654 4 November 1943

The 1st, 4th and 6th Divisions, all surrounding Wewak, launched the final assault on the 1st. In three days of fighting they had eliminated the last Japanese pocket in New Guinea. Morshead's troops had suffered lighter casualties than expected, only 288 killed and 694 wounded, a high percentage of the remaining Japanese not being combat troops and with little in the way of supplies, training or fixed defences. Over 30 flame tanks were used to breach the initial defences and this had broken some Japanese units and allowed his experienced troops to get inside the perimeter. He had taken 300 prisoners and killed over 3000. The campaign in New Guinea, with the exception of the Japanese trapped in far West Papua, was over. Many of the units now in country would be able to be redeployed for other tasks.

1008 3 November 1943

It was a large fleet that pulled out of Scapa. Two battleships, *Queen Elizabeth* and *Valiant*, a battlecruiser, *Renown*, two carriers, *Illustrious* and *Unicorn*, the escort carriers *Battler, Shah and Begum,* heavy cruisers *London* and *Suffolk,* light cruisers *Ceylon, Kenya* and *Nigeria,* 12 modern destroyers, two frigates, two sloops and four submarines, the escort carriers, frigates, sloops and submarines traveling separately.

All would have the same destination, Trincomalee. Admiral Somerville's Eastern Fleet, largely a paper tiger over the last 18 months, would see a changing of the guard, many of its older ships, particularly its two *R Class* battleships *Ramillies* and *Royal Sovereign,* as well as carrier *Hermes* and a handful of *C and D Class* cruisers would be heading back to England, for either decommissioning or reserve.

1209 5 November 1943

Kreuger, Blamey and Kenney sat and discussed the information that had been received from Nimitz. The next major island-hopping operation in the Central Pacific had been decided. Saipan on the 8th February 1944. Its precursor would be a massive raid on Truk in early January 1944.

Once Saipan had been captured and air bases established, the next objective would be a meeting of advances from the South West Pacific and Central Pacific theatres. Admiral King had indicated that a separate SouthWestPac command may be abolished by mid-1944. The next objective after Saipan would have to be either the Philippines or Formosa, or perhaps both.

As the three commanders saw it, they would have to complete their own operations by roughly the time of the Saipan operation. Kreuger had already indicated where he wished the next attack to fall, New Ireland, the operation to be conducted by 1st Marine Division and the Americal Division, with landings in the North near Kavieng by 1st Marine and in the South by the Americal, the operation scheduled for 9 December.

With three relatively fresh divisions freed up in New Guinea, Blamey had drawn up a list of locations he believed should be occupied to provide forward bases on the way to either the Philippines or Formosa. Firstly, the Admiralty Islands and New Hanover, which could be conducted in conjunction with the New Ireland operation, cutting New Britain and Rabaul completely off.

Secondly, the islands of Biak and Noemfoor off the North Coast of West Papua and the West Papua town of Sansapor, the location of the last three Japanese airfields now the island of Watkte had been occupied two weeks ago. He had thought this could be attempted in January.

Lastly, a landing on the island of Morotai in the Dutch East Indies and Bitung in North Sulawesi, both of which would provide excellent location for air bases to dominate the Celebes Sea, East Borneo and the Southern Philippines. This wold a late February operation.

1423 15 November 1943

Fred David's CAC 15 Cockatoo had performed even beyond his expectations. He had three prototypes, completing the third with a three-stage supercharger and had then constructed four "pre-production" machines with full armament. He had been hampered by an undercarriage failure on the second machine, resulting in its loss.

Last week's trials at Point Cook had involved a direct competition between the Cockatoo and Hencall's Griffin engine He 100 F1, plus trials versus a US P-51 and a Portuguese Spitfire V, plus a captured Zero. The CAC 15 had been judged to be superior to all of them. Faster than any of the other four machines, it was much longer ranged than all except the Mustang, within which it was comparable. It was marginally less manoeuvrable than the He 100, but had slightly higher speed, much greater range and a greater rate of climb.

He had been promised orders, with production to commence in January 1944, with both Hencall and CAC producing the new machine. Only the navy had not been interested, the fighters high landing speed and more fragile undercarriage disqualifying it for carrier-based operations.

1515 16 November 1943

The Japanese offensive had commenced on the 6th November in Burma, with the monsoon season barely finished. Lt General Slim's 14th Army had allowed them to exhaust themselves on the prepared defensive positions they had spent the last six months constructing. Some penetrations had occurred, with his forces driven back as much as five miles in some sectors, but he still had 36th Infantry Division and most of the 81st West African Rifles Division in reserve. After the Japanese had exhausted themselves, he would bring them forward for a counter attack.

Chiang Kai-shek had agreed to mount an offensive into North-eastern Burma from Yunnan and his best divisions were still in the Shan States. Once the Japanese offensive ran out of steam, he would attempt to switch over onto the offensive at the same time as Chines forces in the North.

2349 20 November 1943

Pridi Banomyong had achieved his main aim. Lieutenant General Seriroengrit had agreed, that in the event of a breakthrough he would hold the Prime Minister Plaek Phibunsongkharam under "house arrest". His large Northeaster army, comprising four divisions would then hold the highlands and a advance on Bangkok, where he had armed 90,000 irregulars and co-opted the 1st Division including the Royal Guard, who had arranged for members of the royal family still in Thailand to leave Bangkok on the 23rd on an "inspection tour" of the ersatz new Capital, Phetchabun. If the allies broke through, they were ready to make their move.

2016 22 November 1943

Keith Park again reviewed how things had changed since the last aircraft review board figures in May 1943. Older types had now been retired, little now remaining on active squadron service and types had been standardized. Numbers by type now read:

Fighters:
CAC Boomerang 190
CAC 15 Cockatoo 4 (in limited production until Jan 1944)
Curtis P40 412
Hencall He 112 124
Hencall He 100 643(Currently in production-numbers count RAN machines)
Hencall He 119 192(Currently in production)
Republic P43 52
TOTAL 1611 NEED 1600

Bombers/Patrol:
Avro Anson 489
Bolton Paul Defiant 28
Consolidated Catalina 82
de Havilland Mosquito 26(in limited production)
Douglas A20 51(12 ex Dutch East Indies)
Fairy Swordfish 91
Grumman Avenger 183
Hencall He 111 54

Hencall He 211 159(in production)
Lockheed Hudson 119
Lockheed Ventura 74
Martin Mariner 20
North American A36 172
North American B25 21
Vickers Wellington 41
Vultee Vengeance 281

TOTAL 2001 NEED 2000

Transports:
Airspeed Oxford 267
De Havilland Dragon 90
Douglas DC 2 8
Douglas C47 132(in production)
He 70 30
Junkers Ju 52 4
Wackett Garnet 6

TOTAL 528 NEED 800

Things had much improved, with only transports being in shortfall. No more Lend Lease was no expected, although the possibility of equipping the RAAF with a B-24 wing had been floated by the USAAF, which would allow replacement of the badly aging Anson.

2317 24 November 1943

With the He 100 likely to be reduced in production around February 1944, probably ceasing aside from RAN machines in March or April, his own factory would still be producing the CAC 15 under license.

However, it was a replacement for the He 211, an evolution rather than a revolution from a pre-war design, that had filled Hencall's thinking during 1943. With the Gunter brothers, he had spent many hours going over design specifications and conducting wind tunnel tests and had come up with a radical new design that on its first flight had performed beautifully. It would need further development but at this stage seemed a winner and Keith Park, who had attended personally, was very keen. He had decided to call it the He 200 Falcon.

0556 25 November 1943

Lt General Slim's 14th Army had spent 16 days blunting the Japanese offensive and bleeding their forces, being pushed back up to ten miles at certain points. After two days spent reorganising, he was now ready to launch his own offensive. He had air superiority and planned to use that to add a cutting edge to his attacks.

He had two completely fresh divisions to fling into the fray, along with Chinese forces numbering five divisions, one of those armoured in the North. He hoped the breach the exhausted Japanese front lines and then advance quickly, under cover of air and naval forces. He had only enough landing craft for a small amphibious operation, but had two Brigades, one jump capable in reserve. If he broke through, he hoped to land in the Japanese rear near the island of Phuket, backed by a mass paratroop drop. He hoped to push the Japanese out of Burma this campaigning season.

0807 4 December 1943

Lt General Renya Mutaguchi's 15th Army was in complete disarray. His air assets, comprising many out-dated types had suffered against the new allied aircraft and now, harassed consistently by allied aircraft in the South, counterattacked by two fresh divisions, his forces were in full retreat, the gains of his offensive already wiped out and a large hole in his defensive lines having been torn, with enemy troops moving rapidly towards the important road junction of Toungoo. He had little but disorganised light forces to stop them.

In the North, things were even worse. A general offensive from Yunnan Provence had caught the flank of his forces whilst they had already been in retreat from a three-division offensive near Kentung. His troops had no option but to withdraw into Indochina North of the Mekong, leaving the front into Northern Thailand defended only by Thai troops and isolated, cut off units. It was a disaster of the first order and could well get worse.
Burma 4 December 1943(Purple line)

2216 4 December 1943

Plaek Phibunsongkharam had deliberately kept the man waiting as long as possible. He no longer entirely trusted the motives of the regent any way, strongly suspecting Pridi

Phanomyong of pro allied leanings.

When the Regent was shown in, he came with a full squad of royal guard soldiers. Half an hour later the Prime Minister was being shoved into the back of a truck and Pridi Phanomyong spent the night contacting army commanders. Tomorrow night the uprising in Bangkok would start. In the meantime, he had instructed his army commanders to contact allied forces and offer them free passage and to resist any Japanese troop movements through territory held by the Royal Thai Army, effective 1800 tomorrow.

0616 5 December 1943

Commander Robert McWard's *Sailfish* was a veteran, on her 10th patrol, which took her south of Honshū. She had been alerted of a fast convoy of Japanese ships before she arrived on station. About 240 mi (390 km) southeast of Yokosuka, she had made radar contact at 9,000 yd (8,200 m).

The group consisted of a Japanese aircraft carrier, a cruiser, and two destroyers. Despite high seas, *Sailfish* moved into firing position shortly after 2200, dived to radar depth and fired four bow torpedoes at the carrier, at a range of 2,000 yards, scoring two hits. She went deep to escape the escorting destroyers, reloaded, and at 0200, surfaced to resume the pursuit. She had found a mass of radar contacts, and a slow-moving target, impossible to identify in the miserable visibility. As dawn neared, she fired another spread of three bow "fish" from 3,000 yards, scoring two more hits on the stricken carrier. Diving to elude the Japanese counter-attack, which was hampered by the raging seas, *Sailfish* came to periscope depth, and saw the carrier lying dead in the water, listing to port and sinking the stern. Preparations to abandon ship were in progress. As *Sailfish* watched, the escort carrier *Chuyo* slipped beneath the waves.

0535 6 December 1943

Lt General Renya Mutaguchi's 15th Army was now trapped and isolated in Southern Burma. The Thailand Government had declared Phibun's 1942 declaration of war was unconstitutional and legally void and had in turn declared war on Japan for violating its "territorial sovereignty". With the allied armies in full pursuit, the British controlling both the air and now the sea routes and the only recently opened Thai-Burma railway now cut by the Thai army, his forces were in a hopeless position, completely cut off in Southwestern Burma. With the Thai Army now advancing to cut the Isthmus of Kra, even a land-based escape of any type would soon be impossible.

1432 8 December 1943

Sommerville's Eastern Fleet had left Akyab, which they had been using as a forward base to assist Slim's advance, carrying with them all of their limited amphibious assets and embarking the 268th Indian Motorised Brigade and a Battalion of Orde Wingate's Chindits, the second Ghurkha Rifles.

They would be supported in a landing at Tavoy, a location on the coast of Burma by 142 Commando Company and 50th Indian Parachute Brigade, who would drop directly on the city after the landing. Its objective was to assist in the capture of Bangkok, where fierce battles had started to rage. The city was less than less than 100 miles away. His five carriers would, once the beachhead was established, strike at Japanese positions around Bangkok.

2115 8 December 1943

The disaster in Burma had predictably brought the army to the navy's door. Vice Admiral Kiyohide Shima was the new commander of the Mobile Fleet and had received a briefing from Toyoda that afternoon. He was to rendezvous at Brunei with the elements of the fleet based at Truk and proceed, via Singapore to the Bay of Bengal, there to relieve and evacuate the trapped Burma Area Army.

He would sail on the night of the 16th, the earliest the new carriers *Shinyo* and *Kaiyo* could be made ready with:
CV Kaga
CVL Nisshin, Ryuho
CVE Shinyo, Kaiyo, Eikyo
BV Ise, Hyuga
BB Yamato, Nagato

He would pick up the BB *Musashi* and CVE *Taiyo* at Brunei, with a number of cruisers and destroyers, before proceeding on.

2212 8 December 1943

The Eastern Fleet was at an all-time high, thought Somerville, as he had not as yet detached the older ships back to the U.K, with the need to support the current amphibious operations even the old *R Class* were useful. His force currently consisted of:

CV Illustrious
CVL Unicorn, Hermes
CVE Begum, Shah, Battler, Pretoria Castle
BB Royal Sovereign, Ramillies, Valiant, Queen Elizabeth, Resolution
BC Renown, Repulse
CA London, Cornwall, Dorsetshire, Suffolk, Sussex
CL Newcastle, Kenya, Gambia, Ceylon, Nigeria, Emerald, Durban, Dauntless, Danae
24 DD

1012 9 December 1943

3rd Fleet had now become 5th Fleet, under the command of now full Admiral Raymond Spruance. His forces now consisted of *CV's Lafayette, Essex, Lexington(2), Yorktown(2) and Enterprise(2), CVL's Princeton, Independence, Belleau Wood, Monterey, Cabot* and *Cowpens, BB's Washington, South Dakota, Massachusetts and, North Carolina* and *Alabama*, plus numerous cruisers and destroyers that included two of the new *Baltimore Class* heavy cruisers. All of his CV's had now been equipped with the new diver bomber, the Helldiver and some of his light aircraft carriers as well.

His force was also accompanied by Vice Admiral Kincaid's "brown water" fleet, consisting of eight older battleships and eight escort carriers. He had covered the shore assault of two U.S divisions, the 1st Marine in Northern New Ireland, just south of Kavieng and the Americal Division in South-eastern New Ireland.

An attack on the landing forces by 20 Japanese bombers, escorted by a similar number of fighters, from Kavieng had been rebuffed, with only the heavy cruiser *Boston* taking a bomb hit and one LST sunk. Losses among the attacking planes had been almost total, only seven aircraft escaping. He had reports from FRUMEL of upcoming Japanese Naval movements, so their remained a possibility the main Japanese fleet would try and intervene.

1056 9 December 1943

Vice Admiral Collins SWPac Fleet was covering the invasion of both New Hannover and the Admiralty Islands, both assaults going in near simultaneously on the morning of the 9th at 0555. His covering forces consisted of *CV Australasia* and CVL's *Christchurch, Melbourne, Sydney*, as well as the battleship *Pacifica*, plus cruisers and destroyers.

With no Japanese air units located in either location, the only likely response had been from the small airfield at Sansapor on the far West of Papua or the small airfield at Biak or from Rabaul, now much reduced.

A small strike from Biak, eight Mary bombers escorted by nine Zeros had been easily swept aside, but a low-level strike of 12 G4Ms and six A6M's had been missed by radar and only met when virtually on top of the invasion force. They had torpedoed and sunk both the assault transport *Monowai* and the destroyer escort *Murray*, the latter with heavy loss of life and the former with a great loss of equipment, including 20 tanks. Although fighters had later shot down ten of the eighteen attackers, it was a bad result.

0617 11 December 1943

Brigadier Orde Wingate had accompanied the 2nd Gurkha Rifles on the landing at Maunmagan Beach near Tavoy. The combination of the seaborne landing that he had participated in and the airborne landing later that same afternoon had quickly overwhelmed the 4 to 500 Japanese in the small city/large town.

With his forces now secure and a follow up Brigade set to be landed within a week, the priority now was to assist in the capture of Bangkok, still being fiercely contested between Royal Thai Army forces and Thai irregulars and Japanese garrison troops.

Situation in Burma/Thailand after the Thai change over government 11 December 1943 (Purple line)

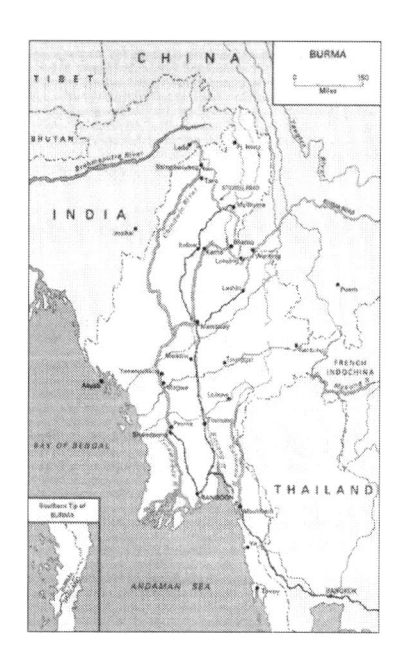

1617 15 December 1943

Morsehead was happy with the progress of the New Hannover and Admiralty Islands campaign. There was a fair bit of fighting to do yet, but both locations had only approximately 2000 Japanese troops. Now cut off with no resupply against superior numbers of Australasians, it was only a matter of time. "Tubby" Allen's 1st Division, the most experienced formation in the army had quickly and efficiently established a beachhead and both operations to clear the defending Japanese were well advanced.

0716 16 December 1943

Major General John Reed Hodge's 23rd Infantry (Americal) Division and the 1st Marine Division had so far not launched major offensive operations on New Ireland, merely building up their own formation's and moving North from Nabuto Bay (Americal) and South from Lagagagon Bay (1st Marines) to link up their forces. After a battle costing near 200 casualties but leaving over 700 Japanese dead, they had linked up near the town of Konos.

The remaining Japanese forces were either trapped in the South of the island, South of Elizabeth Bay, facing the Americal, or in the far North, North of Fangalawa Bay, near the main Japanese stronghold, Kavieng, facing 1st Marines.

1600 17 December 1943

Vice Admiral Shima's Mobile fleet, slightly delayed, sailed from the Inland Sea on their way to Brunei. The situation of the Japanese army in Burma could hardly be any more desperate. Personally, if it had been up to Shima, he would have left the army to stew in their own juices. The Kido Butai had only just been reformed in strength and the quality of pilots and air groups on board his newly built units such as the three escort carriers, did not bear thinking about. They, along with his hybrid battleship conversions, had not been able to handle the more modern types, still operating the old D3A and B5N. The hybrid conversions were of even less utility in his mind, operating only the old A5M, the Zeros landing speed being too fast.

0549 19 December 1943

Commander Edwards Stephens *USS Greyback* had provided the first confirmed sighting that the Combined Fleet was at sea. Southeast of Okinawa, he had sighted the main formation, but had been attacked by escorting destroyers before he could achieve an attack position. He had stayed near the surface too long, being surprised by a Jap destroyer and had been lucky enough to escape by dint of a "down the throat" snap shot by all forward tubes that had hit the tin can twice, sinking IJN *Numakaze* quickly. Not able to get a full count, he had simply reported "multiple carriers and battleships".

0640 25 December 1943

Shima's fleet was being refuelled in Brunei Bay. They had only lost the one destroyer during the transit, although he had no doubt their movement had been reported. He now had his complete force on hand, consisting of:

CV Kaga
CVL Nisshin, Ryuho
CVE Shinyo, Kaiyo, Eikyo, Taiyo
BV Ise, Hyuga
BB Musashi, Yamato, Nagato
CA Tone, Chokai, Ashigara, Haguro, Chikuma, Myoko
CL Naka, Natori, Isuzu, Kuma
21 DD

He would sail tonight, urgency being required due to the ever deteriorating situation in Burma, with the land bridge between forces from Malaya/Southern Thailand and Thailand itself/Burma now cut off.

0546 28 December 1943

Captain Leslie W. A. Bennington's RN *T Class* submarine *Tally Ho* had sighted the main Japanese body proceeding at speed some 30miles South of Penang. He had taken what target was available and was pleased to see that of seven torpedoes launched, two solid hits had been obtained on the port side trailing cruiser. He made a sighting report and rapidly submerged to get away from the inevitable retribution.

0808 28 December 1943

HMAS Taipan, alerted by the sighting report from *Tally Ho* had positioned the boat on the perceived course of the Japanese force and had been rewarded when they had come into sight only 10 miles North of Penang.

He had been lucky, very lucky, a zig taking them into the perfect firing position for the submarine. It was a queer looking beast, the target, a weird combination of heavy ship forward and carrier aft. Commander Rex von Steiglitz had decided to hit her with everything he had and then go deep. He had already gotten off another sighting report. At 0821 he fired probably the heaviest salvo ever fired by a submarine, ten torpedoes, and without waiting to see the results, dove deep. Five torpedoes hit IJN *Hyuga* at 0825, with *Taipan* proving as deadly as her name.

0859 28 December 1943

It had been a poor morning for Shima. Trapped in the narrow yet deep waters off Penang, he had firstly lost the light cruiser *Kuma* to one submarine. Hit by two torpedoes, she had slowly sunk over a period of ninety minutes. Most of the ships company had been rescued but the submarine had escaped.

Now an even worse setback. The hybrid battleship/carrier *Hyuga*, hit along her length by five torpedoes, had violently exploded sixteen minutes after the torpedo hits, showering the *Ise*, over 800 meters away with debris. Whilst destroyers prosecuted the submarine, he was searching for survivors. There seemed to be pitiably few.

0902 28 December 1943

The sighting reports had alerted Admiral Somerville to the presence and intention of the Japanese fleet. It was just like 1942 all over again. Fight or flight? He could not afford to abandon the beachhead and jeopardize the chance for a stunning success on land, not when it was within their grasp.

This time, he felt, it would be fight. The only logical reason for the appearance of this much of the IJN in force was to force its way through to Rangoon and evacuate its troops. That being the case, he could concentrate his own forces, withdrawing them back Northwards towards Rangoon, drawing the Japanese away from their own land based air support and closer to his own.

It would be hard for the men on the forward beachhead at Tavoy, but as yet they were not facing substantial Japanese pressure and they could cease offensive operations of their own. If his carriers and land-based air could blunt the Japanese offensive air capacity, he should be safe. He could not imagine them successfully forcing their way past seven capital ships.

1535 3 May 2014(flash forward)

They had gone to Williamstown to view *HMAS Taipan*. There were very few RAN World War 2 vessels preserved in Australasia, only four to be exact, but *Taipan* was one of them, being preserved at Williamstown along with the *Bathurst Class* corvette *HMAS Castlemaine*. *HMAS Whyalla* was preserved at Whyalla, South Australia and the *River Class* destroyer escort *HMAS Tamar* at Wellington.

Whilst her father had functions, she had been stuck with the brat pack, although the younger two had loved scrambling through the old submarine. She was famous, the highest scoring of all World War 2 RAN subs. Unlike some other *T Class* RAN boats, two of which had been given to East Indonesia, she had been kept after the war, not being retired until 1963. She had asked her minder Chris Hills to take a photo to send back to her mum, currently sick. She would get some brownie points for looking after her hyper younger two brothers.

World Map end 1943

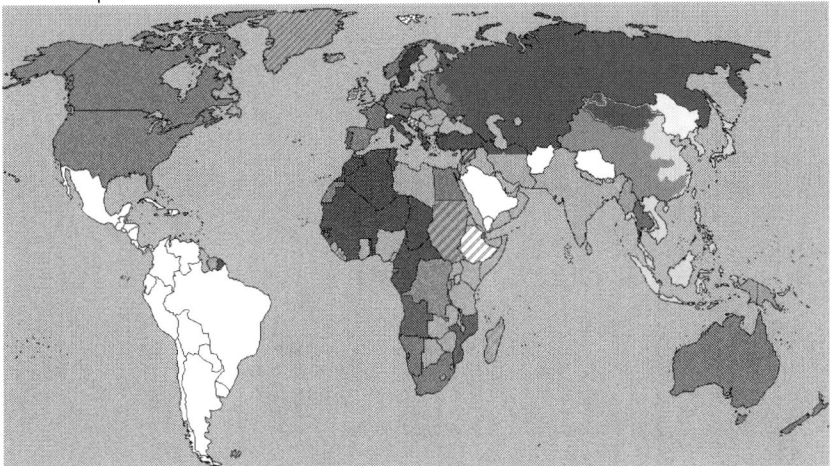

0926 28 December 1943

Hencall's secretary Judy Bordin had delivered the buff envelope this morning and had been overjoyed when he had slit it open and read it. It was an order for 50 machines. The second prototype had also flown well and clearly the RAAF had decided they wanted it. He would wind back He 211 production to complete the existing airframes and then commence production immediately after, probably within a month.

Much like the early days with shortages of Merlin engines, the shortages of the new Griffon engine would mean the CAC 15 would receive priority, but he hoped to get his 50 machines order completed by June 1944. The first machines would hopefully see squadron service around the same time. It was a much bigger plane than the He 211, higher flying, faster, carrying a bigger bomb load, indeed more advanced in every way.

He was not blind to the coming of jet powered aircraft, but nothing like that had yet been attempted in Australasia. The British had promised a prototype engine with a two to three months to work with. It would take quite a while to adapt a design to such a new concept, however. In the meantime, he had the upgrades to the He 100 to work on, along with the 119, but it was the designing, the new aircraft, that really excited him.

It had been a good couple of days for the aircraft industry he though. Yesterday he had gone to CAC to celebrate the release of the first production CAC 15. In actuality, it had not been the first, all nine prototype and pre-production machines having already been brought up to A1 standard, so it was really the tenth machine. It was hoped to have it with a squadron by February.

Performance figures CAC 15 and He 200
He 200 Falcon
Length: 68 ft
Wingspan: 128 ft
Empty Weight:42,220lb
Loaded Weight:98,800lb
Power Plant: 4 Rolls Royce Griffon Engines
Crew:8
Maximum Speed:373 mph
Cruise Speed:235 mph
Armament:8 20mm cannon
6000lb of bombs internally
Range:9,850 miles
Service Ceiling:31,400 ft

CAC 15 Cockatoo
Length:36 ft
Wingspan:36ft
Empty Weight:7540lb
Loaded Weight:9500lb
Power Plant:1 Rolls Royce Griffin
Crew:1
Maximum Speed:457 mph
Cruise Speed:310 mph
Armament:4x20mm cannons
Provision for one 1000lb bomb or drop tank, either 10 rockets or ten 20lb bombs on wings
Range:1165 miles
Service Ceiling: 39,000 ft

0932 28 December 1943

She had slipped out of the Clyde, escorted by the old destroyer *Newmarket*. Both had a long journey to go on their way to service under their third flag. *HMAS Wellington,* ex *HMS Archer*, was ferrying a full load of Corsairs for the RN, but had been commissioned into the RAN two days prior. As she ploughed through the wash, her sister *HMAS Perth*, ex *USS Long Island*, was just leaving Tonga on her final journey to Sydney.

1003 28 December 1943

Colonel Reizo Takahashi's conundrum for the Third Air Army, from his headquarters in Singapore, was how to get his land-based bombers at the British Fleet. As Chief of Staff he had pondered this last night and today. All raids so far on the fleet had been repulsed with some losses. He had no access to Thai airfields anymore and the airfields around both Toungoo and Rangoon in Burma were under constant allied attack, mainly from cannon armed Hurricanes. Air strength in Burma, or what was left of it, was not sufficient to allow bombers or fighters to be staged out of Rangoon and the allies were attacking those airfields at will, with Toungoo on the verge of being overrun anyway. With the Thai airfields out of consideration that left only the Burmese airfields in the isthmus and Malaya. In Southern Burma and surrounds were three bases, however two, Port Blair and Victoria Point were only seaplane bases and the last, Mergui, was small, had no operational aircraft left and had been hammered by British battleship and air bombardment. That left only bases in Malaya, the largest and most accessible being at Butterworth near Penang on the West Coast.

Therein lay the problem. With the British fleet pulling back towards Rangoon, a strike could be a 1300 nautical mile trip, possibly a bit more, possible from bombers but at the absolute limit of range for fighters such as the Zero, so any bombers sent would have to go unescorted or escorted by his limited numbers of twin engine Ki 45's and J1N's, both held in limited numbers only.

1302 29 December 1943

Shima's force, held to the slow cruising speed of 15.5 knots by its escort carriers, was now slightly North of Point Victoria. The British had been slighted by his own land-based reconnaissance float planes, having left their beachhead at Tavoy to its own devices yesterday, they were cruising near the Gulf of Martaban, still over 320 nautical miles to the North. With sunset at 1730, a strike seemed unlikely today, but would have to be fully prepared in the morning.

1414 29 December 1943

On New Ireland, William Henry Rupertus's 1st Marine Division had the remaining Japanese forces pinned into a two to three-mile perimeter around Kavieng. He had brought up artillery and his naval gunfire support was pounding the Japanese, who were trapped in the small area. He had scheduled a final attack for the morning of the 31st, hoping to infiltrate men into positions during the previous night.

The Japanese had tried to land reinforcement by barge during the campaign, but PT boats had been swiftly station on the island and had done much to interdict passage. He had suffered little from air raids from Rabaul, juts the occasional aircraft, at most 3 or 4. The base appeared to have been beaten down and largely moribund. To the South the Americal Division had compressed the Japanese into the Southernmost 9 miles of the island, having just captured the village of Melion, South of the Weitin River.

1548 29 December 1943

Morsehead's Admiralty Island and New Hanover campaign was drawing to a close. The Admiralty Islands had been subdued, the final Japanese strongholds falling on the 27th, with some minor mopping up on the 28th. In exchange for 2106 Japanese dead and 78 captured, he had lost 368 dead and 679 wounded. Operations on New Hanover were in their final stages, the island having been swept and cleared aside from a two-mile perimeter around the town of Taskul, still held by an estimated 700 Japanese.

1644 29 December 1943

Lt General Renya Mutaguchi's 15th Army's position was scarcely less desperate. Under supplied, underfed and with little in the way of heavy equipment, nearly all of which had been lost in the retreat, they were now totally isolated in Southern Burma. Toungoo had been lost to the Chinese, Prome and Scwedaung to the British. The bridgehead at Tavoy had expanded to link up with Thai forces, cutting off his command completely.

The only airfields at his disposal were at Rangoon and Moulmein, both constantly attacked, with his strength in operational aircraft down to 7. Little help could be expected. Bangkok had also fallen to the enemy. Unless he was able to evacuated by the navy, his command had no hope.

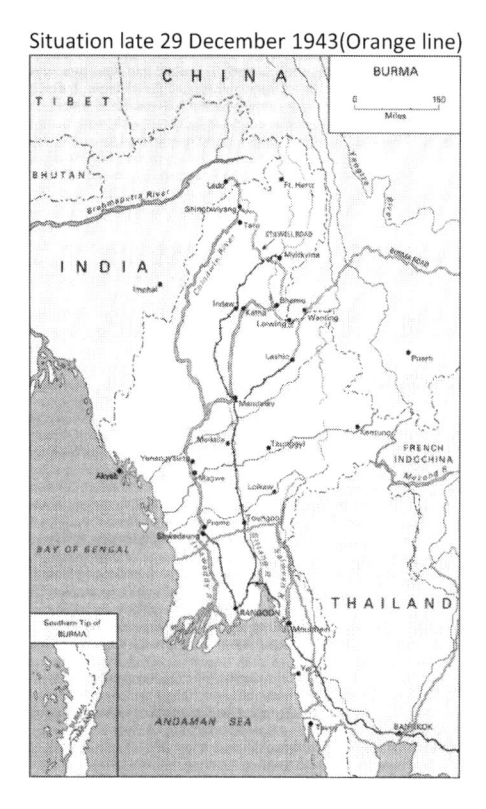

Situation late 29 December 1943(Orange line)

1708 29 December 1943

Somerville now faced a decision as to what to do with the Eastern Fleet. Should he wait until morning and fight an air battle against a possibly numerically superior enemy force, or should he take the initiative and attempt a night surface action against a fleet inferior to his own in battleships. With seven capital ships and his own confidence of RN night fighting doctrine, it was a possibility he was certainly entertaining. He had a small number of ASV equipped aircraft and the Japanese seemed to be stubbornly ploughing on to Rangoon. Either way, he would have to make a decision soon.

0249 30 December 1943

Contacts had started to appear on the scope of radar scope of Somerville's flagship *Queen Elizabeth* at 0243. It was the most powerful concentration of surface forces the RN had fielded since World War 1. Seven capital ships carrying 52 15inch guns, five heavy cruisers, nine light cruisers and 18 destroyers. At the rear of the formation, he had two carriers, *HMS Hermes* and *Pretoria Castle*, both with ASV equipped Swordfish on board.

Somerville had to reversed course back to the North, planning to eventually cut across the Japanese track by moving Northwest, cutting across the Japanese line at approximately 50 degrees, not exactly crossing their T but not far from it. He thought it likely the Japanese possessed surface search radar now, but he assumed it would be inferior to the latest set mounted in his flagship, *Renown*, *Ramillies* and *Valiant*. He planned to track the Japanese long enough to launch a night strike from both carriers, which he had detached and then cut across their bows and engage in the confusion.

0343 30 December 1943

It took almost an hour of time for his carriers to clear the field of advance to the East far enough for a strike to be launched with a degree of secrecy and during this time his forces had been matching the Japanese fleet at 16 knots due North, his old *R Class* battleships huffing their way through the seas with some difficulty, particularly *Resolution*, which was straining to keep pace with the other six ships. Finally, he had received a ready signal from Captain Davis on *Hermes*, indicating the strike was in the air. Ten minutes later he altered course North West to close the range and cut ahead of the Japanese line.

0359 30 December 1943

The low drone of the Bristol Pegasus engine was a giveaway for some Japanese sailors who had heard the sound before, notably off Malaya. One to two minutes before the aircraft hit, searchlights started to probe the sky and crews closed up on anti-aircraft guns. It was far too late in almost every case.

Although two planes were badly damaged enough to cause them to pull out of their attack and one was unfortunate enough to be hit twice by 3.9-inch shells from an *Atkizuke Class* destroyer, that still left twenty aircraft and they bored down on their favourite targets, enemy aircraft carriers. Three carried flares, the rest torpedoes.

The Japanese formation immediately lost all cohesion, with ships darting in all directions to avoid the missiles aimed at them. Many torpedoes missed, but some hit. The carrier *Ryuho*, set on fire by an early hit, became a convenient target for many aircraft, being hit twice more by two of the last four planes to attack, the carrier being beautifully silhouetted by the fire with the flares light dying. The carrier *Taiyo* also took a hit, causing her to immediately slow and list, as did the cruiser *Myoko* and the flagship *Musashi*, although the last two ships were relatively unimpaired.

0429 30 December 1943

The operator of the surface search radar on *Musashi* had not been concerned when he had received a contact at 18,900 yards. With the fleet disorganised, he and the communications officer had thought that it was probably scattered ships returning to the formation. Chastened, he had not raised it again until the contact became a series of contacts, some now as close as 15,800 yards, cutting across the Japanese ships at an oblique angle.

By the time Shima was aware of the contact, the range had fallen to less than 15,000 yards and the Japanese fleet, having made a turn away to the South followed by a turn back to the North and East, were actually closing the range on each other.

0435 30 December 1943

Shima had ordered action stations and the firing of star shell over the suspected enemy ships to receive a positive identification. In the meantime, he had ordered his ships to turn to starboard, with his carriers to conduct a battle turn away to the South to try and clear the area.

It was all quite sensible stuff, if executed perfectly, which it was not. The carrier *Taiyo*, already lamed, swung around slowly and continued to swing, looming in front of the destroyer *Shimikaze*, assigned to escort the carriers away from the area. As the destroyer ploughed into the side of the carrier, the star shells confirmed Shima's worst possible fears.

British battleships, not just one or two, at least five or six looming out of the dark. His course had taken his ships towards them but had stopped his line being crossed at least. At less than 11,000 yards, the fleets passed each other, one heading South East, the other North West. Then all hell broke loose.

0435 30 December 1943

Somerville had watched and waited as the range wound down until the Japanese had made a course change, straitening up on a converging course less than 10,500 yards apart. As the star shells were first fired, he gave the order to his own ships to "engage the enemy with all weapons at your disposal." Most of his ships possessed surface search radar and his newer battleships had a solution on the leading Japanese ships for some time. His first three salvos were to go in before the started enemy had begun to reply.

0508 30 December 1943

The entire engagement toe to toe had lasted less than ten minutes, but the damage inflicted to his command was frightful, thought Shima. As he retreated South, he was still under a small amount of long-range fire, although it was nothing compared to the passing engagement that he had just suffered. His battle line, formerly consisting of the *Musashi*, *Yamato*, *Nagato*, had been scared beyond recognition.

His own flagship had one main turret still in action, thankfully the rear, which was still firing. Hit over twenty times by 15-inch shells, she had fires all over her. Behind the flagship, *Yamato* was much the same, except her captain had also reported a torpedo hit. Listing to port but still capable of 18 knots, she was maintaining station to the rear.

Nagato, however, was not. Hit by a torpedo strike in the engine room after being the target of two enemy battleships, she had lost all power and then been targeted by every enemy ship in the line as they passed. Battered beyond all recognition, he could still see the light of her fires to the North.

Of the heavy cruisers, *Ashigara* and *Haguro* still maintained station, despite severe damage to their upper works, as did *Chokai*, miraculously only hit once only by 8-inch shells. *Tone*, targeted by HMS HMS *Repulse*, had been hit 23 times by 15-inch shells and numerous times by smaller calibre shells. She was settling deeply in the water. Her sister *Chikuma's* location was unknown, but believed sunk. *Myoko*, already having taken one torpedo hit, was hit numerous times by battleship shells before taking two more torpedo hits and had turned turtle and sunk.

The last ship in the line, the light cruiser *Isuzu* had simply disintegrated, ceasing to exist under a ruthless pounding of heavy shells. In the skirmishes between the light forces, he had also lost a light cruiser and four destroyers, with two more destroyers badly damaged and three more lightly damaged but all damaged destroyers were sticking with his forces. His carriers, by turning away, were at least spared the slaughter, however, the *Taiyo* had been left behind, her fate unknown, the carrier and the destroyer *Shimakaze* locked together after their collision. There was no question of going on, none whatsoever.

0616 30 December 1943

As the first rays of sunlight peeked over the Eastern Fleet, Vice Admiral Sir Arthur Power was able to take stock. They had hammered the Japanese, sinking many ships, a heavy cruiser and a *Nagato Class* battleship having taken the plunge in the last twenty minutes, but had certainly not come off unscathed themselves.

The most serious loss had been HMS *Queen Elizabeth*. The flagship, second in line, had been the target of salvos from the two huge Jap battlewagons. Hit badly, with Somerville dead on her bridge, she had also been hit three times when the Japanese had responded with their inevitable "get out of jail" card, torpedoes. Still afloat, she clearly had no more than ten to twenty minutes left in the sun. He had also lost the light cruiser *Danae* and the destroyer *Norman* to torpedoes, with the destroyer *Nizam* so badly damaged by 6.1 inch and 8-inch shells she would have to be scuttled. Many other ships had taken shells hits, but the only other ships badly hit was the *Royal Sovereign*. Hit once by a "long lance", she was in trouble, barely able to make way. Whilst he would have to shepherd his damaged ships back, his carriers would be launching a strike first thing. With Somerville dead, he wanted blood.

0618 30 December 1943

It was a disaster that would take some explaining, thought Shima. Too far away for fighter support, he was preparing to launch his own CAP and would launch all his strike planes at the British, despite running South, hopefully delaying any such action by themselves.

0715 30 December 1943

It was the Japanese who got the first strike away, the veteran deck crews of the *Kaga* having its strike aircraft readied before the inexperienced escort carrier crews were anywhere near ready to launch. Originally intending to launch a large combined strike, in the finish Shima let *Kaga's* strike depart at 0715.

They were over the RN Task Force at 0741, 24 B6N's, 18 D4Y's and 15 A6M's. With only two carriers covering the Task Force, the escort carrier *Pretoria Castle* and the small *Hermes*, the Japanese for once faced little opposition, both carriers having spotted up strike aircraft they had not, as yet, launched, still rearming aircraft from last night's strike.

The two carriers did manage to get all their fighters into the air, nine Seafires and six Martlets. They identified the torpedo carriers as the main danger and for the loss of two Seafires and two Martlets, shot down six B6N's and eight of the fifteen Zeros, the Japanese pilots inexperience showing. AA was very heavy indeed, downing one Zero, four B6N's and four D3Y's. For the torpedo bombers surviving, the almost immobile *Royal Sovereign* was a prime target and of the eight aircraft that launched, two hits were obtained. Three more that targeted *Hermes* all missed, but the dive bombers hit her twice with 500lb bombs, starting fires on the flight deck.

0818 30 December 1943

It was the strike from the main RN carrier group, over the horizon and 45 miles Northwest of the RN battleships, that arrived next.

It consisted of:
Illustrious 14 Barracudas, 19 Corsairs
Unicorn 4 Swordfish
Begum 12 Avengers
Shah 10 Avengers, 6 Wildcats
Battler 9 Seafires

The Japanese CAP, consisting of thirty-six Zeros and six A5M's, was fully alerted by both the expectation of attack and radar. Despite their inexperience, they shot down a Seafire, four Avengers, a Barracuda, a Swordfish and two Corsairs, however, they lost four A5M's and 15 Zeros doing so. AA removed two Avengers and another Swordfish, but the torpedo bombers picked *Shinyo* as their main target, Avengers striking her twice, before the Barracudas hit her twice more, causing her to rapidly stop, quickly assuming an unrecoverable list. Four more targeted the battleship *Yamato*, but failed to gain a hit.

0902 30 December 1943

It was large strike that arrived over the RN battleship force, 55 B5N's escorted by 22 A6M's and 11 A5M's. By this stage the RN carrier force had thrown much of its fighter cover over the group and the CAP consisted of nine Seafires, four Martlets, 12 Corsairs, as well as ten P36 Mohawks from No 155 squadron in Burma.

Although outnumbered by the Japanese aircraft, they gave an excellent account of themselves against the largely novice pilots from the newly commissioned escort carriers and hybrid carrier. 21 B5N's, 12 A6M's and seven A5M's were downed(some by AA) at a cost of only seven aircraft, three Mohawks, a Seafire, a Martlet and two Corsairs(one by collision).

Agitated by the rough treatment, only one hit was obtained by the Japanese, on the small carrier *Hermes*, although her fires were added to by a damaged A5M seemingly deliberately diving into the damaged carrier after being hit. By the time they left at 0928, the little carrier was well alight and would sink later that day.

Aside from an attack by RAF Wellingtons later in the day that sank the Japanese light cruiser *Naka* with a torpedo hit, it was the last action of the day, both forces happy to lick their wounds. For the Japanese navy, despite sinking two RN battleships and a small carrier, as well as a light cruiser and two destroyers, it was a defeat. For the Imperial Japanese Army in Burma, it was a disaster, a death knell.

Losses:

CVL Ryuho
CVE Shinyo, Taiyo
BV Hyuga
BB Nagato
CA Tone, Chikuma, Myoko
CL Naka, Isuzu, Kuma
6 DD

CVL Hermes
BB Royal Sovereign, Queen Elizabeth
CL Danae
2 DD

1708 30 December 1943

The bulk of Vice Admiral Sir Arthur Power's Eastern Fleet was heading back to Ceylon, with all battleships damaged aside from *Repulse* he needed to dry dock some of his ships for repair and then sort out in the light of the day's happenings which of his ships he would release back to the UK.

Early in the morning on the 24th, IJN *I-166* under Lt Commander Nakayama Denshichi had landed six Indian National Army agents at Kirinda, West coast of Ceylon and was returning to the joint Japanese and German submarine base at Penang. Sound quickly established the presence of many vessels and she was lucky enough to be in a position to intercept. It was a commander's dream, battleships and one large carrier.

Firing six torpedoes at the carrier, they hit *HMS Pretoria Castle* in a grouping along her length. Carrying damaged and dud aircraft back to Ceylon, she was to sink slowly at 1939. By that stage *I-166* had been on the bottom an hour and a half, sunk by the destroyer *Quickmatch*.

1809 3 January 1944

William Henry Rupertus's 1st Marine Division had cleared Kavieng in a final, bloody battle.

His campaign to capture the Northern part of the island had been expensive, 800 killed and 2,943 wounded, most of them in this assault, where the Japanese had made excellent use of prepared positions and fought, as usual, to the last man, only auxiliary troops and labourers surrendering. However, when the Americal finished its own campaign in the South, which was drawing to a close and the Australasian captured New Hanover, it would remove the need to ever land troops on New Britain.

1119 5 January 1944

Taskul on New Hanover had fallen to the troops of 1st Australasian, signalling the end of the Admiralty Islands/New Hanover campaign. It had cost 368 dead and 1982 wounded, in exchange for almost 5000 Japanese dead and 127 captured. Morshead's command could now draw breath until early February, when the islands of Noemfoor and Biak off the North Coast of New Guinea and Sansapor in West Papua would be the next targets.

1345 10 January 1944

With the last Japanese positions around Lanisso Bay secured, the Americal Division had secured Southern New Ireland. Their fight had been less bloody than 1st Marines, with a lower concentration of Japanese troops in the South of the island, but had still cost 235 dead and 986 wounded.

1704 10 January 1944

Krueger sat with Blamey discussing the situation. With the Japanese facing a disaster of the first magnitude in Burma and the New Ireland/New Hanover/Admiralty Islands campaigns all completed, they could move their focus away from Rabaul. With airfields being operational on New Ireland, New Hanover and the Admiralties within a month at most, New Britain and Rabaul would become nothing more than a giant prison camp, surrounded to the North and North East by New Ireland, the East by Bougainville, the West by Lae, the South East by Milne Bay, the North by New Hanover and the North West by the Admiralties, the island as completely cut off. The upcoming operations against Noemfoor, Biak and Sansapor would be the end of the New Guinea and Solomons campaign.

All further operations would be directed against severing the Dutch East Indies communications and capturing ground to support the invasion of the Philippines.

2233 11 January 1944

Lt General Renya Mutaguchi's 15th Army was still stumbling back to Rangoon, now fighting on with no hope of relief. His forces had abandoned the coastal areas to the West of the Irrawaddy in an attempt to find a line with natural defences to at least bleed the Anglo-Chinese army as much as possible. Thai forces had control over nearly all Thai territory except the East of the country and the far South. British and Chinese troops, unimpeded in their advance and with total mastery of sea and air communications had rushed forward to check Japanese advances in the East and South of Thailand and a front had stabilized. His own Army, however, cut off and supplied only by a few submarines based at Penang, was slowly losing cohesion, lack of ammunition after intense fighting being a critical issue.

0705 20 January 1944

Spuance's Third Fleet was going after the main Japanese naval base at Truk. It was a huge cloud of aircraft that had formed up in the first wave, launched from the following carriers: *Lafayette, Essex Class Essex, Enterprise(2), Yorktown(2), Lexington(2)* and *Saratoga(2)*, plus *Independence Class* light carriers *Independence, Princeton, Belleau Wood, Cowpens, Langley(2), Monterey* and *Cabot*, with 784 aircraft embarked. Five fast battleships escorted the carriers and a separate surface action group based on the *USS Iowa* and five heavy cruisers was circling to the North of Truk to cut off any Japanese ships attempting to escape.

It was the perfect weather for such an operation, intermittent cloud covering the carriers but clear sky over Truk. It was to be the first strike in a series of continuous strikes lasting a full two days.

0806 25 January 1944

Vice Admiral Masami Kobayashi looked at the letter, recalling him home to Japan and confirming his "retirement" from the navy. He prepared and packed his own belongings, not trusting himself to remain stoic yet in the presence of others.

They had effectively cashiered him on the basis of the events of the 20th and 21st at Truk. The initial American strike had concentrated on his aircraft strength, catching many on the ground, destroying or badly damaging 130+ aircraft of his almost 330 machines. Follow up strike had destroyed more and of the 334 aircraft on Truk on the 19th, only 52 remained active.

He had, of course, attempted to strike back at the enemy, but it had been a largely futile task. One G3M had obtained a torpedo hit on a U.S carrier late on the 20th, another two D3A's had hit both an American battleship and an American cruiser loitering to the North on the 21st. The shipping in the formerly safe anchorage, largely ignored in the first wave, had been destroyed at leisure once his air defences had been beaten down.

The toll had been heavy. The light cruisers *Kashii* and *Katori*, as well as the destroyer *Maikaze* had been sunk by a U.S battleship, with heavy cruiser support, attempting to escape.

All other units had been sunk either in Truk or attempting to escape by air attack. The list was huge and included:
Light Cruiser *Nagara*
Destroyers *Fumizuki, Matsukaze* and *Tachikaze*
Armed Merchant Cruisers *Aikoko Maru* and *Hokoko Maru*
Submarine Tenders *Heian Maru* and *Rio de Janiero Maru*
Aircraft Transport *Fujikawa Maru*
two minesweepers
4 sub chasers
1 patrol boat
Submarines *Ro36, Ro42*

27 transport and freighters
2 fleet tugs
5 tankers
1 ammunition ship

It was a shambles that was to finish Truk as a fleet base, only two undamaged and two damaged destroyers, the damaged fleet repair ship *Akashi*, one damaged submarine, one damaged target ship, one damaged patrol boat, two damaged transports, three small undamaged transports and one hospital ship remained. It had cost him his career.

1909 25 January 1944

It had been a more than successful operation thought Spruance. His losses, aside from the carrier *Enterprise*, badly holed by a torpedo strike and limping back to Pearl, were small. Battleship *USS Iowa* and heavy cruiser *Baltimore*, both hit by 500lb bombs, with both ships damage being only slight. He had lost only 40 aircraft, a paltry amount considering the amount of ships and aircraft destroyed.

0905 26 January 1944

John Curtin, not a religious man, had none the less been moved by the inter denominational service at the Shrine of Remembrance. It was a day he was proud to be an Australasian. He had a cabinet meeting to tomorrow, but for the moment would have some time at home, a rare luxury. The war itself seemed to have turned the corner, the Japanese now well on the defensive, although it was a long way from won as yet, in Europe as well as the Pacific. This afternoon he had a publicity stunt, seeing off the first squadron of CAC 15 Cockatoos, due to fly out for Darwin supposedly this afternoon for the media, although actually not until the following day in reality.

1843 26 January 2015(flash forward)

The limo had pulled around and she was still flicking through the notes of her speech, her own nervousness palpable despite many hours of training in speaking over the years.

At times she wished he was one of her brothers-it was a curse being the eldest, the expectations. If her grandfather had not died so early in 1969, her father would not be King, she would be less in the public eye and have less of this sort of thing thrust upon her, having years extra to "ease in" to it. Crown Princess Maree Drake-Brockman had just returned from her family's estate in Fiji. She had sat on the jetty and talked for a long time with Wesley Adams, whose father managed the island estate for the family. They had been friends for years, born two days apart had grown up together, with Wesley boarding in Melbourne for Uni. She knew his family well, knew his own Great Grandfather had worked as a Kanaka labourer in the Queensland cane fields. She looked at the holiday snap of her and Wes. She owed it to him and others to get this Australasia Day speech to the Australasian Indigenous Commission exactly the way she wanted it.

"For Catholics, reconciliation is one of the seven sacraments of the Church. It's also known as confession although admission of wrong is only one part of it. The most important part is absolution from sin. People going through the sacrament today learn that reconciliation has two essential elements – being sorry and receiving forgiveness. Most religions embrace a reconciliation concept in one form or another. Some use language like atonement or grace. We also see it in non-religious contexts. In world affairs, we have peace processes and amnesty. Post-apartheid South Africa had the Truth and Reconciliation Commission that publicly acknowledged past wrongs and granted many offenders amnesty from prosecution if they confessed their wrongdoing under the Apartheid regime. Through this, it was hoped that that the different sides of the South African conflicts could live together in a new society, despite a past that could not be undone. However, you define it, the common theme is that reconciliation involves both the wrongdoer and the wronged taking steps towards each other to restore or establish a relationship after a conflict or estrangement.

As a nation, Australasia and its citizens have taken major steps of remorse and amends, both symbolic and practical. The 1946 Referendum and the National Apology were major steps by the Federal Government and, importantly, were overwhelmingly supported by the Australasian people. Today both governments and the private sector are devoting substantial funds and resources to overcome the ongoing consequences of past wrongdoing and close the gap between Indigenous and non-Indigenous Australasians in health, employment and education. There have been many successes. Community attitudes have radically changed. There has been real reform in land rights and anti-discrimination laws, access to education and employment.

Racism against Indigenous people in Australasia used to be a fairly mainstream attitude and one that was perpetuated in the important institutions – media, government, schools and universities, business and legal system. It is now very much in the minority. Indirect and unconscious biases do remain issues, and they are particularly complicated issues to overcome. I don't mean that racism doesn't exist. I mean that it now occupies the margins.

We would all be aware of the incident last year when a child hurled a racial slur at Adam Goodes during a football match between Collingwood and Sydney. What really struck me about this incident, however, was the overwhelming support for Adam Goodes, and condemnation of the conduct by the mainstream of Australasia and its institutions. Some years ago, no-one would have cared. Indigenous sporting players regularly experienced racial taunts on the field, by fans and other players alike. In the past our media, institutions and the majority of people expressed racist sentiments intuitively. Now it is the reverse – most people intuitively reject racism.

However, for real reconciliation, it is not enough that the country says sorry, feels remorse, rejects racism and seeks to make amends. It would not even be enough to close the gap. For real reconciliation, all of us need to forgive. I'm not suggesting that Indigenous people should forgive wrongdoers as individuals. However, the time must come when Indigenous people forgive Australasia as a nation.

Indigenous people have every reason to be aggrieved and angry about the past. As a people, and as a nation, we must never forget it. These events cannot be undone. Indeed, the most heinous wrongdoings against Indigenous people were committed by people who are now dead. This is a permanent, irreversible part of our history. Indigenous people now have two options: continue to feel anger at the nation for something the nation cannot change. Or leave these events in the past, draw a line in history and allow the nation to start with a clean slate. Drawing a line in history means Indigenous people permitting themselves to love their country, express patriotism, take pride in Australasia's successes and achievement, and feel part of Australasia as a nation.

It is important that experiences and perspectives of Indigenous people, and the events that occurred are acknowledged and embedded in Australasian history, as much as the stories of the early pioneers and explorers and the gold rushes. Indigenous people can't be expected to draw a line in the past and have the nation move on from a clean slate if these events are unacknowledged and if Indigenous people and their experiences are invisible in history. History is not about imputing the past onto the people of the present or making people feel shame or looking at events of the past through a modern mindset. And it's not about editing out the bits we prefer not to emphasise. It should not be sanitised to make people feel better or worse.

We need to build a solid foundation for economic development for Indigenous people. The outcomes achieved in the past 60 years have not always matched the good intentions. Welfare and government assistance at best allows people to tread water. At worst it embeds them in poverty. People can only be lifted out of poverty with commercial and economic development and jobs and education are the key here.

Australasia Day is arguably the most unique national day in the world because, rather than unite, it can divide Australasians into different viewpoints. It is celebrated on January 26, which is the anniversary of the arrival of the first fleet of criminals in 1788. Previous governments have been reluctant to acknowledge this history. With this, the majority of Australasians just use the day to have a barbeque, go to the beach, play cricket or do some other pastime that takes advantage of the great things about our lifestyle. Making matters difficult for many indigenous people is the date of Australasia Day and alternative dates are suggested. One of these dates is July 1, which is the anniversary of the first sitting of Federal parliament. Such suggestions may have hit a wall because it is generally accepted that whilst there is nothing wrong with having a convict in your ancestry, the same cannot be said for a politician. In all seriousness, this is still an issue that requires much thought and consultation.

In many ways, the date of Australasia Day can perhaps be appropriate precisely because not everyone feels the same way about it. It produces an opal definition of who Australasians are. Like an opal, the date diffracts light to produce a spectrum of views, backgrounds and colours. While this bothers those who want conformity, morality and something to salute, it gives individual Australasians the freedom to really define what being an Australasian means to them."

1444 30 January 1944

Nimitz's thoughts now turned back to Saipan. It had taken longer than expected to seize Enewetak Atoll in the Marshall's, the 2300 well-fortified defenders holding out for over two weeks, causing 478 dead and 1155 wounded. That had pushed back the time frame for the Saipan operation to 24th February. Once they had secured both bases, the feasibility of long-range bombing with the new bombers he had been assured were coming could be investigated.

1203 2 February 1944

Juho Kusti Paasikivi, former Finnish ambassador to the Soviet Union, had been given the task of putting out the feelers for an arranged meeting, hopefully with Molotov, who he knew well and knew he could deal with. It took time to get replies back through the neutral Swedish embassy.

He had been advocating for month that it was time to end this foolishness. Anyone with brains could see which way the wind was blowing. Come summer, the Germans, their protectors so far, would be blown away like leaves in the wind by the Russian summer offensive. Leningrad had already been relieved.

0934 5 February 1944

Blamey received the early reports of 6th Division, which had landed on Biak Island at 0705 that very morning. So far progress had been good, with little resistance on the beaches. Air opposition had consisted of only 8 bombers and 12 fighters and these had been swept aside quite easily. It seemed like things were going well.

In actual fact, it was the start of what would be a daily struggle. The Japanese were determined to keep Biak and its airfields and had over 10,000 men on the island. Their commander Kasumi Naoyuki had stockpiled food and ammunition and had constructed a series of honeycombed bunkers and both natural and artificial caves and tunnels.

Whilst the landings five days ago at Sansapor and Noemfoer Island had been accomplished quickly and easily, the town of Sansapor and its airstrip being captured in three days with less than 50 killed and just over 100 wounded, the 800 Japanese being killed or driven off. On Noemfoer, operations were already almost complete, with only mopping up of a few stragglers from the original 1800 Japanese on the small island. The airfield at Kamiri was already secured. Casualties had been low, less than 50 killed and about 200 wounded. 6th Division on Biak would not be so lucky, with operations on Biak becoming a daily struggle that would last a full ten weeks.

0806 12 February 1944

Lt General Takuzo Numata, the Chief of Staff of the 2nd Area Army, had assembled the force at Singapore with the intention of assisting the 15th Army in Burma. Any chance of that had well and truly passed. His initial reaction to the allied landings at Biak had been to send reinforcements quickly, however, he had been assured that the island could hold for some time.

With his white uniformed colleagues seemingly almost helpless, it seemed the army would have to be the force that picked up the slack. The enemy had withdrawn all but two of their small carriers and a few escorts from the invasion force. At Singapore he had assembled the amphibious assault ship *Shinshu Maru* and the assault carriers *Akitsu* and *Nigistu Maru*, as well as the 18,000-ton ex French passenger ship *Jaiko Maru*, now converted to an armed merchant cruiser by the army, plus two torpedo boats lent by the navy. He would use these to land another 5,000 troops on the island and wrestle back the initiative from the Australasians. If the navy could not raise a finger to assist, he would do it himself with the army's own fleet. The force would sail tomorrow.

1643 12 February 1944

Lt General Renya Mutaguchi's 15th Army in Burma was slowly melting away, his under supplied and trapped forces exchanging unequal casualties with the surrounding allied forces almost every day. The only way he could even hope to sell the lives of his remaining 22,000 men was to withdraw into Rangoon and conduct a street fighting campaign. He had given such orders on the 5th, having given up any hope for further outside assistance. He had received some supply drops by air, but a massed effort by 38 bombers on the 26th January had been met heavily by allied fighters and he had frankly been told further such efforts could not be attempted.

Accordingly, he had been withdrawing his lines back to Rangoon, the allies pursuing behind him. With further advances made by them in Southern Thailand, the gap between his own forces and any relief had widened again. It was a hopeless situation and all they could do was take as many as possible with them.

Situation 13 February 1944 Burma/Thailand-gains represented by new Green line

1707 13 February 1944

The situation must truly have turned against the navy, thought Captain and naval constructor Jiro Chichu. He watched, as, in the fading sun, work continued on the old battleship *Settsu* alongside the new one *Shinano*, now only a few months from completion. The old battleship had her fore and aft turrets refitted, but, out of commission as a battleship for twenty years, would surely have no hope against modern vessels. The navy's hunger for ships much be desperate to consider putting the old girl back in harm's way.

2012 13 February 1944

It was a curious collection of ships that left Singapore, the two 12,000 slab sided assault carriers, each carrying twelve aircraft and 800 troops, the 7,100 ton assault ship *Shinshu Maru* carrying 2,000 troops and the 17,880 ton Armed Merchant Cruiser *Jaiko Maru*, with its curious armament of one 12 inch and nine 5.5 inch guns and 1400 troops, two torpedo boats and two sub chasers.

In a curious quirk typical of Japanese inter service rivalry, the Imperial Japanese Army was on its way for its own sea battle.

0802 17 February 1944

Rear Admiral Harold Bruce Farncomb's RAN escort carrier force was still off Biak Island, supporting what had turned out to be extensive operations on land. The big carriers such as *Australasia, Melbourne, Sydney* and *Christchurch* had suppressed all enemy air activity and his two small carriers plus the even smaller *Noumea* were on station, the *Noumea* having just arrived on an aircraft replenishment mission.

The two sisters, so long separated, were now back together, newly renamed *Perth* and *Wellington*, each embarked an air group of nine Swordfish and six older He 112's, the little carriers being a bit small for the He 100. Only light forces remained on station, his flagship the AA cruiser *Hamilton*, the old destroyer *Clifton*, six *River Class* escort destroyers and five *Bathurst Class* corvettes. He was hoping that the campaign on the island would be over soon, but at the moment only little progress was being made against the extensive defences and his aircraft had been required to give much support.

1555 17 February 1944

Generalissimo Chiang Kai-shek smiled inwardly when he received the report. Four hundred and fifty-five AN-M76 incendiary bombs had been delivered by the Americans as he had specifically requested at the Cairo Conference at the end of 1943, detailing in secret the Japanese bio warfare releases in China as well as their extensive use of mustard gas.

He was looking forward to executing a tit for tat response of his own with the napalm filled bombs. He had also put aside 160 of the missiles for other purposes. He now just needed a complete schedule of Mao's daily itinerary, currently not something he was able to get; however, his contact had put in for a transfer back to Mao's field headquarters. That still left 295 bombs to use against the Japanese, along with the 90 mustard gas 500lb bombs and the ten Lewisite bombs that had been smuggled out of Japanese stores by his own collaborators.

1457 18 February 1944

It had been a major raid, 20 Ki-21 "Sallys" and eight Ki-48 "Lilys". It had been detected a long way out, almost 40 miles from *HMAS Hamilton's* brand-new air search radar. The Task Force, despite the *Noumea's* aircraft ferry, was not strong in air cover, however, they had arrived at a time when the roving CAP of He 119's from Wewak, some three in number, had been on station. These, together with three He 112's, moved out to engage whilst six more He 112's in readiness commenced launch.

The range from the nearest IJA air bases, over 1000 miles, meant the bombers were unescorted. The six fighters had a rich harvest, bringing down five Ki 21's and four Ki 48's in a running battle back to the ships. Four miles out another six He 112's joined in. Losing one to a bombers defensive fire, hey accounted for six more Ki-21's, leaving only nine "Sallys" and four "Lilys". Despite claiming a hit on a carrier, no ships at all were hit, the attack, intended as a precursor to tomorrow intervention, proving to be a dismal failure.

0808 19 February 1944

Lt Commander Kubo Kyuji's torpedo boat still moved through the waves at a sedate 15 knots, on a fool's errand to his own mind. Yet the "experts" from the army still thought they could just appear and dominate the beachhead at Biak, because "they had the bigger ships and guns".

He had been amazed that they had gotten to within almost ninety miles of the beachhead itself without being seen. It would not last for long, he was sure of that. Two big Australasian single engine fighters had passed over the ships an hour ago, rocketing through the two Kawasaki Ki-10 "fighters" over the ships, before coming back two shoot both down with leisure. He hoped yesterday's bomber strike had done their job, even if both carriers had been sunk, as reported, it would be a very dicey operation. The two assault carriers had launched their aircraft, such as they were. With the eight Ki-30 bombers unable to land back on, their mission would involve a one-way trip, an "innovation" that personally sickened him.

0843 19 February 1944

The Japanese strike consisted of eight Mitsubishi Ki-30 "Ann" bombers, escorted by ten Kawasaki Ki-10 "Perry" fighters. Intercepted by 10 He 112's, the Australasian fighters were amazed to see the old biplane fighters, knocking down four bombers and eight of the ten fighters trying to protect them before they had even gotten to the ships, losing only one He 112.

The four remaining bombers went into steep dives, losing one more aircraft to fighters before the final three descended into the ships AA envelope. One was blotted out of the sky by a 4-inch shell from the AA cruiser *Hamilton*, firing at a furious rate. Another overshot his target, the carrier *Perth*. The last hit in the middle of the flight deck and penetrated the tiny carrier *Noumea*, almost immediately igniting avgas tanks on the small and weakly protected ship, which immediately erupted in a fireball. The first deliberate Kamikaze attack of the war had taken its first victim, although only one of the 18 aircraft that had set of was to return.

0909 19 February 1944

The landing back at Nabire had been by the two highest scoring RAAF pilots, Wing Commander Clive "Killer" Caldwell and Squadron Leader Edgar "Cobber" Kain. With a victory each over the antiquated biplanes they had encountered, they had taken their scores to 30 and 33 respectively.

Their opposing aircraft had not done justice to the new machine, which both pilots raved about afterwards. No 54 Squadron had been the first RAAF squadron equipped with the CAC 15 Cockatoo and would have traded in the last of their He 100 E's by 28 February.

0912 19 February 1944

Farncombe had been shocked at the spectacular destruction of *HMAS Noumea* and aware of the Japanese ships, had launched a strike of his own, consisting of 14 Swordfish escorted by four He 112's. He had thought the escort light, but had wanted to keep as many aircraft as possible in light of the recent threat. He need not have bothered, as the only aircraft left on the poorly equipped for air operations IJA escort carriers were three more Ki 10 biplane fighters and two Ki 76 low wing monoplanes, normally used for anti-submarine work. All were shot down by the He 112's without loss, although one Ki-10 briefly engaged a Swordfish in what must have been the last biplane to biplane dogfight of the war.

The Japanese ships miserable AA did a fantastic job, downing two Swordfish, however, the experienced pilots knew what to do in anti-shipping work and released close to their targets. One torpedo found the assault ship *Shinshu Maru*, tearing open a large hole to starboard and dropping her speed down to 9 knots, listing heavily to Starboard. The assault carrier *Nighitsu Maru* was not so lucky, taking two hits that left her crippled and down badly by the bow.

1148 19 February 1944

Farncombe had put a second strike in the air and it would quickly find the Japanese ships not more than twenty miles from their previous location. The 16 Swordfish carried the last of the two carriers' torpedoes, anti-shipping operations not having been expected. Their escort of 4 He 112's was entirely unnecessary, as no Japanese aircraft rose to meet the, the four fighters in the finish contenting themselves with strafing the sub chaser F34, leaving her riddled with bullets and barely seaworthy.

The Swordfish went about their work with relish, hitting the *Nighisu Maru* with two more "kippers", dooming the ship. The damaged *Shinshu Maru* was hit again, causing her to slowly capsize at 1354. Lastly, the biggest ship in the fleet, the *Jaiko Maru* was also hit once, but was still seaworthy.

1506 19 February 1944

Lt Commander Kubo Kyuji heaved a sigh of relief. Short two of the four large ships plus one sub chaser, with another of the remaining two large ships damaged, they had decided to turn around less than 60 miles from Biak. They had lost all their aircraft, much equipment and 1200 men. It was an ample example as to why the army should stick to land operations.

2355 22 February 1944

Lt Kimamura had taken the decision to allow himself to be rescued. Despite what had been said, he wanted to live. His ship, the 550-ton mine layer *Natsushima*, had been had been caught laying a field North of Kavieng by the U.S destroyers *Ausburne, Dyson* and *Stanley*. With a main armament of 2 3-inch guns and a speed of 18 knots, the little ship had no hope and had been quickly sunk.

0907 24 February 1944

Third Fleet and Spruance had arrived at the next stop, Saipan. It would be his last operation before being relieved by Halsey. The bombardment had begun that morning at first light and would continue for four days. Fourteen battleships were involved, and 286,000 shells were fired. Six modern fast battleships delivered 3,956 16-inch shells. The following day the eight old battleships and 13 cruisers under Rear Admiral Oldendorf replaced the fast battleships, each group alternating day by day until the landings occurred on the morning of the 28th.

With an estimated 30000 to 40000 Japanese on the island, the assault was to be made by three Marine Divisions, 2nd, 3rd and 4th. Air cover was provided by 17 fleet and light carriers and eight escort carriers.

0904 26 February 1944

Lt Commander Jens Van Tipplekirk's long patrol out of Fremantle had finally hit pay dirt. A huge Japanese liner, armed, clearly heading back to Singapore, less than 70 miles away. He fired all four forward tubes on *O19* and was rewarded with three solid hits. It was to take two more hours for the large *Jaiko Maru* to finally succumb and Van Tippelkirk was to receive a bird's eye view, surfacing again 90 minutes after firing to watch her final plunge.

1034 27 February 1944

Lt General Renya Mutaguchi's 15th Army in Burma was now reduced to the city of Rangoon; all troops having been withdrawn into the city itself. It would be their final stand. Now reduced to less than 18,000 men, many not combat effective, he had prepared the city as best as possible for combat, baring civilians from leaving for the last week. Their presence should hamper the allied troops more than his own.

2311 27 February 1944

Juho Kusti Paasikivi had finally received his reply very late at night. It was a personal note from Molotov, a good sign surely. A meeting had been arranged for Stockholm on the 22nd of March. It would surely be a bitter pill to swallow, but if the demands were not too onerous, Mannerheim surely must accept.

1013 1 March 1944

Lt General Vandegrift's 1st Marine Corps had landed the on the morning of the 28th. The Japanese had strategically placed barbed wire, artillery, machine gun emplacements, and trenches to maximize the American casualties. However, by nightfall the 2nd, 3rd and 4th Marine Divisions had a beachhead about 6 miles wide and 3/4 mile deep. The Japanese had counter-attacked at night but had been repulsed with heavy losses.

He now had more than 40 tanks ashore and still running and hoped to enlarge his beachhead and capture the vital airfield over the next couple of days. Further inland, Japanese dead lay everywhere from the previous four days intense bombardment.

1533 3 March 1944

Lt General Slim's forces had reduced the Japanese pocket to the urban boundaries of Rangoon only. It was now time to launch the final assault to capture the city. He would allow his troops a brief respite, after all the Japanese were not going anywhere. On the 9th they would move in and attempt to take the city. A quick capture may allow a redistribution of his forces prior to monsoon season in May, although if the Japanese remained true to form, they would fight it out to the last.

0708 10 March 1944

After the disasters off Burma, Vice Admiral Shōji Nishimura had been made commander of the Mobile Fleet. The Americans had landed at Saipan but he had bluntly told Toyoda he was in no position to intervene. He looked at his repair and build schedule. He could, however, expect many ships back into the fleet or newly commissioned over the next few months.

The arrival of the new carrier *Taiho* had given him two fleet carriers to go with *Kaga* to form Car Div 1, the small *Nisshin* and the two escort carriers formed Car Div 2. The new fleet carriers *Amagi* and *Unryu* were due in May, followed by the *Katsuragi* in August. The *Kasagi* would not be due until the very end of 1944, two more not until 1945.

In regards battleships, he had only the old *Yamashiro*. However, that would change. The *Yamato* he expected back from repairs in early May, the *Musashi* in late March. A refit of the old *Settsu* was meant to complete June. The new *Shinano* in July. Plus, he still had the hybrid *Ise*.

He had only four heavy cruisers, a horrific statistic since the navy had started the war with 18, however, a new ship, the *Ibuki*, was scheduled for late July. The light cruiser *Niyodo* was due in April, as was her sister *Kiyodo* in August. The most worrying aspect as this represented all of Japan's strength. They were no other large ships building or planned. What would come later, if these were destroyed?

0808 18 March 1944

General 'Hap" Arnold had exploded when he had read the report from Major Clarke, his aide, on his visit to Kansas and the state of the B-29 production and combat readiness. He had seen the aircraft in early 1944 on the production line and had immediately wanted it in numbers. It was a hard aircraft to manufacture, sure, but a quantum leap over all other options available and could bomb the Japanese home islands from Pacific Island bases.

They had manufactured 144 machines and reported operational ability was 16 aircraft. It was pathetic. More time seemed to be spent with tinkering with the design, each aircraft being slightly different than manufacturing and deploying it to units. He was going to personally go down to Kansas to light a fire under these people, booking a visit for the 22nd.

1919 24 March 1944

Saipan had been secured but at a terrible cost, thought Vandegrift. The battle on Saipan was hopeless for the defenders, but the Japanese were determined to fight to the last man. The Japanese line had been anchored on Mount Tapotchau in the defensible mountainous terrain of central Saipan. The nicknames given by the Americans to the features of the battle — "Hell's Pocket", Purple Heart Ridge" and "Death Valley" — indicate the severity of the fighting. The Japanese had used the many caves in the volcanic landscape to play hide and seek with the attackers, "popping up" out of caves for night operations. The Americans developed tactics for clearing the caves by using flamethrowers, in particular.

By 22 March, the Japanese had nowhere to retreat. The Japanese commander Saito made plans for a final suicidal charge. On the fate of the remaining civilians on the island, he had said, "There is no longer any distinction between civilians and troops. It would be better for them to join in the attack with bamboo spears than be captured." At dawn, with a group of 12 men carrying a great red flag in the lead, the remaining able-bodied troops — about 3,000 men — had charged forward in the final attack. Amazingly, behind them came the wounded, with bandaged heads, some on crutches, others unarmed. The Japanese surged over the American front lines, engaging all comers, causing the Americans 650 killed and wounded. However, the fierce resistance of the U.S Marines resulted in over 4,300 Japanese killed. It was the largest Japanese Banzai attack in the Pacific War, with three Medal of Honour's awarded to defenders, unfortunately all posthumous.

Saito committed suicide in a cave. In the end, almost the entire garrison of troops on the island, at least 30,000, had died. For the Americans, the victory was the costliest to date. 2,788 Americans were killed and 10,802 wounded. Being a former Spanish and then German territory, Saipan became a Mandate of Japan by the League of Nations after World War I, and thus a large number of Japanese civilians lived there, some 25,000.

Weapons and the tactics of close quarter fighting had resulted in high civilian casualties. Civilian shelters were located virtually everywhere on the island, with very little difference noticeable to attacking marines. The standard method of clearing suspected bunkers was with high-explosive and/or high-explosives augmented with petroleum (e.g., gelignite, napalm, diesel fuel). In such conditions, high civilian casualties were inevitable.

In March, Hirohito sent out an imperial order encouraging the civilians of Saipan to commit suicide. The order authorized the commander of Saipan to promise civilians who died there an equal spiritual status in the afterlife with those of soldiers perishing in combat. By the time the Marines advanced on the north tip of the island, in the last three days of the campaign, they met a horrible sight. Over 1,000 Japanese civilians had committed suicide in the last days of the battle to take the offered privileged place in the afterlife, some jumping from "Suicide Cliff". Over 22,000 civilians had died in the campaign.

0702 29 March 1944

It was only five days after the battle on Saipan that they were back in action, the newly formed 5th Marine Division hoping to emulate the deeds of their more famous comrades with an assault on the islands of Guam and Tinian. It was a symbolic recapturing of U.S territory, with only the Philippines and Wake left in Japanese control, aside from Guam. From what Major General Keller Rockey had heard of the Saipan campaign, he hoped it would not be another repeat.

1800 2 April 1944

Lt General Renya Mutaguchi's 15th Army had been eliminated completely and Rangoon, or what remained of it, had fallen. It had been a massacre, equal in ferocity to many of the Central Pacific battles on a grand scale. The Japanese, well prepared, had discovered the best defensive positions. After blowing up every outlying facility of even marginal value, like bridges and footpaths, Mutaguchi had set up minefields, barbed wire, interlocking trenches, and hulks of trucks, cars and trolleys, to create bottlenecks and traps. He then ordered his ragtag troops into the defensive zone.

The battle quickly came down to a series of bitter street to street and house to house struggles. Subjected to incessant pounding and facing certain death or capture, the beleaguered Japanese troops had taken out their anger and frustration on the civilians caught in the crossfire, committing multiple acts of severe brutality, even using their scarce ammunition to spray civilians feeling or attempting to flee the battle area, boarding up houses and setting fire to parts of the city to cover their retreat further into the centre on occasions.

For a month the British, Indian and Chinese troops mopped up resistance throughout the city. With the city centre secured on 1st April, Rangoon was officially liberated, but enormous areas of the mainly wooden city had been levelled, or more commonly, burnt. The battle left 1,916 allied soldiers dead and 7,012 wounded. An estimated 75,000 Burmese civilians were killed, both deliberately by the Japanese and from artillery, naval and aerial bombardment by the allied military forces. 17,234 Japanese dead were counted, but many more remained buried in rubble.

The last pocket of Japanese resistance at the historic Edward Hotel, which was already reduced to rubble, was flushed out by heavy artillery on 2 April. Mutaguchi had publicly committed seppuku the day before in the lobby.

0904 3 April 1944

Juho Kusti Paasikivi had reported back to Mannerheim the conditions that the Soviets wanted. It would mean the losses of their war gains and also Pestamo. A hard price, but perhaps not as hard as may be imposed if they broke through in their planned 1944 summer offensive. It was now in the Field Marshal's purview. He had done all he could.

1633 8 April 1944

"Tubby" Allen's 6th Division had finally secured Biak Island. It had been a long and bitter campaign as well, the Japanese, in their usual fashion, honeycombing all their fortifications together. The Australasian's had used explosives, flamethrower tanks, air power, including the extensive use of napalm for the first time and had sealed up some enemy strong points simply by burying them alive using bulldozer tanks.

It was the stuff of nightmares, with no quarter given. 10,000 Japanese lay dead, only 232 prisoners taken and the nine Japanese light tanks on the island had been destroyed by the Australasian's Sentinels. In return, 6th Division had taken 388 killed, with just over 2,000 wounded.

1208 10 April 1944

Admiral Lord Louis Mountbatten had decided to suspend further offensive operations in Burma and Thailand for the season. Monsoon was less than a month away and he intended to spend that time consolidating his not inconsiderable gains in the face of stiffening Japanese resistance.

Taking Rangoon had been a costly exercise and he now needed to hold what he had, train and integrate his new Thai allies and bring forward new forces that were coming into the theatre to plug gaps that would be created.

The Chinese had now expressed a desire to withdraw their own forces gradually from the theatre now that Burma had been secured. Considering the fact that the Japanese occupied so much of their own country, it would be churlish to refuse and a schedule of replacement had been set. He had new forces coming from both the Indian Army and African divisions. He also needed to equip many of the lightly armed irregular forces that had popped up all over Thailand.

Next season, if the war lasted that long, he would be in a position to liberate Southern Thailand and what was left of Burma, then push into Malaya. The Japanese also occupied a substantial part of Eastern Thailand, as well. By next season he would have substantial naval and air reinforcements as well, making the job that much easier.

0856 12 April 1944

They had been training with the aircraft for over a month and whilst it was a queer looking bird, very modern in appearance, it had proved itself both responsive and reliable. For Squadron Leader James Lockett and No 15 Squadron, it would be their first mission. Many Australasian squadrons had changed aircraft over the last two months, the old Anson's finally being phased out. In the last two months alone, 14 squadrons had been reequipped with the Consolidated Liberator, two with the last issues of He 211's, but No 15 had been the only one so far equipped with the new He 200 Falcon. Using the aircraft's phenomenal range, the squadron was taking off from Darwin to raid the naval yard at Singapore, a near 6,000-mile trip.

1809 15 April 1944

Major General Keller Rockey's 5th Marine Division had completed the conquest of Guam. Despite little real intervention from both Japanese air and naval assets, it had been a hard grind. The extensive reef system around the island made supply, except via certain narrow points, difficult.

After their initial assault, the 77th Infantry Division had also landed and exploited the beachhead. The Japanese, however, had 20,000 troops on the island and, whilst not as well dug in as in some other locations, had resisted fiercely at every turn. The smaller island of Tinian had fallen on the 8th of April.

The operation had cost over 1500 dead and over 5000 wounded, the Japanese garrison being practically wiped out. Now the Sea bees could move in, with airfields being the priority of the Tinian invasion, in particular. The Central Pacific campaign had only one more step to take, Palau.

2224 18 April 1944

Halsey had been disappointed by the results of the raid, which had hit Palau hard. Over 800 aircraft had pounded the island, strafing, bombing and destroying. They had also caught the destroyer *Ikazuchi,* patrol boat *No 31*, minesweeper *W7* and light cruiser *Yubari,* sinking them all. He had expected to catch more of the Japanese navy, but the strike had none the less prepared the way for the island's invasion on the 1st May.

2344 18 April 1944

General Walter Krueger had a meeting with the war council on 24th April. It would be the final chance to talk to Curtin and the Australasian government about the post South Pacific operations and the countries possible involvement and to talk about what the prevailing opinion was post New Guinea operations.

Two more operations were planned, Nimitz invading Palau on 1st May and his own operations at both Morotai Island and Bitung on North Sulawesi, both part of the Dutch East Indies, scheduled for 12th May. He had a conference at Pearl on the 26th of May. That would take the final decision as to what the definite next step would be, with proposed operations against either Formosa or the Philippines or even both scheduled for August.

0600 19 April 1944

Field Marshall Shunroku Hata watched the tremendous barrage start on the Chinese positions. He had amassed almost 400000 men and more than 800 tanks for the offensive, which he hoped would take him all the way to the Indo China border and capture the bulk of Hunan Provence.

His army had drawn the bulk of the crack units from the Kwantung Army, including virtually all their armour. After many stories of reverses in the Pacific Theatre and what he knew had been a disaster in Burma it was good to take the offensive against the old foe. Operation Ichi-Go had started.

0104 23 April 1944

Mannerheim started glumly at the late-night fire. He had always hated Stalin, the Soviets and all they had ever stood for. However, both his country and himself had little further choice. The Axis had without doubt lost the war, their Japanese allies in the Pacific taking a massive beating and the Germans drained to a bloodless corpse, still being pushed back, virtually to the Rumanian border, in the South.

He needed to forestall any further German build up in the country and he owed it to his erstwhile allies to not let them commit any more troops to a worthless cause, even if he could not, as yet, tell them why. He would accept the Soviet terms, humiliating though they were.

1319 23 April 1944

Chiang Kai-shek had finally received the information he required. Mao's daily schedule. The operation would have to be temporarily shelved, however, as the Japanese had launched a massive offensive on his own forces.

He could not afford, at present, to decapitate the communists, as he may still need their assistance. His units were battling hard, but he eagerly awaited the return of his crack Divisions, the first two of which were on their way back from Burma and Thailand. Their better weapons and armour would blunt the Japanese attack.

1413 24 April 1944

Major General Sadatake Nakayama, normally chief of staff of 11th Army, was in temporary command of 3rd Tank Division, they army's only armoured spearhead. It's normal commander had actually been killed by a Chinese sniper and he had stepped in to continue the advance over the Yellow River, which he currently had forces on either side of.

He had been surprised at the scale of the Chinese air raid, normally the IJA had air control, but the appearance of over twenty stubby bodied fighters he had not seen before had swept away the Japanese air presence over the bridgehead.

It had been followed by the appearance of over 50 Chinese fighters, a mix of P-39's and P-40's. They had dropped bombs on his tank units, but he had not been concerned, knowing each would only have one 500lb at most. Each bomb, however, had released a flame compound that had spread all over his tanks, causing many to "brew up". A raid by 8 ancient Ju 52 had scattered more of these bombs about into his suddenly panicked forces.

Finally, Twenty B-25's had arrived and headed to his beachheads on the near side of the Yellow River. The bombs, when dropped had released clouds of orange/yellow gas, which quickly engulfed both men and machines on the windless, cloudless day. Mustard gas, his men had no protection from mustard gas.

As he continued watching two aircraft detached from the stream and headed straight for his headquarters. Seemingly frozen in time, he watched the release, dropping bombs not 150 yards away. One aircraft dropped a series of bombs to the South of his headquarters, another to the North. A cloud of deep violet gas started to envelope him and he fell to the floor, choking violently.

2118 24 April 1944

The war council meeting had gone on long into the day and night. Meeting with Kreuger had become a pleasure. His slight Germanic burr when speaking reminded her slightly of her own father.

Blamey would be the only Australasian representative going to the Pearl conference and the main topic of conversation had been the upcoming potential operation(s) against the Philippines and Formosa. Whilst many had not said so, they feared the potential dissolution of the SW Pac Command and the reduction of Australasian influence that would mean with a unified, Pacific command. It would be Curtin's last war conference for a while, his departure to the Prime Ministers Conference in London being followed by a visit to Roosevelt in the US. It was the first such meeting of countries either currently part of the British Empire, such as South Africa, Rhodesia and India and those part of the new British Commonwealth, such as Australasia and Canada. She worried about his health, he at times looked pale and drawn. Peter Fraser was carrying an almost Herculean workload as deputy and Defence Minister but seemed as unflappable as usual, as did Scullin, who seemed almost ageless.

Their needed to be a great deal of thinking in regards to Australasia's further role in the war post mid-1944, that much was clear. The country still had seven active AIF divisions in the Pacific Theatre, along with two Brigades and 12 Independent Companies. It was not planned to reduce this; however, it had been proposed to cut the militia back to five divisions from mid-1944. Air Force strength would stay constant, as would the RAN, although no further purchases would be made and lend lease would not be further utilised.

Blamey had proposed to split the AIF Corps commands between Morshead and Freyberg, with the command of the militia devolving on Laverack. The former two were the two generals in whom he had the most confidence.

May operations would push into the Dutch East Indies and if SW Pac was dissolved, as may seem likely, future operations may be conducted in conjunction with Commonwealth, rather than U.S forces, so this would require some thought as well. Her forces had taken some terrible casualty figures, but the country must still participate to have a voice post war, finding their own way and also winning the peace.

The country had gone in a different direction over the last five years, she had sensed the drifting away from its Anglo Saxon roots and it's sense of Empire. She hoped it would be a good thing. Karl was a saint, as he had handled most of the arrangements for her daughter's 16th birthday party on the morrow. As she lay back on the couch in the red drawing room, she sensed she was going to sleep and dragged herself up. A big day today would be followed by another tomorrow.

1906 30 April 1944

Field Marshall Shunroku Hata's Operation Inci-Go had not been the unqualified success he had hoped. It was achieving its initial objectives, but at a slow pace and its cost in both men and material had been much higher than expected. His crack 3rd Tank Division had been decimated by a gas attack, losing its Commander and had been caught half on one side and half on the other near its Yellow River beachhead, being thrown back with serious losses.

He had, of course, responded in kind, as he had in previous campaigns, but the Chinese were clearly expecting such an approach and had left their own attack to a perfect day, hot, still and with zero wind. Their fighters were much more modern and in larger numbers and he no longer had total air superiority that he was used to plus they had returned some of their better divisions from Burma. He was still winning, but it was a struggle.

1116 1 May 1944

1st Marines had stormed ashore at Palau, to limited resistance. Over the past 18 months to two years the Japanese had learned that their previous tactics of trying to stop U.S forces on the beaches were doomed to failure, their own forces being much more susceptible to naval gunfire support and air support.

Instead, they had learned to rely on entrenching and fortifications to allow them to hold on with their inferior firepower and second-class weapons were less of a handicap and they could make use of their own troops indomitable spirit. The landing at Palau was not initially contested but would result in some of the most bitter fighting seen so far in the Pacific War and result in the cancellation of further planned operations against bypassed islands.

1909 3 May 1944

Mannerheim had already called in the German ambassador at 1000 that morning. Now he received the new Soviet delegate Pavel Orlov and stated his position. In return for no Soviet occupation, he would accept all conditions and Finland would pull out of the war, effective in an announcement he would make on 11th May. He now only needed to await a final agreement from the Russians.

1908 5 May 1944

Marshall Aleksandr Mikhaylovich Vasilevsky's Ukrainian Front had finished it's 1943-44 operational offensives. His forces had liberated 98% of the Ukraine and had even penetrated the North-eastern border of Romania.

Exhausted and near out of supply, his forces would now receive the rest they deserved. The next offensive would be in the North and he had received a confidential communique indicating the Finnish were going to withdraw from the war, possible in only a few days' time. The Central Front offensive, Operation Bagration, was scheduled for late June, but now may even be brought forward.

1202 8 May 1944

The U.S 32nd Infantry Division made the initial landing at the island Moratai under no fire at all, which was just as well as the jagged coral reefs proved more difficult to manage than anticipated and in fact 68 casualties were incurred in the mornings landings, none to enemy fire. The Japanese garrison on the island, numbering only 452 men of the 2nd Provisional raiding Unit under Major Takenobu Kawashima, with 22 attached Korean labourers, had withdrawn into the hills. The Japanese had planned a response later in May to attempt to retake the island, but this was cancelled after the greater threat posed by the invasion of North Sulawesi materialised on the 13th.

1723 9 May 1944

Keith Park again reviewed how things had changed in his regular six-monthly reports to the aircraft review board. The infusion of 287 B-24 Liberator bombers since the end of 1944 had changed things dramatically and allowed retirement of many Anson's with others converted to transport use. For the first time, the air forces, needs in relation to squadron aircraft had largely been met. Numbers by type now read:

Fighters:
CAC Boomerang 179
CAC 15 Cockatoo 68 (in production)
Curtis P40 390
Hencall He 112 30(all naval)
Hencall He 100 721(Currently in limited production-numbers count RAN machines)
Hencall He 119 266(in production)
Republic P43 49
TOTAL 1703 NEED 1700

Bombers/Patrol:
Avro Anson 211
Consolidated Catalina 76
Consolidated B24 Liberator 284
de Havilland Mosquito 83(in limited production)
Douglas A20 50(some ex Dutch East Indies)
Fairy Swordfish 81
Grumman Avenger 198
Hencall He 111 51
Hencall He 200 34(in production)
Hencall He 211 208
Lockheed Hudson 112
Lockheed Ventura 71
Martin Mariner 20
North American A36 183
North American B25 20
Vickers Wellington 41
Vultee Vengeance 271

TOTAL 2104 NEED 2100

Transports:
Airspeed Oxford 258
Avro Anson 212(transport conversion)
De Havilland Dragon 87
Douglas DC 2 8
Douglas C47 210(in production)
He 70 29
Junkers Ju 52 4

TOTAL 789 NEED 800

0616 13 May 1944

Major General Gordon Bennett, newly appointed to 7th Division, watched the LST go in as part of the first wave for the invasion of North Sulawesi. His Division was being supported by fully four Independent Companies, the 3rd, 4th, 8th and 10th, as well as a battalion of tanks from 1st Armoured, with a second to follow.

They would be here on Sulawesi for some time. The initial objective was the town of Bitung, but the objective was not to capture the whole island, only to capture and hold the Northeast tip. His forces were supported by a good portion of the RAN, including six carriers, which was just as well, because only long-range air support could be expected, from He 200's in Darwin and some B24's based on Biak near West Papua.

1209 24 May 1944

General Tang Ebo was still trying to hold onto the strategically important city of Lyoyang. His increased air forces presence and his use of napalm and chemical weapons had both shocked, surprised and delayed the Japanese. yet they had committed much of their crack forces to this offensive. He had bled them, bled them badly, but they were now driving on the city and he had not enough of China's best forces back from Burma, as yet.

1233 25 May 1944

After remaining static for months, all of a sudden, the situation had become very fluid as the Germans were falling back quickly. The road to Rome had been opened by the fall of Monte Cassino two days ago. Oliver Leese's army was pushing on rapidly, now facing only scattered opposition. Rome itself would fall within no more than a fortnight.

1715 27 May 1944

Well, Kreuger's SW Pac Command was not going to be disbanded after all, even though they were probably being diverted to a secondary axis of advance. Nimitz's forces would be making a landing at Leyte Gulf in the Philippines on 31 August 1944.

SW Pac were expected to make a landing in support of this operation on Borneo, commencing in early-mid September. The first location would be Tarakan, but five points of landing had been identified in what would be a large campaign.

He still had current operations in North Sulawesi and had taken the decision to commit the 41st Division back to New Guinea to support the Australasian Militia Brigade in West Papua with the objective of wiping out the Japanese presence on the island. It would free forces for other operation, with both King and Marshall talking about 1945 operations in support of Slim and Mountbatten in Malaya.

0904 29 May 1944

What had been formerly Somerville's Eastern Fleet had been much reduced after the action off Burma, but now some of the damaged ships, picked out as not required for the still secret Overlord, now only six days away, sailed from Scapa under the command of Admiral Sir Bruce Fraser, victor of the North Cape, who would take over the Eastern Fleet. These forces included both *HMS Renown* and *Valiant*, returning after repairs. The French battleship *Richelieu*, carriers *HMS Indomitable* and *Victorious*, light cruiser *Phoebe* and nine destroyers.

The RN still kept all four *KGV Class* battleships in home waters, along with *HMS Nelson, Rodney, Ramillies* and *Warspite* for bombardment duties. *Malaya* had been refitted for transfer to the Soviet Navy and the old *Resolution* had been decommissioned.

0546 4 June 1944

Hauptmann Joachim Kuntz peered out into the early morning Channel mist as the shape of hundreds of ships hove into view near his Normandy coastal battery of 152cm guns. There were hundreds, thousands. Operation Overlord had commenced.

10 June 2013(Flash Forward)

The demonstration, in the New South Wales highlands, had been bitterly cold and she was glad to get inside. Her brothers and father had enjoyed the day more. It had been her cousin that had commanded the troops that had performed the demonstration, hence the show of family support. Prime Minister John Key was also present.

Now starting to supplant the M113 as the standard APC for first and second line mechanized formations, it would probably spread further into the army since the chassis was a concept vehicle that covered APC, light tank and self-propelled AA vehicle.

It would help supplement the existing AUSLAV and Bushmasters, as well as Abrams tanks, allowing troops to enter higher threat environments than Bushmaster equipped units. In a reversion to a World War 2 name, it had been decided to call it the Dingo.

1119 5 June 1944

Field Marshall Shunroku Hata's forces were finally in a position to threaten and take his primary objective, the city of Luoyang. It had taken much longer than anticipated and cost nigh on 26,000 casualties so far. Casualties that had been mainly taken from his better units.

He was already having second thoughts about phase two of his operation, which encompassed a drive South to the Indo China border, as the cost so far had been much worse than anticipated and he was well behind schedule.

0818 6 June 1944

It was all over, Rommel knew that-he could not see how others could not see it. With the situation in the East unfavourable, the enemy now secured in France and the Italian Front now fluid, at was just a matter of time. Like the water and the rock, the water would eventually be the victor, except this was not like to take anywhere near as long. Something needed to be done to stop it.

1534 8 June 1944

General "Hap" Arnold had done his job well. As promised, the last of the initial batch of B-29's had arrived at Tinian and the island, still a hive of construction activity, now housed 188 B-29's. They still needed shakedown and training with their new machines, planned at this stage for four weeks. After that time, raid would commence against the Japanese Home Islands, with an expected first raid on July the 7th. Long range P-51 escorts were also expected and there were even rumours of an Australasian unit being deployed.

1706 11 June 1944

Major General William Rupertus 1st Marines were still taking a beating on Palau. Umurbrogol Mountain, a collection of hills and steep ridges located at the centre of Palau overlooking a large portion of the island, including the crucial airfield, was the main stumbling block.

It contained some 500 limestone caves, inter-connected by tunnels. Many of these were former mine shafts that were turned into defence positions. Jap engineers had added sliding armoured steel doors with multiple openings to serve both artillery and machine guns. Cave entrances had been built slanted as a defence against grenade and flamethrower attacks. The caves and bunkers were connected to a vast system throughout central Palau, which allowed the Japanese to evacuate or reoccupy positions as needed, and to take advantage of shrinking lines as his forces gradually, painfully and bloodily pushed them back in a series of barbaric close quarter shootouts involving shell and flame, bayonet, bullet and shovel.

1312 18 June 1944

Luoyang had finally fallen to the Japanese and General Tang Ebo's forces were in retreat from the pocket. It had been a costly campaign so far, perhaps 40,000 casualties, but this time he knew his opponents had not gone unbloodied. With his lines now straightened, he now had the support of the majority of Chinese crack forces from Burma. There would be no more retreats.

2030 20 June 1944

It had taken heavy fighting, but Gordon Bennet's 7th Division had taken both Bitung and

Mando, the local population proving most supportive in assisting his troops. Yesterday they had also taken Kotomabago, half way to his objective of Limboto.

Engineers had started airfield construction a week ago and all haste was being made. The carrier *Christchurch* had to withdraw with a bomb hit and the escort *Swordsman* had been sunk by a submarine, whilst the old cruiser minelayer *Adelaide* had been declared a constructive total loss after being torpedoed by a lone G4M 'Betty" the CAP had missed. Fighting had been very heavy and casualties had been high, the Japanese throwing in troops to try and reinforce their positions.

1300 22 June 1944

So far the first stages of Operation Bagration, launched early that morning, had been a success thought Colonel General Konstantin Rokassovsky, his 1st Belorussian Front seemingly achieving complete surprise against the Germans, who had expected the blow to again fall on the Southern Front.

The Stavka had committed approximately 1,700,000 combat and support troopers, approximately 24,000 artillery pieces and mortars, 4,080 tanks and assault guns and 6,334 aircraft to the attack.
Within a week several massive holes had been torn in the front of Army Group Centre, some more than 20 to 30 miles wide, through which poured Soviet armour, surrounding and trapping German units. It would be a disaster that would rival Stalingrad for the Germans.

World Map 22 June 1944

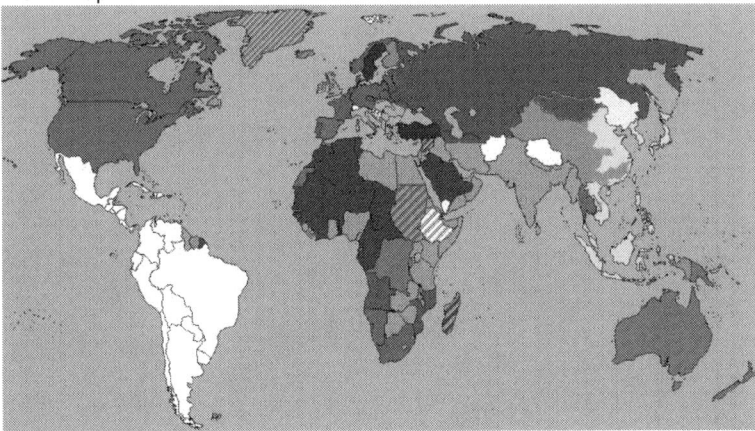

1219 24 June 1944

Hencall had been running bench tests for two weeks on the new jet engines, like a kid in a toy shop, he supposed. He had even given up his Sunday afternoon fishing trips in favour of more work and testing. It was all very exciting. Perhaps another month of tests and they would then have enough data to start work on a design that they could then wind tunnel test. It was a completely new concept, so time would be required to master the aspects required to produce a good design.

1555 10 July 1944

Gordon Bennet's 7th Division had fought their way down to the stop line, despite fierce Japanese resistance every step of the way. For the last two weeks engineers had been working on airfield construction and hoped to have two airfields operational by the end of the month. It would be needed as the fleet had been subject to a number of Japanese attacks, suffering two carriers lightly damaged, one light cruiser, one destroyer, one frigate and one corvette lost, as well as two transports.

It had been an expensive operation in terms of casualties to, 1,152 killed and 2,221 wounded. However, the road was now open to Borneo, with airbases, when constructed, within easy reach for fighters.

0818 12 July 1944

Palau had finally been secured, but at a terrible cost. For the first time in the Pacific, a Marine Division had to be withdrawn with the objective not secured. 1st Marine Division had taken almost 6,300 casualties and its replacement, 27th Infantry Division, would take 3,000 more before the island was finally secure.

The Japanese garrison of almost 11,000 had been wiped out, less than 200 prisoners taken. The Japanese use of spider holes, caves, trenches, mines and barbed wire, plus not, for the first time, sacrificing men pointlessly, had bled the Marines white. It was to have the effect of cancelling further island operations that were considered not absolutely necessary, including planned operations against Wake and Yap in the Caroline Islands.

0705 16 July 1944

The second part of Operation Inch-Go, a planned drive Southwards all the way to the Indo China border, had commenced this morning. Field Marshall Shunroku Hata's command had taken far more casualties than anticipated in the first part of the operation, well over 40,000, and had not succeeded in capturing or encircling any Chinese units. They had, however, achieved their territorial objectives. His army's push South would be accompanied by a breakout and push North from the Hong Kong garrison.

1216 18 July 1944

John Curtin was happy with the results of the Commonwealth Prime Minister's Conference. Things in India seemed to have died down and the second front, so long awaited, had happened. Churchill had promised increased resources to the Indian Ocean and Pacific, with Curtin acquiescing to basing the British Fleet out of Sydney, with Australasia largely supplying it in terms of food, dockyard support and the like. It would require an upgrade of facilities at Sydney, which had commenced. In return, he had gotten Churchill's agreement not to directly support the Dutch in any Colonial adventures in the East Indies if it degenerated into a war after the Japanese were expelled, which he had been assured of intelligence operatives that it might.

His meeting with Roosevelt was very cordial and the relationship, initially prickly, had now advanced to an excellent stage. He had complimented the President on his appointment of

Kreuger, who Curtin considered an outstanding man.

His main concern was now his own health. He was often starting to feel short of breath and only himself and his doctor knew he had heart disease. He would let his wife and probably Scullin and Fraser know soon enough. He hoped he could see it through, but if not, needed a succession plan.

0901 19 July 1944

The light cruiser wallowed in the light seas, her back broken by two amidships torpedo hit. As the crew of the *USS Flasher* watched, taking turns looking through the periscope, the light cruiser *Tama* slowly turned turtle and sank, 570 miles South on Hong Kong.

0934 20 July 1944

It had taken somewhat longer than expected, though "Hap" Arnold, but Tinian was a hive of activity as the first of 174 B29's started taking off, their objectives the Imperial Iron and Steel Works at Yawata, on Kyushu. The Japanese home islands, unless one counted small scale raids on the Kuriles, had not been bombed since the Doolittle Raid in 1942.

Two squadrons of Australasian He 200's had arrived on the island yesterday, with another B29 bomb group also due. Although this may be the first raid, it was going to be a large one and operations would now commence a series of raid that would continue for the duration of the war, sapping Japan's remaining industrial strength.

1519 24 July 1944

General Temosuki looked over the destruction of Yawata and the damage to the iron works. It was not too bad, the bombing not being terribly accurate. The main issue was the number of the aircraft involved and the almost helplessness of the defenders. It was mostly second line units, with second line equipment that provided Japan's home air defence, attack not having been expected. He would have to withdraw his more modern, high performance aircraft from other theatres in an attempt to engage the high flying, fast bombers. Heavier AA guns would have to be placed around strategic targets, the light guns not having the ceiling to engage.

1214 7 August 1944

Captain Nakahara's light cruiser *Yahagi* had departed Kagoshima for Sasebo with a sub chaser and two float planes as aerial cover. Lt Commander John E. Lee's may have had a new submarine, *USS Croaker*, but he was a veteran submariner even if *Croaker* was on her first war patrol. He had let the light cruiser close to 1,300 yards and fired a salvo of four stern torpedoes.

At 1222, *Yahagi* is hit starboard aft by two of the torpedoes. At 1240, she had sunk off Amakusa Shoto. Only 215 of her almost 600 crew were to be rescued, the ship sinking fast. She had not been able to be assisted by the sub chaser *PG 45*, which has caught a torpedo herself, going down quickly with almost 60 men.

1909 9 August 1944

Major General Jens Anderson Doe's 41st Infantry Division, in conjunction with Australasian Militia Brigade 51 plus Australasian Forces advancing from Sansapor, had eliminated the final Japanese presence from New Guinea.

In a series of grinding battles, they had overwhelmed the half-starved Japanese forces, who had resorted to the gardening and farming, as well as more gruesome practices, to keep themselves alive in the isolated tip of West New Guinea. Japanese fortifications were poorly constructed, sparse and often not manned and for the first time, Japanese forces had proven willing to surrender, over 800 being taken of the 12,000 in the area. It had cost the allies 786 dead and 3,016 wounded and injured. Post war, many would say for little real gain.

0644 10 August 1944

Admiral Toyodo had good reason to believe that the next American blow must fall on the Philippines. The very direction of their advance pin pointed it as a target. Borneo or Formosa were the only other possible targets, but nothing would hurt Japan more than the loss of the Philippines, which would isolate her Southern Possessions.

The Mobile Fleet was split at present, it's heavy surface units at Brunei where they had access to their fuel sources. The Kido Butai was still in the home islands, training and working up its air groups.

He had worked hard to try and rebuild the navy after it's disastrous losses and had arrived at the conclusion that every ship, and he meant every ship, must be committed to the defence of the Philippines.

At Brunei had had:
Bat Div 1 (*Yamato, Musashi*)
Bat Div 2 (*Shinano, Ise*)
Bat Div 3 (*Yamashiro, Settsu*)
Cru Div 1(4 CA's)
Cru Div 2(1 CA, 3 CL's)

At Kure he had:
Car Div 1(*Taiho, Kaga*)
Car Div 2(*Amagi, Unryu*)
Car Div 3(*Katsuragi, Nisshin*)
Car Div 4(*Kaiyo, Eikyo*)

He had also made plans to sail a diversionary force to Tarakan, to both back up the defences at Borneo and provide a distraction from his main units if the U.S forces landed at the Philippines. It would be tough on these ships and crews, but they were considered expendable anyway.

1607 10 August 1944

Nimitz had chatted with King about the Leyte operation, the largest the U.S would have attempted so far. There would literally be thousands of ships, all under the operation control of Spruance. It would take months to secure the island chain, in his opinion and the Japanese navy would surely try and intervene, after remaining passive for over six months. After this operation and the soon to follow operation on Borneo, Japan would be cut off from her Southern possessions totally, deprived of her oil. They could then turn their attention to the subjection of the home islands in 1945.

1834 11 August 1944

It was an eclectic collection of ships that departed Kure under cover of darkness. Rear Admiral Keizō Komura had not expected conduct his first assignment as an admiral with such a collection. His "fleet" consisted of *Kamakura Maru, Okatisan Maru* and *Kumano Maru*, standard 8,000 ton cargo ships converted to auxiliary aircraft carriers, with no catapults, no arrestor gear and no proper hangers, capable of carrying ten aircraft each, two former Thai coastal defence ships mounting 4 8 inch guns and capable of barely 18 knots, two even smaller 1,400 ton Thai coastal defence ships mounting four 6 inch guns, the armed merchant cruiser *Gokoko Maru*(the last in the navy), the old light cruisers *Tsushima* and *Hirado*, out of commission for four years previous, the ancient 19th century armoured cruisers *Izumo, Iwate* and *Yakumo*, five small and old *Momo, Momi* and *Watatake Class* destroyers, the destroyer *Tanikaze*, the oldest in the fleet and nine ex Thai torpedo boats.
He had no earthly idea what use anyone could possibly think these ships, or their collection of inexperienced crews, could possibly be.

18 August 1944

General Marc Clark's forces had liberated Florence and his troops would shortly face the new German defensive line, the Gothic, as the allies continued to push North in Italy.

0616 19 August 1944

The Red Army's summer's offensive had brought them all the way to the Vistula, within spitting distance of Warsaw, which was now in uprising. What was needed from now on in was resolute defence, absolute ruthlessness. In the Adolf Hitler's unceasingly addled mind, he saw the perfect candidate for the Vistula Command, his loyal Heinrich, Heinrich Himmler would make the ideal candidate.

0719 19 August 1944

The old battleship *Ramillies*, a veteran of two wars, recoiled under the back blast of her own guns. Despite being old and slow, she was a lovely ship thought Captain Hugh Hopkins, still in good condition. With the allies at the gates of Paris and German resistance in France seemingly collapsing, the invasion of Southern France had begun.

1908 23 August 1944

The broadcast died away. The 22-year-old King Michael I, who was initially considered to be not much more than a figurehead, had deposed the Antonescu dictatorship. The King then offered a non-confrontational retreat to the German ambassador of German units out of Romania. But the Germans considered the coup "reversible" and attempted to turn the situation around by military force. The Romanian Army were now under orders from the King to defend Romania against any German attacks. King Michael had put the Romanian Army, which had a strength of nearly 1,000,000 men on the side of the Allies. Another of Germany's satellites had fallen, joining Italy and Finland.

1444 25 August 1944

The small convoy, consisting of the escort carrier *Junko Maru*, a large transport and three escort destroyers had been decimated off Manila by the two U.S submarines. The *Harder* had sunk two destroyers and the escort carrier, the *Haddo* one destroyer and the transport. Nothing remained of the five-ship force at all, which had been pursued and attacked by the two submarines since noon yesterday.

2358 31 August 1944

So, the Americans had landed at Leyte. It was the location he had picked, thought Toyoda, so it made the implementation of the plan that he had devised that much easier. His carriers, or Northern Force, which he would personally command, would immediately sortie South to engage the U.S Forces, destroying or at least damaging and distracting the U.S Fleet aircraft carriers and battleships.

With their forces drawn off, his main surface striking force, Centre Force, under Nishimura, based on four battleships, would dash to attack though the San Bernadino Strait, enveloping the U.S forces in a bear hug with Southern Force, under Abe, coming though the Surigao Strait. Komura's Far Southern Force would leave Tarakan, pass South of the Davao Gulf and move North to engage enemy forces. In actuality, he was hoping this force, which would look impressive from the air, would simply draw off US forces, leaving Centre and Southern Force open.

0003 1 September 1944

Field Marshall Shunroku Hata's Ichi-Go offensive had largely failed in its second part. His army had taken another 50,000 casualties and had only advanced very slowly, fierce Chinese counter attacks, many by armoured forces superior to his own had bled his army badly of its better units.

From the start line he had advanced Southwards and captured the city of Changsha on the 30th. When he had consolidated his positions around the surrounds of the city, the offensive would be called off. It had achieved too little and his opponents appeared as combative as ever. With the news of the American landings in the Philippines, he had also anticipated that in the coming months, many of his units would be needed elsewhere.

0506 1 September 1944

General William Joseph Slim had the task of commanding all allied land forces in Burma and Thailand. The front had been stable since April 1944, with the Japanese seemingly content to sit in place, although they had been conducting aggressive operations in China.

He had not minded the wet season wait. Whilst he had not necessarily received all the land reinforcements that he would have liked, he had integrated the Thai forces into his command and had equipped and trained many of their previously irregular forces, plus had brought units forward that were no longer required in India with the brightening political situation there.

In regards to air and naval forces, he was now lavishly equipped in comparison to his opponents. The surrender of Italy and the destruction of most of the German fleet, along with the waning of German air power, had brought him additional units.

Fraser's fleet was planning a raid for the 5th September on the Dutch East Indies. He then planned to use that fleet to support an amphibious landing at Phuket in Thailand on the 15th September, two days after he kicked off his own offensive in Southern Burma/Thailand on the 13th. With the Australasian's invading Borneo on the 11th and the US invading the Philippines, it would come as a series of hammer blows at the Japanese.

0558 1 September 1944

With Russian troops right on the border, even though no state of war existed between Bulgaria and the Soviet Union, the Russians had made their demands on the 26th and the Fatherland Front had risen in rebellion. Kimon Georgiev, its leader, had received the news ten minutes ago. The government had capitulated to the Fatherland Front's demands.

Sworn in as the new Prime Minister later that day, by 2nd September Bulgaria had repudiated its alliance with Nazi Germany and declared for the allies. Another Axis domino had fallen. Only Slovakia, currently in rebellion and Hungary remained.

RN Eastern Fleet
Commander: Admiral Bruce Fraser
Location: Trincomalee

CV: *Illustrious*(30 Corsairs, 27 Barracudas), *HMS Indomitable*(31 Seafires, 22 Avengers), *Victorious*(30 Corsairs, 24 Barracudas), *Unicorn*(mainly used as a maintenance carrier -12 Barracuda, 6 Sea Hurricanes)
CVE: *Ameer, Battler, Begum, Shah*(usually 12 Avengers, 6 Wildcats each)
BB: *Howe*(Flag), *Richelieu*(French)
BC: *Renown, Repulse*
CA: *Cornwall, Cumberland, Dorsetshire, London, Sussex, Suffolk*
CL: *Ceylon, Gambia, Kenya, Newcastle, Nigeria, Phoebe*
DD: 20

BB *Valiant* had been sent home badly damaged in August when the dry dock in Trincomalee had collapsed on her

RAN Covering Fleet:
Commander: Vice Admiral John Collins
Location: Darwin
CV *Australasia*(24 He 100, 12 Avengers, 12 A36), *CVL Christchurch*(9 He 100, 6 Avengers, 6

A36), *Melbourne*(12 He 100, 9 Avengers), *Sydney*(12 He 100, 9 Avengers)
BB *Pacifica*(Flag)
CA *Dunedin, Auckland*
CL *Launceston, Hobart, Darwin, Nashville, Boise, Phoenix*
DD *Wik, Wiri, Nasoqo, Kurnei, Alawa, Warramunga, Tagalag, Koko, Palawan, Maori*(all *Tribal Class*)

RAN Invasion Force:
Commander: Rear Admiral Roland de Righi
Location: Darwin
CVE *Perth*(9 He 100, 9 Avengers), *Wellington*(9 He 100, 9 Avengers), *Brisbane*(Flag)(9 Swordfish)
CLAA *Tromp, Jacob van Heemskirk, Hamilton*
DD *Stuart*
DE *Waikato, Tamar, Clutha, Darling, Todd, Waimbula, Derwent, Hawkesbury*(all *River Class*)
3 Assault ships
8 Transports

RAN Support Force
Commander: Rear Admiral Harold Farncombe
Location: Darwin
DD *Vampire, Valhalla*(Flag), *Attack*
Sloops *Swan, Warrego*
2 AO
1 PT Depot Ship
1 Hospital Ship
2 Stores Ships
12 Corvettes(*Bathurst Class*)

IJN Northern Force
Commander: Admiral Toyoda
Location: Inland Sea
CV *Kaga* (30 A6M, 24 B6N, 18 D4Y), *Taiho*(30 A6M, 24 B6N, 18 D4Y)(Flag), *Unryu, Amagi, Katsuragi* (all 24 A6M, 18 B6N, 12 D4Y)
CVL *Nisshin*(15 A6M, 12 B6N)
CVE *Eikyo, Taiyo* (both 12 A6M and 12 B6N)
5 DD
10 *Matsu Class* DE

IJN Centre Force
Commmander: Vice Admiral Nishimura
Location: Brunei
BV *Ise*(30 A6M)
BB *Yamato, Musashi, Shinano*(Flag)
CA *Haguro, Kumano, Ashigara, Ibuki, Chokai*
CL *Oyodo, Niyodo, Kiyodo, Noshiro, Natori*
24 DD

IJN Southern Force
Commander: Vice Admiral Abe
Location: Brunei
BB *Yamashiro*(Flag), *Settsu*
CL *Abukuma*
11 DD

IJN Far Southern Force
Commander: Rear Admiral Komura
Location: Tarakan
CVE *Kamakura Maru, Okatisan Maru, Kumano Maru*(each 6 A5M, 2 B5N)
CA(old) *Izumo, Iwate, Yakumo, Asama, Aso*(Flag)
CL(old) *Tsushima, Hirado, Hizen, Hiko*
AMC *Gokoko Maru*
6 DD
9 TB

IJN Replenishment Force
Location: Inland Sea
2 AO, 1 DD, 4 TB

IJN Reinforcement Force
Location: Inland Sea
AV *Akitsushima*
CL *Kashima*
4 DD
2 AO
2 Transports

USN "Big Blue Fleet" 5th Fleet
Commander: Admiral Raymond Spruance

TG 38.1(Vice Admiral John McCain)
CV *Wasp, Hornet, Saratoga*
CVL *Cowpens, Monterey*
CA *Boston, Quincy, Astoria, Chester, Salt Lake City*
2 CL AA
14 DD

TG 38.2(Rear Admiral Gerald Bogan)
CV *Enterprise*
CVL *Independence, Cabot, Bataan*
BB *Iowa, New Jersey*
CA *Vincennes*
CL *Biloxi, Chattanooga, Miami*
15 DD

TG 38.3(Rear Admiral Frederick Sherman)
CV *Essex, Lexington*

CVL Princeton, Langley
BB Massachusetts, South Dakota
CL Santa Fe, Mobile, Birmingham
15 DD

TG 38.4(Rear Admiral Ralph Davidson)
CV Lafayette, Intrepid
CVL San Jacinto, Belleau Wood
BB Washington, Alabama
CA New Orleans, Wichita
11 DD

USN "Brown Water Fleet" 7th Fleet
Commander: Vice Admiral Thomas Kincaid

Leyte Landing Group
Commander: Vice Admiral Thomas Kincaid
40 DD
Numerous transports APD's etc)

Close Support Group
Commander: Vice Admiral Jesse Oldendorf
BB Tennessee, California, Idaho, Mississippi, New Mexico, Pennsylvania
CA Portland, Minneapolis
CL Honolulu, Denver, Columbia, Cleveland
29 DD

Escort carrier Groups(Vice Admiral Theobald)
Taffy 1(Vice Admiral Theobald)
CVE Sangammon, Chenango, Suwanee, Santee
3 DD
4 DE

Taffy 2(Rear Admiral Stump)
CVE Natoma Bay, Manila Bay, Marcus Island, Kadashan Bay, Buka Island
3 DD
4 DE

Taffy 3(Rear Admiral Clifton Sprague)
CVE St Lo, White Plains, Kalinin Bay, Kitkun Bay, Gambier Bay
3 DD
3 DE

Taffy 4(Rear Admiral Thomas Sprague)
CVE Fanshaw Bay, Liscombe Bay, Ommaney Bay, Nehanta Bay, Rudyerd Bay
3 DD
3 DE

Support Force:

6 CVE
18 AO
16 DD
15 DE

6 August 1949(Flash Forward)

They were three of Australasia's most prominent wartime leaders, Leslie Morshead, Keith Park and John Collins. All were there for different reasons. As they watched the ceremony, the guard being inspected by Queen Alice, the flag being pulled down on the old *HMAS Australasia*, Collin's flagship on a number of occasions.

She was being returned to mercantile service, hence Morshead's presence as General Manager of the Orient Steam Navigation Company. This was Park's last function as head of the Defence forces, before his retirement on 15th August. His replacement was Collins. They were now raising the flag on the new carrier *HMAS Sydney* and the new cruiser *HMAS Melbourne*, both ships having made the trip from the U.S two months ago. Both ships were surrounded on one side by the old carrier *Christchurch*, not long for the breakers and four new *Daring Class* destroyers.

Overhead was a fight of He 2 strategic bombers, with the unfamiliar screams of the new He 280 jet fighters accompanying them.

1202 1 September 1944

It was just a tick over noon when Nishimura could almost imperceptibly feel the slight movement of the ships as she pulled away from the jetty. They were on their way. He had no real illusions about the task in front of them. Intelligence reports put the size of the US forces off Leyte as far beyond anything that the Imperial Navy could muster any more. All he could do is the best with the forces that he currently had. What he had was the cream of what was left of the IJN, at least it's surface forces. His three *Yamato Class* battleships represented the core of his command. They would have to bullock their way past the U.S Forces, which is what their design was for after all.

He was at least in a better position than Southern Force, with its older ships and equipment, or Far Southern Force, with its antiques. He thought again of his son, dead now four months. He would be joining him soon enough. His final mission was to cause as much damage as possible to the enemy and he was determined to carry it out to the letter. This would be his last mission, he was sure. Hopefully Northern Force would get in good blows to the U.S carriers. The combination of this and the apparent threat provided by Far Southern Force, would hopefully draw them off, allowing his force to break through to the enemy "soft" forces.

He had selected *Shinano* as his flagship. She was so new he could still smell the glue on the wood panelling in his day cabin. She had, however, received the pick of the crews that had been raised for this mission. Far Southern Forces crews were as new as its ships were old. At least he had been spared that. As he finished his lunch, the ship started to slowly pick up speed. The die was cast.

1313 1 September 1944

Rear Admiral Komura's far Southern Force was already at sea. Restricted to about 13.5 knots as a cruising speed, he had had to leave earlier than Nishimura's force. Komura had also thought breakdowns were not out of the question. Some of these ships had not seen the open sea for a number of years. He had made no attempt to disguise his ships at all. After all, he was quite sure their main purpose was to be spotted. With that in mind, he had fitted and painted wooden slatting over the superstructure of the armed merchant cruiser *Gokoko Maru*, giving her the appearance of a carrier from the air.

From the air his force could quite possibly look impressive, up to four carriers and 5 other ships that could easily be mistaken for battleships or at least heavy cruisers. Plus, the very number of ships, 29, would also add to its imposing nature.

However, that is all it would do, look impressive. His three old armoured cruisers were only good for 16 knots, possibly 17 at maximum speed. His ex-Thai coastal defence vessels were even slower, even if they were in better condition. His light cruisers were ancient. In fact, he had to be supported by two coal hulks at Tarakan, so many of his old ships were requiring coal that 8000 tons had to be brought in. Nine of his escort ships were tiny 430-ton Thai torpedo boats with a main armament of three 3-inch guns. Only one of his 14 escort massed over 1000 tons.

His crews were the worst of the worst, new recruits, in many cases boys or older, unfit men, little trained, in some cases even troublemakers. His twenty or so aircraft were manned by green pilots as well. He was under no illusions. His forces sole aim was to draw and attract enemy forces, his ships purpose to draw bomb and torpedo hits that may find homes in other, more useful ships.

1018 3 September 1944

Toyoda's Force, consisting of eight carriers, had slipped out of the Inland Sea and was on his way South. Logically, he knew that they were underprepared. Every effort had been made over 1944 to rebuild the air strength of the Kido Butai, however, it was true combat experience that so many were short of.

On the positive side, the stocks of older aircraft had been dispensed with, the air groups reequipped with the new D4Y and B6N. With almost 400 air craft, he was confident that they could deliver a blow of some substance to the Americans. His task forces escort, however, was weak. Only five new *Atkizuke Class* fleet destroyers and ten new *Matsu Class* Escort destroyers, not fleet destroyers in the true sense of the word. It was withstanding a counter blow that he worried about. He had moved more land-based air from Formosa and the Netherlands East Indies to the Philippines to support operations. If they did not check the Americans here, the war was effectively unwinnable. The Americans taking the islands would cut off the fleet from its fuel sources, making the possession of heavy ships pointless, for they would be immobilized by lack of fuel. Therefore, he was not concerned by casualties, only the infliction of damage that would make the Americans give pause.

In many ways all three forces were decoys for Centre Force, whose mighty battleships would hopefully obliterate the Yankee invasion fleet. If not, the only thing to fall back on would be the introduction of "crash dive" tactics, which had so far been resisted, although the few aircraft in Far Southern Force would be doing just that.

0444 6 September 1944

Nishimura's Centre Force had avoided the Palawan Passage. It's shallow waters and lack of room to manoeuvre offered all that would be required for a submarine commander. He had assessed the other two possibilities.

The first option, sweeping out into the South China Sea and then East into Mindoro Straight would have been his preferred option, however, a lack of tankers and of fuel prevented this. The second option he had finally decided on was using the Balabac Strait, then crossing the Sulu Sea. Much less dangerous from a submarine perspective, but within range of American and Australasian air recon units based at Morotai.

He had accepted the risk of being spotted simply because he did not believe that he could avoid allied air reconnaissance in the first place anyway. In his opinion the possibility of being not spotted was almost non-existent. It also offered the opportunity to stay merged with Abe's Southern Force slightly longer, providing more group protection.

0754 6 September 1944

Admiral Sir Bruce Fraser was happy with the results of the Eastern Fleet's raid, even if a bit disappointed with what had been found in port at Surabaya, where only one transport and a minesweeper were sunk. The oil refineries and storage tanks on Java had taken a large hit, the second time that Eastern Fleet had devastated Japanese production during the war so far. Over fifty Barracudas and twenty Avengers had conducted the strike, escorted by over 50 Corsairs. They had been met by 12-15 Japanese fighters, but these had largely been brushed aside. Only five aircraft had been lost, two to accidents.

A counter attack by 18 Japanese bombers, escorted by ten old Ki 43's had been easily broken up by the Seafires on CAP. Overall the Japanese response had been quite muted, but morning recon by RAAF P43's had indicated quite severe damage, so they had been hit hard.

0654 7 September 1944

Today would be the start of the battle, thought Nishimura. He anticipated that Northern Force would make its presence known during the course of the day. Reports from both Southern and Far Southern Force indicated both had possibly been spotted late yesterday.

The army had promised to assist with strikes on the U.S carriers today with their 4th Air Army under General Tominaga, although they had lost many planes over the last few days opposing the American invasion. Meanwhile 1st and 2nd Air Fleet had carefully husbanded their resources, using their aircraft only for defence of their own airfields. Today they would add their strength to attacks on the Americans, hoping to overwhelm their defences.

Map of the direction of the planned advance of the various Japanese Task Groups.
Red= Northern Force
Green = Centre Force
Purple = Southern Force
Blue = Far Southern Force
Orange=Leyte landings

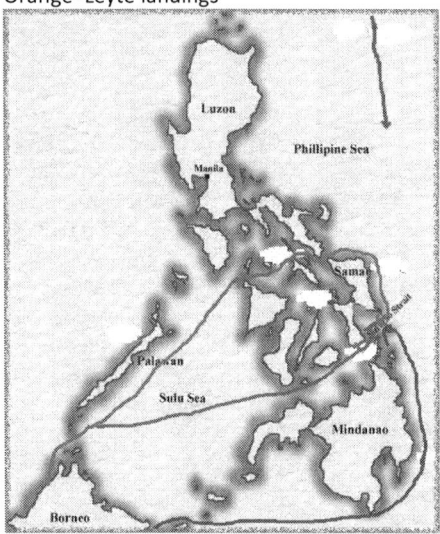

0738 7 September 1944

Admiral Raymond Spruance's brain was whirring like a computer. The sighting report of a Japanese force, to the North and obviously the main threat, had come in only 20 minutes ago. Three separate Japanese Task Groups had all been sighted late yesterday, now this one, the fourth.

He reviewed the reports. To the North eight carriers, five cruisers, ten destroyers. Heading probably for San Bernadino Strait, four battleships, eight cruisers, 20+ destroyers. Cutting South through Surigao Strait two battleships, one cruiser and ten destroyers. Cutting South of Mindanao four carriers, three battleships, six cruisers and 15 destroyers. Everything heading for Leyte and the planned destruction of the essentially helpless support ships. Every threat much be met. By 0754 he had consulted and made his decisions. It would involve splitting his forces, never that desirable an outcome, but he felt that he had no choice.

He would take the bulk of 5th Fleet North in pursuit of the Japanese carriers, consisting of TG38.1, 38.2, and 38.3, minus four battleships, four heavy cruisers and 12 destroyers. He should not need the heavy ships as it appeared the Japanese force was only carriers, light cruisers and destroyers.

To deal with the Southern Force he would detach his Southernmost force, Rear Admiral Davison's TG 38.4, in its entirety, including two battleships. To deal with the force coming at the Surigao Strait, he felt confident that Oldendorf's six old battleships should be enough. For the force coming at San Bernadino, he would use his escort carriers to launch strikes today and would detach Lee with four battleships to back up the "Taffy's" in case the Japanese broke through.

It seemed like a fair compromise. It divided his forces, but there seemed little other option in light of multiple threats, none of which could be ignored. It was as well he decided quickly, for at 0802, multiple contacts appeared on air search radar.

0816 7 September 1944

The first strike of the day had been directed at Vice Admiral John McCain's TG 38.1. Radar had picked up what turned out to be 66 Japanese aircraft at a range of 48 miles. They had picked poorly in their choice of target, as McCain's TG 38.1 was by far the most powerful of all the four US Fleet carrier forces. 18 Hellcats went forth to intercept from CAP, bringing down 16 Japanese aircraft for the loss of two Hellcats, 22 miles out. Four miles out the remaining 16 Hellcats were joined by 25 more that had been launched by the five carriers and these proceeded to savage the Japanese formation, shooting down 33 more Japanese aircraft and badly damaging 5 others in exchange for only four more Hellcats. The remaining 17 Japanese aircraft, stunned by their losses, were unable to mount a coherent attack and achieved no hits at all and suffered another four losses to AA. First round had definitely gone to the USN.

0901 7 September 144

No sooner one strike had departed than another appeared for TG 38.1 and Jon McCain. Again, his men had handled themselves superbly. What later records were to divulge was a strike of 58 aircraft was again detected on radar. This time TG 38.1 had more fighters aloft and fully 24 Hellcats intercepted 15 miles out, joined later by 12 more. For the loss of five Hellcats, they again clawed most of the Japanese aircraft from the skies, downing 34 and badly damaging 6 more, with AA claiming four more.

The Japanese attack was again poorly executed and the only ship hit was the AA cruiser *Oakland*, which took a 500lb bomb hit which fortunately did not explode. It had been a poor morning for the IJN land-based air units, with almost 80 aircraft expended for little result.

0918 7 September 1944

Vice Admiral Theobald's "Taffy 1", as the Northernmost of the four "Taffy's", was the first to come under attack, in this instance by IJA bombers based mainly on Luzon. The size of their formation had grown considerably, with Vice Admiral Lee's four battleships of TG 58 having integrated themselves amongst "Taffy 1", Lee having deduced quite correctly that the Japanese would be likely to simply hit the closest formation of ships, and so it had proven.

The four *Sangamon Class* escort carriers of TG "Taffy 1" were bigger, beamier and carried more aircraft than their smaller Casablanca Class sisters and still retained 12 Wildcats each even after dispatching a strike on Canter Force 36 minutes ago. They put up a strong CAP of over thirty Wildcats to meet the first strike of 40 Japanese aircraft at 0743 and, with assistance from nearby Taffy 2 and some extras from Taffy 3, was still able to keep that number over themselves over the next hour and a half, during which time three Japanese strikes appeared, each numbering 40-55 aircraft.

Each of these strikes was driven off with a disproportionate number of Japanese losses, an estimated 70 Japanese aircraft being shot down or badly damaged in exchange for nine Wildcats lost and three so badly damaged they were ditched. A terrific curtain of AA fire was to knock down 14 more Japanese aircraft, the only two hits obtained being one on USS New Jersey, a starboard hit that demolished a 5 inch mount and caused extensive casualties and another that hit Suwanee a glancing blow on the starboard dual 40mm mount, carrying it away and killing all the crew thereon.

0944 7 September 1944

John McCain's TG 38.1's attempts to do virtually anything beyond defend had been severely hampered by the almost constant series of Japanese attacks. Yet again another strike of 40+ aircraft had been seen off, with almost thirty blotted from the sky.

This time he had not survived unscathed, the light carrier Cowpens on fire from a bomb hit from one of the aircraft that had gotten through. Damage control's initial reports were that they had things under control, but it had penetrated the middle of the flight deck and she was nonoperational at present. He would be delayed in meeting the rendezvous point for the trip North.

1011 7 September 1944

General Tominaga's IJA 4th Air Army had hurled 136 aircraft at the Americans and had lost 68, with another 11 being write offs. It was an expensive proposition attacking the carriers off Samar and only two ships had been reported hit, a carrier and a battleship. He had promised the Navy maximum cooperation, never the less, and would launch another massed strike this afternoon.

1123 7 September 1944

Nishimura's Centre Force had been attacked three times by small strike over the course of the last 45 minutes, firstly by 17 Avengers and 12 Wildcats, secondly by 18 Avengers and 11 Wildcats and thirdly by 31 Avengers and 23 Wildcats. All had come from "Taffy 1" and "Taffy 2".

Warned by the latest in Japanese air search radar on the Shinano, he had launched 29 of his A6M fighters, one stubbornly refusing to start and also through in the four land based Ki 61's he had as top cover.

It had seemingly been an uneven fight. His aircraft had shot down four torpedo bombers and two fighters from the first American strike in exchange for eleven Japanese defenders. AA had shot down another two bombers, however, a torpedo hit had been obtained on Ise, slowing her to 20 knots and causing a five-degree list to port. The remaining 19 Zeros and three Ki 61's lost nine more aircraft in shooting down two Wildcats and two Avengers of the second strike, but again the struggling Ise was hit, twice more to port with torpedoes.

By the time the third, larger strike had arrived, only 12 Zeros and a lonely Ki 61 remained to defend. They shot down an Avenger, with intense AA destroying three more and the fighters downed two Wildcats. However, seven more Zeros were lost. That left 28 Avengers, who concentrated initially on the crippled *Ise*, now reduced to 7 knots. The first three aircraft missed, although one torpedo ran on and hit the light cruiser *Natori*, crippling her with engine room damage. The next eight, however, achieved four hits, ripping open the battleships hull and causing her to rapidly capsize. Six more aircraft hit the *Natori* twice more, dooming the light cruiser.

The last eleven aircraft concentrated on the *Yamato*, hitting the giant battleship once to starboard, causing no significant damage, but a taking on board of 1100 tons of water lowed her speed by almost two knots.

1148 7 September 1944

Rear Admiral Davidson's TG 38.4 had been the subject of a curious attack 20 minutes earlier. Picked up well out on radar, it had translated to 6 older B5N's and 12 even older A5M's. Met by 24 Hellcats, all had been eventually destroyed, although one A5M, along with two others, had made it to the Task Force. One had been shot down by a Hellcat, another by AA. A third had dived at the *Lafayette*, but seeing it was going to be intercepted by two Hellcats, had reversed course and plunged directly into the destroyer *Gridley*, crippling her.

Davidson wondered about his own strike on the Southernmost Japanese formation, which should be pretty much at the target now. He had dispatched two waves, each comprising over 50 attack aircraft.

1201 7 September 1944

Rear Admiral Komura's Far Southern Force had been hit hard. 36 Helldivers and 38 Avengers, with 22 Hellcats as escort, had arrived over his old relics and his only protection had been six old A5M's plus three old Ki 43's flying as escort. All had been rapidly dispatched by the U.S fighters at a loss of only one Hellcat, although one Avenger had been downed by the simple expedient of an A5M ramming it. AA from his own task force, weak on all his old ships, had brought down a Helldiver and damaged an Avenger, but that left 35 Helldivers and 36 Avengers to concentrate on his old and slow ships.

The armed merchant cruiser *Gokoku Maru*, hit twice by bombs, was left sinking and one fire. The small carrier *Kumano Maru* had been hit three times and was also stopped and on fire, clearly sinking by the stern. The small carrier *Kamakura Maru*, hit once, was slowed to 12 knots and badly damaged. The destroyer *Kuri*, hit by an 1000lb bomb had already broken up and sank.

The Avengers had concentrated on his "battle line" and destroyed it. The old *Izumo*, hit twice to port with torpedoes had rolled over and sunk. The *Iwate*, also hit by one torpedo, was clearly settling. The two ex-Thai coastal defence *Hizen* and *Hiko* had both been hit, one torpedo being more than enough for *Hizen*, now sinking. *Hiko* had simply exploded after only one hit. The torpedo boat *Tral* had taken a hit by a torpedo probably not intended for it and sunk rapidly. The old light cruiser *Hirado* was also badly lamed after a hit. His Task Force was now defenceless and worse still, 21 minutes later, had detected another strike inbound.

1243 7 September 1944

26 Helldivers and 34 more Avengers arrived escorted by 21 Hellcats over Far Southern Force. They faced no air opposition at all. It was already a scene of sad destruction and this batch of over 80 aircraft only added to it.

Whilst the Hellcats concentrated on strafing the small and weak ex Thai torpedo boats, the dive bombers again concentrated on the carriers. The crippled *Kamakura Maru*, hit three more times, rapidly succumbed. The last remaining escort carrier, *Okatisan Maru*, was hit four times by 1000lb bombs and also sank rapidly. The last Helldiver hit the torpedo boat *Trut*, immobilized by strafing, obliterating the small ship.

The ex-Thai coastal defence ship, now the Japanese *Aso*, sank rapidly after a torpedo strike cut her speed to five knots, listing to starboard. A second strike was the finishing blow. The crippled light cruiser *Hirado*, hit again, was to turn turtle half an hour later. The old armoured cruiser *Yakumo*, hit twice in rapid succession, simply exploded. The old destroyer *Hasu* was also sunk by a torpedo strike. Finally, the torpedo boat *Yure*, so badly strafed that she was barely able to make way, had to be scuttled.

By 1330, Far Southern Force had been reduced to the ex-Thai coastal defence ship *Aso*, the old light cruiser *Tsushima*, four destroyers and six torpedo boats. It had distracted the U.S forces alright, perhaps far too successfully, with a huge cost in lives. Sixteen of Far Southern Forces 28 ships had been sunk.

1249 7 September 1944

Toyoda's Northern Force had released its strike planes, the final group of 92 taking off just over an hour ago. Almost 250 aircraft were now winging their way towards the US carriers, representing the last gasp of Japanese Naval Aviation. Toyoda inwardly hoped they would slash through the U.S fighter blanket to cause some critical losses amongst their carriers, for he was more than aware that a counter strike would eventually be on its way.

1318 7 September 1944

Spruance had not launched any strike planes as yet. He had accurate intelligence on the Japanese fleet activity from his own patrol aircraft had told him they had already started launching before 1200, so he had held his own strikes in the hope of absorbing the first Japanese strikes whilst having nothing "spotted up" and then launching his own large counter strike later in the day, before reengaging tomorrow.

The first Japanese strike was detected at 1254 and consisted of 20 D4Y's and 39 B6N's escorted by 30 A6M's. It was detected and engaged 22 miles out from the now combined US carrier force, a running battle ensued that lasted all the way back to the fleet with 55 Hellcats that had been put up for fleet defence. The U.S fighters savaged both the strike aircraft and the Zeros, shooting down 17 A6M's, 10 D4Y's and 23 B6N's for the loss of seven Hellcats. Another five aircraft were "splashed" by AA. The only ships hit were the light cruiser *Birmingham*, which took a torpedo hit that badly damaged her and the smoking *Cowpens*, which was hit by a 500lb bomb, restarting fires recently put out.

1401 7 September 1944

The second Japanese strike, consisting of 23 D4Y's and 36 B6N's escorted by 31 A6M's ran into the same wall of U.S fighters still aloft after the last strike. In fact, Raymond Spruance had launched another 15 Hellcats so it was almost 60 of the tubby fighters that first engaged the Japanese strike 19 miles out. The Japanese were even more roughly handled than in the last strike, losing 18 A6M's, 22 B6N's and 13 D4Y's to fighters and another five aircraft to AA fire in exchange for six Hellcats. Concentrating their attacks on the crippled *Cowpens*, the Japanese obtained a torpedo hit that slowed and caused a list to port on the light carrier.

It was the third and final attack, consisting of 32 D4Y's and 30 B6N's escorted by 30 Zeros that caused the most damage. It caught some of the Hellcats on deck, after being recalled to refuel and rearm and a lesser number were airborne, some 42. These still knocked down eight D4Y's and 22 of the B6N's which were the most heavily engaged, as well as 14 A6M's, in exchange for seven Hellcats. AA fire would bring down another three D4Y's and three B6N's, as well as an A6M. However, two hits were obtained on the *Cowpens* with bombs, setting the light carrier ablaze from end to end. In addition, the carrier *Enterprise* was also hit by a 500lb bomb, but the damage was right near the front of the flight deck and easily repairable. The Japanese had scored some hits and damage, but the cost had been horrendous, 163 aircraft of the 271 aircraft being sent failing to return. Seven more would crash on landing.

1538 7 September 1944

Spruance's 5th Fleet had gotten itself into range and had flown off two huge strikes, with a third in preparation when radar again indicated a large Japanese strike, probably land based, inbound. It consisted of 68 aircraft, mainly older B5N's and D3Y's, escorted by A6M's, with a few newer types.

He was able to put up 47 Hellcats as a defence and these savaged the Japanese aircraft in a similar manner to this morning, shooting down 46 aircraft in exchange for only four losses. AA downed five more. However, the carrier *Independence*, with aircraft still on deck was hit twice by bombs and rapidly caught fire. The *Cowpens*, immobile and still on fire, was also torpedoed, sealing her fate.

1614 7 September 1944

The size of the first strike was an unpleasant surprise to Toyoda. He had kept back a substantial amount of A6M's, 66 machines still being available for use as CAP when the first U.S strike hit. It was, however, huge, 56 Avengers, 69 Helldivers and 44 Hellcats.

Despite being outnumbered, the Hellcats did well against the Japanese fighters and in exchange for seven losses shot down 31 A6M's. Five Avengers and four Helldivers were shot down by the Japanese aircraft, with another two Helldivers shot down by the weak

AA. The remaining strike aircraft were harassed as best as possible by the Japanese fighters, but hits were inevitable, and so it was shown.

The Helldivers scored hits on both *Unryu*(three) and *Amagi*(two), as well as the weakly protected *Taiyo*, setting all three alight. The destroyer escort *Sugi* broke in half after a heavy bomb hit. The Avengers then swooped in and hit the old Pearl Harbour veteran *Kaga* three times with torpedoes, slowing her almost to a stop. Escort carrier *Taiyo* was also hit badly and left listing and on fire.

As Toyodo looked out over the fleet he knew he was in deep trouble, half his carriers already badly or critically damaged.

1633 7 September 1944

Commander "Tommy" Dykers *USS Jack* had departed Fremantle on the 8th August and would probably have been on her way home already if the appearance of the Japanese fleet had not interrupted the situation. He had been trying to get into attack position for some time, but now his job had been made easier. The Japanese were obviously now concerned only with aircraft, allowing him easy passage through to the crippled carrier. He had to make this count, as he had only five torpedoes left, four forward and one aft.

He fired all four at the large carrier and then swung to fire at the escort uncomfortably close on the port side. He was rewarded with three solid hit and, almost immediately after, another on the offending escort. Within twenty minutes, both the carrier *Amagi* and the escort Ume had reached the bottom. *USS Jack* had come up aces.

1635 7 September 1944

It was Rear Admiral Thomas Sprague's "Taffy 4" that took the next Japanese strike from land-based air. Approximately sixty aircraft strong, escorted by 12 Ki 61's and 12 Ki 43's, they were met by almost 40 Wildcats, losing 44 aircraft in the attack in exchange for six U.S fighters. On this occasion, however, they drew blood. The escort carrier *USS Rudyerd Bay*, hit twice by bombs dropped by two successive "Vals", was to explode violently after burning for 33 minutes post the hits. She was to sink two hours later.

1648 7 September 1944

The second large U.S strike, consisting of 44 Helldivers, 58 Avengers and 39 Hellcats came up against a reduced Japanese CAP of only 40 A6M's. In exchange for 22 A6M's, they lost only two Avengers to fighters and two more to AA, as well as four Hellcats to Japanese fighters. That left a huge number of strike aircraft to attack the seven Japanese carriers still afloat.

The torpedo planes quickly finished off the cripples, hitting the *Amagi* three more times, the *Kaga* four more and the *Taiyo* twice. All were clearly doomed. Another torpedo, meant for *Nisshin*, was deliberately intercepted by the escort *Take*, sinking her. None the less, the *Katsuragi* was hit twice and the *Nisshin* once, slowing both and crippling the *Katsuragi*, which had had her screws sheared off to port. The Helldivers then targeted the carrier, hitting her five times, leaving her a blazing wreck and then also hitting *Taiho* once, although causing only moderate damage.

When the U.S aircraft drew off, only three of the original eight carriers, two of those, both damaged, remained.

1742 7 September 1944

Spruance's last strike had been a gamble that would cost him 27 aircraft ditched as they made their way back to 5th Fleet in almost full darkness for the last 45 minutes of their journey, some aircraft missing the mark and ditching and others "pranging" their landings in the gloom. Despite the loses, it had been an acceptable gamble as they effectively finished off Northern Force.

The last strike of the day, consisting of 39 Helldivers and 47 Avengers, escorted by 36 Hellcats, encountered only three Japanese carriers and 23 A6M's. Losing only two Hellcats in exchange for the destruction of 18 A6M's and one Avenger and one Helldiver to AA, they proceeded to attack the Japanese ships. The light carrier *Nisshin* was hit three times by torpedoes, leaving her sinking. *Eikyo* was also hit twice and then four times by 1000lb bombs, also leaving her ablaze from end to end and sinking. *Taiho* was also hit once in the middle of the flight deck by a 1000lb bomb, starting serious fires and the escort *Momo*, separated from the main body whilst pursuing a submarine contact was rapidly dispatched.

1806 7 September 1944

As the sun sank beneath the horizon, Toyoda viewed the scene of destruction, both on board his flagship and in his Task Force in general. He could now only hope that Nishimura and Centre Force could come through and save the day with a penetration of the American beachhead. The Kido Butai, so painstakingly built up over the course of 1944, had been destroyed as an effective force. Of the eight carriers that had sailed, only one, the damaged *Taiho*, remained. Four of his ten *Matsu Class* escort destroyers had also been sunk.

Losses amongst his three hundred aircraft had been almost total. With many of the remaining CAP A6M's damaged on landing on the holed flight deck, most of the remainder had ditched. He now 27 aircraft left on board *Taiho*, some of those damaged. It was time to retreat. With Far Southern Force also defeated, it was up to Centre Force alone.

Counting the destruction of *Ise* in Centre Force, the three CVE's in Far Southern Force and his own losses, an amazing 11 IJN carriers had been sunk on 7th September. Only the damaged *Taiho* remained. In terms of aircraft for the day, an incredible 378 carrier based and 284 land-based planes had been lost. Japanese aviation in and around the Philippines had been gutted like a fish.

1934 7 September 1944

I-58 had worked hard to get into position, attracted initially by the plume of smoke from the crippled carrier. Commander Yamata had positioned the submarine on a possible course back to Leyte Gulf and he had been rewarded.

The small convoy of the carrier, the light cruiser *Birmingham* and two destroyers crossed directly across his course and he saluted it with a full spread of six torpedoes. Three hits finished the light carrier *Independence*. *I-58* and Commander Yamata escaped to cause more problems 10 months later.

2012 7 September 1944

USS Growler had evaded pursuit and had had the satisfaction of watching her victim, the destroyer *Suzutsuki*, sink. Commander William Lewis had been unable to get a solution on the heavy Jap carrier, but the *Atkizuke Class* destroyer on the far port side of the formation had taken two hits and broken up quickly off Cape Engano. Northern Force had taken another loss.

2315 7 September 1944

Lt Commander Van Heemskirk's O19 had had a barren patrol so far, but the sighting of the Japanese formation, consisting of two larger and ten smaller ships had rapidly brought the boat to action stations. He had expended only one torpedo so far on patrol, so had plenty in reserve. *O19* fired all four bow tubes, swinging quickly and firing another four from the stern. Van Heemskirk was rewarded with two solid hits on one ship and two more on another that immediately exploded.

Unfortunately he had not much tie to celebrate the destruction of the old light cruiser *Tsushima* or the torpedo boat *Shrugu*, for his surface search radar, malfunctioning, had not picked up the old destroyer *Kuratake*, which sliced through the pressure hull of *O19* two minutes later after looming through the darkness. Like the torpedo boat *Shrugu*, there were no survivors from *O19*. *Kuratake*, herself badly lamed, had to be scuttled an hour later, leaving Far Southern Force short a light cruiser, a destroyer and a torpedo boat.

0204 8 September 1944

Admiral Toyoda's Northern Force was continuing to suffer attrition, losing the destroyer escort *Momo* 90 minutes ago to a submarine as they retreated North, although this time at least a measure of revenge had been taken with the destruction of her assailant. It had been more bad news when they had rendezvoused with the support group, whom had also lost the tanker *Gyoko Maru* to a submarine, along with the old destroyer *Shiokaze*.

It had been a disaster so far mused Toyoda. Unless the other two groups could pull off a miracle, it would be a disaster the navy never recovered from. He knew full well that aside from three more *Unryu Class* carriers, only destroyers, submarines and escorts were building, no other heavy units. He also knew that the allied heavy bombing attacks on the home islands would only increase, not decrease, with attendant production and raw material problems that would make laying new ships difficult soon.

0238 8 September 1944

Vice Admiral Lee TG 58 had started to receive reports of the Japanese Fleet coming through the San Bernadino Strait a little before 0130 from picket destroyers he had left near the entrance. He was still receiving regular updates and they were now moving East across the North Coast of Samar.

He had no intention of engaging at night, despite the advantage his gunnery radar would give him. He was well aware of the potency of Japanese torpedoes and wanted to be able to exploit the Japanese lack of air cover. By delaying the time of engagement, he drew the Japanese further South in search of targets. When dawn came, TG 38.4 would hopefully also be in a position to intervene. It was currently hurrying North from its pursuit of the Japanese Far Southern Force. When dawn came, he intended to be ideally just over the horizon South and East of the Japanese. He had withdrawn all the "Taffy" back near the landings at Leyte, giving the Japanese a reason to continue their advance. They would be of limited use in this battle, having expended nearly all their torpedo stocks yesterday.

When dawn came, hopefully he could follow a strike from TG 38.4, by cutting his battle line back across the Japanese line of advance and engage. His own forces had been supplemented by two destroyer divisions from the landing site, now giving him a large screen of 23 destroyers.

0501 8 September 1944

Vice Admiral Kincaid was more than satisfied with events. PT Boats had first picked up the Japanese force at 0037, advancing North up Surigao Strait. They had made repeated attacks, but the strong Japanese screen had driven them off, destroying three boats with no known damage inflicted in return. He had his six old battleships slowly cruising back and forth, blocking the Strait completely. His destroyers were positioned to the starboard and port of the advancing Japanese formation, with another squadron to the North.

The Japanese were now slightly over 40,000 yards away. He anticipated they would be within his radar envelope within the next 15-20 minutes. When that occurred, he would order his destroyers in to attack, adding their torpedoes to the confusion he was sure his gunnery would wreak.

0528 8 September 1944

Vice Admiral Abe's Southern Force were writhing at the centre of a terrible ambush. His two battleships were taking a terrific storm of shellfire and the situation was further complicated by the fact that his own flagship, *Yamashiro*, had just taken two torpedo hits. Badly damaged and listing heavily to port, on fire from constant hits from enemy heavy units that his surface search radar had not, as yet, picked up, he was able to reply only feebly from A turret(B was already disabled) and from the *Settsu* astern, using visual sightings from muzzle flashes only.

In addition to the damage on his flagships, the light cruiser *Abukuma* had been struck by two torpedoes, rapidly finishing the old ship. He had dispatched his own destroyers to try and guard his own flanks. They had some success, torpedoing one American destroyer, but those on the starboard side had come under heavy gunfire from American cruisers and three had taken hits from U.S destroyer's torpedoes. Already he had lost the *Yayoi*, *Mutsuke* and *Shirayuki* to torpedoes, plus the lead ships in his line, the destroyer *Fubuki* had taken so many heavy calibre hits she was also clearly doomed.

Going on further was clearly not an option. He had to get his force out of here to at least save what he could. The *Yamashiro* itself was probably already past saving, but perhaps the other ships could escape. He ordered a turn way.

0536 8 September 1944

The Japanese had turned away and now Kincaid authorised his battle line to follow and pursue. Even though his old ships were only good for 16-17 knots, knots, the Japanese line seemed to be held to about 15 knots, so he could continue to hold them within his range.

He had already sunk or critically damaged five smaller ships plus a Japanese battleship was also clearly finished, the other well alight as well. It had come at a cost of only one casualty, the destroyer *McDermut*. Another destroyer *Mertz* had taken a heavy shell hit. Of his battleships, only the *Pennsylvania* had been hit and then only once for limited effect.

0558 8 September 1944

Captain Yori Namashita's destroyer *Asagiri* was fleeing back down the Surigao Strait. With him were the destroyers *Uranami*, *Ayanami* and *Mochizuki*. The rest of Southern Force had been left behind, sunk or sinking. He had finally drawn away from the American fire and with dawn only 15-20 minutes away, he needed to put as much distance as possible between his forces and the US ships.

Yamashiro with Admiral Abe had gone some time ago, the light cruiser *Abukuma* had been destroyed almost on contact with the Americans. They had also lost five of their seven destroyers, one, the *Hatsuyuki*, simply blowing up. He had to leave the old battleship *Settsu* behind. Reduced to five knots, on fire and a wreck, he had not been able to stay with her as U.S forces closed in, although he had had the satisfaction of torpedoing a U.S destroyer that had come in to close. Southern Force had been crushed.

0609 8 September 1944

There was a certain melancholy as the first smudge of light started to appear on the horizon in watching the old battleship slowly turning over and sink. She followed two Japanese destroyers sunk in the last half hour.

In all, Kincaid's forces had destroyed two battleships, one light cruiser and seven destroyers in exchange for the loss of the destroyers *McDermut* and *McGowan* and heavy damage to the *Mertz*. A few other ships had suffered some damage, but in all cases this was minor. It was a crushing victory.

0614 8 September 1944

The first rays of dawn were spreading across the sea and Nishimura was baffled. The new surface search radar in *Shinano* had detected nothing during the course of the night and he had expected to have a visual on American units upon the dawn. However, the sunshine had brought nothing but empty seas, with the radar screens of his operators remaining defiantly empty.

He was halfway down the East Coast of Samar, opposite Dolores and the U.S forces had seemingly vanished. He was less than three hours steaming from Leyte Gulf with three battleships, five heavy cruisers and four light cruisers, as well as 24 destroyers. It was baffling. He needed to get recon from somewhere so had decided to catapult off a pair of floatplanes from *Oyodo*.

0620 8 September 1944

Rear Admiral Ralph Davison's TG 38.4 had launched their first strike for the day. Taking into account the Japanese lack of air cover, he had gone almost totally for strike aircraft, 44 Avengers and 37 Helldivers, escorted by only 12 Hellcats. He had launched only eight fighters for CAP this morning, giving over most of his assets to offensive operations.

His ships were only 98 miles from the oncoming Japanese, so flight time would be short. He had taken his cue from Vice Admiral Lee and had instructed his aviators to not worry about "finishing off" cripples, but to concentrate on inflicting damage on as many enemy ships as possible. His own battleships, along with two heavy cruisers and five destroyers had continued on ahead almost an hour ago when he had commenced launch operations. He was now working on a second strike which he hoped would be about the same size.

0657 8 September 1944

Nishimura's Centre Force had suffered a large air strike that without air cover he had been ill equipped to repel. Only three lonely A6M's had arrived to give air cover and these had been quickly swept aside. He had also lost the second float plane he had just launched to scout to the East, even if its tail gunner had destroyed an American fighter. He was not to know that the *Oyodo's* first launched "Jake" had suffered a similar fate, being "bounced" by a Hellcat without getting off any sort of report.

The enemy force had seemingly plastered ships randomly, both the *Musashi* and *Yamato* suffering bomb hits, the *Musashi* also suffering a torpedo strike that caused her to ship 1400 tons of water and slowing her top speed by two knots. These were painful but not critical hits, however, the heavy cruiser *Ashigara* had taken a torpedo hit that knocked out the port side boiler rooms, created a 7-degree list and slowed her speed to 14 knots. Light cruiser *Oyodo* had also taken a hit that had both slowed her and started a fire forward, necessitating the flooding her forward magazines. The destroyer *Michishio* had taken both a 1000lb bomb and a torpedo hit and was sinking. The destroyer *Yudachi* had also taken a 1000lb bomb hit and was in a bad way and may have to be scuttled.

He had radioed for more air cover and still had no idea what he faced. He now decided to use the time the task force was stationary to catapult more recon planes off, this time from *Shinano* herself.

0808 8 September 1944

Nishimura's force had no sooner gotten itself going South again, having completed some basic repairs, search and rescue and scuttled the destroyer *Yudachi*, which could not be repaired, when he received another blow. The Task Force had been attacked by approximately 30 U.S Avengers at 0740, but these had caused little damage, only two hits from what appeared to be HE bombs on his own flagships that had easily been brushed off, although the suffering cruiser *Ashigara* had also taken a hit, starting a fire.

A miserable six A6M's had arrived as CAP over his ships, but any cheer he may have felt from that had been snuffed out by the appearance of another large U.S raid, in the vicinity of 100 aircraft. That and the two reports he had received, one at 0805 and another at 0808. Two enemy battleships, two cruisers, six destroyers only 20 nautical miles to the South. With another gaggle of eight destroyers five miles astern.

Even worse, to the Northeast, effectively behind and to seaward of him, four enemy battleships, four cruisers and over 20 destroyers, also approximately 20 nautical miles away. The gateway to Leyte, seemingly only two hours steaming away, was far from open and his forces were about to be attacked from the air again.

0823 8 September 1944

Nishimura's Centre Force had again taken casualties. A large U.S raid had quickly swept aside the six A6M's he had as cover, shooting them all down for the loss of a single aircraft. His AA defences were not functioning the way he would have liked, his 18.1-inch fragmentation shells having performed poorly. His ships had only shot down five, four and now four more aircraft respectively from the three US strikes.

The crippled *Ashigara* had taken two more torpedoes and been sunk. His own flagship *Shinano* had taken another, meaning all three of his battleships had taken torpedo hits that cut their speed to 23-25 knots. Light cruiser *Noshiro* had taken two hits and was clearly finished as well. The destroyer *Asashio* had also been sunk, taking both a torpedo that immobilized her and then a 1000lb bomb hit. *Yamato* had also been hit with a 1000lb bomb, but this had hit No 1 turret and been deflected. Finally, the already damaged *Oyodo* had been hit and stopped by a 1000lb bomb. Quickly becoming a priority target, she had been hit three more times and was ablaze from end to end and obviously finished. Although not sinking, she would clearly have to be scuttled.

With the U.S aircraft now gone, he could only await whatever assistance that would come from 1st and 2nd Air Fleets, which had promised all they could give. Now he had to fight his way past U.S battleships. North or South, that was the question? He was now down to three damaged battleships, four heavy cruisers, two light cruisers and 21 destroyers.

0827 8 September 1944

Rear Admiral Edward Hanson had waited for the destroyer division to catch up. Now with two battleships, two heavy cruisers and 14 destroyers, he had been in contact with Lee. He was currently still 19 nautical miles South of Centre Force. Lee had closed into 17 nautical miles to the Northeast of Centre Force. He now ordered his own Task Force into action.

Centre Force had six battleships closing in from two different directions, both now less than 38,000 yards away. He remained worried about air attack, but had eight Hellcats as top cover from *Lafayette*.

0848 8 September 1944

Nishimura was in a quandary. Shells had started splashing down around Centre Force and he had visual contact with enemy battleships to the Northeast. However, 60 seconds ago new fire had started from the South, from battleships as yet unseen.

He had to make a decision. He had come to the conclusion that it could not be South. His ships were damaged, he had received reports that Abe's Southern Force had been smashed by U.S battleships and a run South could only take him further away from air support and closer to U.S carriers, and, from what had happened to Abe, probably more U.S battleships. He ordered a turn back to the North, just as the first hit had gone in, two shells impacting *Yamato*. He could now just see the fighting tops of ships to the South, the range being approximately 31,000 yards. The ships to the Northeast had closed to 28,000 yards. He would have to force his way through and attempt and escape. Held to 23.5 knots, he knew that would be a hard task. He was already mentally committing his destroyers to a torpedo attack to try and cover his heavy units escape.

0914 8 September 1944

Nishimura's force had completed a turn back to the North some time ago and was still coming under fire. He had detached ten destroyers and the light cruiser *Niyodo* to conduct a torpedo attack and would send the second division after the first had completed their attack. His force was only being gained on slowly by the two U.S battleships astern and these had gained no hits in any case. His main issue was the U.S battleships to the Northeast, for, as he turned North, the range had steadily dropped and was now down to 20,500 yards.

Yamato had been hit four more times, *Musashi* three and as yet he had yet to reply in kind. His own gunners clearly lacked the skills to hit at long ranges and he ordered a course correction starboard towards the U.S battleships to close the range.

0941 8 September 1944

Vice Admiral Lee had his own problems. The battleship *South Dakota* had taken two 18-inch shell hits, one of which had penetrated near B turret, knocking it out and starting a dangerous fire that was still being fought, the magazine of the turret being flooded to prevent any danger. The Japanese fire was becoming more accurate as the range had fallen and he had dispatched 18 of his own destroyers to fend off the Japanese attack. He had instructed his four heavy cruisers to concentrate on the enemy light units, but only limited success had been achieved, with one destroyer clearly sinking with multiple hits. He was getting consistent hits on the enemy battleships now, but nothing seemed to stop them, despite him concentrating two battleships on one of the enemy's, the third ship not being targeted.

1006 8 September 1944

Centre Force had received a reprieve, with the U.S battleships having turning away from the torpedo strike some time ago, although Nishimura had no doubt they would be back. The force to the South continued to dog him, with the *Yamato* at the rear of the line suffering hits from this force in addition to those previous from the battleships at the Northeast that had recently turned away. She was well ablaze and, worse still, her speed had dropped with penetrations aft of No 3 turret in the engineering spaces damaging her steam lines.

His destroyers had also suffered from their attack, which had produced only a hit on a U.S destroyer that had broken it in half. In return he had lost the *Hamanami* torpedoed, the *Okinami* to gunfire from U.S cruisers and the *Kiyonami* to the maddeningly accurate and sustained U.S destroyer gunnery. The *Yamagumo* was also crippled by gunfire. He still had a long way to run to the San Bernadino Strait.

1017 8 September 1944

1st and 2nd Air Armies had launched a strike to assist Nishimura with all of their remaining strength. They had managed to cobble together 30 strike aircraft escorted by 13 A6M's and had added seven A5M's from their training squadron and six Nakajima G5N "Liz" four engine heavy transports armed with bomb racks to make a total of 56 aircraft.

When they arrived over Lee's force, they encountered a CAP of ten Hellcats that quickly tore into the Japanese aircraft. The aircraft left had been brutally winnowed from yesterday's attacks and many of the pilots were the best of those available to the Philippines, therefore only 19 aircraft were lost with four more badly damaged for four Hellcats lost and one badly damaged. Heavy AA from the four battleships in particular was to shoot down six more attackers. That left 20 strike aircraft and these achieved some success, a G4M torpedoing the *USS South Dakota*, by far Lee's most damaged battleship already, having been hit four times by 18-inch shells. Another G5N had dropped a stick of bombs directly over the destroyer *Luce*, hitting her twice and crippling the small ship.

1032 8 September 1944

TG 38.4 has put up another large strike, this time including Hellcats in the mix, for total strike numbers of 24 Hellcats with rockets, nine more as top cover, 28 Avengers and 33 Helldivers. The Hellcats had concentrated on the destroyers and also sister ships *Hatsuharu* and *Hatsushimo*, leaving both little more than smoking wrecks. The Avengers had concentrated on the limping *Yamato*, off the back of the Japanese formation and had hit her four times with torpedoes, slowing her to 11 knots and giving her a large list to starboard. The Helldivers had divided their attentions between *Musashi*, which took three damaging bomb hits and the heavy cruiser *Kumano*, which took four and was left limping at 7 knots and ablaze.

It had been a cheap strike in terms of losses, with only five aircraft lost and three damaged badly, four to AA and one to a batch of four Ki 43's that appeared and shot down one Avenger before being swept aside themselves.

1043 8 September 1944

Nishimura had little choice. With *Yamato* now making only 7 knots, afire and listing heavily, he had to leave her, along with the crippled heavy cruiser *Kumano* and two crippled destroyers. They would no doubt be overtaken by the force trailing to the South, but with the U.S force to the North now back in contact he had little choice. His own force's gunnery had been bitterly disappointing, the U.S ships landing four or five hits for every one of his own.

He was committing his destroyers to another attack, he had little choice in the matter, but this time his own heavy ships would follow them in, closing the range. He needed to inflict enough damage to convince the Americans to sheer off. Nothing else was going to save his force. If that did not work then, like Von Spee, he may have to sacrifice his heavy units to allow his cruisers and destroyers a chance to escape.

1115 8 September 1944

Vice Admiral Lee's battleships were again coming under intense fire and it was again the *South Dakota* that was suffering. She had been hit four more time by 18.1-inch shells and was starting to lose touch with his other four battleships as he sent his destroyers out to repel yet another torpedo attack from enemy light forces, with twelve enemy destroyers and two cruisers closing the range on his battleships. His other ships were only lightly damaged, although the *Wichita* was one fire from three eight-inch shell hits and her speed was reduced to 26 knots.

1138 8 September 1944

Nishimura had made his decision. With fires raging on board *Musashi*, the ship down to 14 knots with accumulated damage and only No 3 2 turret still in action, both battleships were shuddering and jerking under an almost constant barrage of hits. All of his destroyers and cruisers had launched, putting over 140 torpedoes into the water. The U.S forces had turned away, but he needed now to press and allow his other forces to disconnect. *Musashi* was near finished and his own ship badly damaged as well and only capable of 20 knots. He would follow the torpedoes in and allow his other forces to disconnect.

His own forces had been cut down further as well, the destroyer *Urakaze* and light cruiser *Kiyodo* both taking torpedo hits which had sunk the destroyer and crippled the light cruiser. The destroyer *Shiranui* was also crippled by U.S destroyer fire. Only three heavy cruisers, one light cruiser and twelve destroyers would be attempting to escape.

1154 8 September 1944

Vice Admiral Lee's ships had run East to avoid the torpedo strike but *South Dakota* was simply too lamed to hold the range open. The ship had taken two torpedo strikes, as had the trailing destroyer *Stephen Potter*. The destroyer had broken apart under two hits and the battleship was now virtually stationary, listing drunkenly to starboard, now facing two Japanese battleships coming towards her like juggernauts.

1155 8 September 1944

Rear Admiral Edward Hanson's ships had dispatched the two Japanese destroyers and the heavy cruiser and had battered *IJN Yamato* into scrap. He had now steamed past in pursuit again of the rest of Centre Force. As he watched, the destroyer *Cotten* put four torpedoes into the cripple, which slowly turned over and started to go own by the bow.

1218 8 September 1944

The US battleships were now pouring fire into the two oncoming Japanese battleships and the crippled light cruiser following them. They contented themselves with pummelling the *South Dakota* from 8,000 yards rather than trying to hit his other units at 18,000. His own destroyers had been ordered in to conduct a full attack on the two battleships and had reported light fire only from the enemy units, probably due to the devastation inflicted on their secondary mounts.

The second enemy battleship was blazing merrily and had fallen out of the loose three ship formation. Lee could see the *South Dakota* was almost finished. Now he needed to make the Japs pay for what had occurred.

1242 8 September 1944

The game was almost up for both Nishimura and *Shinano*. *Musashi*, hit by four torpedoes was burning fiercely and listing heavily to port, her guns no longer in action. On board *Shinano*, only No 3 turret was still operational under local control. Most, if not all, of the secondary batteries had now been silenced. At least they had taken one of the enemy with them and possibly allowed the escape of the other ships, pathetically few though they may be. The light cruiser *Kiyoda* had also succumbed to battleship calibre fire. He calmly awaited his fate. He had known from the start this would his last mission. Soon he would see his son again.

1331 8 September 1944

It had taken a hail of shell and nine more torpedoes to finish the last Jap battle wagon, but now all three had been dealt with. *South Dakota* was still afloat but not for long. She had turned turtle at 1323 and would clearly slip under soon.

He was not going to take his damaged ships in pursuit, although *Lafayette* and TG 38.4 had indicated that they would be launching a last strike, their own supplies or anti shipping ordinance now reaching a low ebb. It had been a long afternoon for Lee's forces and his excitement at the victory had been dampened by the loss of the *South Dakota*.

1536 8 September 1944

With the remnants of Centre Force now only half and hours steaming from San Bernadino Strait, they must have been down heartened to see another huge cloud of U.S aircraft descend on them. Thirty rocket equipped Hellcats, 291 Avengers and 24 Helldivers again converged.

When they had left, the cruiser *Haguro* had taken three torpedo and three bombs hit and was clearly finished. The destroyer *Asashimo* had taken a 1000lb bomb hit and would have to be scuttled. Destroyer *Murasame* had taken multiple rocket hits and was sinking and the destroyer *Isokaze* had taken so many rocket hits that she would have to be abandoned. Only heavy cruisers *Chokai* and *Ibuki*, light cruiser *Niyodo* and nine destroyers remained of Centre Force.

1907 8 September 1944

Admiral of the Fleet Osami Nagano considered the reports as they had come in. The damage caused to the enemy had been nowhere near what was expected and the losses sustained had crippled the Navy, finishing it as a viable threat. He looked over the losses suffered:

From 8 CV/CVL/CVE only one damaged CV, *Taiho*, survived
From 6 battleships, none survived
From 1 seaplane carrier, 1 survived
From 10 heavy cruisers, 3 survived
From 11 light cruisers, two survived
From 1 armed merchant cruiser, none survived
From 51 fleet destroyers, 25 survived
From 10 destroyer escorts, 5 survived
From 13 torpedo boats, 10 survived

The navy had been crippled as striking force. Its naval aviation assets were completely destroyed. Tomorrow he would cancel the last two *Unryu Class* carriers, not scheduled to complete until mid-1945. Only the *Kasagi*, scheduled for completion in December, would go ahead. In addition, this war, seemingly so hard on Japanese admirals, had killed another two, Abe and Nishimura.

2018 8 September 1944

Spruance reviewed the losses from the battle. Although serious, they were, in his estimation, acceptable given the virtual elimination of the IJN. They consisted of BB *South Dakota*, CVL *Independence*, *Cowpens*, CVE *Rudyerd Bay* and four destroyers. A number of other ships had been damaged, including all three of Lee's remaining battleships.

The landings, however, had been secured and the enemy's fleet, a threat in being for so long, had been eliminated. Tomorrow his air groups would take up the pursuit of Southern and Centre Force, but for now, at least, they could have a night's rest.

1334 9 September 1944

Centre Force, or what was left of it, had suffered again with the U.S committing to two long range strikes against the retreating ships. By the time these aircraft had finished the second and last strike of the day, he had lost another four ships, with the light cruiser *Niyodo*, the destroyers *Kiyoshimo*, *Naganami* and *Akatsuki* all sunk. Only two heavy cruisers and six destroyers remained. Captain Shutoku Miyazato aboard *Chokai* was now senior officer.

What he was to see when he anchored at Brunei Bay late on the 10th was even grimmer. Back in the Inland Sea was the damaged carrier *Taiho* and four *Atkizuki Class* destroyers. At Brunei were the heavy cruisers *Ibuki* and *Chokai*, seaplane carrier *Akitsushima*, plus fourteen fleet destroyers, four of these older types. He discounted the relics at Tarakan under Rear Admiral Komura, which included the coastal defence ship/heavy cruiser *Aso*, light cruiser *Kashima*, three destroyers and five small torpedo boats.

With the smaller *Matsu Class* escort destroyers released back to escort command, it was all that remained of the strike elements of the IJN. With only one carrier, one light cruiser and four more destroyers being built, reinforcements could not be expected. Leyte had been the last ride of the IJN.

0639 11 September 1944

Aerial reconnaissance had warned Vice Admiral Collins that there was a Japanese fleet at Tarakan that would try and oppose the landings, which he had consequently delayed by a day. He hurriedly moved his four carriers *Melbourne, Sydney, Christchurch* and *Australasia* forward and had launched a strike of 33 Avengers, 18 A36's and nine rocked equipped He 100's escorted by 24 He 100's against the port at 0618. He would follow this up with a second strike as and if required.

0801 11 September 1944

It had been the final blow to Rear Admiral Komura's command. Refuelled and rearmed, he had expected to sail for Singapore tonight. Instead, the anchorage had been filled with aircraft, these ones Australasian. Destruction had been almost total. The ex-Thai Coastal defence ship *Aso* had capsized after two torpedo hits, the light cruiser *Kashima* had also taken two hits and was sinking slowly by the stern. The destroyers *Kuratake* and *Yugao* had suffered a similar fate. Three torpedo boats, the *Rate, Hinku* and *Yoge* had all been sunk by bombs. A fourth, the *Tingu*, had taken so many rocket hits and a bomb hit that she had settled. All that was left was the old destroyer *Tanikaze*, the oldest DD in the fleet and the slightly damaged torpedo boat *Prut*. The defending fighter squadron, consisting of 12 Ki 43's, had little impact, destroying three Australasian aircraft in exchange for ten of their twelve. Ashore when it had happened, he ordered both small ships to make ready. By 1200, he had cleared the harbour with both on their way to Singapore.

1319 11 September 1944

Chiang Kai-shek had instigated Operation Rat Poison. He had been alarmed that many in the United States Army Observation Group that had visited and established relations with Mao's Communists had declared them more organized and less corrupt than his own forces.

Mao was traveling to an army demonstration outside Yanan and he had given the go ahead when he had received the news from his contact. Twelve B-25 Mitchells thundered over the small column, escorted by 10 P40's. They easily brushed off the escort of three old I-16's. By the time they had finished, every vehicle had been engulfed by the flames of the napalm. To be sure, the three P40's left that had not engaged dropped three 500lb bombs and a creeping brownish orange gas marked the scene of destruction. Later that day, communist troops recovered the horribly burnt but recognizable corpse of Mao Zedong.

0907 12 September 1944

Covered by the battleship *Pacifica*, two heavy and six light cruisers, 1st Division had gone ashore at Tarakan. Resistance had been light, with little in the way of fixed defences. Japanese defenders consisted of two battalions only, which were poorly supplied with heavy equipment, their main task since 1942 having been the continuation of oil production from the Island off the East Coast of Borneo. Air defences had also been small and now consisted only of a flight of "Mary" light bombers and three Ki 43's. These had been easily swept aside by the attackers and so far, Vice Admiral Collins had been happy with the morning's events.

0934 14 September 1944

Rear Admiral Komura had arrived in Singapore with heavy cruisers *Ibuki* and *Chokai*, seaplane carrier *Akitsushima* and fifteen fleet destroyers. He had been instructed to pick up a large cargo of strategic materials to ships them back to Japan, leaving only five older destroyers at Singapore. The Anglo-Chinese offensive in Burma and Thailand had commenced yesterday and the South East Area army was again under pressure. It seemed everywhere Japan was losing, an unpalatable reality.

1116 15 September 1944

Slim's Forces had battled their way ashore at Phuket and Phang-Nga in Thailand against only scattered opposition, placing themselves with a substantial force almost 150 miles behind the Japanese front lines and in a position to completely cut off all Japanese forces in the Isthmus of Kra in what would be a disaster for the Japanese Southeast Area Army.

This had been Slim's plan all along and with the amphibious left now available for the operation, he intended to continue to reinforce his beachhead and then grind the cut off Japanese forces to pieces between his two armies. He had launched offensives in Eastern Thailand, with his objectives the capture of the cities of Roi Et and Surin, but this was more for political reasons to keep his Thai allies happy and would not be the main axis of advance, which would be to the South.

0454 22 September 1944

As another disaster in Thailand/Burma loomed for the IJA, with allied forces now not more than 8 miles from the city of Surat Thani, Rear Admiral Komura's forces at Singapore had been re tasked to attack the allied bridgehead at Phuket. Firstly, ordered to transport strategic materials to Japan, the hold, then unload at Singapore, then hold, they were finally on their way and had just arrived at Penang. They would sortie that night to hopefully be off the bridgehead at daybreak on the 23rd. Although his command was considerably more modern this time, he held out little hope for his two heavy cruisers and 15 destroyers.

1909 22 September 1944

Admiral Sir Bruce Fraser had conducted a series of raids against the Japanese airfield in Northern Sumatra, mainly in Aceh province, as these had proven to be a constant nuisance to the landings at Phuket and a danger to his ships, with *Repulse* hit by two 500lb bombs two days ago. He had sent her back to Trincomalee with the *Unicorn* and four destroyers and had left the beachhead covered by his four escort carriers, the light cruiser *Pheobe* and six destroyers.

2118 22 September 1944

Kreuger was happy with the way things were going in the Leyte operation. After 23 days of combat operations, the Sixth Army had all of its first and second phase objectives under control, as well as some third-phase objectives, such as Abuyog. In addition, elements of the 7th Division had pushed across the island from the southern end of the XXIV Corps sector and controlled approaches to the town of Baybay on the west coast. Only one key area, Ormoc Valley on the west side of the island, remained to be taken and he would commence a pincer offensive against the Valley tomorrow with armour and artillery support.

The destruction of the Japanese navy had hastened operations, as their almost unescorted attempts to reinforce their garrisons and bring in extra troops had been almost universally unsuccessful.

0632 23 September 1944

In the finish it was an Avenger launched for an early warning anti-submarine patrol that alerted Captain Frederick Court on board the escort carrier *Shah* to the presence of the Japanese force not more than 42,000 yards away.

It was the RN forces that had been caught by surprise, with naval intelligence confirming that no Japanese naval forces of consequence were at Singapore, which was obviously not the case, with two cruisers and 15 destroyers reported. His small carriers, with top speeds of 17 knots were not going to be able to outrun the Japanese, therefore he needed to use the only defence they did have, their aircraft.

He signalled Fraser for assistance from his fleet carriers, but these may not be able to intervene immediately, being nearly 260 nautical miles away. He instructed his destroyers and the light cruiser *Pheobe* to act as his shield. The Japanese would not be in gun range for probably an hour. He needed to use that time to launch a strike.

0733 23 September 1944

They had just closed to 22,300 yards and his heavy cruisers had commenced firing against the enemy carriers, partly sheltered as they were by a smoke screen. It was easier for *Ibuki*, as she carried the very latest IJN surface search radar that was good enough to direct gunnery by and she had already obtained a hit. Now yet again, he had been attacked by what was seemingly the curse of every IJN admiral. Aircraft. Thirty-three Avengers and seven rocket armed Wildcats had appeared over his ships.

0754 23 September 1944

The *Chokai* had taken a torpedo hit which had lamed the large heavy cruiser, cutting her speed to 18 knots. Also hit had been the old destroyer *Kamikaze*, which had broken up under the hit. The destroyer *Hamakaze* had also taken a hit that had badly damaged her and left her capable of a mere 10 knots. The old destroyer *Akikaze* had been hit repeatedly by rockets and constant strafing and had been left a smoking wreck. He contacted the *Ibuki* and urged her to go on pushing the attack.

0823 23 September 1944

Captain George Dunbar led the light cruiser *Pheobe* and four destroyers, HMS *Quadrant, Quality, Quickmatch* and *Quilliam* out to block the nine Japanese destroyers attempting to close. The two Japanese heavy cruisers were still holding their distance at 22,000 yards, along with four destroyers.

0845 23 September 1944

It had been a short, vicious little battle that had cost him the destroyer *Quilliam* to a Japanese "long lance", with his own cruiser *Pheobe* having taken ten 5 inch shell hits. In return, they had torpedoed one Jap destroyer and crippled another with gunfire from his cruiser. A third, hit repeatedly by his destroyers had been also hit by three Wildcats with rockets. With three of their nine destroyed, the Japs had retreated.

0901 23 September 1944

In the finish it was the appearance of a fresh batch of strike planes from Fraser's fleet carriers that forced the Japanese away, thought Captain Court aboard *Shah*. His own ship had taken two eight-inch shell hits but the most serious was HMS *Ameer*. A series of 8-inch shell hits had started a fire near her aviation gas storage tanks that at 0848 had culminated in a huge explosion that had blown the ship apart. In addition to many ships damaged, he had lost her and the destroyer *Qulliam*.

0947 23 September 1944

Captain Ajiro Suzinoko on board the heavy cruiser *Ibuki* was fleeing South with the remnants of what had been Rear Admiral Komura's fleet. They had caused some damage to the British, but the odds were hopeless in face of such large air superiority. They had lost the *Chokai* and ten of their 15 destroyers. All that was left was the *Ibuki*, damaged by a bomb hit, the new destroyers *Suzumani, Kishinami, Yukikaze* and *Shigure* and the ancient *Tanikaze*, which had somehow survived three battles without a scratch.

0745 28 September 1944

It had taken a fierce three-day battle but the city of Surat Thani had fallen to the troops of the 82nd West African Division. With three divisions ashore in Southern Thailand and a solid line stabilized, Japanese force in Southern Thailand and Southern Burma, pressed hard already by a renewed offensive in the North, were hopelessly cut off.

Slim was ecstatic, everywhere the Japanese forces, whilst resisting strongly, were being pressed hard and the allied advantages of total air superiority and vastly superior firepower and logistics was taking its toll. Even in Eastern Thailand where he had conducted a weak offensive, ground had been gained, with the border city of Paoy Pet captured by Thai forces and Roi Et and Surin threatened.

1907 29 September 1944

Keith Park was again reviewing how things had changed in his regular six-monthly reports to the aircraft review board. The RAAF was at its most modern and powerful, even if it had been reduced in strength by 16 squadrons in light of the now non-existent threat to the Australasian mainland. Like the army, which was in the process of reducing to twelve divisions, seven regular and five militia. The country, which had mobilized more men per capita than most, was now returning to a more normal footing, with many returning to essential industries instead. In regards to aircraft, the new CAC 15 Cockatoo was proving a winner and was rated by many who flew it as the best fighter they had ever flown. The new He 200, three squadrons of which were based at Tinian, were involved in the aerial offensive against Japan, using their longer range to bomb targets in the Northernmost Island, Hokkaido and in fact had just completed a week of offensive firebombing against Sapporo, conducted over three nights 8 days apart. Numbers by type now read:

Fighters:
CAC 15 Cockatoo 204 (in production)
Curtis P40 356
Hencall He 100 701(Currently in limited production-numbers count RAN machines)
Hencall He 119 310(in production)
Republic P43 34
TOTAL 1605 NEED 1600

Bombers/Patrol:
Consolidated Catalina 91
Consolidated B24 Liberator 270
de Havilland Mosquito 148(in limited production)
Douglas A20 48(some ex Dutch East Indies)
Fairy Swordfish 77
Grumman Avenger 176
Hencall He 200 92(in production)
Hencall He 211 200
Lockheed Hudson 106
Lockheed Ventura 70
Martin Mariner 19
North American A36 175
North American B25 20
Vickers Wellington 40
Vultee Vengeance 265

TOTAL 1796 NEED 1800

Transports:
Airspeed Oxford 249
Avro Anson 218(transport conversion)
Douglas C47 304(in production)

Hencall He 70 27

TOTAL 798 NEED 800
1618 10 October 1944

The meeting in regards to ship production had resulted in a drastic cutback in orders and production for the USN. It had not been escorts and destroyers that suffered, rather heavy surface ships. With the allies pushing through France and into Belgium and Holland, the Soviets on the gates of Warsaw, the end of the war in Europe was in sight. The German surface fleet had largely been sunk, only *Tirpitz* in Norway remaining a threat.

In the Pacific, the Japanese had been decisively defeated in the Leyte engagement and the resultant encounters at Tarakan and Phuket had weakened them further. Their fleet consisted of no more than 2-3 carriers and a couple of cruisers. With this in mind, the need for heavy surface ships was much lessened. Currently building were:

13 *Essex Class* CV's(one more ordered)
3 *Midway Class* CV's(one more ordered)
1 *Iowa Class* BB
9 *Baltimore Class* CA's
4 *Oregon City Class* CA's(6 more ordered)
11 *Cleveland Class* CL's
1 *Oakland Class* CLAA
8 *Fargo Class* CL's(5 more ordered)

It was resolved that all ships not laid down were to be cancelled. The navy was keen to look at laying down examples of the new *Worcester Class* light cruiser, who's design was finalised and the new *Des Moines Class* heavy cruiser, which was nearing a completion of design work. Two and four respectively would be authorized and all five of the six would be laid down 1945, with one in early 1946

Accordingly, it was also decided to cancel two *Cleveland Class*, two *Fargo Class* and two *Oregon City Class* cruisers that had all been laid down only within the last three and a half months and scrap them. The extra manpower and resources could be used towards completing the ships on the slips and more submarines and escorts.

0908 19 October 1944

With operations on Leyte progressing very well, Kreuger had conducted his second amphibious landing, this time on Mindoro. Mindoro was only lightly occupied by the Japanese Army, and much of it was held by Filipino guerrillas, so he hoped it would be quickly overrun. Besides being close to Luzon, Mindoro has another advantage: good flying weather nearly all the time, this being a part of the Philippines that was relatively dry – quite unlike Leyte which often received torrential rains for most of the year, not only giving it poor flying weather, but making it very muddy and difficult to construct airfields.

1116 26 October 1944

General Kenji Doihara had written off the forces trapped in Southern Thailand and Burma and had instead concentrated in building a defensive line to protect Malaya and, more importantly, Singapore. The 22,000 troops trapped in a thin pocket of land near Victoria Point were beyond any assistance but he had made sure that all likely points of entry into the much better defended Malaya peninsula were garrisoned and defended well. He had formed a new defence line based on the city of Songkhla that utilized both the narrow peninsula at that point and the lakes near the city.

He had received numerous pleas from assistance both from his own staff and the cut off forces. He was aware that he was not a popular man, even in the Japanese army, after some of his more questionable activities in Manchuria, where he had been the unofficial kingpin of both the drug and prostitution trades. How he wished he was back there, in its quiet, backwater rear areas. In any case, with a lack of air superiority and no naval assets to evacuate the men, it was the only practical decision.

1645 26 October 1944

Lt General Leslie Morshead had been satisfied with the progress after two days. 2nd Division and three Independent Companies had gone ashore yesterday at Brunei at three separate locations in the bay after two days naval bombardment and "softening up". There had been little left in the once important port, only two transports, a tanker, a frigate and two small minesweepers being sunk. His troops had already established a two-mile-deep penetration in some areas and casualties were moderate only.

With the battle at Tarakan now finished, the island being captured at a cost of 400 dead and 900 wounded, it was hoped to switch those forces to Borneo itself and eventually link up, sealing off the Northern part of the island.

Front lines 26 October 1944 Burma/Thailand

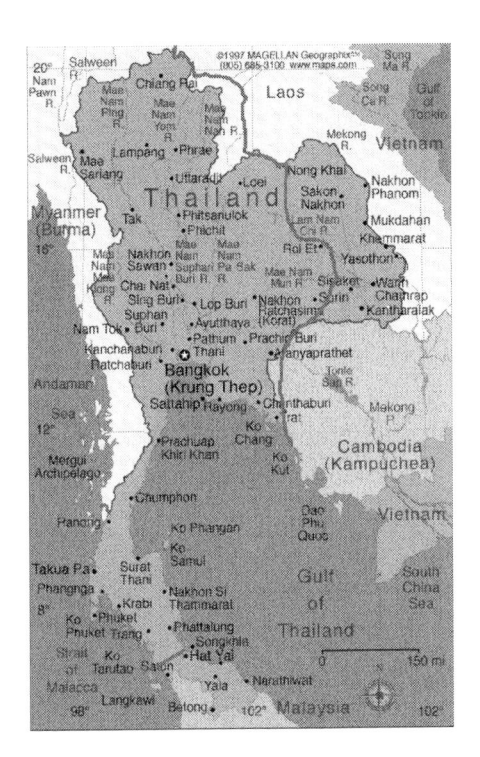

1414 2 November 1944

General Curtis LeMay had just taken over command of strategic bomber operation and had come rapidly to a conclusion that had not been reached by his predecessor, Brigadier General Haywood Hansell. Whilst the B29's had certainly interrupted Japanese shipyard and aircraft production with their raids on factories, it had not achieved the results that had been hoped for.

At veteran of the 8th Air Force, LeMay had seen firsthand what area bombing could do and the results of the two raids conducted on cities, on Tokyo by B-29's from 24th September to 3rd October and from Australasian He 200's on Sapporo from 25th September to 2nd October. He now had even greater numbers of aircraft and would spend the next week drawing up potential targets. He now had large stocks of M69 incendiary cluster bombs and it was with these he would carry the fight to the Japanese on a more personal level. By 15th November, LeMay was ready to conduct an all-out air offensive upon Japanese cities.

1446 18 November 1944

With the campaign in Borneo now gathering momentum and the Northern part of the island secure, Morshead's forces had made two more landings in three days on Borneo, with the 3rd Division landing at Balikpapan to secure the oil refineries on the 15th and the second at Kutching, the capital of Sarawak. Resistance had been heavy at Balikpapan, with over 350 casualties during the landing but a large beachhead had now been secured. 7th

Division had landed at Kuching to very light resistance. He now had four Divisions and over 80,000 men on Borneo and expected a hopefully speedy resolution to the campaign.

0809 21 November 1944

Kreuger's next operation, a major landing on Luzon had started this morning. The landings, on the south shore of Lingayen Gulf on the western coast of Luzon, had started well. Almost 175,000 men were to follow across the twenty-mile beachhead within a few days. With heavy air support, it was planned to push inland, with the first objective being the taking of Clark Field, some 40 miles northwest of Manila. Japanese naval forces had not contested any of the landings beyond the titanic battle at the commencement. Their air units also seemed spent. Only the infantry was fighting with their usual fanaticism.

1506 24 November 1944

Slim's forces had finally ground down and eliminated the trapped Japanese forces at Victoria Point. Much like Rangoon, they had fought to the last. Only 515 prisoners had been taken from an estimated 22,000 plus enemy troops. Even with complete air and naval support, it had cost 3,224 dead and 6,573 wounded, a very stiff price.

He could now take some time to re-orientate and redeploy his forces to Southern Thailand. In January he would start a push for Malaya with the ultimate objective, Singapore. Capture of Butterworth and Kota Bahru in Northern Malaya would give him airfields to hit Singapore with tactical aircraft.

1414 28 November 1944

Admiral Onoshi read the report with satisfaction. The "Special Attack Units" training in Formosa had been completed, with the other units near Kagoshima and Osaka due to finish within the week. It was a hard fate on the men involved, but with no ships left and a dwindling stock of experienced pilots this was the only option. One aircraft, one ship. That was still a ratio that Japan could still afford. Conventional methods had failed dismally. This seemed the only way forward, the only way to give their enemies pause. Fuel would also soon become an issue. Kamikaze operations would go much easier on the limited stocks available.

1203 30 November 1944

Chiang Kai-shek had started withdrawing his forces from Thailand, with many units freed up after the fall of Victoria Point. He would not be committing his own troops to the recapture of Malaya. He still had troops in North-eastern Thailand although he would be replacing many of the front-line units with second line units now that his limited offensive in conjunction with Thai and British troops to straighten the line in the North East was drawing to a close. 85% of Thailand had been recaptured and some progress had been made in Western Indo China. Although the Thai's were naturally keen to push on, the troops were close to exhaustion and casualties had been heavy.

His next offensives, scheduled for February 1945, would all be in China, where he hoped to recapture some of the territory lost in 1944 and hopefully push on to open a up a port. The communists would also get some of his attention. The Thai's would have to be happy with controlling most of the country. It was more than could be said for China.

0214 14 December 1944

General Kreuger's troops had pushed into the Northern suburbs of Manila. So far operations were ahead of the predicted schedule. Clark Field had been retaken on the 8th and Japanese resistance, whilst fierce, had been hampered by a lack of any effective air defence and a shortage of supplies and heavy weapons. He knew the campaigns would have months to run as yet, the jungles, mountains and large land mass making the retaking of more remote areas a lengthy proposition.

0909 25 December 1944

As the technicians from the ABC set up, Queen Alice went over the final text of her speech. Despite the cost in human lives, which had been appalling, it could only be judged a good year for the country. The tide had finally, hopefully irrevocably, turned. Everywhere the enemy was in retreat and whilst, like a wounded animal they could be dangerous, as the Ardennes operation showed, they seemed increasingly punch drunk. In the Pacific, the Japanese were being pushed back in Thailand and probably soon, Malaya by the British. By her own forces in Borneo. By U.S forces in the Philippines, where a terrific struggle was going on for possession of Manila.

For the first time, as Ben Chifley had coined the phrase, we could see the light on the hill. She went back to her speech. After it was finished, she could briefly at least join her own family in celebration of Christmas.

"I hope and pray that the coming year will see the story of liberation and Allied triumph completed. Some of the beacons of freedom which the Germans and Japanese had put out all over the world are being rekindled and are beginning to shine through the fog of war. I count it a high privilege to be able to use these moments to send a Christmas message of good will to men and women of whatever creed and colour who may be listening to me throughout Australasia and overseas-on the battlefields, on the high seas, or in foreign lands. At this Christmas time we think proudly and gratefully of our fighting men and women wherever they may be. May God bless and protect them and bring them victory.

Our message goes to all who are wounded or sick in hospital and to the doctors and nurses in their labour of mercy. And our thoughts and prayers are also with our men who are prisoners of war, and with their relatives in their loneliness and anxiety. To children everywhere we wish all the happiness that Christmas can bring. Among the deepest sorrows I have felt in these years of strife, the one I feel most is the grief of separation. Families rent apart by the call of service, people sundered from people by the calamities that have overcome some, while others have been free to continue to fight. I have rejoiced in the victories of this year, not least because they have broken down some of the barriers between us and our friends and brought us nearer to the time when we can all be together again with those we love.

For the moment, we have a foretaste of that joy and we enter into the fellowship of Christmas Day. On this day, more perhaps than at any other season of the year, we long for a new birth of freedom and order among all nations, so that happiness and amity may prevail and the scourge of war may be banished from our midst. Yet, though human ingenuity can show us no short cuts to the very heart of the Christmas message the goal is still before us and I for one believe that these years of sacrifice and sorrow have brought us nearer to it. We do not know what awaits us when we open the door of 1945, but if we look to those earlier Christmas days of the war, we can surely say that the darkness daily grows less and less. Already it is giving way to confidence, and let us hope before next Christmas Day, God willing, the story of liberation and triumph will be complete.

We have shared many dangers and the common effort has bound us together. Yet labour and devotion, patience and tolerance will still be needed for the experiment of living as nations in harmony. The defeat of Germany and Japan is only the first half of our task. The second is to create a world of free men, untouched by tyranny. We have great Allies in this arduous enterprise of the human spirit-man's unconquerable mind and freedom's holy flame. In the meantime, in the old words that never lose their force, as your Queen I wish you from my heart a happy Christmas and for the coming year a full measure of that courage, faith and lastly, happiness."

Map 25 December 1944

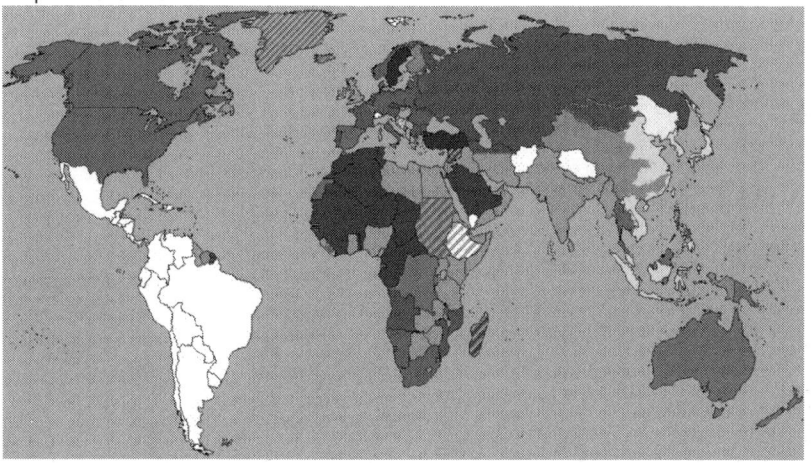

0608 26 December 1944

As the year drew to a close Admiral Onoshi's "Special Attack Units" were ready. Japan had no hope of retaining the Philippines and the lack of airfields there and the possibility of destruction on the ground rendered their use moot. He had stockpiled both aircraft and volunteers in both Formosa and Japan, with a small amount at Singapore. When the Americans and their running dog allies made their next move, he would be ready.

0705 27 December 1944

The new fighter looked sleek and deadly though Captain Edwards Pulsudski. It would prove a good delayed Christmas present for his squadron, based in San Francisco but shipping out soon to Luzon had been the first to be equipped with them. They were likely going to be a vast improvement from the A-20's that they currently fielded. They had called the new aircraft the Grumman F-7F Tigercat.

1415 28 December 1944

Admiral of the Fleet Osami Nagano had attended the commissioning ceremony, with four new ships freshly commissioned into the navy. It had all been a massive public relations exercise that had seen the fleet carrier, the light cruiser and the two new destroyers commission on the same day.

What was not widely known was that on the day that these units commissioned, laying down of further seagoing ships was discontinued. Only two *Atkizuke Class* destroyers were still building as well as 19 *Matsu Class* escorts. Damage to the yards and a shortage of steel may well see not even these completed. Since Leyte he had lost a seaplane carrier and a destroyer to one torpedo attack in November, two destroyers attempting to evacuate the Andaman Islands to Royal Navy destroyers and another off Yokosuka to a submarine that his forces had succeeded in sinking, plus a new small escort carrier and a destroyer just over a week ago.

His active "fleet" now consisted of fleet carriers *Taiho* and *Kasagi*, heavy cruiser *Ibuki*, light cruisers *Sakawa*, *Aktizuki Class* destroyers *Hanazuki, Haratsuki, Suzutsuki, Niizuki* and *Fuyutsuki*, *Yagumo Class* destroyers *Suzunami, Hayashimo* and *Kishinami*, destroyers *Yukikaze, Shigure, Asagiri* and the ancient *Tanikaze*, sixteen ships in all. The disastrous losses of 1944 had been suppressed and the general public knew nothing of them.

1645 1 January 1945

It had taken 5 days of bitter fighting but the landing on Corregidor by airborne and amphibious forces had finally seen the fortress taken after a series of intense battles that often came down to hand to hand fighting and the individual, casual, heroism of the men involved. It had provided a New Year propaganda coup for the newsmen as well, the symbolism being a role reversal from 1942.

With the battle for Manila getting ever bloodier and still raging Kreuger could use all the good news he could get. On 8th January he would be landing forces on Palawan, a strategically important chain but supposedly only held lightly by the enemy. It would be proceeded by a large naval effort by Nimitz's forces centred on the island of Iwo Jima commencing on the 6th, the same date that Slim's Malaya offensive was due to kick off.

2113 5 January 1945

Prime Minister Bela Miklos had negotiated safe passage out of besieged Budapest, where Hungarian and German forces battled to hold the city and break the surrounding Soviet and Romanian forces. He had been promised safe transit via Soviet lines and his eventual destination was Moscow.

Hungary was Germany's last remaining ally, but he hoped that this would be a state that lasted only a short time. When he got to Moscow, he would be asking for an armistice if the conditions offered were anything like bearable.

0630 6 January 1945

It was daylight and the start of one of the most intensive naval bombardments and air bombardments ever seen had started 35 minutes ago. A massive assembly off ships had arrived of the island of Iwo Jima, the biggest ever seen.

It would be the foretaste of a long and bitter struggle, the island's Japanese commander, Lieutenant General Tadamichi Kuribayashi, had his men construct a huge series of fortified bunkers and tunnels to support his defensive preparations since mid-1944. He had stated that he was prepared to fight to the last man. The next month would prove him to be bitterly correct.

0555 7 January 1945

Slim's offensive had been delayed a day by the need to bring forward some final units to the start line. At 0550 he had started a large artillery barrage that had been supported by the battleships and cruisers of the Eastern Fleet off the West Coast in some areas. He had six fresh, fully equipped divisions to press the attack with in what he hoped would be a reverse of 1942. Yesterday his air units had attacked and strafed many Japanese airfields and heavy bombers from Darwin had struck the Singapore airfields at night five times in the last two weeks.

1212 10 January 1945

It had taken almost four weeks of intensive fighting but Manila had finally been captured. The battle had quickly come down to a series of bitter street-to-street and house-to-house struggles that had resulted in gains being couched in terms of street, rather than suburbs, captured. Large areas of the city had been levelled, with the older Spanish style building being largely razed to the ground and never rebuilt. The battle left 987 U.S dead and 4.867 wounded. An estimated 85,000 Filipinos civilians were killed, both deliberately by the Japanese and from artillery and aerial bombardment by American forces. Over 20,000 Japanese dead were estimated.

Kreuger's forces had suffered badly during the campaign, with many men scarred by images they would never forget. His forces had landed on Palawan yesterday and he was eating up the ground held by the Japanese in the islands with every passing day. Only Mindanao was still held by the Japanese of the large islands in the chain. It was scheduled for Mid-February. For now, he needed to make Luzon free of Japanese forces.

1435 10 January 1945

Admiral Onoshi walked away from the meeting happy. Although further away than was desirable, he had agreement to conduct an initial series of attacks on the 12th and was authorized to expend fully 900 aircraft in the first up trial attacks. With success, more would come.

1706 11 January 1945

After four days of relentless attacks by troops, armour, aerial, naval and artillery bombardment, General William Slim's 5th Army Group had broken through the Japanese lines at two points, both North and South of the town of Hat Yai. He had poured units into the gap and was exploiting it despite fierce enemy resistance. So far, he had cut off 2,000 Japanese in the town and this was not the only front where his troops were on the verge of a significant victory. To the South the Japanese troops North of Satun had suffered a major buckle in their line and his forces had started to penetrate the Northern suburbs of the city, the last in Thailand before crossing over to Malaya.

2113 11 January 1945

Admiral of the Fleet Osami Nagano had decided against committing the fleet, or what remained of it, to operations over Iwo Jima. He would wait a little longer and see where the Americans struck next. If must surely be Okinawa, the Ryukyus' or Formosa. In either case, he would release the rest of the fleet. He did not have enough pilots to man both carriers, however, Onishi was keen to convert one ship to a launching platform for the new Okha flying bombs. Two attempts to transport them to the Philippines had both failed, resulting in the sinking of an escort carrier and a seaplane carrier. Nagano though the man was mad, a chronic waste for an untried weapon, a weapon that brought him some distaste. None the less, Onoshi had a great deal of influence, arguing, what use is a carrier without weapons. In that sense, at least, he had a point.

2314 15 January 1945

Admiral William "Bull" Halsey sat in his cabin and contemplated the last three days events. Masses attacks by Japanese aircraft had been the order of the day. In many cases obsolete types, escorted by fighters. They had fought their way through to the Task Force and commenced deliberately diving their aircraft into his ships.

It was a new, horrifying version of war. It had occasionally happened in the past when a wounded pilot of plane had decided to "take some of them with him", but never, obviously, systematically, such as had occurred over Iwo Jima. He had taken some measures to counteract, pushing bigger numbers of fighters onto CAP and spreading out radar equipped destroyers from the task force for earlier detection as well as roving CAP flights further to the North and North East.

It had been a costly three days that had resulted in the loss of the escort carrier *Kitkun Bay*, which had exploded when hit, two modern destroyers and the old destroyer minesweeper *Ruebens*. Damaged had been the Intrepid, battleship *New Mexico*, cruiser *Salt Lake City* and four destroyers. A transport had been sunk and two LST's had also been sunk, although one of those was by submarine.

1916 20 January 1945

Hungary had surrendered, as had Slovakia. Germany had no allies and the Soviet offensive on the Vistula was gathering momentum. East Prussia had been overrun as had most of Poland. Only cut off pockets remained in Konigsberg, Danzig and Memel. General Gotthard Heinrici had been brought forward to command the East, now that Hitler's "loyal Heinrich" had reported sick and confined himself to a sanatorium.

How typical that when the fat fell in the fire, they called for him, though Heinrici. All he could do was attack their flanks and hope to slow them down. Logistics may then eventually work in his favour. He remained unaware that on this day the first of the concentration camps had been liberated, the sights seen shocking even battle-hardened Red Army veterans.

1208 21 January 1945

Slim's forces had won a decisive battle at Jitra, capturing the first Northern Malay city and sundering the Japanese line. His forces were pushing forward to exploit the advantage they had gained. On the East coast progress had been slower, but his forces were assaulting the last Thai city, Yali and were within 35 miles of the border and Khota Bharu and its important airfield.

0616 31 January 1945

General Stilwell has prepared the plans for the offensive for months in conjunction with Chinese officers. He had stockpiled the better equipped divisions with US advisors and communications and the six Divisions from Burma, lavishly equipped with the best and newest equipment had been added to his order of battle. Over ten divisions were in reserve, six equipped with the latest equipment. He had 42 divisions committed to the attack, near to a million men and 1,800 guns.

1436 7 February 1945

The battle for Iwo Jima was finally over. As advertised, Tadamichi Kuribayachi's men had fought to the last. Over 19,000 had been killed, only 200 or so taken prisoner. Although all ground had been taken and the island declared secure, over 2,000 Japanese actually were still alive in the maze of tunnels and caves and would gradually emerge to be killed or surrender over the next year. This four-week battle comprised some of the fiercest and bloodiest fighting of the war. The Japanese positions on the island had been heavily fortified and, in many cases, immune to bombardment.

Iwo Jima was the only battle by the Marines in which the overall American casualties (killed and wounded) exceeded those of the Japanese, although Japanese combat deaths were thrice those of the Americans throughout the battle. U.S casualties were 6,214 killed and 17,345 wounded. The battle was immortalized by the photograph of the raising of the US flag on top of the 545-foot Mount Surabachi.

U.S forces were one step closer to Japan, with only one more landing being planned, Okinawa, thought Nimitz. It was just as well, as the new Japanese Kamikaze tactics had taken some getting used to. They had expended 2,200 aircraft, sinking an escort carrier and damaging another, damaging two fleet carriers, a battleship and two light cruisers, sinking three destroyers and damaging eight others, as well as sinking two merchant ships and an LST and damaging four more LST's. Naval casualties had been almost 868 killed and over 2,000 wounded. It had been an unpleasant new surprise that went a long way to explaining just how desperate the Japanese had become.

1807 11 February 1945

Lt General Morshead's Borneo campaign was now three months in and was still continuing. His forces had pushed on and secured the Northern part of the huge island completely, compressing the remaining Japanese forces into the Southern fifth of the island. Casualties had been 1,612 killed and 3,456 wounded with an estimated 14,000 Japanese killed. He had re-orientated his forces, with his latest offensive gathering momentum in a move he that was only 15 miles from cutting the Japanese forces in two and surrounding the city of Pontianak. After reducing this pocket, he could concentrate on the remnants of the Japanese forces trapped in the South centred on Banjarmasin.

1653 14 February 1945

General Kenji Doihara's forces were in full retreat, and as Captain Wilhelm von Prilowitz of the Kriegsmarine looked behind, he could see the large cloud of greasy black smoke from the oil storage tanks from the joint Japanese/German submarine base at Penang. Like all naval staff, he had been meant to be evacuated by ship, but his ride and most of the vessels in the harbour had been sunk by RN carrier aircraft. He now found himself traveling South on the jammed road, ironically in an old Mercedes staff car, fleeing South like most of the Japanese troops.

He would be going South to Singapore, unlike most of the troops who he had discovered hoped to form an improvised defence line at Kuala Kangsar 50 miles further South. With monsoons on the West Coast not expected before early April, they had to hold until then.

0543 15 February 1945

From the lofty bridge of *HMS King George V*, Admiral Sir Bruce Fraser monitored the preparations for Operation Rapier. It was a huge force, fleet carriers *Illustrious, Indomitable, Victorious, Indefatigable* and *Unicorn*, battleships *King George V, Howe, Renown* and *Richelieu* plus cruisers and escorts from the RN. Carriers *Sydney, Australasia, Melbourne, Christchurch* and battleship *Pacifica* from the RAN plus their escorts.

Two years ago, or even 12 months it would have been unthinkable in the face of Japanese air power, but now he planned to launch over 250 aircraft at Singapore, its naval dockyard, its ships and its airfields.

0555 15 February 1945

As dawn approached the carrier steamed serenely onward, unaware of her danger. *USS Tautog*, under Commander Thomas Baskett, had picked up the contact at 0234 and had raced to stay ahead, attain position and dive. He now watched the fruits of his labour as four solid hits impacted on the carrier. As a bonus, the fifth torpedo went ahead and exploded in the stern of the escorting destroyer. Over the next 48 minutes, he had the pleasure of watching both go under. *IJN Kasagi*, returning from an aircraft ferry mission to Formosa, would never carry the Okha flying bombs that were being designed for her.

1539 15 February 1945

It had been the first time that a P-43 had landed on a fleet carrier, but the RAAF pilot seemed unfazed by the task and the reconnaissance P-43 had brought back photographs that Admiral Fraser had been very keen to obtain.

They showed a scene of chaos at the docks and at least ten merchant ships of some size sunk, in addition to smaller vessels. Also clearly sunk were at least three destroyers or escorts, two being upside down, on at a pier. His staff had counted at least 50 destroyed aircraft on the Singapore airfields. Another 40-45 had been shot down by his own CAP whilst attacking the fleet, although he had taken a hit, *HMS Unicorn* taking a torpedo that killed 12 men and lamed the light carrier. Overall, however, it had to be called a success. The navy's support had been instrumental in the rapid advance of British forces on the West Coast.

1809 17 February 1945

Admiral of the Fleet Osami Nagano walked away from the Imperial Command conference a troubled man. The Americans had invaded the island of Okinawa with a huge fleet yesterday. There was little realistic hope the defenders could defeat them. It was just a matter of time and totals. Time it would take to subdue the island and totals of those killed.

As if that was not bad enough, the Emperor had asked the navy if they could not relieve or attempt to assist those on the island. What pitiful remnants remained of the fleet, just the carrier *Taiho*, heavy cruiser *Ibuki*, light cruiser *Sakawa* and a few destroyers were to be committed, purposelessly and to their deaths.

The war was over, he failed to see how they could not grasp it. It required a political, not a military solution, now. The country was starting to show the first signs of food shortages. Before the war it had been postulated 6 million tons of merchant shipping was needed to sustain a war. Two million was required to import and feed Japan adequately. They had commenced the war with 6.4 million tons. Now no new merchant ships, like no new warships were being laid. Japan's shipyards and shipbuilding industry was at a halt. Only some ships near completion were being attempted to be finished. In 1944 alone an incredible 2.7 million tons of shipping had been lost. Less than 1.9 million tons remained and food was not all that was transported on that tonnage.

Plus the firebombing of Japans cities was shocking. Twenty-nine cities had so far been firebombed, including Tokyo. Some more than once. He had no doubt more would follow. Onoshi had at least gotten his way. Massed Kamikaze attacks would follow over the next few days. Some would involve the new Okha flying bomb.

1802 21 February 1945

Rear Admiral Kokura had the task of leading the "intervention" force to Okinawa in what would constitute the IJN's last sortie of World War 2. His forces consisted of Fleet carrier *Taiho* (14 A7M, 36 A6M, 20 D4Y), heavy cruiser *Ibuki*, light cruiser *Sakawa*, Aktizuki Class destroyers *Hanazuki*, *Yiozuki*, *Suzutsuki*, *Niizuki* and *Fuyutsuki*, Yagumo Class destroyers *Suzunami*, *Hayashimo* and *Kishinami*, and the ancient *Tanikaze*, twelve ships in all. It was all the fleet units left to Japan, the few destroyers at Singapore having been sunk recently.

What chance they had against hundreds he could not conceive. At least, unlike far Southern Force, his ships were modern. Perhaps like Far Southern Forces lucky survivor, *Tanikaze*, he would somehow make it back. His appearance tomorrow was designed to be masked by the first mass application of Kamikazes at Okinawa.

2012 21 February 1945

Stillwell's offensive was grinding forward, opposition from the Japanese being strong indeed. None the less, nearly all the ground lost in last year's Ichi-Go offensive by Japan had been recaptured and whatever losses he was taking were being more than matched by the enemy. Although that would eventually cause his attack to peter out, he had only thrown the last of his fresh formations into the attack yesterday, so there was still ground to be gained. His tank units, using M4 Sherman's, had been particularly effective. Much of Hunan and Guangxi had been retaken and his eventual aim, Canton was very much still a possibility. Its possession would open up a port in mainland China, a port that could now be exploited with the Japanese Navy seemingly prostrate.

23 March 1952(flash forward)

Admiral John Collins had reached a final decision on the proposals in regards to rank standardisation within the defence forces. He had come to the conclusion that overall it represented a good idea and whilst it would require a departure from standard British rank it was not drastic and would help to better integrate the services for combined operations and the like, plus make simple tasks like pay easier to reconcile. The proposed new ranks were:

Army / Navy / Air Force
O11 Field Marshal / Admiral of the Fleet / Marshal of the RAAF
O10 General / Admiral / Air Chief Marshal
O9 Lieutenant General / Vice Admiral / Air Marshall
O8 Major General / Rear Admiral / Air Vice Marshall
O7 Brigadier / Commodore / Air Commodore
O6 Colonel / Captain / Group Captain
O5 Lieutenant Colonel / Commander / Wing Commander
O4 Major / Lieutenant Commander / Squadron Leader
O3 Captain / Lieutenant / Flight Lieutenant
O2 Lieutenant / Sub Lieutenant / Flying Officer
O1 2nd Lieutenant / Ensign / Pilot Officer

C2 Officer Cadet / Midshipman / Officer Cadet
C1 Officer Candidate / Officer Candidate / Officer Candidate

E9 Warrant Officer / Warrant Officer / Warrant Officer
E8 Sergeant Major / Master Chief Petty Officer / Sergeant Major
E7 Staff Sergeant / Chief Petty Officer / Flight Sergeant
E6 Sergeant / Petty Officer / Sergeant
E5 Corporal / Master Seaman / Corporal
E4 Lance Corporal / Leading Seaman / Lance Corporal

E3 Private First Class/ Able Seaman/ Leading Aircraftsman
E2 Private / Seaman / Aircraftsman
E1 Private Recruit / Seaman Recruit / Aircraftsman Recruit

Very little in the way of changes of rank badge would need to be made. O 11 would normally be only a ceremonial rank, only Blamey had ever been promoted to it. He would, of course, ultimately need both the Minister, the Government and the Queen's approval, but as the uniformed Chief of the Defence staff, he believed it in the best interests.

Borneo Map 22 February 1945

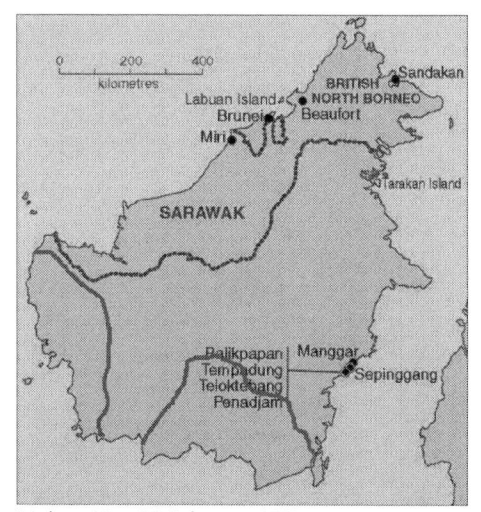

Malaya Map 22 February 1945

0947 22 February 1945

What had surprised Admiral Halsey so far had been the muted Japanese response to the

Okinawa invasion. Just a handful of 20-30 aircraft each day since the landing making conventional attacks. Iwo Jima had certainly taught the U.S Navy that every effort must be made to provide an integrated defence network against the potential menace of Kamikazes and the lessons learned had been implemented at Okinawa.

Radar picket destroyers, much larger CAP, battleships integrated into carrier task forces, heavier AA, proximity fuses, he even had two damaged ships and one broken down LST moored to the North as "tethered goats" to absorb attacks. Yet for all these measures, it was hard to protect both his men and his ships against opponents prepared to kill themselves.

He had been scarcely surprised when full scale attacks had started at first light this morning. So far, he had escaped major damage, only one destroyer being hit, although that had been badly. What had surprised him was the sighting report from an Avenger that had gone off the air soon after delivering it. A hostile carrier, plus a battleship, a cruiser and nine destroyers, 140 miles to the North. He immediately ordered a strike launched.

1001 22 February 1945

Rear Admiral Kokura's A7M's had downed the US intruder, but he had no doubt that his position had been reported. He had gotten off his strike, 20 D4Y's escorted by 20 A6M's. That left only his fighters from fleet defence, A7M's and A6M's. He had no doubt they would see action soon enough. He had resumed course South to Okinawa towards what he assumed with be ascension.

1112 22 February 1945

Halsey had gotten off his strike but had still been subject to relentless attacks. He had seen off another group of 80 or so Kamikazes as well as a conventional strike by D4Y's, possibly from the Japanese carriers. Another picket destroyer had been hit badly, a second less so. Plus, the battleship *North Carolina* had taken a hit but had shrugged it off her heavy armour. The light cruiser *Birmingham* had been less fortunate and he was witness to her burning fiercely a mile away. Radar had picked up another heavy Jap formation almost 50 miles out.

1135 22 February 1945

Ensign Kenzi Hamira sat jammed into the confined space of the flying bomb. If he had any second thoughts, it was too late now. The twenty-five G4M "Bettys" trailed 30 miles behind the huge cloud of Kamikaze aircraft, 108 in total, with 28 A6M's escorts. His own force had six fighters as escort. It was hoped the new weapon would inflict heavy casualties on the Americans, provoking a response and a willingness to come to terms. Either way, Kenzi Hamira would not get to know about that.

1146 22 February 1945

As he looked over at the fireball that was *USS Shangri-La* it remained obvious that the Japanese had hit them with a new weapon, aircraft launched flying bombs. The carriers had been hit hard, with *USS Saratoga* being hit as well, although in that instance the plane had come in shallow and mainly skidded across the flight deck. A destroyer had also been hit. Thankfully the flying bombs appeared to be poor maneuverers as many ships had avoided them with evasive manoeuvres at the last minute but *Shangri-La* had taken two hits that had started an inferno. Newly arrived only a few weeks ago, she was in large trouble already. That Japanese had lost over 250 aircraft so far today, which made him wonder how long they could keep this up.

1158 22 February 1945

Rear Admiral Kokura's force had taken the brunt of the massive US strike, actually two 110-120 aircraft strikes that joined together on their way to the target. When it finally arrived, it had consisted of 98 Helldivers, 94 Avengers and 45 Hellcats. The defending 14 A7M's and 16 A6M's tried their best and were piloted by experienced pilots, but they could only shoot down two Avengers and nine Hellcats for the loss of 15 A6M's and 11 A7M's. AA shot down two Avengers, a Hellcat and two Helldivers. Sadly, it left over 180 attacking aircraft.

By the time they broke off at 1154, the left little behind them that resembled a fleet. *Taiho* had been the prime initial target. Hit five times by torpedoes, all to starboard, she had capsized. Light cruiser *Sakawa* had also been targeted by the torpedo bombers, who hit her four times and sunk her rapidly. Destroyer *Hayashimo* had gone the same way.

The dive bombers had hit *Ibuki* nine times with 1000lb bombs, leaving her on fire and sinking. Two hits to *Niizuki* had left her sinking, as had two to *Hanazuki*. Another hit to the destroyer *Kishinami* in the engine room had brought her to a stop and the U.S fighters had taken out their frustrations on her leaving her immobile and crippled. Only five destroyers remained.

Rear Admiral Kokura had gone down with *Taiho*. The remaining four fighters, along with the two surviving planes from Kokura's strike had to ditch, with nowhere to land. The Imperial Japanese Navy had gone down with a fight, but on 22nd February 1945, it had ceased to exist as a seagoing strike force.

1708 22 February 1945

It had been a huge day for attacks, with Halsey's staff counting over 600 Japanese aircraft destroyed for the loss of 29 U.S aircraft, not counting those lost aboard *Shangri-La*. He had been unable to keep the further attacks off the ships, her plume of smoke, visible from 40 miles acting like a carcass for flies. She had probably been finished before, but a strike by two A6M's had added fuel to the fire. Thankfully the plume of smoke and fire had kept the pressure of his other ships and only one more destroyer had been "clipped" and lightly damaged.

He had launched another 90 plane strike at the fleeing Japanese destroyers that remained, all strike aircraft, but the little ships had proven nimble and only two more had been sunk, with another damaged. For Halsey and the Okinawa fleet, it was the foretaste of a daily struggle, although 22 February remained by the far the largest and bloodiest attack, although two other days of the campaign were to witness mass attacks as well.

0712 23 February 1945

Captain Kento Dohara looked over what had returned from Okinawa. *Aktizuki Class* destroyers *Yiozuki* and *Suzutsuki*, the second heavily damaged by a bomb hit, plus the old *Tanikaze*, which seemingly led a charmed life. The Imperial Japanese Navy had exactly one *Atkizuke Class* destroyer still building. For all intents and purposes, it had ceased to exist.

Although Dohara did not know it, the successful arrival of a convoy on 2nd February three weeks ago would represent the last of Japan's East India oil and had effectively ended the chance for future fleet operations anyway. However, it was hard not to argue that 2,000 men had been killed needlessly.

1546 2 March 1945

It had taken a month and a half, but Palawan Island was finally secured. The last major landing in the Philippines, on Mindanao, had occurred on the 25th February 1945. All of the large islands of the Philippines had been secured except isolated small islands and Mindanao, excluding hold outs, most of whom were located in the strategically unimportant mountains of Luzon.

Some further lightly held islands in the Sulu Sea were to be invaded over the next two months, but these were very much sideshows. 75 to 80% of the Japanese in the Philippines had been killed, captured or expelled. With Okinawa continuing to slog onwards, with a bitter price in blood being paid, Kreuger would be glad to see the end of this damn war.

2019 7 March 1945

General Omar Bradley could hardly believe the reports. The one great tactical question left on the Western Front was how to get a foothold over the Rhine. Incredibly, First Army found an intact bridge across the Rhine at Remagen. It crossed the river in force quickly and was now well established on the East Bank. The gateway to the heartland of Germany and indeed the end of the war in Europe was in sight. With the Russians paused along the Oder-Neisse line, it was now a race to get to Berlin.

1617 12 March 1945

General Slim's army was pushing ever Southwards, although logistics had become difficult. Since capturing the Northern Malaya airfields, he had achieved total air superiority and the navy had kept the pressure on the Japanese, not allowing resupply by sea into Singapore in most cases. The monsoon was not far away at all, perhaps only a week. He had decided to take a break and reorganize when it hit, but wanted to push on and capture Kuala Lumpur and Kuantan before that occurred. Currently he was not more than eight miles from either. The campaign for Johore and Singapore could resume in June after a two-month break in April-May.

1818 15 March 1945

Lt General Morshead's Borneo campaign was almost completed, perhaps only a week or so remained. He had trapped the remaining Japanese in a small pocket in Southwest

Borneo, not more than 10 miles deep and eight miles wide. His forces had already eliminated the pocket in the Southeast, killing over 14,000 enemy troops. This would represent the last act on a long campaign.

The air forces long range CAC 15 Cockatoos, now based in Southern Borneo, has swept Japanese fighters on Java from the skies. With the Philippines secured and Malaya falling, the end was surely near.

0715 22 March 1945

Lt General Morshead's four Divisions had finished operations in Borneo, the whole island being secured. It had been an expensive campaign, 3,256 killed and 7,147 wounded. Japanese casualties had been near to 25,000, if not higher.

With the islands secured and the British driving on Singapore, the Chinese driving the Japanese back in China, the allies were on the offensive everywhere. The war in Europe also seemed to be coming to an end. It was a possibility that this may be his last operation. In any case, he was due to rotate back to Australasia for rest and leave.

0909 2 April 1945

The monsoon had arrived almost like clockwork, thought Slim. Rain on the 30th had been followed by more on the 31st and torrential rain had been falling since that night. Yesterday had marked the last days of offensive operations. His troops could now rest and reequip. They had done a sterling job in pushing the Japanese back to the gates of Johore. Yesterday had cleared the city of Melacca. His forces had their foot firmly on the throat of the Japanese. Whilst a tow month break would only make his army stronger, his enemy seemed to be faltering.

Malaya Map 2 April 1945(new front line in green)

1543 4 April 1945

General Stilwell's offensive had been called off. It had not achieved its objective of Canton, but it had cleared the Japanese back to their pre Ichi-Go start lines in most cases. In a few areas they had gained ground. More importantly, they had shown that they could now drive the previously superior Japanese back. They would take a break, resupply and evaluate another offensive in June.

China front lines in red 4 April 1945

1246 14 April 1945

Prime Minister John Curtin rose to address the house. "I beg that an humble Address be presented to Her Majesty to convey to Her Majesty the deep sorrow with which this House has learned of the death of the President of the United States of America and to pray Her Majesty that in communicating his own sentiments of grief to the United States Government, she will also be graciously pleased to express on the part of this House their sense of the loss which the Australasia and Empire and the cause of the Allied Nations have sustained, and their profound sympathy with Mrs. Roosevelt and the late President's family and with the Government and people of the United States of America."

"My friendship with the great man to whose work and fame we pay our tribute to-day ripened during this war. I had met him, only in 1944 but immediately discerned a warm, engaging, generous man, confident of his position and abilities who maintained a personal charm it was impossible to ignore.

When the Pacific war broke out in all its hideous fury, when our own life and survival hung in the balance, I was already in a position to telegraph to the President on terms of an association which was to become most intimate and, to me, most agreeable. This continued through all the ups and downs of the world struggle until Tuesday last, when I received my last messages from him. These messages showed no falling off in his accustomed clear vision and vigour upon perplexing and complicated matters. Indeed, I shall always be grateful that the President sent a man of such sterling qualities as General Kreuger to us in 1942. I thoroughly enjoyed my time of staying with him at the White House or in his retreat in the Blue Mountains, which he called Shangri-La.

I conceived an admiration for him as a statesman, a man of affairs, and a war leader. I felt the utmost confidence in his upright, inspiring character and outlook and a personal regard-affection I must say-for him beyond my power to express to-day. His love of his own country, his respect for its constitution, his power of gauging the tides and currents of its mobile public opinion, were always evident, but, added to these, were a generous heart which was always stirred to anger and to action by spectacles of aggression and oppression by the strong against the weak. It is, indeed, a loss, a bitter loss to humanity that those heart-beats are stilled for ever. President Roosevelt's physical affliction lay heavily upon him. It was a marvel that he bore up against it through all the many years of tumult-and storm. Not one man in ten million, stricken and crippled as he was, would have attempted to plunge into a life of physical and mental exertion and of hard, ceaseless political controversy. In this extraordinary effort of the spirit over the flesh, the will-power over physical infirmity, he was inspired and sustained by his devoted wife, whose high ideals marched with his own, and to whom the deep and respectful sympathy of the House of Representatives flows out to-day in all fullness. There is no doubt that the President foresaw the great dangers closing in upon the pre-war world with far more prescience than most well-informed people on either side of the Atlantic and Pacific, and that he urged forward with all his power such precautionary military preparations as peace-time opinion in the United States could be brought to accept. There never was a moment's doubt, as the quarrel opened, upon which side his sympathies lay.

In 1941, in deep and dark and deadly secrecy, the Japanese were preparing their act of treachery and greed. Japan, Germany and Italy had declared war upon the United States and both our countries were in arms, shoulder to shoulder. Since then we have advanced over the land and over the sea through many difficulties and disappointments, but always with a broadening measure of success. I need not dwell upon the series of great operations which have taken place in the Pacific, to say nothing of that other immense war proceeding at the other side of the world. The extraordinary Lend Lease scheme, of which he was the architect, speaks volumes for the man.

Nothing altered his inflexible sense of duty. To the end he faced his innumerable tasks unflinching. One of the tasks of the President is to sign maybe a hundred or two hundred State papers with his own hand every day, commissions and so forth. All this he continued to carry out with the utmost strictness. When death came suddenly upon him, he had finished his mail. That portion of his day's work was done. He had brought his country through the worst of its perils and the heaviest of its toils. Victory had cast its sure and steady beam upon him. He had broadened and stabilised in the days of peace the foundations of American life and union.

In war he had raised the strength, might and glory of the great country to a height never attained by any nation in history. With her left hand she was leading the advance of the conquering Allied Armies into the heart of Germany and with her right, on the other side of the globe, she was irresistibly and swiftly breaking up the power of Japan. And all the time ships, munitions, supplies, and food of every kind were aiding on a gigantic scale her Allies, great and small, in the course of the long struggle.

But all this was no more than worldly power and grandeur, had it not been that the causes of human freedom and of social justice to which so much of his life had been given, added a lustre to all this power and pomp and warlike might, a lustre which will long be discernible among men. He has left behind him a band of resolute and able men handling the numerous interrelated parts of the vast American war machine. He has left a successor who comes forward with firm step and sure conviction to carry on the task to its appointed end. For us. it remains only to say that in Franklin Roosevelt there died the greatest American friend we have ever known and the greatest champion of freedom."

Roosevelt had died with victory in Europe seemingly within spitting distance. Life was an unfair master at times, though Curtin, who had begun to think about his own mortality.

1806 14 April 1945

Keith Park submitted his latest report to the aircraft review board. The RAAF was reducing its types, handing some lend lease machines back. He had attended Hencall demonstration with a jet powered prototype only last week. It had been a success and now he was working on a production design, already conducting wind tunnel tests for a suitable body shape. It wold be followed by tests of the He 200 with four jet engines, although this would require turbine manufacture, which had just started to be investigated and was not scheduled to start until July or August. The new He 200 was split between strategic bombing of Singapore and Japan, although the squadrons currently hitting Singapore would shortly be switched to Java. Numbers by type now read:

Fighters:
CAC 15 Cockatoo 278 (in production)
Curtis P40 271
Hencall He 100 686(Currently in limited production-numbers count RAN machines)
Hencall He 119 366(in production)

Bombers/Patrol:
Consolidated Catalina 88
Consolidated B24 Liberator 264
de Havilland Mosquito 188(in limited production)
Douglas A20 46(some ex Dutch East Indies)
Fairy Swordfish 74
Grumman Avenger 170
Hencall He 200 138(in production)
Hencall He 211 193
Lockheed Hudson 100
Lockheed Ventura 69
North American A36 169

Vickers Wellington 40
Vultee Vengeance 260

Transports:
Airspeed Oxford 244
Avro Anson 169(transport conversion)
Douglas C47 361(in production)
Hencall He 70 26

0908 15 April 1945

Vice Admiral John Augustine Collins days as an operational officer were numbered. He had been told that he would be taking over from Admiral Guy Royle as the uniformed head of the Australasian navy on 1 June 1945. Previously an operational admiral, his service would now be desk bound.

He reviewed the state of the navy:
BB *Pacifica*
CV *Australasia*
CVL *Christchurch*
CVE *Sydney(2), Melbourne(2), Brisbane(2)*{Landing ship carrier}, *Perth, Wellington*
CA: *Auckland, Dunedin*
CL: *Launceston, Hobart, Darwin, Hamilton*
DD(Tribal Class): *Wik, Wiri, Nasoqo, Kurnei, Alawa, Warramunga, Tagalag, Koko, Palawan, Maori*
DD(old): *Vampire, Valhalla, Stuart, Attack*
DD(*Clemson Class*) *Barnes, Albany, Newmarket*
Destroyer Escorts: *Waikato, Tamar, Clutha, Darling, Todd, Waimbula, Derwent, Hawkesbury*
Sloops: *Swan, Warrego*
Frigates: *Success, Stalwart, Swordsman*
Submarines: *Otway, Taipan, King Brown, Death Adder, Brown Snake, Copperhead, Tiger Snake, Black Snake, Dugite, Shortnose Snake, Whip Snake, Diamond Python*
Corvettes/Minesweepers: 51
Assault Ships: *Kanimbla, Manoora, Westralia*
Hospital ships: *Oranje, Wanganella, Manunda, Maunganui*
Sub Depot Ships: 2
PT Boat Depot Ships: 3
Oilers: 4
MTBS: 92

In addition, the navy had operational control over two Dutch AA cruisers and two submarines and two Portuguese destroyers and two sloops. It had been a long war, but it felt like it was coming to an end, although he had no doubt that with what the U.S navy was facing at Okinawa, an invasion of Japan would prove a costly and bloody affair, both for the RAN as well as land forces.

0558 16 April 1945

General Gotthard Heinrici prepared to fight what he knew full well would be the last battle of the eastern Front. It was a battle against hopeless odds. Although he controlled the dominating terrain of the Seelow Heights, his forces were vastly inferior to his opponents. He had received some ad hoc reinforcements three days ago, the 9th Mountain Division from Norway, a loose collection of units that was more the strength of a brigade and the 303rd Assault Gun Battalion, actually a collection of vehicles from both the proving grounds at Zossen and units withdrawn from Norway. It included such items as heavily armoured Panzer 1's, the largest tank he had ever or probably would ever see, some old French types and a triple turreted tank. He doubted their half-trained crews could do much so he had moved them up to thee Wotan Line, his last fixed line of defence and dug them in as fixed pillboxes in 90% of cases.

He had slightly over 120,00 men and 649 tanks. His opponents had over a million men and over 3,000 tanks. The result was inevitable; however, he had his duty. He looked skywards as the first Soviet artillery started, landing on the trenches he had already ordered abandoned. It had started.

By 20th April, the Russians, held for four days by Heinrici's forces, had finally broke through. By 22rd April, Berlin was being shelled and on the 24th the city was encircled. By the 26th US and Soviet forces had met in small groups and in force on the 27th at Torgau.

0805 29 April 1945

Whilst General Heinrich von Vietinghoff was signing the instrument of surrender for all German forces in Italy, to become effective 0001 2 May 1945, the body of the former Il Duce, Benito Mussolini, was hanging upside down on a meat hook from the roof of an Esso petrol station in Milan, being stoned and spat on by the general populace.

Such was the end for the first of the three "great dictators". The campaign in Italy was over, or near enough. Field Marshall Harold Alexanders forces would surge forward from the next morning against broken units, gaining as much ground as possible before the war's end.

1102 1 May 1945

Eva had bitten down on the capsule and now it was his turn. As he bit down on the Luger and pulled the trigger, he contemplated how it has all gone wrong. How had he been defeated by the Jewish/Bolshevik hordes? Two hours later his corpse was being unceremoniously burnt as Russian troops advanced towards the bunker, now only a few hundred meters away. The second "great dictator had also suffered an ignominious end.

On 2nd May he was followed into death by Goebbels and his wife. By the night of 2-3rd May the last units were attempting to break out from Berlin, not to continue the fight, but to get to the West and surrender to British or US forces. The last holdouts in Berlin were not subdued until the morning of the 4th May.

0908 5 May 1945

Field Marshal Bernard Law Montgomery watched the Germans sign the instrument of surrender for all forces in Northwest Germany, Holland and Denmark. It effectively marked the end of the war in Europe for his Army Group, although U.S forces were still advancing into Czechoslovakia facing very light resistance. It was to take effect at 0001 6th May. For Monty, the war was over.

1906 5 May 1945

Halsey could finally draw a sigh of relief as the battle for Okinawa concluded earlier in the day and darkness had fallen. He could finally withdraw his fleet, which had suffered at the hands of the Kamikazes. Losses had been extensive, and had included (including ships not sunk but constructive total losses) the carrier *Shangri-La*, 23 destroyers, 12 Destroyer Escorts/fast transports/minesweepers, 10 LST's, five transports. Two fleet carriers, a light carrier, two escort carriers, two battleships, three light cruisers and eight destroyers had been seriously damaged. Only one destroyer and one transport had been sunk by conventional attack. In all, over 300 ships had been sunk or damaged, some small and some only lightly, but in any case, it had been the most expensive operation of the war. The navy had suffered 5,209 dead and nearly 16,234 wounded.

The Army and Marines had also paid a bitter price in blood, 9298 dead, over 30,000 wounded or injured. More than 110,000 Japanese troops had been killed, for the first-time appreciable number surrendered, over 7,000, many being recent conscripts. Civilian casualties matched military ones at least, perhaps more than 110,00 killed, most of the island homeless. It had been a mini bloodbath. He shuddered to think what the home islands conquest would be like.

1605 9 May 1945

The final surrender document of Germany had been signed, to take effect from 0600 10 May 1945. As Keitel and Jodl both signed, they placed themselves in the hands of the three allied great powers. They would both hang at Nuremberg. For the moment, however, it was smiling all around among the allies. The war in Europe was over, although isolated fighting in Yugoslavia would continue for up to a week. Only Japan remained of the Axis powers, alone and without allies.

Final areas held by Germany 10 May 1945(not including French ports or Norway)

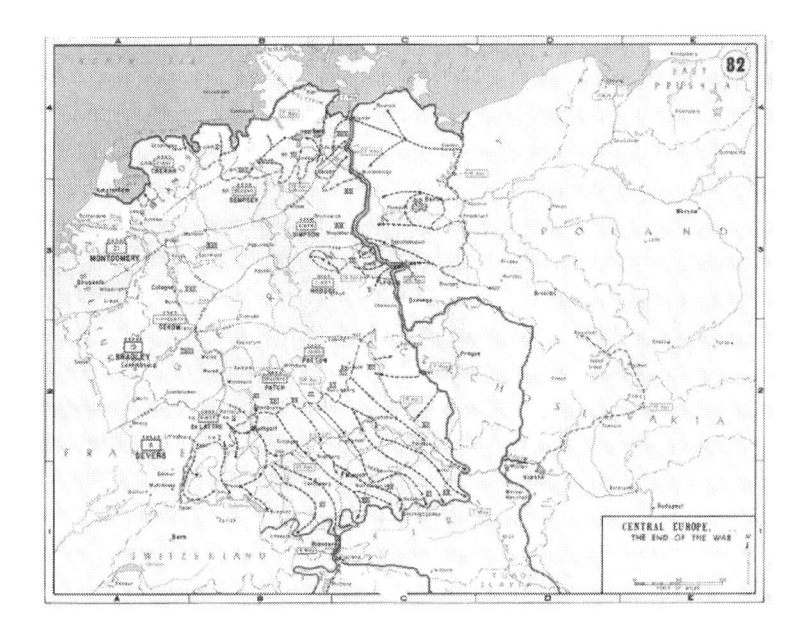

2046 10 June 1945

Admiral Raymond Spruance had struck at both Kure on the 6th June and Sasebo on 10th June with 13 fleet carriers, six light carriers and eight battleships. It had been the U.S Navy's revenge for Pearl Harbour but the tally of ships sunk had been woefully low. The Imperial Japanese Navy probably had no ships to think, he thought. The cost in aircraft had been low, the fighter cover for both bases being less than expected and only 39 aircraft had been lost, 15 of those to accidents. More than 60 defending fighters had been shot down.

Ships sunk had included two old armoured cruisers, both of which had been disarmed, the Japanese army escort carrier *Chigusa Maru*, the *Matsu Class* destroyer escorts *Tsubaki*, *Kaba* and *Nashi*, a frigate, four small escorts and five minesweepers, along with a 3,000 former target ship converted to an escort. It was a lean haul, which more than underlined the impotence of the IJN. None of Spruance's ships so much as took a scratch.

1854 11 June 1945

Slim's forces had resumed their advance in an attempt to take Singapore, already breaking through the Japanese lines after two days of constant artillery, both land and naval, and air bombardment. His troops had gone forward this morning and had already battered their way through the main Japanese line in the West. With the West Coast road now open, he was less than 80 miles from Singapore.

2314 11 June 1945

In the late-night stillness on board the battleship *Pacifica* newly promoted Vice Admiral Harold Farncombe contemplated the forces he had in the bay at Kuching, Sarawak. He had transported Charles Vyner Brooke, Rajah of Sarawak and his newly appointed heir, his daughter Leonora Margaret, along with her son, back to Kuching to resume his rule as Rajah of Sarawak.

Resting in the bay were the carrier Australasia, light carriers *Christchurch, Melbourne, Sydney*, along with escort carriers *Brisbane, Auckland* and *Perth*, two heavy cruisers, eight light cruisers, 12 destroyers, six destroyer escorts, three amphibious assault ships and five transports. They contained 2nd Division, 1st Armoured Brigade and 2nd, 4th, 5th, 7th, 9th and 11th Independent Companies, under the command of Lt General Freyberg. He would sail tomorrow to land these troops on the East Coast of Malaya at Bandar Penawar, 12 miles from Singapore. It would be his first big test as a fleet commander.

1236 12 June 1945

Stillwell's next 1945 offensive had begun. The Japanese army in China had a huge bulge in its line encompassing the strategically important cities of Hankow and Wuchang. It was the closure of that bottleneck that was his objective and it was nearly all of his US trained formations that had been committed to the task. Cutting the less than 100-mile-wide bottleneck would trap almost 80,000 Japanese soldiers and spell the doom of Japanese power in Southern China. Further to the South, a secondary spoiling offensive led by two of his crack divisions, the 200th and 300th, would thrust forward to Canton on the 16th.

0705 13 June 1945

In what would be one of the last opposed amphibious operations of the war, 2nd Australasian Division and supporting forces had gone ashore at Bandar Penawar. By nightfall, a comfortable beachhead had been established. The attack had clearly caught the Japanese by surprise and no fixed defences and only a company of garrison troops had been available. By nightfall he had established a strong beachhead and was ready to advance by daybreak on the 14th.

Vice Admiral Farncombe had not expected anything in the way of resistance from Singapore, it's aerial and naval forces had been beaten down over the last 6 months of 1945 and the British Eastern Fleet had long ago pulled any teeth that Sumatra may have had in relation to air power. It was only from the airfields of Indo China that he feared any air activity, but so far none had been forthcoming. That would change on the 14th.

0116 14 June 1945

Curtin's lungs had become congested. After several weeks in hospital in May he had insisted on returning to Miegunyah, the Prime Ministerial residence in Toorak. "I'm not worth two bob", he had told his driver, Ray Tracey, but he had kept up a cheerful front with his wife Elsie, although he thought his daughter could see through the facade. Lately he had fallen into summoning old friends for a chat. With the war in Europe successfully completed, only Japan remained. Singapore seemed on the verge of fall and he hoped to recover many of the men captured in 1942.

These late-night coughing fits had become more common and he was having trouble sleeping. He still wanted to see it through, both for the capture of Singapore and for the fall of Japan. Kreuger was also coming back to Melbourne for what would likely be a farewell meeting of the war council, only one operation remaining, the invasion of Japan. he wanted to make sure he was there for that. He had developed a real fondness for the firm, yet clever and gently spoken American. He would talk to Peter Fraser and the Queen none the less. It would pay to be well prepared for the worst and to have a succession plan in place.

0606 14 June 1945

General Kenji Doihara's Malaya army was now in full retreat, alarmed by the prospect of being cut off from Singapore, their only viable source of supply. If they lost Singapore to the newly landed forces, their position would be hopeless, if it was not already. Without ammunition, any amount of bravery was of little use.

0616 14 June 1945

There were two separate "special attack" squadrons in Southern Indo China, each consisting of 60 aircraft. Spurred into action by the panicked cries of Doinhara's Malaya Army, they had committed themselves to the attack on the fleet. Too far South to be escorted normally, 20 A6M's none the less accompanied them, with the option to fly on to airfields in Sumatra, refuel and return. Only 6 of the Okha flying bombs had been able to be delivered on board the destroyer *Yoikaze* in early May, but 118 aircraft, including six Bettys with flying bombs had lifted off by 0648, escorted by 20 fighters.

1108 14 June 1044

Vice Admiral Harold Farncombe's forces had taken a heavy hit. At 1017, he had detected a large cloud of oncoming enemy aircraft 45 miles out. The fleet was well covered by CAP, as he had first hand reports as to what had taken place both at Iwo Jima and Okinawa. In addition to a CAP of 18 He 100, he was able to launch 24 more to cover the task force. In addition, he was covered by 12 CAC 15 Cockatoos led by the RAAF's most experienced ace, Wing Commander Edgar "Cobber" Kain, who had amassed 40 victories.

The RAAF and RAN pilots tore into the Japanese aircraft, which included many older types, downing much of the escort and by the time the battle had been joined a mere three miles from the ships, 30 of the attackers and 13 of the twenty escorts had been shot down in exchange for a single CAC 15 and three He 100's. The addition of 24 fresh fighters took a heavy toll on Japanese aircraft, with another 47 being shot down, four of these escorts.

That left 45 suicide aircraft, plus the six Okha's. One flying bomb lost control and turned over, plunging into the sea. AA shot down nine more planes. That left 34 and not all of these missed. A flying bomb streaked in and hit the escort carrier *Perth*, creating an immediate fireball. The transport *Cardigan Bay* was rapidly hit twice, to sink two hours later. Destroyer escort *Clutha* was hit twice as well, capsizing the small ship plus the heavy cruiser *Dunedin* was also hit badly by a twin engine "Betty" that had previously shed its load.

Only two Japanese aircraft from 138 returned, Kain increasing his score to 46, the 12 CAC

15's destroying 31 aircraft between them, but it had been a costly attack, sinking three ships and damaging two others.

1534 14 June 1945

Freyberg's forces, advancing through the night with light forces, were only seven miles from Singapore at daybreak. Freyberg had approved a plan devised by Major General "Black Jack" Galleghan, in conjunction with Z force operatives. As his troops pushed past scattered light resistance towards the Johor causeway, they found it as yet unblown.

Galleghan produced his piece de resistance, six Chi-Ha and three Ha-Go Japanese tanks, in this instance "commanded" by Z force operatives of Asian extraction. Whilst a "breakdown" was feigned on the causeway, frogmen who had entered the water cut the explosive charges placed on the bridge supports. When Freyberg's advance elements appeared late in the afternoon, only one small charge detonated, allowing him to have three independent companies and over 40 additional Sentinel tanks across the weakened but still usable bridge by night fall.

By morning, the bridgehead had withstood two night attacks by the poorly equipped and trained Japanese fortress troops in Singapore, although at a cost of over 70 dead and 160 wounded. Daylight would bring the massed parachutes of the British 50th Parachute Brigade from 0809.

1635 16 June 1945

Fierce fighting had left Australasian and British forces in possession of two airfields, the dockyard and most importantly, both bridges into Singapore. Although much mopping up remained to be done, Singapore, defended by only poorly training second line and garrison troops had been taken "on the bounce".

The Australasian 1st Armoured Brigade and 2nd Infantry Division and the British 50th Parachute Brigade controlled all key areas of the town and later that day elements of the British Lushai Light Brigade would start flying in to the captured aerodromes.

What had shocked Freyberg was the condition of the men at Changi Prison in Singapore, liberated three hours ago. Many were emaciated skeletons and it had required strong intervention to stop some of the men shooting the Japanese guards out of hand. As it was, twenty-two had surrendered and four had met that fate before other troops had intervened.

2012 17 June 1945

It had been an expensive week for the RAN thought Farncombe. He had lost the escort carrier *Perth* with over 220 dead plus the *DE Clutha*. In addition, he had sent the *Dunedin*, badly damaged, back to Sydney under escort.

The light cruiser *Hamilton* and the old *Clemson Class* destroyers *Barnes* and *Albany* had arrived with the old destroyers *Attack, Stuart, Valhalla* and *Vendetta*, both the later converted to fast transports. They carried three more Independent Companies and equipment to reinforce the bridgehead at Bandar Panawar.

With the airfields at Singapore now secure, the British would be flying in the 28th East African Infantry Brigade. The allies could them hold Singapore and grind the remaining Japanese troops, of supply, to death in Johore.

Malaya situation 0600 18 June 1945(purple front line)

1647 18 June 1945

General Kenji Doihara's Malaya Army's situation was hopeless. Trapped in Southern Johore, he had been falling back to Singapore when the city itself had fallen. Reports indicated that the allies now controlled 95% or more of the city itself and would likely eliminate the last Japanese forces by tomorrow, if not tonight. His own forces were still being engaged by British troops and his front line was still 30 miles from Singapore. He had only two weeks of ammunition supply left and no place to get more from, plus, dependent on a fighting retreat to Singapore, he had no fixed fortifications behind him.

What he would do when that ran out, he had no idea. There was no army to cut through to, no navy to evacuate his troops, no airfields to land supplies even if he had any aircraft left to carry them.

1435 21 June 1945

General Kisaburo Hamamoto's South China Area Army line had been shattered by attacks from two Chinese divisions, one mechanised and one armoured, followed by more than 12 Infantry Divisions that had exploited the subsequent breaches in his line. He had managed to hold the integrity of his front line, but only by gradually withdrawing under the pressure, back towards Canton. If he could not stabilise the line, he would retreat back into the city itself and make a stand there.

The Chinese were attacking with renewed vigour and his own troops morale was low, not having received replacements or supplies for some time. Some of his men were even grumbling about their fate being stuck in Southern China for so long.

1645 1 July 1945

General Stilwell's offensive had not achieved its primary purpose, the cutting off and trapping of Japanese forces in the Hankow/Wuchang pocket, however, it had achieved its secondary objective. The Japanese were attacking his flanks to slow his progress and were withdrawing back through the corridor to avoid being trapped. By the second half of July he would have possession of both cities and would have recaptured a substantial part of the Central industrial heartland of China. With offensives in the South driving the Japanese back to Canton, it finally seemed they were in retreat for good.

0606 2 July 1945

Oppenheimer had settled on a day for the first test. It would be a tight squeeze in regards time as they still had some issues to sort out, but early in the morning on the 16th had been the time decided. The cruiser Indianapolis was due to leave San Francisco later that day in the event of a successful test. President Truman was to start the Potsdam Conference the following day.

For the test, "the gadget", would be hoisted to the top of a 100-foot steel tower, as detonation at that height would give a better indication of how the weapon would behave when dropped from a bomber. Detonation in the air maximized the energy applied directly to the target, and should generate less fallout. The gadget was to be assembled under the supervision of at the nearby McDonald Ranch House on 13 or 14th July, and winched up the tower the following day ready for detonation. The nuclear age was about to begin.

2234 2 July 1945

Foreign Minister Shigenori Togo heard the distant crump of bombs, perhaps only a single bomber this time. Peace, they had to make peace. But the Emperor and the majority of the council were still against, even with the USSR not renewing the treaty of friendship in April, a sure sign that an attack would be coming with the war in Europe now over and their German allies prostrate.

The bombing of Japanese cities was taking a terrible toll, Yokohama, Tokyo, Toyama, Nagoya, Osaka, Nishinomiya, Siumonoseki, Kure, Kobe, Omuta, Yawata, Kawasaki, Wakayama, Kagoshima, Okayama, Sasebo, Amagasaki, Maikonoio, Nobeaka, Miazaki, Moh, Hbe, Saga, Imabari, Sapporo and 44 other cities had all been firebombed. Millions were homeless.

The air force was getting weaker; aircraft production having fallen. Only slightly less than 1.6 million tons of merchant shipping remained, not enough to import food at required levels. Singapore had fallen. U.S forces were on their doorstep at Okinawa. China was suffering reverses. The Philippines had been lost. The Dutch East Indies cut off. There was limited access only to oil.

The once mighty navy had been reduced to four destroyers and a handful of destroyer escorts, 14 by the look of it. Surely it was now time to put aside honour and think of the futures of their own children.

1602 3 July 1945

General Kenji Doihara's Malaya Army had been pushed back to the city of Johor Bahru, just North of Singapore. He still had 34,000 men, with another 8,000 cut off at Pontian. His force, however, had disintegrated as a unified command, with no heavy equipment and in most cases, no automatic weapons either. Many men had used all their ammunition and some had already given their lives in human wave attacks, some committed by men armed only with bayonets.

Whilst he could not officially allow his men to surrender, he realised that further resistance would not last more than a day or two at most. Accordingly, he had instructed his men to use what little supplies they had to eat a last meal. Those who wished to do so would conduct a final attack at 0200 tonight.

1542 4 July 1945

It was the largest scene of wholesale slaughter that Slim had ever seen, and he had been a military man since the turn of the century. Bodies piled up made little mountains in certain areas and twelve hours later medical troops were still finding some fallen men alive.

The huge human wave attack, committed on a broad front and in a number of sectors had completely overwhelmed his front-line units in many cases. The enemy, seemingly short on ammunition had killed over 1,800 British troops and wounded 2.916 more. In some cases, troops had been bayoneted to death, in a few they were even kicked and punched to death. Whilst an estimated 30,000 Japanese had died, some 2,000 actually breaking through allied lines, it was interesting to note that nearly 3,000 Japanese had not moved, simply waiting for capture.

With the elimination of the Pontian pocket on the 6th, the Malayan campaign would be over. For Japanese General General Kenji Doihara, pimp and drug lord, he had taken the way of seppuku at 0300 on the 4th. By the afternoon of the 7th the last Japanese strongholds had been mopped up and Slim was able to cable London from the main Post Office at Singapore.

2012 5 July 1945

The war council meeting had broken up at the palace and the Queen was finishing her own private correspondence to her sister, now back in Athens after four years on Crete. She had been shocked by how badly John Curtin had deteriorated in the week since she had seen him last. He had struggled to last the meeting out and, although he articulated himself well, he had paused between sentences, almost to get his breath. The news of the virtual end of the Malayan campaign had brought him much cheer, he had said.

Kreuger, who had not seen Curtin for some time, was obviously shocked by his wan and haggard appearance. For the American General, it was a farewell. Promoted to a 5-star rank, he had been delegated as the allied land commander for the proposed Operation Downfall, the planed invasion of Japan, scheduled for 26 September 1945, although preliminary landings were to commence on outlying islands on the 21st. Nimitz was to be the overall commander, Spruance the commander of naval forces. For the first phase, Operation Olympic, the invasion of Kyushu, no Australasian troops were to be committed. Three divisions were planned for the later invasion of Honshu.

After some tidying up and taking some of his own staff with him on his move to Manila, Kreuger would cease to be Commander SWPac, with Blamey taking over on the 10th July. He would be elevated to Field Marshal on the same date. SW Pac was now an inactive theatre, only air operations and an occasional naval bombardment remained ongoing against the surviving Japanese troops concentrations, mainly centred on New Britain, Java and Sumatra. She had officially presented a specially forged 18 carat gold ceremonial pistol with a carved, Kangaroo and Emu, Kiwi and Coconut carved grip to him to commemorate his time in Australasia, as well as the freedom of the cities of Melbourne and Brisbane, plus a signed US flag from all of them as late 4th July present. He had accepted all these with his usual modesty.

After the meeting had broken, she had buttonholed Peter Fraser, asking him to look after Curtin as much as possible. She had also asked him that in the event of the worst, if he was prepared to take over, which he had indicated she was. As Defence Minister, he had thrown himself tirelessly into the prosecution of the war. She had asked him to thinking about the peace. If it broke out and the war ended, what would become of the British and in particular the Dutch Colonial empires on the country's doorstep? She was well aware it would be just as important, if not more important, to win the peace as well as the war.

0909 15 July 1945

Chiang Kai-shek's forces, led by the crack 200th and 300th Divisions had pushed the Japanese steadily back until they held a perimeter around all three cities, Macau, Hong Kong and Canton. Japanese forces had withdrawn back into all three urban areas in anticipation of fight to the finish and it would be now up to the fourteen Chinese Divisions involved in the Southern Offensive to winkle them out.

0530 16 July 1945

The gadget exploded with an energy equivalent of around 20 kilotons of TNT, leaving a crater of Trinite, or radioactive glass, in the desert 250 feet wide. The shock wave was felt over 100 miles away, and the mushroom cloud reached 8 miles in height. It was heard as far away as El Paso, so a concoction was issued a cover story about a huge accidental ammunition magazine explosion at Alamogordo Field. Later that day, Truman was informed of the success of the operation. That night, *USS Indianapolis* left San Francisco with the first operation bomb "Little Boy".

1458 18 July 1945

The meeting of the "big six" had broken up, still with no agreement as to what was to be done. Navy Minister Mitsumasa Yonai had joined Togo as being supportive of surrender, but the other four remained firmly opposed.

On June 10, the Emperor's confidant Marquis Koichi Kido had written a "Draft Plan for Controlling the Crisis Situation," warning that by the end of the year, possibly in the last quarter of the year, Japan's ability to wage modern war would be extinguished and the government would be unable to contain civil unrest. "... We cannot be sure we will not share the fate of Germany and be reduced to adverse circumstances under which we will not attain even our supreme object of safeguarding the Imperial Household and preserving the national polity." Kido proposed that the Emperor take action, by offering to end the war on "very generous terms." Kido proposed that Japan withdraw from the formerly European colonies it had occupied provided they were granted independence, that Japan disarm provided this not occur under Allied supervision, and that Japan for a time be "content with minimum defence." Kido's proposal did not contemplate Allied occupation of Japan, prosecution of war criminals or substantial change in Japan's system of government. With the Emperor's authorization, Kido approached several members of the "Big Six." Tōgō was very supportive. Suzuki and Admiral Mitsumasa Yonai were both cautiously supportive; each wondered what the other thought. General Anami, the Army Minister, was opposed, as were the other two.

In late June, the Emperor had lost confidence in the chances of achieving a military victory. The Battle at Okinawa had been lost, Singapore was endangered and he was aware of the failing of the Japanese army in China, of weakness the Kwantung Army in Manchuria, of the navy, and of the army defending the Home Islands. The Emperor had received a report which concluded that "it was not just the coast defence; the divisions reserved to engage in the decisive battle also did not have sufficient numbers of weapons." According to the report's author "I am told that the iron from bomb fragments dropped by the enemy was being used to make shovels."

On June 28, the Emperor summoned the Big Six to a meeting. Unusually, he spoke first: "I desire that concrete plans to end the war, unhampered by existing policy, be speedily studied and that efforts made to implement them." It was agreed to solicit Soviet aid in ending the war. Other neutral nations, such as Switzerland, Sweden and the Vatican, were known to be willing to play a role in making peace, but they were so small they were believed unable to do more than deliver the Allies' terms of surrender and Japan's acceptance or rejection. The Japanese hoped that the Soviet Union could be persuaded to act as an agent for Japan in negotiations with America and Britain. Negotiations had so far, however, proceeded at a slow pace, with much backwards and forwards but little in the way of concrete proposals.

Front line in Thailand/Indo China 20 July 1945(unchanged at war's end-crimson line)

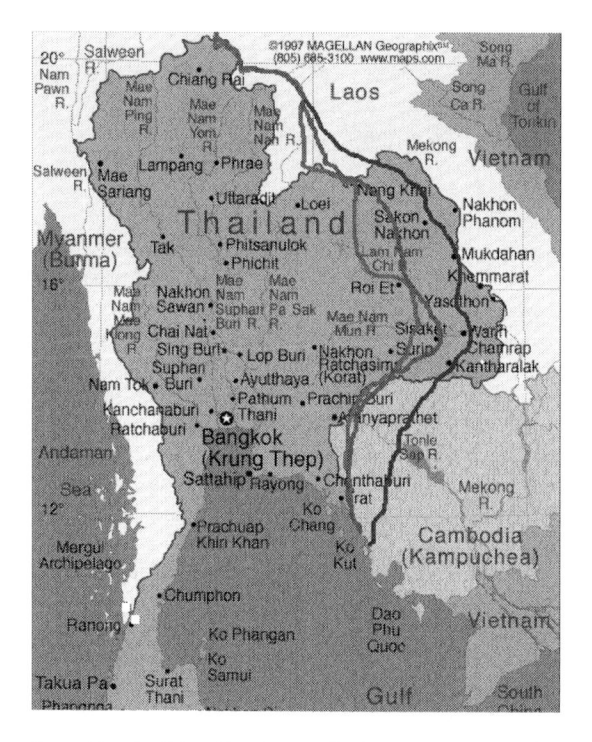

Front Line in China 20 July 1945 (only active operations after this point are against Canton, Hong Kong and Macau)

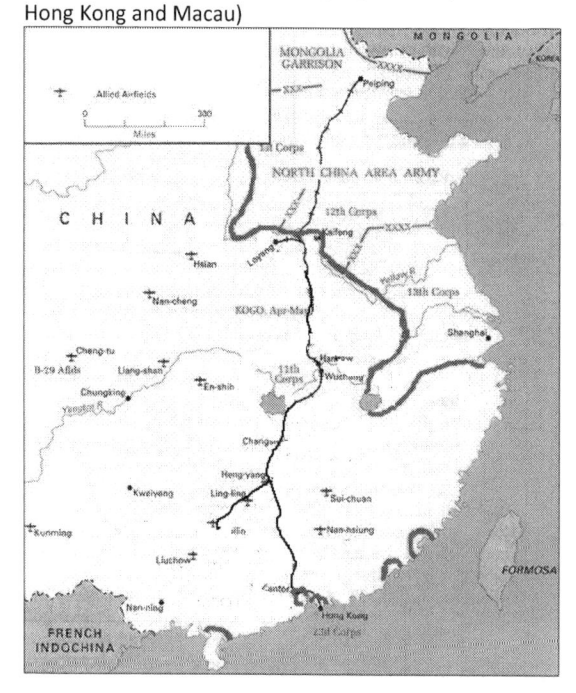

0314 20 July 1945

The urgent ringing of the telephone next to her bed startled Queen Alice out of a rare deep sleep. The palace had its own switchboard so the call would not have been put through at this time of night unless it was of the utmost importance.

As she put down the receiver, she turned back to her now awake husband Karl, visibly upset. Prime Minister John Joseph Curtin had been found by his wife Elise just after two o'clock, having gotten up coughing, he had not come back to bed. This had been a regular occurrence for some time now. She found him in the armchair, a half-drunk cup of tea beside him, having passed away.

He had been argued by many to be Australasia's greatest Prime Minister. As Kreuger, who flew back to Australasia for his funeral was to remark "the preservation of Australasia from invasion will be his immemorial monument." Sadly, he had died within spitting distance of the end of the war, which, although he did not know it, was now just 35 days away.

Whilst many focus on his wartime legacy, he had left an indelible mark on Australasia's social makeup as well, extending welfare to all, regardless of race and had introduced such things as Child Endowment and Widows Pension, plus he had finally with his famous 1942 speech steered the country away from its traditional ties to the U.K and into the Pacific rim and the special relationship enjoyed with the U.S.

0616 25 July 1945

As the dawn rose over the scene, Lt Commander Shokichi watched the ship slowly roll over and sink. He had hit her with four torpedoes at 0518. Unescorted and following a straight course, she had probably thought her high speed at 25 knots would be enough to protect her.

She had simply been unfortunate to run directly across the course of one of the few Japanese submarines left operational. She had been dispatched, along with *I-58, I-363, I-366* and *I-367* to patrol the area and this ship would be a fine feather in her cap and in *I-47's*. As the USS *Indianapolis* dipped beneath the waves, so did "Little Boy" slated to be delivered to Tinian on the 26th.

1415 26 July 1945

As Bedell Smith read the Potsdam Declaration, Molotov remained confident the Japanese would not acquiesce and had informed Stalin of such. This would be to the advantage of the USSR, which had readied their own operations to commence 10 August 1945.

It had announced the terms for Japan's surrender, with the warning, "We will not deviate from them. There are no alternatives. We shall brook no delay." For Japan, the terms of the declaration specified:

- the elimination "for all time [of] the authority and influence of those who have deceived and misled the people of Japan into embarking on world conquest"
- the occupation of "points in Japanese territory to be designated by the Allies"
- "Japanese sovereignty shall be limited to the islands of Honshu, Hokkaido, Kyushu and Skikoku and such minor islands as we determine." As had been announced in Cairo in 1943, Japan was to be reduced to her pre-1894 territory and stripped of her pre-war empire including Korea and Taiwan, as well as all her recent conquests.
- "The Japanese Military forces, after being completely disarmed, shall be permitted to return to their homes with the opportunity to lead peaceful and productive lives."
- "stern justice shall be meted out to all war criminals, including those who have visited cruelties upon our prisoners."

On the other hand, the declaration stated that:

- "We do not intend that the Japanese shall be enslaved as a race or destroyed as a nation, ... The Japanese Government shall remove all obstacles to the revival and strengthening of democratic tendencies among the Japanese people."
- "Japan shall be permitted to maintain such industries as will sustain her economy and permit the exaction of just reparations in kind, but not those which would enable her to rearm for war. To this end, access to, as distinguished from control of, raw materials shall be permitted. Eventual Japanese participation in world trade relations shall be permitted."
- "The occupying forces of the Allies shall be withdrawn from Japan as soon as these objectives have been accomplished and there has been established, in accordance with the freely expressed will of the Japanese people, a peacefully inclined and responsible government."

The only use of the term unconditional surrender came at the end of the declaration:

- "We call upon the government of Japan to proclaim now the unconditional surrender of all Japanese armed forces, and to provide proper and adequate assurances of their good faith in such action. The alternative for Japan is prompt and utter destruction."

Contrary to what had been intended at its conception, the Declaration made no mention of the Emperor at all. Allied intentions on issues of utmost importance to the Japanese, including whether Hirohito was to be regarded as one of those who had "misled the people of Japan" or even a war criminal, or alternatively, whether the Emperor might become part of a "peacefully inclined and responsible government" were thus left unstated.

2019 27 July 1945

To say that the nonappearance of the *Indianapolis* had produced an out and out panic in high ranking circles within the U.S civilian and military government who were "in the know" was a massive understatement.

It at least had the beneficial effect of creating a massive search umbrella which rapidly located the life rafts of the surviving crew. By nightfall, the full story had been revealed and the comfort that the weapon was at a depth that would allow it to never be recovered was at least some consolation.

0718 28 July 1945

Oppenheimer had been shocked to hear what had happened to "Little Boy". The "Fat Man" device core had been arranged to leave for Tinian today by air transport, the rest of the components leaving tomorrow.

He did not have time or the available Uranium to build another "gun type" device, but more plutonium based implosion weapons were in the process of being made ready and he would have another available to leave for Tinian in about one-two weeks. He expected to have another by the end of the month and three more in September.

The main issue was reliability. He had been almost certain "Little Boy" would work. "Fat Man" he was less sure of. The Uranium gun type device had almost no features that could go wrong and had been tested. "Fat Man" he was fairly sure of, but not 100%.

2332 29 July 1945

Halsey's 3rd Fleet, huge now in numbers with 14 fleet and seven light carriers, as well as seven battleships and two large cruisers had struck again at the harbours and shipyards of Japan, now lying virtually impotent. This time the targets had been Yokosuka and Kagoshima, hit on the 25th and 29th respectively. Again, there had been little left to sink, however, they had destroyed 55 Japanese aircraft in the air and 26 on the ground for the loss of only 17 planes.

They had also sunk two destroyer escorts, three minesweepers and three submarines at Yokosuka and four patrol boats and two minesweepers at Kagoshima. Afterwards, his larger surface ships had bombarded Kagoshima for two hours, totally destroying the port and its facilities. It was to be last operation of 3rd Fleet.

1536 30 July 1945

Peter Fraser had received the confidence of his own Labor members at the 29th July Caucasus meeting and seen the Queen earlier today to be sworn in as the new Prime Minister of Australasia. He had big shoes to fill and a war still to fight.

1436 7 August 1945

General Curtis LeMay had been aware of the Manhattan project, so in the absence of "Little Boy", had designed a different operation for Hiroshima, it's intended target. With only the occasional raider from Japan now hitting Okinawa, he had moved the Australasian He 200's, now numbering over 70 aircraft, to Okinawa. There they had been joined by the first of other components of "Tiger Force", 40 aircraft in two RAF squadrons, equipped with Avro Lincolns.

Tonight he would launch the largest raid ever against a Japanese city, 398 B29's hitting Hiroshima with incendiaries, followed two hours later by over 100 He 200s and Lincolns. That would warm the Japs up for what he knew was coming to Nagasaki on the 9th.

0923 8 August 1945

The dry day and high winds had combined to make what was left of Hiroshima a firestorm that still continued to burn unchecked. Super-heated air starved trapped people of oxygen and created what was later described as tornado like gusts of fire, seemingly living itself as it reached out to touch those still alive themselves.

No one would ever know how many died from the over 2,400 tons of mainly jellied incendiaries dropped on the city, but estimates are upwards of 110,000. It was without doubt one of the most destructive raids in World War 2. It had cost the allies 11 aircraft.

1053 9 August 1945

The Japanese had ignored the five B-29's over Nagasaki, assuming such a small number were merely there for the purposes of aerial reconnaissance. The city was in a sense unlucky, having not been on the target list at all when it was originally drawn up. The five cities originally being Kyoto, Hiroshima, Kokura, Yokohama and Niigata. Nagasaki was listed as a "reserve", along with Akita, these representing pretty much the remaining Japanese cites not destroyed by firebombing. However, Henry Stimson had vetoed Kyoto over many objections and Hiroshima had been obliterated. That had elevated both onto the list.

With cloud forecast over Kokura, Nagasaki had been promoted to No 1. At 1053, the rather unusually named Captain Kermit Beahan released the device from the B29 Bockscar. The resulting flash "brighter than 1000 suns" heralded in the nuclear age.

1807 10 August 1945

The landings at Causeway Bay on the 8th had rapidly been exploited and the last Japanese resistance around Aberdeen had been extinguished 45 minutes ago. Hong Kong had been recaptured and secured, as had Macau three days ago. It had been a bitter and bloody battle, requiring as usual, the virtual extermination of the Japanese defenders. Only in Canton did bitter house to house fighting, which had started back in mid-July, continue.

If Major General Po-Lan thought it incongruous that Chinese troops had liberated the ground of the middle kingdom for reoccupation by Western, Colonial powers, he outwardly at least gave no sign of it.

2300 10 August 1945

Molotov had informed Japanese ambassador Sato that the Soviet Union had declared war on the Empire of Japan, and that from August 11 the Soviet Government would consider itself to be at war with Japan.

At one-minute past midnight August 11, 1945, the Soviets commenced their invasion simultaneously on three fronts to the east, west and north of Manchuria. Under the command of Marshal Aleksandr Mikhaylovich Vasilevsky were 1.6 million men, 30,000 artillery pieces, 5,800 tanks including such powerful recent types as the T44 and JS-3, over 5,500 aircraft. Even the Soviet Far Eastern Fleet, with its two *Kirov Class* heavy cruisers *Kalinin* and *Kaganovich* was now more powerful than the Japanese navy. Their objectives were to cut deep into Manchuria and reach through to Korea and even Northern China.

2012 12 August 1945

The council meeting on the 12th had broken with still no agreement, although Foreign Minister Togo had sensed that Suzuki had drifted towards their position, giving the council itself a 3-3 split. The news of the Soviet invasion and particularly the bombing of Nagasaki had been twin shocks. At first, some refused to believe the United States had built an atomic bomb, even after they had announced on the 10th that this was the cause of destruction. The Japanese Army and Navy had their own bomb programs and therefore the Japanese understood enough to know how very difficult building it would be. Admiral Soemu Toyoda, the Chief of the Naval General Staff, argued that even if the United States had made one, they could not have many more and, unbelievably to Togo, this seemed the prevailing opinion, even with Suzuki.

1536 16 August 1945

With Kokura selected as the second target on 19th August and Niigata as the third on 2 September, Le May wanted to make another demonstration to the Japanese and had selected two more locations to do so.

The city of Akita would be the subject of another firebombing raid tonight, consisting of 368 B-29's. On the same night, 58 more B-29's, 71 Australasian He 200's and 42 RAF Lincolns would strike the nearly small city of Oga. Although Le May was not to know it, it was to be a fateful mission.

0304 17 August 1945

Kimiko Odate tried to move the children quickly towards the air raid shelter. The smaller city had little in the way of air defences and had been considered relatively safe due to its isolation in the North and its strategic unimportance. This is why the children had been brought here from Tokyo and its dangers. Tonight, it was its closeness to Akita that doomed it. Atsuko was the first to make it into the tunnel, running ahead of her younger siblings, including her slightly chubbier older brother, and her older but less fit sister. Flung further into the shelter, she suffered only a broken arm and abrasions from the blast and subsequent fire that killed her sister and two brothers.

1645 18 August 1945

The remaining Japanese troops in Canton, cut off and surrounded, had been forced back into a one square mile region centred on Liuhua Lake and Shaecun Island. Invested from all sides, it was now just a matter of time.

The fighting for the city had been terrible and bloody, but with no relief likely, Lt General Abuto Mori had no choice but to fight it out. Bodies were everywhere, both Japanese and Chinese, but he was down to less than 20,000 men. There could be only one ending.

2115 18 August 1945

The council meeting scheduled for the 19th had been put back to the 21st. The Emperor had been inconsolable in his grief but at this stage Togo considered every day precious. The Soviets had smashed through General Otsuzo Yamad's Kwantung Army like a knife through hot butter and were driving their tanks around Manchuria like they already owned it. He had to make a decisive plea on the 21st.

1036 19 August 1945

Colonel Paul Tibbet's B-29 Enola Gay had become the second aircraft to release an atomic bomb. It had been a sobering experience to see the mushroom cloud boiling up from what had been the arsenal city of Kokura. He understood this was war but the sheer power of the force itself was more than a little frightening.

0434 22 August 1945

The War Cabinet had met all day on the 21st and had still been unable to meet a consensus, now deadlocked 3-3. At around 0200, Suzuki had finally addressed Emperor Hirohito, asking him to decide between the two positions.

The Emperor stated: "I have given serious thought to the situation prevailing at home and abroad and have concluded that continuing the war can only mean destruction for the nation and prolongation of bloodshed and cruelty in the world. I cannot bear to see my innocent people suffer any longer. I was told by those advocating a continuation of hostilities that by July new divisions would be in place in fortified positions ready for the invader when he sought to land. It is now August and the fortifications still have not been completed. There are those who say the key to national survival lies in a decisive battle in the homeland. The experiences of the past, however, show that there has always been a discrepancy between plans and performance. Since this is also the shape of things, with these terrible bombs and the rain of fire on our cities that has caused heartbreak to both myself and so many others, how can we hope to repel the invaders? It goes without saying that it is unbearable for me to see the brave and loyal fighting men of Japan disarmed. It is equally unbearable that others who have rendered me devoted service should now be punished as instigators of the war. Nevertheless, the time has come to bear the unbearable. I swallow my tears and give my sanction to the proposal to accept the Allied proclamation on the basis outlined by the Foreign Minister."

Once the Emperor had left, Suzuki pushed the cabinet to accept the Emperor's will, which it eventually did after two more hours of debate. At 1105, the Foreign Ministry sent telegrams to the Allies announcing that Japan would accept the Potsdam Declaration, but would not accept any peace conditions that would "prejudice the prerogatives" of the Emperor. That effectively meant no change in Japan's form of government—that the

Emperor would remain a position of real power. Togo hoped that it would be resolved quickly. The Russian's had almost captured Changchun and Mukden, encircling huge numbers of troops in Manchuria. In addition, they had made landings in the Kuriles and Northern Korea as well as Sakhalin. The Kwantung Army was dissolving and very soon their bargaining position would be even worse.

0559 22 August 1945

As the first light of dawn started to glow golden on the surface, Lt Commander Sakamoto Kaneyoshi commanding I201 had powered through the escort at 18 knots submerged, seemingly attracting little attention. SubDiv 34, comprising *I-201, 202, and 203*, all brand-new concept submarines, had sortied on the 4th August. He waited until the solution was perfect and then fired all four torpedoes, being rewarded with two hits.

He and *I 201*, hunted by three *Fletcher Class* destroyers would not live to see the light cruiser USS Dayton slowly sink from the two torpedoes that had hit her port stern over four hours later. Aside from an LST sunk at Okinawa on the 23rd, she was the last U.S warship sunk in World War 2, some 120 hours from the end of hostilities.

2116 25 August 1945

The allied response had arrived on the 24th. On the status of the Emperor it said: From the moment of surrender the authority of the Emperor and the Japanese government to rule the state shall be subject to the Supreme Commander of the Allied powers who will take such steps as he deems proper to effectuate the surrender terms. The ultimate form of government of Japan shall, in accordance with the Potsdam Declaration, be established by the freely expressed will of the Japanese people.

The debate was again dragging on, the same 3-3 split now evidenced with the allies second response. The council had been throughout alarmed as the allied bombers spent August 25 dropping leaflets over Japan, describing the Japanese offer of surrender and the Allied response. The leaflets had a profound effect on the Japanese decision-making process, as many now feared civil unrest. By 0200 on the 26th, it was decided to reconvene at 1600 to again discuss.

2212 25 August 1945

Reduced to a 100-yard perimeter around the Zhudao Garden Plant Institute building and less than 800 men, Lt General Abuto Mori had decided to personally lead a last charge. By daybreak on the 26th, Canton had been secured by Chinese forces at terrible human cost, over 39,000 Japanese, 22,000 Chinese and upwards of 100,000 civilians. It was to be the last land battle of World War 2, excluding Soviet operations.

0344 27 August 1945

The meeting had again dragged on for hours, debating the latest development when B29 had daylight bombed the Nippon Oil Company refinery at Tsuchizaki on the northern tip of Honshū. This was the last operational refinery in the Japan Home Islands and it produced 67% of their oil. Now the news was in of a huge fire raid on Yokohama, with much of the city destroyed. All key locations in Manchuria had been taken, with much of the Kwantung Army destroyed.

The Emperor had met with the most senior Army and Navy officers. While several spoke in favour of fighting on, Field Marshal Hata did not. As commander of the Second General Army, the headquarters of which had been in Hiroshima, Hata commanded all the troops defending southern Japan—the troops preparing to fight the "decisive battle". Hata said he had no confidence in defeating the invasion and did not dispute the Emperor's decision. The Emperor had then asked his military leaders to cooperate with him in ending the war.

At a conference with the cabinet and other councillors, Anami, Toyoda, and Umezu again made their case for continuing to fight, after which the Emperor said "I have listened carefully to each of the arguments presented in opposition to the view that Japan should accept the Allied reply as it stands and without further clarification or modification, but my own thoughts have not undergone any change. ... In order that the people may know my decision, I request you to prepare at once an imperial rescript so that I may broadcast to the nation. Finally, I call upon each and every one of you to exert himself to the utmost so that we may meet the trying days which lie ahead."

The cabinet immediately convened and unanimously ratified the Emperor's wishes. They also decided to destroy vast amounts of material pertaining to war crimes and the war responsibility of the nation's highest leaders. Immediately after the conference, the Foreign ministry transmitted orders to its embassies in Switzerland and Sweden to accept the Allied terms of surrender. The text of the Imperial Rescript on surrender was finalized by 2100 transcribed by the official court calligrapher, and brought to the cabinet for their signatures. Around 0100 on the 28th, the Emperor, with help from a recording crew, made a recording of himself reading it, before going to bed.

1400 28 August 1945

Hirohito stepped up to make the broadcast. It was over.

"Despite the best that has been done by everyone—the gallant fighting of the military and naval forces, the diligence and assiduity of Our servants of the State, and the devoted service of Our one hundred million people—the war situation has developed not necessarily to Japan's advantage, while the general trends of the world have all turned against her interest. Moreover, the enemy has begun to employ a new and most cruel bomb, the power of which to do damage is, indeed, incalculable, taking the toll of many innocent lives. Should we continue to fight, not only would it result in an ultimate collapse and obliteration of the Japanese nation, but also it would lead to the total extinction of human civilization.

Such being the case, how are We to save the millions of Our subjects, or to atone Ourselves before the hallowed spirits of Our Imperial Ancestors? This is the reason why We have ordered the acceptance of the provisions of the Joint Declaration of the Powers.

The hardships and sufferings to which Our nation is to be subjected hereafter will be certainly great. We are keenly aware of the inmost feelings of all of you, Our subjects. However, it is according to the dictates of time and fate that We have resolved to pave the way for a grand peace for all the generations to come by enduring the unendurable and suffering what is insufferable.

1806 5 September 1945

The war in the Pacific had come to an end, though Captain William Davis, USN. After the Japanese broadcast on the 28th, holdouts had still continued to attack US ships, with Kamikazes attacking on the 29th and even ten more on the 30th. Japanese fighters had ceased to intercept allied aircraft of the 31st and the Soviets had even finished operations yesterday. The first occupation troops had also landed yesterday without incident. With the surrender due to be signed in Tokyo on the 12th, this meeting had looked at US ship production and what needed to be cancelled, and what was worth continuing with. The cutbacks in late 1944 had ensured that most ships were reasonably well advanced and under construction still were:
8 *Essex Class* CV's
2 *Midway Class* CV's
1 *Iowa Class* BB
1 *Baltimore Class* CA
4 *Oregon City Class* CA's
4 *Des Moines Class* CA's
1 *Cleveland Class* CL
8 *Fargo Class* CL's
2 *Worcester Class* CL's

It had been decided to suspend two *Essex Class* CV's and five *Fargo Class* CL's and to proceed with other construction at much reduced pace.

1212 12 September 1945

Fleet Admiral Chester William Nimitz looked out from the *USS Missouri* over the mighty armadas of warships from so many allied nations, the US, UK, Australasia, China, USSR, France, Canada, Netherlands, Portugal, even Thailand in Tokyo Bay. Japan had been crushed and the surrender duly signed. It was a testament at the United States Navy and indeed all the allied nations. At last the Axis finally lay prostate and utterly defeated.

Maybe now they could concentrate on the peace, yet already there were ominous signs, civil war in Greece, conflict in China and colonial powers returning to South East Asia, hoping to rescue their empires. They had won the war, he hoped they could also win the peace. Fleet Admiral Raymond Spruance would be the new master of Japan, Walter Kreuger having elected to retire.

0709 15 September 1945

Fleet Admiral Raymond Spruance sighed. It was an order that was already creating problems. He scanned again the offending parts of General Order No 1:

a. The senior Japanese commanders and all ground, sea, air and auxiliary forces within China (excluding Manchuria, Formosa and French Indo China north of 16 degrees North latitude shall surrender to Generalissimo Chiang - Ki-shek.

b. The senior Japanese commanders and all ground, sea, air and auxiliary forces within Manchuria, Korea north of 38 degrees North latitude and Karafuto shall surrender to the Commander in Chief of Soviet Forces in the Far East, Marshal Vasilevsky.

c. The senior Japanese commanders and all ground, sea, air and auxiliary forces within the Andamans, Nicobars, Thailand, French Indo China south of 16 degrees North latitude, Netherlands East Indies and Bismarcks, shall surrender to the Supreme Allied Commander, South East Asia, Field Marshal Blamey.

d. The senior Japanese commanders and all ground, sea, air and auxiliary forces in the Japanese Mandated Islands, Ryukus, Bonins, and other Pacific Islands shall surrender to the Commander in Chief, U.S Pacific Fleet, Fleet Admiral Nimitz.

e. The Imperial General Headquarters, its senior commanders, and all ground, sea, air and auxiliary forces in the main islands of Japan, minor islands adjacent thereto, Korea south of 38 degree North latitude, and the Philippines shall surrender to the Commander in Chief, Occupying Forces Japan, Fleet Admiral Spruance.

The cutting in two of French Indo China and Korea was already causing problems and Indonesia had declared its independence on 1st September, a declaration that had already brought angry Dutch protests. Plus, he had to deal with Hirohito. That was going to be sticky.

Japan 1 October 1945-31 March 1950

Japan's colonial empire had preached a coalition of Asian races, directed by Japan, against the imperialism of Britain, France, the Netherlands, the United States, and European imperialism generally. This approach celebrated the spiritual values of the East in opposition to the crass materialism of the West.

In practice, however, the Japanese installed organizationally-minded bureaucrats and engineers to run their new empire, and they believed in ideals of efficiency, modernization, and engineering solutions to social problems. It was fascism based on technology, and rejected Western norms of democracy. After 1945, the engineers and bureaucrats took over, and turned the wartime techno-fascism into entrepreneurial management skills.

Japan had never been occupied by a foreign power, and the arrival of the Americans with strong ideas about transforming Japan into a peaceful democracy had a major long-term impact. Japan came under the direction of American Admiral Raymond Spruance, until replaced by General Marc Clark in May 1949. The main American objective was to turn Japan into a peaceful nation and to establish democratic self-government. The occupation transformed the Japanese government into an engine of production, wealth redistribution, and social reform. Political reforms included a freely elected Japanese Diet and universal adult suffrage, including women, previously excluded. The Occupation emphasized land reform so that tenant farmers became owners of their rice paddies, and stimulated the formation of unions that gave workers a say in industrial democracy. The great business conglomerates were broken up, consumer culture was encouraged, education was radically reformed and democratised and the Shintō-basis of emperor worship was ended. The reforms were implemented by Japanese officials under indirect American control, so that no Japanese institutions were directly controlled by Americans.

The role of Hirohito was a more complex one. Although the new constitution of 1947 abolished the old system on noble titles, a symbol of the past was still necessary for national unity and Spruance realised that. He had more than enough evidence to implicate Hirohito and his brother Yasuhito, Prince Chichibu, in war crimes, as well as some of his cousins and uncles. In essence, Spruance made a deal with Hirohito and the Imperial Household. If he abdicated, along with Yasuhito, he would ensure they were not prosecuted. Hirohito's third brother Nobuhito, also refused and in the finish the office fell to Takahito, Prince Mikasa, Hirohito's youngest brother, who had dramatically urged him to take responsibility for his wartime mistakes in late 1945. He had publicly clashed with his brother over the activities of Unit 731 in Manchuria pre-war. Upon returning to Japan in 1944, he wrote a stinging indictment of the conduct of the Imperial Japanese Army in China, where the Prince had witnessed atrocities against Chinese civilians. The Army General Staff suppressed the document, but one copy survived.

The Empire was dissolved. Japan was stripped of its overseas possessions and retained only the home islands. Manchukuo was dissolved, and Manchuria and Formosa were returned to China, although Manchuria continued to remain a separate entity with Soviet support. Korea was occupied and divided by the U.S. and the Soviet Union. The U.S. became the sole administering authority of the Ryūkyū, Bonin, and Volcano Islands, while the USSR took southern Sakhalin and the Kurile islands.

Shigeru Yoshida played the central role as Prime Minister between 1946 and 1950. His goal was rapid rebuilding of Japan and cooperation with the American Occupation. He led Japan to adopt the "Yoshida Doctrine", based on three tenets: economic growth as the primary national objective, no involvement in international political-strategic issues, and the provision of military bases to the United States.

Mingling with so many foreign troops, particularly American, opened up Japanese society, helping it become more tolerant of other cultures.

War crimes tribunals were conducted, with 11 prominent politicians were executed. Despite objections from Australasia, Japanese members of the Imperial Family were excluded, but over 1000 eventual executions of Japanese military personnel were eventually conducted. Nor were members of Unit 731 and many of the practitioners of barbary from Manchuria spared. Many others received prison terms.

The country itself, prostrate and in ruins, gradually started rebuilding itself with what is the customary energy and efficiency of its people, often on the back of US support and loans. With no military, it's efforts could be focused upon civilian infrastructure.

Its former arms, including its three surviving destroyers and eight surviving destroyer escorts, went to the Western Allies. Most were scrapped, only the old *Tanikaze*, a new *Atkizuke class* destroyer and a *Matsu Class* DE that went to China surviving. Some aircraft, such as surviving 20 Kawanishi H8K's and over 20 Ki 100's went to China, the rest were scrapped, many countries operating Government run scrapyards through 1946 processing captured spoils of war back to scrap metal.

1632 20 September 1945

Keith Park submitted his latest report to the aircraft review board. This report would now be the basis of reducing operating squadrons and machines, with the war now over a week old. He wished he could be so sure that combat aircraft would not be needed again soon, but the situation directly to the North of Australasia in Dutch New Guinea looked likely to erupt at any moment. In any case, repatriation duties would require transports squadrons to stay fully occupied until well into 1946. Six combat squadrons had already been dissolved. More would surely follow. The primary task of disarming, repatriating and administering the Netherlands East Indies had fallen back on the country and it seemed like it would be a difficult one. The final run down of orders and contracts was now starting, although wartime orders that had been paid for would continue to come off production lines at a reduced pace until March. Hencall's two jet prototypes were both due to debut by the end of the year. If successful, orders would surely follow as they represented the future now of aviation. Numbers by type now read:

Fighters:
CAC 15 Cockatoo 364 (in production) 408(in production)
Curtis P40 72
Hencall He 100 668 310
Hencall He 119 402(in production-terminating November) 292

TOTAL 1492 NEED 1500

Bombers/Patrol:
Consolidated Catalina 85 80
Consolidated B24 Liberator 260
de Havilland Mosquito 224 218
Douglas A20 45(some ex Dutch East Indies)
Fairy Swordfish 72 20
Grumman Avenger 168 124
Hencall He 200 184(in production) 210(in production)
Hencall He 211 188 182
Lockheed Ventura 64
North American A36 162 148
Vickers Wellington 39 36
Vultee Vengeance 256

TOTAL 1754 NEED 1750

Transports:
Airspeed Oxford 240 234
Avro Anson 131(transport conversion)
Douglas C47 406(in production) 456
Hencall He 70 25 24

TOTAL 800 NEED 800

Demobilization was to prove rapid and by the end of 1945, all P40's, A20's and lend lease machines, namely B24's, Lockheed Venturas and Vultee Vengeances had been returned to the US. End 1945 figures are shown above in black.

Soviet Invasion of Manchuria August-September 1945

23 March 1952(flash forward)

Admiral John Collins reviewed the rank insignia. They had reverted to the old 19th century British system for enlisted. He was happy with the officer's insignia for the RAN. Overall, he thought it would simplify matters.

Australasian Defence Forces enlisted insignia post 1952

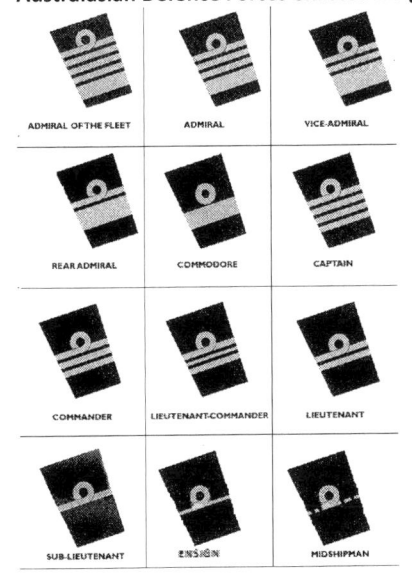

ADMIRAL OF THE FLEET	ADMIRAL	VICE-ADMIRAL
REAR ADMIRAL	COMMODORE	CAPTAIN
COMMANDER	LIEUTENANT-COMMANDER	LIEUTENANT
SUB-LIEUTENANT	ENSIGN	MIDSHIPMAN

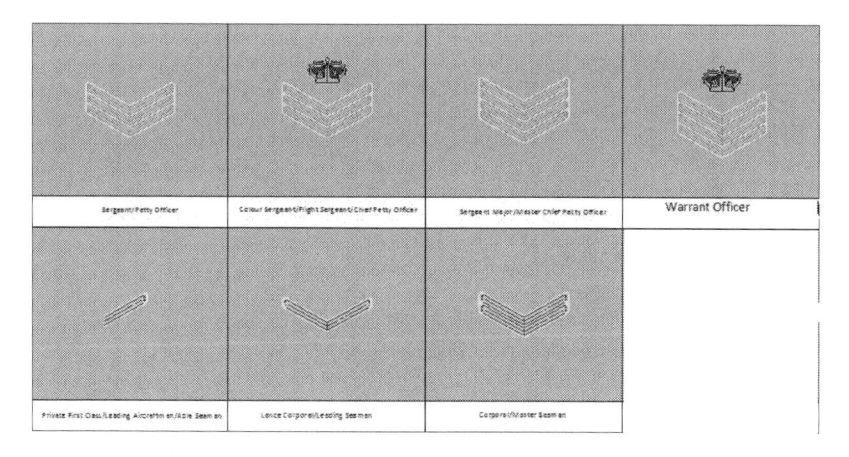

Royal Australasian Army Shoulder Insignia (Officers) post 1952

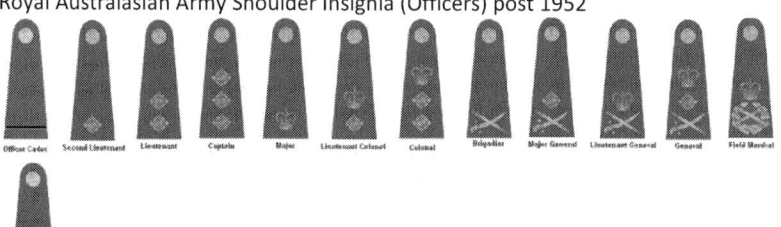

1532 26 January 1948 (flash forward)

Vice Admiral John Augustine Collins watched the decommissioning ceremony for the old girl. *Pacifica* had fought in every major action of World War 2. It was sad to see the old girl go.

The escort carrier *Wellington* had been returned to the USN. Both *Sydney* and *Melbourne* had been converted back to mercantile service as liners. For carriers, only the old *Christchurch* and *Australasia* along with the landing ship carrier *Brisbane* soldiered on, although *Australasia* was due to go later in the year or early 1949 when replaced by a U.S *Essex Class* and one or perhaps two of the U.K *Majestic Class* light carriers.

The heavy cruiser *Auckland* was still active, but *Dunedin* had been broken up, her guns preserved at the war memorial, under a pirate ship display. *Auckland* herself would decommission in 1949, replaced by a U.S built *Des Moines Class* cruiser. One of the four light cruisers were still active, two being sold to China, one to Thailand, as were the ten *Tribal Class* DD's. All of the older destroyers had met the breakers. New *Daring Class* destroyers were currently building. When the first of these arrived the *River Class* DE's would be decommissioned. The 11 *Snake Class* submarines were still in commission, as were many of the *Bathurst Class* corvettes. The war-built conversions such as the assault ships had gone back to mercantile service, and most of the MGB's had been sold. The navy was in draw down, but new ships were being laid.

Pacific Islands Summary October 1945-March 1950

1) New Caledonia
New Caledonia continued to be an Australasian Territory, administered by an appointed Governor through the Australasian Dependencies Office, however, for the first time it's citizens, regardless of race or creed were offered full rights as Australasian citizens on 12 May 1948. It had been untouched by the war. By 1950, these was discussion about Australasian Statehood, the island always being having a large population of mainland expatriates.

2) Tonga
Remained an Australasian Protectorate, with Australasia responsible from Defence and Foreign affairs, but the local Government under its own King administering all other matters. Also untouched by the war.

3) Solomon Islands
The Solomons had been a site of extensive allied basing during World War 2, but no land fighting. In January 1950, the first local councils were elected. The islands themselves remained Australasian colonies.

4) Marshall Islands
The Marshall's administration was taken over by the US from Japan as an UN mandated external territory. Former Japanese colonists were expelled back to Japan. It had seen extensive fighting and money was allocated by the US towards rebuilding, but it came at a cost. The US was to conduct 71 nuclear weapons tests in the Marshalls, leaving it the most radioactive site on Earth.

5) Ellice Islands
The Ellice Islands remained an Australasian Territory. It had been untouched by the war aside from allied basing.

6) Gilberts Islands
The Gilberts, particularly Tarawa, also remained an Australasian Territory. Tarawa, in particular, had been devastated by the war and rebuilding lasted into the 1950's.

7) Wake Island
Wake was retaken by the US after the war and rebuilt as a military base, much of it's previous infrastructure being flattened during the occasional air and naval bombardment.

8) Cook Islands, Niue, Pitcairn and Tokelau
These remained Australasian Territories, it's citizens gaining full rights as Australasian citizens on 12 May 1948.

8) Palau and the Caroline Islands
The islands groups administration was taken over by the US from Japan as an UN mandated external territory. There were many Japanese colonists and these were expelled back to Japan.

9) Nauru

Nauru's native inhabitants were moved off islands as slave labourers for the Japanese, but were brought back to their home by the RAN. The island continued as an Australasian Territory.

10) French Polynesia
Not touched by the war, the French resumed their colonial administration in 1945

11) New Hebrides
French Colonial Administration was resumed in 1945, but only after a series of protests from local islanders, who had little desire to be administered by a colonial power after being used extensively for allied basing during World War 2.

12) Bougainville/Buka
The two islands had seen extensive fighting and needed much post war rebuilding. They had resumed port war as a separate Australasian Territory. It's citizens, regardless of race or creed were offered full rights as Australasian citizens on 12 May 1948.

13) Papua/New Guinea
Both resumed post war as Australasian colonies. Some rebuilding was required and Japanese troops in some cases were discovered hiding in the mountain highlands jungles up to 1950. A fairly large Australasian Army presence was maintained due to unstableness of events in Indonesia, with Port Moresby maintaining a quite large garrison for some time.

China/Manchuria/Mongolia October 1945-March 1950

Things rapidly deteriorated in China after the end of hostilities. The Nationalists seemed to be in the better position, having recently cleared the most of the South of Japanese occupation, with a strong army that had been well fed by U.S Lend Lease.

The communists appeared to be the opposite. With the death of Mao, they seemed leaderless and with only scattered, poorly equipped forces. It was the arrival of Stalin's forces in the August 1945 offensive and the very term of the Japanese unconditional surrender that changed things. In the unconditional surrender dictated by the U.S, Japanese troops were ordered to surrender to KMT(Nationalist) troops and not to the communists present in some of the occupied areas. In Manchuria, however, where the Nationalists had no forces, the Japanese surrendered to the Soviet Union. Chiang Kai-Shek ordered the Japanese troops to remain at their post to receive the Kuomintang and not surrender their arms to the communists. In practice that did not occur.

The USSR's 1945 offensive destroyed the fighting capability of the Kwantung Army and left the USSR in occupation of all of Manchuria by the end of the war. Consequently, the 700,000 Japanese troops stationed in the region surrendered, including all their equipment. Most would see the inside of Soviet labour camps for ten years or, in some cases, permanently. Later in the year, Chiang Kai-shek realized that he lacked the resources to prevent a communist takeover of Manchuria following the scheduled Soviet departure.

Chiang made what he thought was a deal with the Russians to delay their withdrawal until he had moved enough of his best-trained men and modern material into the region; however when the time came the Russians flatly refused permission for the Nationalist troops to traverse its territory by land or air. On November 15, 1945 a Nationalist offensive began with the intent of preventing the communists from strengthening their already strong base. The Soviets had spent the extra time systematically dismantling the extensive Manchurian industrial base and shipping it back to their own war-ravaged country.

The communist forces, outnumbered, resorted to the old leveller practiced so much in Manchuria over the last 15 years. Stalin had commanded Marshal Rodion Malinovsky, the Soviet commander, to give Zhu De, now firmly installed as the Chinese communist leader, access to Kwantung army weapons dumps. They responded by using gas on their attackers.

Chiang Kai-Shek's forces pushed as far as Chinchow, taking casualties all the time, however, and an end of 1945 offensive by communist forces pushed back the Nationalist forces almost to their start lines in some areas. Worse still, exchanges of gunfire in certain sectors had involved Russian troops. Stalin had given Malinovsky authority to conduct his own offensive. He drove the Nationalists back for six days until US protests in the strongest sense stopped them and a cease fire in place was arranged.

In the "interests of peacekeeping and to protect human rights", Russian troops were to stay in Northern China and Manchuria until mid-1949. Whilst solidifying their position, Soviet advisers arranged for a series of distractions for Chiang's forces, including a full scale Islamic communist rebellion in North West Xinjiang province, with a proclaiming of the Second East Turkestan Republic. It was a bitter insurgency that lasted until late 1949, culminating in late 1949 when the five leaders of the ETR were "disappeared" on a visit to Moscow to garner support for their now losing cause, having outlived their usefulness. They also engineered a border incident with Mongolia, now formally a Soviet satellite, all to keep Chiang's forces attention from the Northeast.

In the intervening period, Zhu De had built a totalitarian state modelled on a cult of personality, virtually bankrupted the country accumulating as much military hardware as possible with Soviet support and had emulated a previous Chinese "Emperor", Qin Shi Huang, and built a huge wall across North-eastern China, either to keep his own people in or Chiang's Nationalists out, no one seemed sure.

China had become two nations, Zhu De's pervasive sense of theatre even leading him to recall Henry Piyu, languishing in prison, dress him in his Manchukuo finery and have him formally abdicate his Imperial powers to Zhu De, the country formally reverting to the old name, Manchuria. He even took one of Henry Piyu's former concubines, Li Yuqin, as his lover.

As for the Nationalist's under the KMT, they gradually established control over the rest of China, brutally suppressing any communists on "their side of the fence". By late 1949, Chiang was locked out of the North, but an undisputed master of the rest of China, including restored Formosa, renamed Taiwan. Sadly, his government was still a morass of shady deals and corruption.

China(Blue) and Manchuria(Red)

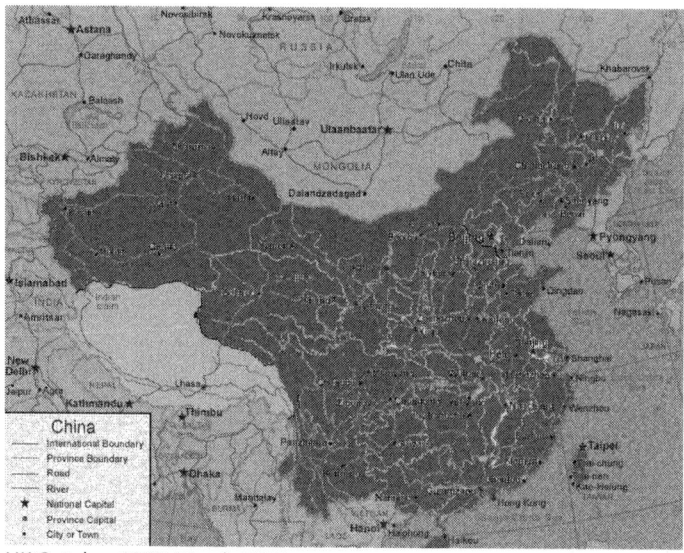

UK October 1945-March 1950

After the war, the landslide 1945 election reflected a desire by many to see the end of wartime austerity and Attlee became Prime Minister of the U.K the Labour Party had clear aims. Nationalisation, later to prove a disaster for Britain. The Bank of England, along with railroads, coal mining, public utilities and heavy industry. A comprehensive welfare state was created with the creation of a National Health Service, entitling all British citizens to healthcare, which, funded by taxation, was for at the point of delivery. Among the most important pieces of legislation was the National Insurance Act 1946, in which people in work paid a flat rate of insurance. In return, they (and the wives of male contributors) were eligible for flat-rate pensions, sickness benefit, unemployment benefit, and funeral benefit. Various other pieces of legislation provided for child benefit and support for people with no other source of income. Legislation was also passed to provide free education at all levels.

Britain was in many respects unable to afford such radical changes and the government had to cut expenditures. This began with giving independence to many British overseas colonies, beginning with those most vocal pre-war, with India in 1947 and Pakistan, Burma and Ceylon in 1948-1949. UK forces withdrew from Egypt and South Africa went its own way, as did Ireland, who cut their last ties. Under the post-war economic system, Britain had entered into a fixed exchange rate of with the U.S of $4.03 to the pound. This rate reflected Britain's sense of its own prestige and economic aspiration and optimism but was badly judged, and hampered growth. In 1949, Attlee's government had little choice but to devalue to USD 2.80/ GBP, permanently damaging the administration's credibility, although they remained popular with employment nearly full.

Britain became a founding member of the UN during this time and also helped found NATO in 1949. During the onset of the Cold War, Britain started developing developed its own nuclear arsenal, although the first test was not carried out until 1952.

Defence expenditures were drawn down, the army reducing in size dramatically, along with the RAF. By the late 1940's the RAF was again starting to modernise, the Canberra bomber having its first flight in 1949. It remained a mixture of piston engine/turboprop and jet aircraft. The RN was dramatically downsized, by March 1950 all the *KGV Class* battleships reduced to reserve, only the *Vanguard* being in commission. The older ships were all scrapped. Many of the war built light carriers were farmed out to other countries after World War 2, Australasia getting one, Holland another, France two more, Canada two. Many were left uncompleted on the stocks, as were a number of the *Swiftsure Class* cruisers.

Distracted by what would be further independence movements in Africa, the UK clearly wanted to move itself away from its remaining Pacific and Asian connections, but was drawn back into territorial disputes and a post war communist insurgency in Malaya, which it had wanted to grant independence to post war, but this would now have to be delayed. It avoided involvement in the growing problems in Indonesia, leaving this to Australasia. Whilst backing France in Indo China, it was not actively involved. The U.K's focus was shifted almost entirely to events in Africa, the Mediterranean and post war Europe, where the Cold War was starting. In Greece it's support for the successful struggle to rid the country of communist elements was particularly strong.

RN March 1950
6 CV's
7 CVL's
4 BB

U.S October 1945 - March 1950

Post war the only major industrial power in the world whose economy emerged intact— and even greatly strengthened—was the United States. Although President Roosevelt thought his personal relationship with Stalin could dissolve future difficulties, President Truman was much more sceptical.

The Soviets, too, saw their vital interests in the containment or roll-back of capitalism near their borders. Stalin was determined to absorb the Baltics, neutralize Finland and Austria, and set up pro-Moscow regimes in Poland, Romania, Czechoslovakia, Hungary, East Germany, and Bulgaria. He at first collaborated with Tito in Yugoslavia, but then they became enemies. Stalin ignored his promises at Yalta when he had promised that "free elections" would go ahead in Eastern Europe. The US was initially naïve in regards to Stalin, Indeed the British government, under the Labour Party, was at first more anti-Communist than the U.S. After making large ad-hoc loans and gifts to the Europeans in 1945-47, the U.S. reorganized its foreign aid program in the Marshall Plan, 1948–51, which gave $12 billion in gifts (and some loans) to help rebuild and modernize the West European economies. The Cold War had begun and Stalin refused to allow his satellites to accept American aid. Both sides mobilized military alliances, with NATO in the west and the Warsaw Pact in the East in operation by 1949.

Wartime rationing was officially lifted in October 1945, but prosperity did not immediately return as the next three years would witness the difficult transition back to a peacetime economy. 12 million returning veterans were in need of work and in many cases could not find it.

Inflation became a rather serious problem, averaging over 10% a year until 1950 and raw materials shortages dogged manufacturing industry. In addition, labour strikes rocked the nation, in some cases exacerbated by racial tensions due to African-Americans having taken jobs during the war and now being faced with irate returning veterans who demanded that they step aside. The huge number of women employed in the workforce in the war were also rapidly cleared out make room for their husbands.

Following the Republican takeover of Congress in the 1948 elections, President Truman was compelled to reduce taxes and curb government interference in the economy. With this done, the stage was set for the economic boom that, with only a few minor hiccups, would last for many years. After the initial hurdles of the 1945-48 period were overcome, Americans found themselves flush with cash from wartime work due to there being little to buy for several years. The result was a mass consumer spending spree, with a huge and voracious demand for new homes, cars, and housewares. Increasing numbers enjoyed high wages, larger houses, better schools, more cars and home comforts like vacuum cleaners, washing machines—which were all made for labour-saving and to make housework easier. Inventions familiar in the early 21st century made their first appearance during this era. The live-in maid and cook, common features of middle-class homes at the beginning of the century, were virtually unheard of by the 1950s; only the very rich had servants.

The U.S military went into a huge draw down, war laid ships gradually being completed, the last of these not until 1950, but no new naval construction laid down at all. There were so many surface vessels that virtually all the pre 1940 navy went to the breakers, or, at best, into mothballs. Only 4 of the old battleships were kept, joining them in mothballs were all but the Iowa Class five ships. Large numbers of older ships were expended at Bikini Atoll in nuclear tests. Only Lafayette and the old BB Texas being kept as memorials. New aircraft were ordered, the air force split off as a separate arm from the army and the jet age truly arriving, most propeller driven planes being retired. Latest equipment was the Convair B-36 and the F 86 Sabre. The army was drastically downsized and much equipment was sold abroad, the armoured units reequipping with the M26.

1950 USN
8 CV's
3 CVL's
3 BB

Dutch East Indies/Indonesia/East Indonesia October 1945-March 1950

For a country already trying to forge a national identity that had been heavily suppressed pre-war, liberation from the Dutch was initially greeted with optimistic enthusiasm by Indonesians who came to meet the Japanese army waving flags and shouting support such as "Japan is our older brother". As the Japanese advanced, rebellious Indonesians in virtually every part of the archipelago killed groups of Europeans and informed the Japanese reliably on the whereabouts of larger groups. Approximately 100,000 European and some Chinese civilians were interned and went to prisoner-of-war camps where the death rates were between 13 and 30 per cent.

Experience of the occupation varied considerably, depending upon where one lived and one's social position. Many who lived in areas considered important to the war effort experienced torture, sex slavery, arbitrary arrest and execution, and other crimes. Many thousands of people were taken away from Indonesia as forced labourers, or romusha for Japanese military projects and suffered or died as a result of ill-treatment and starvation. Between four and 10 million romusha in Java were forced to work by the Japanese military. About 270,000 of these were sent to other Japanese-held areas in South East Asia, only 52,000 were repatriated, meaning that there was a death rate of 80%.

Materially, whole railway lines, railway rolling stock, and industrial plants in Java were appropriated and shipped back to Japan and Manchuria. British intelligence reports during the occupation noted significant removals of any materials that could be used in the war effort. Needless to say, this turned the locals completely against the occupiers.

Sukarno and Hatta proclaimed independence for Indonesia on 29th August. The following day, the Central Indonesian National Committee elected Sukarno as President, and Hatta as Vice President. It was mid-September before news of the declaration of independence spread to the outer islands, and many Indonesians far from the capital did not believe it. As the news spread, most Indonesians came to regard themselves as pro-Republican, and a mood of revolution swept across the country. External power had shifted; it would be a few weeks before Allied Forces entered Indonesia, and the Dutch were too weakened by World War II. The Japanese, on the other hand, were required by the terms of the surrender to both lay down their arms and maintain order; a contradiction that some resolved by handing weapons to Japanese-trained Indonesians.

The resulting power vacuums in the weeks following the Japanese surrender, created an atmosphere of uncertainty, but also one of opportunity for the Republicans. By early September 1945, control of major infrastructure installations, including railway stations and trams in Java's largest cities, had been taken over by Republicans who encountered little Japanese resistance.

Republican leaders struggled to come to terms with popular sentiment; some wanted passionate armed struggle; others a more reasoned approach. Sukarno and Hatta were more interested in planning out a government and institutions to achieve independence through diplomacy. It was common for ethnic 'out-groups' – Dutch internees, Eurasians, Ambonese and Chinese – and anyone considered to be a spy, to be subjected to intimidation, kidnap, robbery, and sometimes murder, even organised massacres. Such attacks would continue to some extent for the course of the revolution. As the level of violence increased across the country, the Sukarno and Hatta led Republican government in Jakarta urged calm. However, many in favour of armed struggle saw the older leadership as dithering and betraying the revolution, which often led to conflict amongst Indonesians.

The Dutch accused Sukarno and Hatta of collaborating with the Japanese, and denounced the Republic as a creation of Japanese fascism. The Dutch East Indies administration had been promised a ten-million-dollar loan from the US to finance its return to Indonesia. Keith Park, who took over from Blamey on 1 October, wrote a stinging protect against this, telling Melbourne that this would only further inflame an already knife edged situation, where he had just landed troops to disarm the Japanese and restore order. He sent copies to both the Queen and Prime Minister Peter Fraser. After protects to Washington, the offer was withdrawn. By early 1946 three Australasian Army Divisions were in Indonesia.

The Australasians were charged with restoring order and civilian government in Java. The Dutch took this to mean pre-war colonial administration and continued to claim sovereignty over Indonesia. Troops did not, however, land on Java to accept the Japanese surrender until mid-September 1945. Blamey and later Park's immediate tasks included the repatriation of some 300,000 Japanese, and freeing prisoners of war. He did not want, nor did he have the resources, or for that matter the inclination, to commit his troops to a long struggle to regain Indonesia for the Dutch.

Park was desirous of removing as many inflaming symbols as possible and diverted soldiers of the former Dutch colonial army and over 10,000 Indo-Europeans and European internees back to Port Moresby, using RAN ships as transport. They could be sorted out there, where there was ample war-built accommodation, away from harm and any trouble they may cause. Many would end up in either the Netherlands, Singapore or Australasia.

It was not until February 1946 that the Dutch landed their forces in Jakarta and other key centres, Australasia refusing any assistance in doing so. Republican sources reported 13,000 deaths up to March 1946 in the defence of Jakarta, but they could not hold the city. The Republican leadership thus established themselves in the city of Yogyakarta with the crucial support of the new sultan. On Java and Sumatra, the Dutch found some military success in cities and major towns, but they were unable to subdue the villages and countryside. On the outer islands (including Bali), Republican sentiment was not as strong. They were consequently occupied by the Dutch with comparative ease, and an autonomous state were set up by the Dutch. The campaign was becoming increasingly bloody and showing little sign of ending by late 1946.

Finally an agreement was brokered by Australasia, partly by threat of using the troops still on Indonesian soil, some 60,000. Concluded on 2 December 1946, it saw the Netherlands recognize the Republic as the authority over Java, Madura and Sumatra, as well as Borneo, still held by Australasian troops. Both parties agreed to the formation of by 1 January 1949, a semi-autonomous state with the monarch of the Netherlands at its head. The Republican-controlled Java and Sumatra would be one of its states, alongside areas that were generally under stronger Dutch influence, including southern Kalimantan, and the East, which consisted of Sulawesi, Maluku, the Sundra Islands and New Guinea. The Central National Committee of Indonesia did not ratify the agreement until February 1947, and neither the Republic nor the Dutch were satisfied with it. Both sides soon accused the other of violating the agreement.

In July 1947, the Dutch launched a major military offensive with the intent of conquering the Republic. Claiming violations of the agreement, the Dutch described the campaign as "police actions" to restore law and order. Soon after the end of World War II, 25,000 volunteers had been sent overseas. They were later followed by larger numbers of conscripts from the Netherlands. In the offensive, Dutch forces drove Republican troops out of parts of Sumatra, and East and West Java. The Republicans were confined to the Yogyakarta region of Java. To maintain their force in Java, now numbering 100,000 troops, the Dutch gained control of lucrative Sumatran plantations, and oil and coal installations, and in Java, control of all deep-water ports.

International reaction to the Dutch actions was negative. Neighbouring Australasia and newly independent India were particularly active in supporting the Republic's cause in the UN, as was the Soviet Union and the United States. It's was the US suspension of Marshall Plan aid, badly needed in the Netherlands and its intention to, in conjunction with the Australasian Navy, blockade Java, that in the finish brought the Dutch back to the table.

Sectarian religious violence had long been a main issue in the Dutch East Indies and consequently, both parties eventually agreed to a referendum on independence for the former colony. It gave five options, full independence, for a separate Muslim Indonesia/Christian East Indonesia split, each entity being fully independent, for the same two options again as an independent Dutch dominion and lastly to remain a Dutch colony. The option of a separate Indonesia/East Indonesia would be deemed to be binding if either designated area voted for it.

East Indonesia encompassed Western New Guinea, West Timor, Flores, Sumba, West Timor and the Southern Malucu's including Ambon. It was the option for full independence as separate states that was decided.

For President Sukarno, it was an option that he opposed, however, it disposed of the Dutch and gave him over 90% of the cake. It would have to do for now. On the plus side it gave him a more homogeneous country with less ethnic, and particularly religious, minorities. From 1 July to 1 December 1948, people were given the option of moving from one state to another, with transport provided by military forces, much like in 1947 India and Pakistan, but with an offer of free passage. On 1 December 1948, official transfer of sovereignty ceremonies marked the transfer of power to both countries.

For The Netherlands itself, it was a stinging slap in the face that affected its relationship with Australasia for some time, but for many enlightened liberals, it was a wakeup call that was marking the end of colonialism everywhere. An exceptionally rich colony, its loss hurt, however, it did allow the Netherlands to concentrate on its own rebuilding and eased the later reactions to pro-independence movements in its South American possessions.

Map showing division between East Indonesia and Indonesia (black line)

Philippines October 1945- March 1950

On July 4, 1946, representatives of the USA and of the Philippines signed a Treaty of General Relations between the two governments. The treaty provided for the recognition of the independence of the Republic of the Philippines as of July 4, 1946, and the relinquishment of American sovereignty over the Philippine Islands.

It came with numerous strings attached. The U.S. retained dozens of military bases, including a few major ones. In addition, independence was qualified by legislation passed such as the Bell Trade Act which provided a mechanism whereby U.S. import quotas might be established on Philippine articles which "are coming, or are likely to come, into substantial competition with like articles the product of the United States" It further required U.S. citizens and corporations be granted equal access to Philippine minerals, forests, and other natural resources.

The Philippine government had little choice but to accept these terms for independence. The US Congress was threatening to withhold post-World War II rebuilding funds unless the Bell Act was ratified, funds the war-ravaged country could not do without. The Philippine Congress obliged on July 2, 1946.

Manuel Roxas became the first president of the new republic. His administration was marred by graft and corruption; moreover, the abuses of the provincial military police contributed to the rise of the left-wing movements in the countryside. His heavy-handed attempts to crush these led to widespread peasant disaffection. Roxas did not stay long in office because of a heart attack as he was speaking at Clark Air Base on April 15, 1948. He was succeeded by his vice president Elpidio Quirino. His six years as president were marked by notable post-war reconstruction, general economic gains, and increased economic aid from the United States. Basic social problems, however, particularly in the rural areas, remained unsolved, and his administration was tainted by widespread graft and corruption.

The country itself also faced a legal challenge from the former Sultan of Sulu, Esmail Kiram 1st, who claimed the Republic had no rights to the Sulu Sea islands to the South of the Philippines and that they had been "stolen by conquest", firstly by Spain and then the U.S and the new republic.

This was defeated, with previous military conquest being ruled a legitimate way that territory could have been acquired at the time. It did, however, throw up many questions about the lease agreement the former British North Borneo Company had acquired on Sabah, that would later bedevil sovereignty there.

Burma October 1945-March 1950

The surrender of the Japanese brought a military administration to Burma. The restored government established a political program that focused on physical reconstruction of the country and delayed discussion of independence. The nationalists opposed the government, leading to political instability in the country. A rift had also developed between the Communists and the socialists, including the most prominent nationalist leader Aung San. In September 1946 the Rangoon police went on strike, this then spread from the police to government employees and came close to becoming a general strike. The British Governor Rance calmed the situation by meeting with Aung San and convincing him to join the Governor's Executive Council along with others. The new executive council, which now had increased credibility in the country, began negotiations for Burmese independence, which were concluded successfully in London by agreement on 27 January 1947. The agreement left parts of the communist and conservative branches dissatisfied, however, sending the Red Flag Communists underground and the conservatives into opposition.

On 19 July 1947 U Saw, a conservative pre-war Prime Minister of Burma, engineered the assassination of Aung San and several members of his cabinet including his eldest brother Ba Win, while meeting in the Secretariat. Thakin Nu, the Socialist leader, was now asked to form a new cabinet, and he presided over Burmese independence on 4 January 1948. The popular sentiment to part with the British was so strong at the time that Burma opted not to join the Commonwealth, unlike India or Pakistan.

The first years of Burmese independence were marked by successive insurgencies by the Red Flag Communists led by Thakin Soe, the White Flag Communists led by Thakin Than Tun, the Yèbaw Hpyu (White-band PVO) led by Bo La Yaung, a member of the Thirty Comrades, army rebels calling themselves the Revolutionary Burma Army (RBA) led by Communist officers Bo Zeya, Bo Yan Aung and Bo Yè Htut – all three of them members of the Thirty Comrades. These were put down by both local troops and Nationalist Chinese troops forces under the command of General Li Mi, China having become the fledgling republic's main ally.

Portugal, Macau, Goa and East Timor October 1945-March 1950

Portugal reoccupied both its colonies in October 1945, with little in the way of resistance from their native inhabitants. Whist they continued to invest in Macau and Goa, in East Timor Portugal continued to neglect the colony. Very little investment was made in infrastructure, education and healthcare. Locally, authority rested with the Portuguese Governor and the Legislative Council, as well as local chiefs. Only a small minority of Timorese were educated.

Sarawak October 1945 - March 1950

Charles Vyner Brooke had returned to Sarawak with the invading Australasian troops not long after the Japanese had been expelled. He quickly gathered back up the reins of government and attempted to steer a middle course that would keep him clear of the troubles in Indonesia. He had withdrawn 200,000 pounds just prior to the Japanese occupation in exchange for constitution amendments that reduced his powers as an absolute ruler. He had hoped to use that to support himself and his three daughters, having little confidence in his original heir, his nephew Anthony.

On reflection, in Australasia, he had changed tack and named his oldest daughter Leonora his heir and set about rebuilding the country, using the 200,000 pounds on renewed capital investment and to restart the countries oil industry.

In contrast to many other areas of the empire, the Brooke dynasty had been intent on a policy of paternalism in order to protect the indigenous population against exploitation. They governed with the aid of the mainly Muslim Malays and enlisted the Ibans as a contingent militia. The Brooke dynasty also encouraged the immigration of Chinese merchants but forbade the Chinese to settle outside of towns in order to minimise the impact on the native Dayak way of life. Brooke continued these policies post war, but, with change sweeping Asia, acceded to demands for elections and set up a constituent assembly, the first elections taking place in 1949. He also reached out to expand the influence of the ever-increasing Chinese population of Sarawak. Brooke's investments in the countries oil and gas infrastructure and refineries, mainly at Miri, paid him handsome dividends and repaid the eventual million pounds investment many times over. One of the few oil producing areas in Borneo and Indonesia not badly bombed and likewise destroyed by the war, Sarawak leaped ahead to prosperity and consolidated the popularity of the White Rajas. This allayed much of the objections from Malay Islamists regarding his daughter being his heir, although his eventual aim was to pass the office to his grandson.

By 1952, his daughter had abdicated her claim in favour of her son, Simon Mackay, renamed Simon Brooke. Now his grandfather's heir, he had already inherited a fortune from his father, via a half share in Inchcape plc, a multinational retail and services company with strong Asian ties, that by 2013 had a turnover of 8 billion pounds per annum. Charles Vyner had at that stage also negotiated with Royal Dutch Shell continued exclusive rights to Sarawak oil, in exchange for increased royalties. In exchange for his initial investment, he contracted 2% of those royalties to the Brooke family, more than repaying his initial investment.

Sabah resumed under a separate colonial administration, still involving the British North Borneo Company, as did Labuan. Brunei resumed much as per war, although much infrastructure needed to be replaced as it had been extensively bombed as a major Japanese base.

0908 25 January 1947

It was the first flight of a fully armed and combat loaded prototype and Hencall was excited to see how it went. It was a much more evolutionary design than his new fighter, being merely a placement of jet engines on the old He 200 body shape.

Never the less, the original body was aerodynamically close to perfect, so the fit had not been hard. her first flight had been on 26 October 1946, but that had not been combat laden. Since then she had been airborne in conjunction with the second prototype over twenty times.

By 1102, she had landed back and the test pilot, "Ginger" Allen had professed himself happy. He hoped to be able to make deliveries of the new machine, which he had named the He 2 to commemorate a new start, by the end of the year.

USSR October 1945-March 1950

Soviet Russia had borne the brunt of World War 2, with quite possibly up to 27 million casualties, two thirds of them civilians. Her industry and infrastructure, particularly in the

West, were devastated.

Stalin was determined to punish those peoples he saw as collaborating with Germany during the war and to deal with the problem of nationalism, which would tend to pull the Soviet Union apart. Millions of Poles, Latvians, Georgians, Ukrainians and other ethnic minorities were deported to Gulags in Siberia. In addition, in 1941, 1943 and 1944 several whole nationalities had been deported to Siberia, Kazakhstan, and Central Asia, including, among others, the Volga Germans, Chechens, Ingush, Balkars, Crimean tartars and Turks. Although these groups were later politically "rehabilitated", some were never given back their former autonomous regions. In 1946 and 1947 the country had the additional burden of a famine and a Ukrainian uprising that was ruthlessly suppressed.

In the aftermath of World War II, the Soviet Union extended its political and military influence over Eastern Europe, in a move that was a continuation of the older policies of the Russian Empire. Some territories that had been lost by Soviet Russia in 1918 were annexed by the Soviet Union after World War II: the Baltic States and eastern portions of interwar Poland. They also gained the northern half of East Prussia from Germany, plus Transcarpathia from Czechoslovakia and Bukovina from Romania. Finally, in the late 1940s, pro-Soviet Communist Parties won the elections in five countries of Central and Eastern Europe (Poland, Czechoslovakia, Hungary, Romania and Bulgaria) and subsequently became People's Democracies. These elections were, of course, rigged, and the Western powers did not recognize the elections as legitimate. For the duration of the Cold War, the countries of Eastern Europe became Soviet satellites — they were "independent" nations, which were one-party Communist States whose General Secretary had to be approved by the Kremlin, and so their governments usually kept their policy in line with the wishes of the Soviet Union, although nationalistic forces and pressures within the satellite states played a part in causing some deviation from strict Soviet rule.

The mild political liberalization that took place in the Soviet Union during the war quickly came to an end in 1945. The Orthodox Church was generally left unmolested after the war and was even allowed to print small amounts of religious literature, but persecution of minority religions was resumed. Stalin and the Communist Party were given full credit for the victory over Germany, and generals such as Zhukov were demoted to regional commands. Even so, the basic structures and tensions that marked the cold war were not yet in place in 1945-1946. Despite the necessary means of the United States to advance a different vision of post-war Europe, Stalin initially viewed the re-emergence of Germany and Japan as the Soviet Union's chief threats, not the United States. At the time, the prospects of an Anglo-American front against the USSR seemed slim from Stalin's stance. This changed with the events of the Greek civil war and the Western powers policy of encirclement or containment of communist ambitions. With the onset of the Cold War, anti-Western propaganda was stepped up, with the capitalist world depicted as a decadent place where crime, unemployment, and poverty were rampant.

Stalin's personality cult reached its height in the post-war period, with his picture displayed in every school, factory, and government office, yet he rarely appeared in public. Post-war reconstruction proceeded rapidly, but as the emphasis was all on heavy industry and energy, living standards remained low, especially outside of the major cities. Weapons production, however, which the USSR was already tooled up to do, continued unabated.

In one sense, the aims of the Soviet Union may not have been aggressive expansionism but rather consolidation, i.e., attempting to secure the war-torn country's western borders. Stalin, assuming that Japan and Germany could menace the Soviet Union once again by the 1960s, thus quickly imposed Moscow-dominated governments in the springboards of the Nazi onslaught: Poland, Romania and Bulgaria. Much of the rest of the world, however, viewed these moves as an aggressive attempt to expand Soviet influence and communist rule. Disagreements over post-war plans first centred on Eastern and Central Europe. Having lost more than 20 million in the war, suffered German and Nazi German invasion, and suffered tens of millions of casualties due to onslaughts from the West three times in the preceding 150 years, first with Napoleon, Stalin was determined to destroy Germany's capacity for another war by keeping it under tight control. U.S. aims were quite different.

By successfully aiding Greece in 1947, Truman also set a precedent for the U.S. aid to anti-communist regimes worldwide, even authoritarian ones at times. U.S. foreign policy moved to the view that the Soviets had to be "contained" using "unalterable counter force at every point", until the breakdown of Soviet power occurred.

The United States launched massive economic reconstruction efforts, first in Western Europe and then in Japan (as well as in South Korea and China). The Marshall Plan began to pump $12 billion into Western Europe. The rationale was that economically stable nations were less likely to fall prey to Soviet influence, a view which was vindicated in the long run.

In response Stalin blockaded Berlin in 1948. The city was within the Soviet zone, although subject to the control of all four major powers. The Soviets cut off all rail and road routes to West Berlin. Convinced that he could starve and freeze the city into submission, no trucks or trains were allowed entry into the city. However, this decision backfired when Truman embarked on a highly visible move that would humiliate the Soviets internationally — supplying the beleaguered city by air. Military confrontation threatened while Truman, with British help, flew supplies over East Germany into West Berlin during the 1948–49 blockade. This costly aerial supplying of West Berlin became known as the Berlin airlift.

Truman joined eleven other nations in 1949 to form NATO, the United States' first "entangling" European alliance in 170 years. Stalin replied to these moves by integrating the economies of Eastern Europe in his version of the Marshall Plan, exploding the first Soviet Atomic Bomb in 1949, and signing an alliance with Manchuria in February 1950. However, the Warsaw Pact, Eastern Europe's counterpart to NATO, was not created until 1955, two years after Stalin's death.

Militarily the Soviet Union remained a first rank power. Its air force bringing on line new jet engine planes such as the Yak-23, the La-15 and the Il-28, the last a two-engine bomber, although many older types remained in service. Their development was hastened by the foolish decision by the UK to allow export of the excellent Rolls Royce Nene engine. Its army was the largest in the world and was lavishly equipped with tanks, including the new and excellent T54, as well as the JS-3.

The Soviet navy was very much the poor relation, but had started the first part of an ambitious program to build 340 *Whisky Class* submarines. Post-World War 2 it had been given the ex-Italian battleship *Roma* and badly needed to renew its aging war-built surface fleet, previously based around two old pre-WW1 battleships and six *Kirov Class* heavy cruisers.

Ceylon October 1945-March 1950

Following World War II, public pressure for independence increased. British Ceylon achieved independence on 4 February 1948, with an amended constitution taking effect on the same date. Military treaties with the United Kingdom preserved intact British air and sea bases in the country and British officers also continued to fill most of the upper ranks of the Army. Don Senanyake the first Prime Minister of Ceylon. In its early years the country remained strongly British in outlook, with most of the top government officials still British.

Malaya and Singapore October 1945-March 1950

The Japanese had a racial policy just as the British did. They regarded the Malays as a colonial people liberated from British imperialist rule, and fostered a limited form of Malay nationalism, which gained them some degree of collaboration from the Malay civil service and intellectuals. The occupiers regarded the Chinese, however, which formed a large percentage of Malaya and Singapore's population, as enemy aliens, and treated them with great harshness, up to 80,000 Chinese in Malaya and Singapore were killed. Chinese businesses were expropriated and Chinese schools either closed or burned down.

Although the Japanese argued that they supported Malay nationalism, they offended Malay nationalism by allowing their early ally Thailand to re-annex the four northern states, Kedah, Perlis, Kelantan, and Terengganu that had been surrendered to the British in 1909. The loss of Malaya's export markets soon produced enormous unemployment which affected all races and made the Japanese increasingly unpopular.

During occupation, ethnic tensions were raised and nationalism grew. The Malayans were thus on the whole glad to see the British back in 1945, but things could not remain as they were before the war, and a stronger desire for independence grew. Britain was quickly in financial trouble and the new Labour government was keen to withdraw its forces from the East as soon as possible. Colonial self-rule and eventual independence were now British policy. The tide of colonial nationalism sweeping through Asia soon reached Malaya. But most Malays were more concerned with defending themselves against the Malayan Communist party (MCP) than with demanding independence from the British; indeed, their immediate concern was that the British not leave and abandon the Malays to the armed Communists, which were the largest armed force in the country.

In 1944 the British drew up plans for a Malayan Union, which would turn the Federated and Unfederated Malay States, plus Penang and Malacca (but not Singapore), into a single Crown colony, with a view towards independence. The Bornean territories and Singapore were left out as it was thought this would make union more difficult to achieve. There was however strong opposition from the Malays, who opposed the weakening of the Malay rulers and the granting of citizenship to Chinese and other minorities. The British had decided on equality between races as they perceived the Chinese and Indians, quite rightly, as more loyal to the British during the war than the Malays. The Sultans, who had initially supported it, backed down and placed themselves at the head of the resistance.

In 1946 the United Malay National Organisation (UMNO) was founded by Malay nationalists. They favoured independence for Malaya, but only if the new state was run exclusively by the Malays. Faced with implacable Malay opposition, the British dropped the plan for equal citizenship. The Malayan Union was thus established in 1946, and was dissolved in 1948 and replaced by the Federation of Malaya, which restored the autonomy of the rulers of the Malay states under British protection.

Meanwhile the Communists were moving towards open insurrection. The MPAJA had been disbanded in December 1945, and the MCP organised as a legal political party, but the MPAJA's arms were carefully stored for future use. The MCP policy was for immediate independence with full equality for all races. This meant it recruited very few Malays. The Party's strength was in the Chinese-dominated trade unions. In March 1947, reflecting the international Communist movement's "turn to left" as the Cold War set in, the MCP leader Lai Tek turned the party increasingly to direct action. These rebels launched guerrilla operations designed to force the British out of Malaya. In July, following a string of assassinations of plantation managers, the colonial government struck back, declaring a State of Emergency, banning the MCP and arresting hundreds of its militants. The Party retreated to the jungle and formed the Malayan People Liberation Army, with about 9,000 men under arms, nearly all Chinese.

The Malayan Emergency lasted from 1948 to 1954, and involved a long anti-insurgency campaign by British and Australasian troops in Malaya. The strategy, which proved ultimately successful, was to isolate the MCP from its support base by a combination of economic and political concessions to the Chinese and the resettlement of Chinese squatters into areas free of MCP influence. The effective mobilisation of the Malays against the MCP was also an important part. From 1948 the MCP campaign lost momentum and the number of recruits fell sharply, by 1952 it was confined to the far North of the country, out of contact with its Manchurian sponsors. With the end of the Malayan crisis, Malaya was on the brink of Independence.

Nepal/Bhutan/Tibet/Sikkim October 1945-March 1950

These sparsely populated, mainly Buddhist countries remained true frontiers. China, occupied mainly with Manchuria, continued to regards Tibet as a province, Tibet continued to self-govern under the Dalai Lama. Tibet continued in 1949 to have very limited contacts with the rest of the world and was closed to foreigners. Very few governments had anything resembling a normal diplomatic recognition of Tibet with the exception of the UK.

Bhutan, Nepal and Sikkim, three alpine monarchies, led largely a life of isolation. Their defence and foreign affairs, handled by the UK prior to Indian independence, fell to India post 1947. They remained absolute monarchies, backward in all senses, slavery being legal until the 1920's.

Thailand October 1945-March 1950

Pridi Phanomyong was the dominant figure in Thailand's politics post war. The country had finished the war with many casualties, no navy, no air force and on the Japanese surrender, still had 7% of its territory occupied.

Democratic elections were held for the first time in December 1945. These were the first elections in which political parties were legal, and Pridi's People's Party and its allies won a majority. In March 1946 Pridi became Siam's first democratically elected Prime Minister. In 1947 he agreed to hand back the French territory occupied in 1940 as the price for admission to the UN, the dropping of all wartime claims against Siam due to its initial Japanese alliance and a substantial package of American aid.

In December 1945, the young king Ananda Mahidol had returned to Siam from Europe, but in July 1946 he was found shot dead in his bed, under mysterious circumstances. Three palace servants were tried and executed for his murder, although there are significant doubts as to their guilt and the case remains both murky and a highly sensitive topic in Thailand today. The king was succeeded by his younger brother Bhumibol Adulyadej. In August Pridi was forced to resign amid suspicion that he had been involved in the regicide. Without his leadership, the civilian government floundered, and in November 1947 the army, the one branch of the armed services that had remained strong, seized power under General Khuang.

Kuang's regime coincided with the onset of the Cold War and the establishment of a Communist regime in North Vietnam. He soon won the support of the U.S., beginning a long tradition of U.S.-backed military regimes in Thailand (as the country was again renamed in July 1949, this time permanently). Once again political opponents were arrested and tried, and some were executed. There were attempted counter-coups by Pridi supporters in 1948, 1949 and 1951, the second leading to heavy fighting between the army and navy before Kuang emerged victorious. In the navy's 1951 attempt, popularly known as the Manhattan Coup, Kuang was nearly killed when the ship he was held hostage aboard was bombed by the pro-government air force.

India, Pakistan and Punjaba October 1945-March 1950

With the finish of the war in September 1945, the most immediate problem for the British was how, war weary and exhausted, they were to deliver on the promises to the people of that "jewel of the empire", India.

In January 1946, a number of mutinies broke out in the armed services, starting with that of RAF servicemen frustrated with their slow repatriation to Britain. The mutinies came to a head with others in Calcutta, Madras, and Karachi. Although the mutinies were rapidly suppressed, they had the effect of spurring the new Attlee government in Britain to action, and leading to the Cabinet Mission to India led by the Secretary of State for India, Lord Lawrence and including Sir Stafford Cripps, who had visited four years before. Also, in early 1946, new elections were called in India. The Indian National Congress achieved electoral victories in eight of the eleven provinces. The negotiations between the Congress and the Muslim League, however, stumbled over the issue of the partition.

Jinnah proclaimed 16 August 1946, Direct Action Day, with the stated goal of highlighting, peacefully, the demand for a Muslim homeland in India. However, on the morning of the 16th armed Muslim gangs gathered in Calcutta to hear the League's Chief Minister of

Bengal, who, if he did not explicitly incite violence certainly gave the crowd the impression that they could act with impunity, that neither the police nor the military would be called out and that the ministry would turn a blind eye to any action they unleashed in the city.

That very evening, in Calcutta, Hindus were attacked by returning Muslim celebrants, who carried pamphlets distributed earlier showing a clear connection between violence and the demand for Pakistan, and implicating the celebration of Direct Action day directly with the outbreak of the cycle of violence that would be later called the "Great Calcutta Killing of August 1946". The next day, Hindus struck back and the violence continued for three days in which approximately 4,000 people died (according to official accounts), Hindus and Muslims in equal numbers. Although India had had outbreaks of religious violence between Hindus and Muslims before, the Calcutta killings was the first to display elements of "ethnic cleansing," in modern parlance. Violence was not confined to the public sphere, but homes were entered, destroyed, and women and children attacked.

Although the Government of India and the Congress were both shaken by the course of events, in September, a Congress-led interim government was installed, with Jawaharlal Nehru as united India's prime minister.

The communal violence spread to Bihar (where Muslims were attacked by Hindus), to Bengal (where Hindus were targeted by Muslims), in the United Provinces (where Muslims were attacked by Hindus), and on to Rawalpindi in March 1947 in which Hindus were attacked or driven out by Muslims.

Late in 1946, the Labour government in Britain, its exchequer exhausted by the recently concluded World War II, decided to end British rule of India, and in early 1947 Britain announced its intention of transferring power no later than June 1948. However, with the British army unprepared for the potential for increased violence, the new viceroy, Lord Louis Mountbatten, advanced the date for the transfer of power, allowing less than six months for a mutually agreed plan for independence. It was accelerated by ever increasing violence in the Punjab. Sikhs and Muslims in particular participating in many violent protests, the Sikhs agitating for their own homeland, seemingly a forgotten minority. Both Congress and League leaders agreed to partition Punjab upon religious lines, a precursor to the wider partition of the country.

In June 1947, the nationalist leaders, including Nehru and Kalam Azad on behalf of the Congress, Jinnah representing the Muslim League and Master Tara Singh representing the Sikhs, agreed to a partition of the country along religious lines in opposition to Gandhi's views. Inspired by events in Indonesia, each religious minority obtained its own homeland. The predominantly Hindu Sikh areas were assigned to the new India and predominantly Muslim areas to the new nation of Pakistan. The Sikhs obtained the own homeland, Panjab, centred to the Northwest in India and between India and Pakistan, centred on the cities of Amritsar (the capital), Ludhiana, Jalandhar and Patiala. The plan included a partition of the Muslim-majority provinces of Punjab and Bengal. The communal violence that accompanied the announcement of the Radcliffe lines, the lines of partition, was even more horrific.

More than 18 million displaced people were to move in an attempt to get within the borders of one state or another. The newly formed governments were completely unequipped to deal with migrations of such staggering magnitude, and massive violence and slaughter occurred on both sides of the border. Estimates of the number of deaths vary, with low estimates at 300,000 and high estimates at 1,200,000.

On 14 August 1947, the new Dominion of Pakistan came into being, with Muhammad Ali Jinnah sworn in as its first Governor General. The following day, 15 August 1947, Punjaba came into existence as a dominion also, under Tara Singh. India, now a smaller *Union of India*, became an independent country on 16 August with official ceremonies taking place in New Delhi, and with Jawaharlal Nehru assuming the office of Prime Minister and the viceroy, Louis Mountbatten, staying on as its first Governor General; Gandhi, however, remained in Bengal, preferring instead to work among the new refugees of the partitioned subcontinent.

On 18 July 1947, the British Parliament passed the act that finalized the arrangements for partition and abandoned British suzerainty over the princely states, of which there were several hundred, leaving them free to choose whether to accede to one of the new dominions.

British India had consisted of 17 provinces and 562 princely states, some large, some very small. The provinces were given to India, Punjaba or Pakistan, in some cases in particular, after being partitioned. The princes, however, won the right to either remain independent or join either nation. Thus, India's leaders faced the prospect of inheriting a nation fragmented between medieval-era kingdoms and provinces organised by colonial powers. The new governments employed political negotiations backed with the option (and, on several occasions, the use) of military action to ensure the primacy of the Central governments and of the Constitutions then being drafted. By the end of 1947 all but two had been resolved, Hyderabad (eventually invaded by India in 1948) and Kashmir.

The area of Kashmir (Muslim majority state with a Hindu king) in the far north of the subcontinent quickly became a source of controversy that erupted into the initial Indo-Pakistan war which lasted from 1947 to 1949. Eventually a United Nations-overseen ceasefire was agreed that left India in control of two-thirds of the contested region, Pakistan the balance. Punjaba kept strictly neutral. Nehru initially agreed to Mountbatten's proposal that a plebiscite be held in the entire state as soon as hostilities ceased, and an UN-sponsored cease-fire was agreed to by both parties on 1 January 1949. No state-wide plebiscite was ever held, however.

The Indian Assembly adopted the Constitution of India on 26 November 1949. India became a sovereign, democratic, republic after its constitution came into effect on 26 January 1950. Rajendra Prasad became the first President.

In Pakistan, by the ending months of 1947, the national government led by Prime minister Ali-Khan was able to settle the core issue of territorial boundaries, Karachi being the state's first capital. Ideological and territorial problems arose with neighbouring states, mainly with India over Kashmir which was a theatre of war in 1947-48.

It was declared "Urdu alone would be the state language and the lingua franca of the Pakistan state", though he called Bengali as the official language of the Bengal province."; nonetheless, tensions began to grow in Bengal.

In Punjaba, Yadvinder Singh Mahendra Bahadur, the former Maharakja of Patiala, was offered the position of Governor General as the country skilfully managed to keep out of the conflicts of its two much larger neighbours.

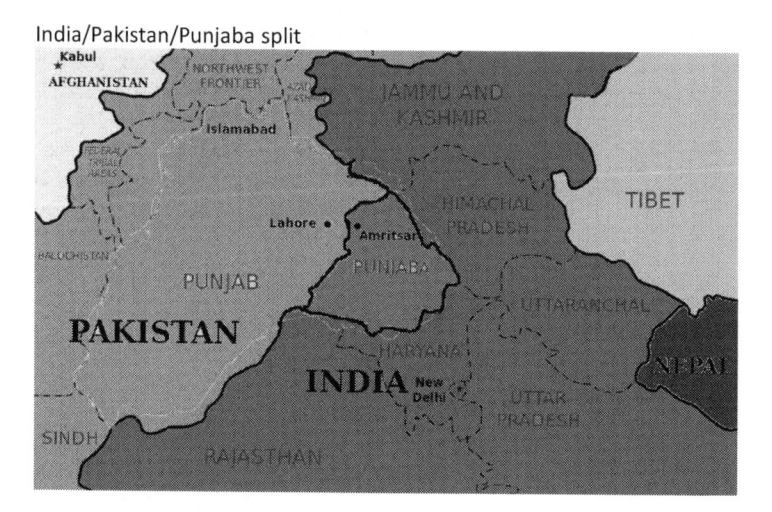

India/Pakistan/Punjaba split

France October 1946-March 1950

After the war and the Provisional French Republic (GPRF) was instituted. With most of the political class discredited and containing many members who had more or less collaborated, Gaullism and Communism became the most popular political forces in France.

De Gaulle led the GPRF from 1944 to 1946. Meanwhile, negotiations took place over the proposed new constitution, which was to be put to a referendum. De Gaulle advocated a presidential system of government, and criticized the reinstatement of what he pejoratively called "the party's system". He resigned in January 1946 in protest at the adoption of the latter. In the 1946 election the socialists and communists won power, but soon quarrelled themselves in 1947, the communist leaving the government. This left the socialists in a minority. The split of the alliance in spring 1947, the departure of Communist ministers, and Gaullist opposition did not create conditions for ministerial stability. Coalitions were composed of an undisciplined patchwork of centre and centre-left parties. Finally, the Fourth Republic was confronted with the collapse of the French colonial empire, which, after the country's humiliations in World War 2, it could not afford to lose, either politically or on the basis of National pride.

French Navy 1950
1BB
2 CVL

French Indo China October 1945-March 1950

This essentially covers three areas, Laos, Cambodia and Vietnam, all with traditional local monarchs.

On 9 March 1945, during the Japanese occupation, young king Norodom Sihanouk had proclaimed an independent Kingdom of Kampuchea, following a formal request by the Japanese. Shortly thereafter the Japanese government nominally ratified the independence of Cambodia and established a consulate in Phnom Penh. After Allied military units entered Cambodia, the Japanese military forces present in the country were disarmed and repatriated. The French were able to reimpose the colonial administration in Phnom Penh in November the same year, over much protest from local noble families. The independence movement continue, however, with the powerful support of the King.

In Laos, independence movements also existed, however, their most staunch opponent was their own King. Sisavang Phoulivong was a lifelong supporter of French rule in Laos, and in 1945 he refused to cooperate with Lao nationalists and he was deposed when the Lao Issara declared the country independent. In April 1946, the French took over once again and he was reinstated as king (the first time a Lao monarch actually ruled all of what is today called Laos).

Vietnam was much more politically sophisticated and its people better educated, therefore its desire for independence was that much greater.

In March 1945, Japan launched the Second Indochina Campaign and ousted the Vichy French and formally installed Emperor Bảo Đại in the short-lived Empire of Vietnam. Post surrender, Japanese forces allowed the Viet Minh and other nationalist groups to take over public buildings and weapons without resistance. After their defeat the Japanese Army gave weapons to the Viet Minh, the communist and nationalist guerrillas that had previously been their main opponents. In order to further help the nationalists, the Japanese kept Vichy French officials and military officers imprisoned for a month after the surrender.

Ho Chi Minh claimed in a speech in October 1945 that due to a combination of ruthless Japanese exploitation and poor weather, a famine had occurred in which approximately 2 million Vietnamese died. The Viet Minh arranged a relief effort in the north and won wide support there as a result.
American President Roosevelt and General Stilwell had privately made it adamantly clear that the French were not to reacquire French Indochina (modern day Vietnam, Cambodia and Laos) after the war was over.

In October 1945 200,000 troops of the Chinese 1st Army arrived in what would become North Vietnam. They had been sent by Chiang Kai-shek under General Lu Han to accept the surrender of Japanese forces occupying that area which had been designated to Chiang Kai-Shek.

The Chinese forces remained there until 1946 and initially kept the French Colonial soldiers interned with the acquiescence of the Americans. The Chinese used the Vietnamese branch of the Chinese KMT to increase their influence in Indochina and put pressure on their opponents. Chiang Kai-shek threatened the French with war in response to manoeuvring by the French and Ho Chi Minh against each other, forcing them to come to a peace agreement, and in February 1946 he also forced the French to surrender all of their concessions in China and renounce their extraterritorial privileges in exchange for withdrawing from northern Indochina and allowing French troops to reoccupy the region starting in March 1946.

Ho Chi Minh was able to persuade Emperor Bảo Đại to abdicate on August 31, 1945. Bảo Đại was appointed "supreme advisor" to the new Vietminh-led government in Hanoi, which asserted independence on September 8.

With the fall of the short-lived Japanese colony of the Empire of Vietnam, the French wanted to restore its colonial rule in French Indochina. The Chinese Government, as agreed to at Potsdam, occupied French Indochina as far south as the 16th parallel in order to supervise the disarming and repatriation of the Japanese. This effectively ended Ho Chi Minh's nominal government in Hanoi.

General Leclerc arrived in Saigon on November 11th. Leclerc's primary objectives were to restore public order in south Vietnam and to militarize Tonkin (North Vietnam). Secondary objectives were to wait for French backup in view to take back Chinese-occupied Hanoi, then to negotiate with the Viet Minh officials.

Conflict was not long in coming and in 1946 fighting broke out in Haiphong after a conflict of interest in import duty at the port between the Viet Minh government and the French. On November 23, 1946, the French fleet began a naval bombardment of the city that killed over 9,000 Vietnamese civilians in one afternoon. The Viet Minh quickly agreed to a cease-fire and left the cities.

There was never any intention among the Vietnamese to give up, as soon 30,000 men to attacked the city. Although the French were outnumbered, their superior weaponry and naval support made any Viet Minh attack impossible. In December, hostilities started in Hanoi between the Viet Minh and the French, and Ho Chi Minh was forced to evacuate the capital in favour of remote mountain areas. Guerrilla warfare ensued, with the French controlling most of the country except far-flung areas.

By 1948, France started looking for means of opposing the Viet Minh politically, with an alternative government in Saigon. They began negotiations with the former emperor Bảo Đại to lead an "autonomous" government within the French Union of nations. Two years before, the French had refused Ho's proposal of a similar status, albeit with some restrictions on French power and the latter's eventual withdrawal from Vietnam. However, they were willing to give it to Bảo Đại as he had freely collaborated with French rule of Vietnam in the past and was in no position to seriously negotiate or impose demands (Bảo Đại had no military of his own, but soon he would have one).

In 1949, France officially recognized the "independence" of the State of Vietnam within the French Union under Bảo Đại. However, France still controlled all foreign relations and every defence issue as Vietnam was only nominally an independent state within the French Union. The Viet Minh quickly denounced the government and stated that they wanted "real independence, not Bảo Đại independence". Later on, as a concession to this new government and a way to increase their numbers, France agreed to the formation of the Vietnamese National Army to be commanded by Vietnamese officers. In the same year, the French also granted independence (within the framework of the French Union) to the other two nations in Indochina, the Kingdoms of Laos and Cambodia.

The United States recognized the South Vietnamese state, but many other nations viewed it as simply a French puppet regime and would not deal with it at all, including Nationalist China. In a strange turn round from their 1945 policy, the United States began to give military aid to France in the form of weaponry and military observers to defeat the Viet Min.

Korea (North and South) October 1945-March 1950

During World War II, Koreans were forced to support the Japanese war effort. Tens of thousands of men were conscripted into Japan's military. Around 200,000 girls and women were forced to engage in sexual services as "comfort women".

After the war, Japanese rule was brought to an end. Korea was divided into two occupied zones in 1945 along the 38th parallel, with the Northern half of the peninsula occupied by the Soviet Union and the southern half by the US, in accordance with a prior arrangement, where UN supervised elections were intended to be held for the entire peninsula shortly after the war.

In August 1945, the USSR established a Soviet Civil Authority in the northern portion of the Korean Peninsula. The Provisional People Committee for North Korea was set up in February 1946, headed by Kim Il-Sung, who had been appointed by the USSR. He introduced sweeping land reforms and nationalized key industries. Talks on the future of Korea were held in Moscow and Seoul but without result. Initial hopes for a unified, independent Korea evaporated as the politics of the Cold War resulted in the establishment of two separate nations with diametrically opposed political, economic, and social systems.

There was sporadic unrest in the South. In September 1946, South Korean citizens had risen up against the Allied Military Government. In April 1948, an uprising of the Jeju islanders was violently crushed. The South declared its statehood in May 1948 and two months later the ardent anti-Communist Syngman Rhee became its President. The People Republic of Korea under Kim followed, established in the North on 9 September 1948.

The Rhee regime consolidated itself through harsh persecution of all suspected opponents. It conducted a number of military campaigns against left-wing insurgents during which 30,000 to 100,000 people lost their lives.

Soviet forces withdrew from the North in 1949 and most American forces withdrew from the South the following year. This dramatically weakened the Southern regime and encouraged Kim Il-sung to consider an invasion plan against the South.

The country now divided, the relationship between the two Koreas became more antagonistic as time passed. The Soviet forces having withdrawn in 1949, North Korea pressured the South to expel the United States forces but Rhee sought to align his government strongly with America, and against both North Korea and Japan. Meanwhile, the government took in vast sums of American aid, in amounts sometimes near the total size of the national budget. The main policy of the First Republic of South Korea was anti-communism and "unification by expanding northward". The South's military was neither sufficiently equipped nor prepared, but the Rhee administration was determined to reunify Korea by military force with aid from the United States. The North, encouraged and lavishly supplied militarily by Manchuria, looked South.

By March 1950 Korea was a powder keg waiting to explode.

0715 30 September 1945

As she sat sipping her tea and nibbling on her toast, Queen Alice reflected that yesterday's football Grand Final was perhaps a metaphor for things in general, perhaps for the last 6 years. It had been a bitter, bloody game that soured Carlton's win and had witnessed five players being knocked out and a couple more attempting to strike the umpire. The Melbourne tabloid "The Truth" had called it "the most repugnant spectacle League football has ever known" in this morning's edition, with ten players reported for a total of sixteen offenses. The scandal sheets of "The Truth" were a secret addiction, she always made sure she read it and burnt it before others noticed.

In truth itself it was a reflection of the last 6 years of bitter and bloody struggle. It had been a horrific war and she had spared herself none of the details of the brutalities inflicted, particularly by the Japanese. Much like the umpires in the game, her own forces were now stuck in the middle of what was clearly going to be a nasty conflict in Indonesia.

It put the country in an unpleasant situation, the Dutch had been strong supporters in the anti-Japanese fight and loyal allies, yet she could not in all good conscience sanction their forcing their way back into the East Indies at the cost of lives when clearly opposed by their own former colonial subjects. Doing so would cost lives, too many of which had already been thrown away. Yet she did not want to give Sukarno free reign to trample over the rights of self-determination of the individual parts of the East Indies. Any federation would clearly be dominated by Sumatra and in particular Java, which she was well aware made many in the Christian East very nervous.

The army had three divisions in the East Indies, with another in Singapore. She just wanted to bring her boys home, but it seemed more conflict was beckoning. She had had discussions with Fraser, Scullin and Evatt. The government's policy would be not to assist or to allow others to assist the Dutch reoccupation and to try and broker a deal. It was one she agreed with.

0909 28 March 1946

Air Chief Marshall Keith Park's main activities these days seemed to be about downsizing and demobilization. There was still, however, much to do, mainly on five separate fronts. Firstly, the occupation of Japan, involving a Brigade of troops under "February" Easther. Secondly, the conflict in Indonesia, where had had over two divisions of troops trying to keep the peace under Freyberg, who he had managed to convince to stay on and not retire. He at least had three competent Divisional Commanders in Frank Berryman, "Red" Robertson and Bridgeford. Thirdly, the mass of material accumulated under all three services needed to be sorted, either allocated, stored, sold to other states or destroyed. Lend Lease materials needed to be returned. Some 27,000 tons of chemical weapons alone needed to be disposed of by either burning, venting (for phosgene) or by dumping at sea. Tanks, aircraft, ships, many needed to go. Much other material would be stored against future need. Fourthly, demobilization, not going fast enough for some. Just the logistics of getting men and equipment home, caring for POW's until they were well enough to be transported and discharged. Plus, the burdens of having to keep men on posts like Indonesia.

Lastly, planning for the future. The government was asking a size that the army and air force should be. At this stage he had asked for a post war army of 40,000 regulars and 60,000 reserves. An air force of 48 squadrons. He did not, as yet, know how that would be received. Plus, his more technology sensitive services, the air force and navy, needed to be renewed, the navy in particular, with most of its ships being pre-war and having seen hard service. He hoped to fund much new construction by selling old or surplus equipment to other countries, many of whom had had their own armed forces wiped out and money obtained from scrap value of older material.

The army alone had suffered a wave of retirements, many war famous names, "Tubby" Allen, Gordon Bennett, Ivan Dougherty, Jack Gallegan, Edmund Herring, Edmund Drake-Brockman, Cyril Barrowclough, John Laverack, Herbert Lloyd, Ivan McKay, John Northcote, Jack Stevens, Howard Kippenberger, Alan Vasey, George Wooten, Henry Wynter and of course Blamey himself. It was still a hectic time.

1907 2 December 1946

Peter Fraser, Prime Minister of Australasia, contemplated the situation in Indonesia. In 1945 he had managed to persuade US President Harry Truman that giving money to the Dutch to help them invade their former Indonesian colony was a huge mistake and a continuation of the sort of Imperialism that the US had declared itself opposed to.

In the finish it had required the threat of military force for the Dutch to finally come to the negotiating table and an agreement had been penned to end the conflict. He had to threaten to actively use the over 60,000 Australasian troops still in the former East Indies to finally bring each party to reluctant agreement. He feared it may have fractured the previously excellent relationship with the Dutch for some time. Like all fair agreements, it left both parties unhappy.

It saw the Netherlands recognize the Indonesian Republic as the authority over Java, Madura and Sumatra, as well as Borneo, still held by Australasian troops. Both parties agreed to the formation of by 1 January 1949, a semi-autonomous state with the monarch of the Netherlands at its head. The Republican-controlled Java and Sumatra would be one of its states, alongside areas that were generally under stronger Dutch influence, including southern Kalimantan, and the East, which consisted of Sulawesi, Maluku, the Sundra Islands and New Guinea. It was to prove an illusion. With Australasian troops completely withdrawn by early March 1947, it was to explode into war again by July.

1017 25 April 1947

Keith Park, as chief of the defence force, reviewed what sales had been made of military equipment to overseas governments. It had so far been a mini bonanza in terms of sales. With so many fledgling countries in need of establishing their own armed forces, despite their being so much surplus World War 2 stock, much had been on sold.

The light cruisers *Launceston* and *Hobart* had been sold to China, along with four *River Class* destroyer escorts and an *O Class* submarine. Similarly, the light cruiser *Darwin* had been sold to Thailand, along with two more *River Class* destroyer escorts. Two sloops had been sold to India, as well as six *Bathurst Class* corvettes.

The light carriers *Melbourne* and *Sydney* had been sold back to Huddart Parker for mercantile service, as had three of the four hospital ships, all three assault transports, one of the two submarine depot ships had been given back to the Netherlands Navy, all three of the PT boat depot ships had been sold back to mercantile concerns, as was the only MAC carrier. The old destroyer *Newmarket* had found her fourth owner, being gifted to Indonesia, along with two *Bathurst Class* corvettes. The ex-Italian cruiser *Dunedin* had been scrapped, as had all the older WW1 vintage destroyers.

The navy had been reduced to *Australasia* and *Pacifica*, the light carrier *Christchurch*, the assault carrier *Brisbane*, heavy cruiser *Auckland*, light cruiser *Hamilton*, 10 *Tribal Class* DD's, one *River Class* DE, ten *Snake Class* submarines and a large number of *Bathurst Class* corvettes, although new ships had been ordered, including replacements for the aging destroyers.

From an aircraft point of view, He 100's had also made popular exports, India purchasing 126 and 48 Mosquitos, Thailand 40, Portugal 24 and China 115 as well as 80 He 119's and 20 He 211's. Indonesia had purchased 12 He 119's and been given 20 Catalinas. Chile had recently signed a contract for 24 He 119's and 12 He 200's.

Army surplus had gone to many countries, with Thailand purchasing 20 Sentinel tanks and India 72 more. Masses of small arms had gone to Indonesia, India, Pakistan, Burma, Thailand, Sarawak and even a small amount to South Korea and Peru.

1807 1 May 1947

It had been a big year for the military, thought Vice Admiral John Collins. The government, alarmed at the unstableness of its neighbours and realising that it's army, air force and navy were in many cases operating with now outdated and aged equipment, had made a series of purchases.

The army, having no shortage of carriers, badly needed a new tank. Accordingly, a contract to supply 100 Centurion Tanks had been signed with the U.K, with 40 tanks, 8 more Centurion hulled bridge-layers and more 12 AVRE's to be built in Australasia. They had also purchased 6 heavy assault tanks, called Tortoise, from the UK.

The air force had purchased no overseas equipment, however, both Hencall jet designs had reached the production stage and an order for 100 He 2 heavy jet bombers had been placed as well as an order for 150 jet He 280 fighters. 120 CAC 15 Cockatoos had been reequipped with the Griffon 101 engine, pushing out performance to 494 mph, making it the fastest piston engine fighter flying. The RAN had ordered 90 navalised versions for its new carriers.

The navy had disposed of much pre-war equipment and with so much on the stocks at the end of the war, had purchased some new ships. The ex-*Essex Class* carrier *Reprisal* had been purchased and should arrive in 1948. Likewise, in late 1948 the ex U.K light carrier *Majestic*. They would replace the *Australasia* and *Christchurch*, respectively. It had also purchased the ex U.S *Des Moines Class* heavy cruiser *Dallas*, due to arrive in 1949. It would replace the old warhorse *Pacifica*. The RAN's other main need had been the replacement of pre-war destroyers. Accordingly, five *Daring Class* destroyers had been laid down and five *Battle Class* already launched in the U.K had been purchased for completion. The *Battle Class* ships would be available late 1948, the *Daring Class* in 1950. This would allow the retirement and possible sale of the old *Tribal Class* ships.

1644 1 July 1947

Ben Chifley had delivered another budget and it was hard to ignore the conclusion that post war the country was doing very well indeed. The last of the troops had been returned from overseas (except the occupation force in Japan, now wound down to only two battalions).

Post war it seemed the public's need was greater than pre-war and what he had most feared, not being able to reabsorb the ex-servicemen back into the work force, had mostly been avoided. Transportation and mining were driving the surge, although manufacturing had been built up extensively during the war and smart operators were now retooling for civilian products.

The railways, converted to a single gauge nationally pre-war, he had nationalized, taking them off the states. It seemed the sensible option, as the states lacked the income to reinvest in the needed upgrades needed to keep the system, rub down over the way years, up to date.

Civil aviation had taken off, Qantas being merged with Tasman Airways Limited in 1946 to form Royal Australasian Airlines, mainly flying DC-3's and Catalinas from ex-military conversions, although Commonwealth Aircraft Corporation were now producing scratch built civilian versions of the DC-3. The government had started operation of its own domestic airline, Trans Australasia Airlines and there were also private operators such as Ansett and Kiwi Air in the market, many using purchased ex-military aircraft, some of which had been in storage during the war, some retired after.

He had no doubt that post war, the rise of the automobile would be felt. There were a number of car manufacturers that had so far established themselves post war. Ford had already been in Australasia, now Holden had also set up as had fellow US company Ford and MACK Trucks, another U.S company. Rootes Australasia was license producing British cars, as was the New Zealand Motor Corporation. Hencall had started his own car company to diversify post war and the Queens brother and sister in law owned Southern Cross, a domestic manufacturer in Adelaide. Todd Motors was an Auckland based truck manufacturer.

The wartime expansion of shipbuilding had also had a spin off for the domestic market. Building itself had been centred on Sydney and Auckland and post war a number of vessels had been converted back into mercantile service. There had been a huge leap forward in demand for post war migration to Australasia and the government had commissioned two 27,090-ton liners to do much of the transporting. Laid in late 1946, one in Sydney and one in Auckland, they would be available by 1949. They were to be named in honour of the two RAN leading ships of World War 2, *Australasia* and *Pacifica*.

Mining had also taken off post war. Western Mining had found huge deposits of copper, silver and uranium at Olympic Dam in South Australia. New deposits of gold had been found at Kalgoorlie. nickel in Tasmania, Bauxite in Queensland and the country already had huge deposits of iron ore.

1208 2 March 1948

It had taken a large round of diplomatic negotiating and, in the finish the threat of military force, but both parties had finally, in some cases reluctantly, signed an agreement to allow a plebiscite to determine the fate of Indonesia. The Dutch had gone on the offensive against the Indonesians on 4 July 1947, just over seven weeks after the last Australasian forces had been withdrawn.

After a number of high-profile atrocities on both sides, Fraser had contacted the U.S and together they had presented a united front. If the Dutch did not stop offensive action and call a halt "in place", the US would suspend Marshall Plan aid and both navies would blockade the East Indies.

This had finally brought both sides to the negotiating table. The plebiscite would be undertaken later this year. The Indonesians had been indignant that there was an option for the East, mainly Christian, to opt out as a separate state, however, they were militarily not in a situation that they could argue. It had at least stopped the killing of thousands. If both sides had left unhappy and that at least had been achieved, Peter Fraser found he could live with it quite well.

1234 16 December 1948

The fleet had arrived back in Sydney from Indonesia on the same day that their new arrivals from the U.K had. The newly commissioned light carrier *HMAS Wellington* had arrived with five *Battle Class* destroyers, *HMAS Gallipoli*, *HMAS Tobruk*, *HMAS Crete*, *HMAS Milne Bay* and *HMAS Lae*. They would be replacing the five or the seven ships that had returned, five *Tribal Class* destroyers and *HMAS Christchurch*, retired after 19 years of RAN service and eight in the RN, fighting in most major WW2 battles.

Admiral Collins would be glad to see the back of the Indonesian conflict, both separate states had now come in to existence and the navy had been heavily involved in population transfer over the last five months from one state to another.

He was due to go to Woomera in remote South Australia next week to watch a test at the new missile testing area set up as a joint UK-Australasia facility. He was also aware that the British had asked Australasia for the provision of nuclear testing facilities, although their program was still perhaps two to three years away from that stage. If that was the case, he wanted to make sure the country availed itself of that research. The demobilization of service personnel had been completed in 1947, the granting of a 40 hours week making their fitting into the workforce somewhat easier.

6 August 1949

They were three of Australasia's most prominent wartime leaders, Leslie Morshead, Keith Park and John Collins. All were there for different reasons.

As they watched the ceremony, the guard being inspected by Queen Alice, the flag being pulled down on the old *HMAS Australasia*, Collin's flagship on a number of occasions.

She was being returned to mercantile service, hence Morshead's presence as General Manager of the Orient Steam Navigation Company. This was Park's last official function as head of the Defense forces, before his retirement on 15th August. He had only two appointments left, both private. He was going to drive out and see Ernest Hencall on the 8th to present him with an Order of Australasia and a private meeting with the Queen on the 12th. His replacement was to be Collins.

They were now raising the flag on the new *Essex Class* carrier *HMAS Sydney* and the new cruiser heavy cruiser *HMAS Melbourne*, both ships having made the trip from the U.S two months ago. Both ships were surrounded on one side by the old carrier *Christchurch*, not long for the breakers and four new *Daring Class* destroyers and on the other side by the old heavy cruiser *Auckland*, also due for the breakers. All of the countries pre 1945 ships had now seen the breakers, aside from the submarines and corvettes, plus the landing ship carrier Brisbane.

On the far side of the harbour was the New Australasian national Line ship *RMS Pacifica*, a 27,000-ton liner that would be used to transport so many of the post war migrants to the country. Her sister ship Australasia was four months from completion in Auckland. Four days ago, the government had removed the requirements of the dictation test, opening the country up to migration from all sources and countries, so the number coming may yet swell further. Overhead was a fight of He 2 jet strategic bombers, with the unfamiliar screams of the new He 280 jet fighters accompanying them.

Perhaps it was a good time to be going, thought Park. He could sense a change in the wind, an election being due at the end of the year. He had ensured all three services had achieved renewal, which was just as well as events in Indonesia/East Indonesia, North Korea/South Korea, India/Pakistan and Manchuria/China were all at a flashpoint. The RAAF had been reduced to forty squadrons, the numbers and types of aircraft being streamlined. It consisted of:

Bomber/Photo Recon
He 2 jet bombers 148
He 200 bombers 167
De Havilland Vampire 80
De Havilland Mosquito 46

Fighters
He 280 jet fighters 142
CAC 15 Cockatoo 278

Transport
Douglas C47 215

RAN
CAC 15 Cockatoo 88
North American A36 42
Fairy Barracuda 68
1916 8 August 1949

Park and Hencall had spent the day together, talking about Park's impending retirement, the way forward in regards to the RAF and what new designs and plans were on the drawing board. Ernest Hencall had been overwhelmed by the Order of Australasia.

Hencall had recently returned from the U.K and had recommended purchasing the English Electric Canberra which he had seen fly in the U.K. He thought it the most advanced design he had so far seen. That combined with the He 2 would give Australasia a modern bomber force. Small amounts of He 200 could be kept for long range maritime patrol, probably reequipped with the more powerful Griffon 101 engine.

Hencall was excited to meet the Canadian delegation and their aviation technical team coming to Australasia on 16 September part of the Canadian royal visit. They were on the verge of test flying their own indigenous fighter and he was excited at the possibilities for cooperation on a design. As they retired to the pub for a beer and a counter meal, Hencall had indicated that he would be going back into civil aviation design and asked Park if he would like a "retirement job" working one day a week or so with the company, mainly liaising with the civil aviation companies to determine what they saw as their post war needs. As they fished for snapper in Port Phillip Bay later that night, Park decided to accept.

2216 29 August 1949

Stalin read the report with satisfaction. The bomb, named First Lightning, had been exploded near Khabarovsk earlier today. It had all gone according to plan. They no longer had to bow down to the Americans diplomatically now that they had their own delivery system, or would have in about six months' time when sufficient other devices had been constructed. Perhaps when that occurred it would be time to let the two tin pot Asian dictators have their way in Korea, just to test the waters as to a possible reaction from the U.S and their allies. It would allow him to dip his toe in the water without risking anything truly important.

1316 18 September 1949

Jim Chamberlain and his colleague from Avro Canada John "Jack Frost" had spent the day at Hencall's works. They had witnessed the modification of the war built He 200 to a maritime patrol aircraft but were eager to discuss the relatively new He 280 fighter and make comparisons between it and their new "bird", due to make its first flight in Jan or February 1950, the CA 100.

They had arrived as part of Queen Patricia's technical and trade mission and Jim Chamberlain had been delighted to talk "shop" all day. He had recounted his own involvements in the design of the Vampire whilst at de Havilland and he was particularly interested in aerodynamic design and cutting wind resistance, one of Hencall and the Gunter Brothers key areas of expertise.

Both countries were in need of a high altitude, all weather interceptor now that the Soviets had proven themselves capable of delivering a nuclear payload soon. It was agreed to put forward to their respective governments a possible joint project to design such an aircraft as well as a possible long-range strategic bomber.

1606 18 December 1949

It marked his last day as Prime Minister of Australasia, in many ways the end of an era. Peter Fraser had been an extraordinary hard worker, particularly during the war years when he had taken on the onerous burden of Minister of Defence. However, the election on 10th December had proved a landslide win to the Liberal/National/Country party coalition.

Perhaps he had been too slow in relaxing wartime restrictions or bringing troops home but the reality of the situation was that the situation in Indonesia had demanded they stay on site. He had also spent more than some thought was required on defence post war, but the armed services had needed renewal of obsolete equipment and he did not want to put the country in a position of being unprepared with so many unstable situations. Robert Menzies would be the new Prime Minister, with a 31-seat majority. Menzies, endowed with great charisma, had appealed more to the electorate in a new radio age.

For him it would mean retirement, his health was not great. It was a changing of the guard. Scullin would also be retiring. "Doc" Evatt was President of the new UN. Frank Forde had missed his chance at re-election. Ben Chifley wold be the new leader.

0918 23 February 1950

Hencall was delighted by the agreement. The two governments would joint fund the two new aircraft. The fighters would be mainly designed and built in Canada, although some of the wind tunnel and modelling would be done in Australasia. The strategic bomber design would be done in his own works, with Canadian assistance in regards to the power plants.

Canada had also signed a contract for 24 He 2D strategic bombers as a stopgap until the new machine was available, since it may have a lead time of 5 years or so. All in all, it seemed a good result for both countries, with potential costs halved. If the design was successful, they would lobby other potential customers.

1308 12 May 1950

Chiang Kai-shek had inspected the troops and had conducted a series of briefings on the still secret operation, scheduled for a kick off on the 23rd May. Tibet had always historically been a part of China, of course and now that things on the Manchurian border had ground to a mutually agreed stalemate, it was time to focus his attention to the South.

He had spent a great deal of time with his cartographical and survey personnel over the last month and had been very keen to impress on his generals the stop line of the operation, both in Aksai Chin, where he intended to cross the Johnson Line. He also intended to claim the previous lost Chinese lands South of the McMahon line on the North-western Frontier and had been in contact with the Chogyal of Sikkim, Tashi Namgyal, who believed India were agitating to annex his small country.

He was sure there would be some condemnation of the action, but at the end of the day, he was simply reclaiming Chinese land given away to Western Imperialists and his fallback position would be the establishment of a protectorate over Tibet where the Dalai Lama could nominally stay in spiritual, if not temporal, power. The 23rd May action (or invasion depending on your point of view) would touch off a series of conflicts across Asia.

1444 24 May 1950

Kim Il-Sung was delighted by the news. The Nationalist Chinese were focusing their attentions to the South and there were reports of exchanges of gunfire between nationalist troops and those of Tibet. It was the ideal opportunity to strike whilst attention was diverted elsewhere and North Korea's largest hostile neighbour was distracted elsewhere.

In the South, Syngman Rhee had about 30,000 alleged communists in jails and about 300,000 suspected sympathizers enrolled in the Bodo League re-education movement. South Korean forces had reduced the active number of communist guerrillas in the South from 5,000 to 1,000. However, he believed that the guerrillas had weakened the South Korean military and that a North Korean invasion would be welcomed by much of the South Korean population.

While the Communists were struggling for supremacy in Manchuria, they were supported by the North Korean government with material and manpower. His North Koreans had donated 2,000 railway cars worth of matériel while thousands of Koreans served in the Manchurian army during the war. North Korea also provided the Manchurians with a safe refuge.

The North Korean contributions to the victory he had made sure were not forgotten after the creation of the People's Republic of Manchuria in 1948. As a token of gratitude, between 50,000 to 70,000 Korean veterans that served were now back, along with their weapons, and they would play a significant role in the initial invasion of South Korea. Manchuria had promised to support the North Koreans in the event of a war against South

Korea.

Throughout 1949 and 1950 the Soviets had continued to arm North Korea. The combat veterans from China, the tanks, artillery and aircraft supplied by the Soviets, and rigorous training increased North Korea's military superiority over the South, which had been armed by the American military.

In April 1950, Stalin had given Kim permission to invade the South under the condition that Zhu De would agree to send reinforcements if they became needed. Stalin made it clear that Soviet forces would not directly engage in combat, to avoid a direct war with the Americans. Kim met with Zhu De in May 1950. Mao was concerned that the Americans would intervene but agreed to support the North Korean invasion.

Soviet generals with extensive combat experience from the Second World War had been sent to North Korea as the Soviet Advisory Group. These generals had completed the plans for the attack on 2nd May. The original plans called for a skirmish to be initiated in the Ongjin peninsula on the west coast of Korea. The North Koreans would then launch a "counterattack" that would capture Seoul and encircle and destroy the South Korean army. The final stage would involve destroying South Korean government remnants, capturing the rest of South Korea, including the ports.

Today, Kim Il-sung had called for a Korea-wide election on 20-22 July 1950 and a consultative conference in Haeju on 1-3 June 1950. Today, Kim Il-Sung requested permission to start with general attack across the 38th parallel, rather than a limited operation in the Ongjin peninsula. In light of the Nationalist's distractions, Stalin agreed to this change of plan. Kim had brought the date for the operation up to the 12th June.

His front-line units comprised more than 100,000 men and he now had an air force lavishly equipped with aircraft. Only his navy was small. Stalin had told him the USSR could not directly intervene; however, he had contributed much in the way of arms and armour and two days ago another contribution had arrived, this one n the form of men. 35,000 Japanese prisoners of war had been sent by train to North Korea, with a promise of freedom if they served in the North Korean Army. Languishing in Siberia, of the slightly more than 100,000 men, these had accepted the offer.

1324 5 June 1950

Tibet's ambassador Ngapoi Ngawang Jigme looked over the terms again. Of course, they were insulting, but what could one do? Chamdo had fallen to the Chinese and he had been instructed by the Regent for the young Dalai Lama to make peace, there was little alternative. They had no natural allies despite the sympathy of some countries and their own army, small and poorly equipped (in some cases still with muskets or bows and arrows) had little hope. They had lost 156 killed and 3,458 captured and inflicted only 97 casualties on the invaders.

The Chinese had communicated a proposal that Tibet be regarded as a protectorate of China, that China be responsible for Tibet's defence, and that China be responsible for Tibet's trade and foreign relations. Acceptance would lead to peaceful "liberation", or otherwise war. The Tibetans undertook to maintain the relationship between China and

Tibet as one of preceptor and patron. He had recommended cooperation, with some stipulations about implementation.

With little choice, he signed. A week later, protests were to follow, as rather than withdrawing and allowing Tibetan internal autonomy, Chinese troops and tanks continued to push on, reaching the border of Tibet and India in Nyingchi Prefecture on the 11th.

On the morning of the 12th, an hour before North Korean troops crossed the demilitarised zone, Chinese troops and tanks crossed into the disputed areas of Arunachel Pradesh. They were two hours behind forces that had crossed into Aksai Chin. Later that same day, the Chogyal of Sikkim was to declare himself independent of India's protectorate status.

0558 14 June 1950

Truman had been shocked by the rapidity of events in Korea. An attack had been predicted so often by U.S intelligence organs that when it finally came it was to achieve complete surprise. The North Koreans had already smashed through the ROK or South Korean defences and were advancing rapidly on Seoul. Although the South Korean army numbered almost 100,000 men, it was short on heavy equipment and armour and had no effective air force. In contrast, North Korean forces numbered 150,000 troops, organized into 10 infantry divisions, one tank division, and one air force division, with 210 fighter planes (piston engine Yak 9's mainly) and 280 T-34-85 tanks, 110 attack bombers, 200 artillery pieces, 78 Yak trainers, and 35 reconnaissance aircraft. In addition to the invasion force, the North KPA had 114 fighters, 78 bombers, 105 T-34-85 tanks, and some 30,000 soldiers stationed in reserve in North Korea.

Already the destroyers *USS Mansfield* and *De Haven* had been required to rescue over 700 US and friendly nationals from Inchon, South Korea. His administration was caught ill prepared and at a crossroads. Before the invasion, Korea was not included in the strategic Asian Defence Perimeter outlined by Secretary of State Acheson. Military strategists were more concerned with the security of Europe against the Soviet Union than East Asia. He was worried that a war in Korea could quickly widen into another world war should the Manchurians or Soviets decide to get involved as well. One facet of the changing attitude toward Korea and whether to get involved was Japan. He saw Japan as the critical counterweight to the Soviet Union and Manchuria in the region. While there was no United States policy that dealt with South Korea directly as a national interest, its proximity to Japan increased the importance of South Korea. A major consideration was the possible Soviet reaction in the event that the U.S. intervened. He was concerned that a war in Korea was a diversionary assault that would escalate to a general war in Europe once the U.S. committed in Korea. He was waiting for more information from intelligence sources in regards to the USSR's likely position.

On the other hand he believed if aggression went unchecked a chain reaction would be initiated that would marginalize the United Nations and encourage Communist aggression elsewhere. The UN Security Council had approved the use of force to help the South Koreans and the U.S. immediately began using what air and naval forces that were in the area to that end. He had refrained from committing on the ground because his advisers believed the North Koreans could be stopped by air and naval power alone, although many of his senior admirals had advised that the navy was so drawn down that it may not even be able to keep up a blockade.

The other huge concern was the happenings in Tibet and Northern India, where Chinese forces had crossed the border into Indian territory after traversing Tibet. He had tried contacting Chiang-Kai Shek but he had been told he was "unavailable". The Indians had a motion before the UN condemning the attack and asking for military assistance, which the Chinese had vetoed. He had talked to Atlee who was furious. It was a mess.

In regards to Korea, he had started contacting his old allies to ask for assistance. Both the U.K, Canada and Australasia had so far committed, as had France although her ongoing struggles in Indo China were likely to curtail any real assistance. Greece had also offered. Others were likely to follow. If the situation was to get any worse, he may have to commit ground forces. In addition, he would perhaps have to consider calling up some reserve formations and reactivating some of the many mothballed ships in the navy.

1619 14 June 1950

Pyotor Ustinov was happy. The ship design had passed the final hurdle, being approved by Stalin. Now the first of the Project 82 ships could be laid down, most likely in early 1951 at Nikolayev. She was going to be fast, brutally fast at 36 knots. Already six of the much smaller Project 68 ships were under construction, the first of a planned class of 25. With the huge expansion of the submarine force, perhaps the Red navy could finally come to the fore.

1646 15 June 1950

Cabinet had met and made the decision. With little prospect of being able to actively intervene in assistance of India, it had been decided to deploy troops to Korea as rapidly as possible to try and stem the rapid North Korean advance. Prime Minister Robert Menzies had immediately offered assistance if required and President Truman had contacted him personally to accept this offer of assistance.

This being the case, Lt Colonel Charles Hercules Green's 3rd RAR Battalion (the last Australasian troops in occupation in Japan) had been placed on notice for redeployment in Korea. The two squadrons of aircraft left in Japan, both CAC 15 equipped and under the command of the legendary "ace" "Cobber" Kain, would also go to Korea, as would the two destroyers on station in Japan.

From Australasia would follow 1 RAR's Infantry Battalion and 4 RAR's Armoured Battalion as well as the 1st Heavy Tank Destroyer Company. The assault carrier *HMAS Brisbane* was to be made ready and would sail with the light carrier *HMAS Sydney* as soon as practicable.

Menzies was more than a little concerned that this new round of conflict may spill over into a renewed war between Pakistan and India or China and Manchuria. The Indonesian situation also bore watching, Indonesia increasing its rhetoric against its relatively undefended neighbour recently.

In the meantime, China's ambassador had been called in for consultations. He had stated that China had no territorial demands on India at all, but was merely reoccupying historic

Chinese territory. It was true that China's forces had stopped their advance in most locations. Even if that was the case, how that would sit with India did not bear thinking about and he had been in contact with Atlee to try and arrange a diplomatic exchange between the two powers.

Australasian Flag 1950

Naval Ensign

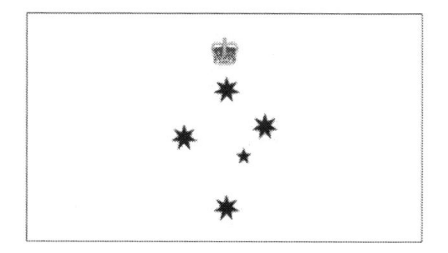

1412 28 June 2014(flash forward)

It was the final flypast of the old aircraft, the He 166 Mammoth. It was the final aircraft that saw service of the many RAAF Hencall designs, not going into service with both Australasia and Canada in 1962 and 1963, respectively, joining the Avro Arrow in the front line. It had been six years after the death of the company founder in the case of Hencall Aviation.

It had been the mainstay of Australasia's nuclear deterrent in the 1960's, 1970's and early 1980's, when the fleet was retired along with the country's nuclear capability. Some aircraft were modified for use as tankers and two more as airborne command posts, however, and the tankers had served in that role until 2013, when the last few units of the massive 85,000 kg former bomber had been retired. As Crown Princess Maree looked up at the flight of F22's escorting the two old bombers, it certainly seemed like a case of the old and the new.

1554 21 June 1950

Captain William Harmison watched the last of the North Korean MTB's make her escape. His light cruiser, *USS Juneau*, along with light cruiser H*MS Jamaica* and the frigate *HMS Black Swan* had encountered a North Korean convoy of 10 ammunition ships (all coasters), escorted by six torpedo boats and three gunboats. After a fierce fight that had resulted in the annihilation of the North Korean force, only one torpedo boat escaping. The last boat had, however, managed to torpedo *Black Swan* at the end of the engagement and it seemed likely that the frigate would have to be scuttled. So far it had been the first definable success for the U.N backed forces of the South.

1432 23 June 1950

It had not taken long for Wing Commander Edgar "Cobber" Kain to add to his tally of kills. With 46 in World War 2, he had downed his first in the Korean War, a Yak 9 and had damaged another. His CAC 15 was a much faster machine, but seemingly not as manoeuvrable as the Yak. Much like the Zero, tactics would seem to be a series of diving attacks using his speed to determine the point of engagement. He wondered how much longer they would remain equipped with the older CAC 15's and whether the newer jets would eventually reach the combat zone.

2015 1 July 1950

The 24th Infantry Division was the first U.S unit sent into Korea to absorb the initial "shock" of North Korean advances, and disrupt the much larger North Korean units. It's mission was simple really-to try and buy time so that the major allied support forces could establish what was hoped to be a defensible perimeter around Pusan that could then be expanded upon.

The 24th division was under-strength, and most of its equipment dated from 1945 or even before due to cutbacks enacted in the first Truman administration. It was also not well equipped and supplied to fight a sustained war. It had no heavy equipment to deal with the North Korean T34-85 tanks and it would be fair to say it's troops had become soft after 5 years of occupation duty in Japan but were now learning the hard way.

Elements of the division had been defeated at Osan, Pyontaek, Chonan and along the Kum River. Earlier today, Major General Dean, the 24th's commander, had ordered the division's three regiments—the 19th, 21st and 34th Infantry Regiments—to cross the Kum River, destroying all bridges behind them, and to establish defensive positions around Taejon. Dean formed a line with the 34th Infantry and 19th Infantry facing east, and held the heavily battered 21st Infantry in reserve to the southeast. Taejon stood as a major transportation hub between Seoul and Taegu, giving it great strategic value for both sides. The division was attempting to make a stand at Taejon, the last place it could conduct a delaying action before the North Korean forces could converge on the unfinished Pusan Perimeter.

The 24th Infantry Division's three infantry regiments, which had a wartime strength of 3,000 each, were already below strength on their deployment, and heavy losses in the preceding two weeks had reduced their numbers further. The 21st Infantry had 1,000 men left, having suffered 1,500 casualties. The 34th Infantry had only 2,000 and the 19th had 2,200 men. There were another 2,000 men in the 24th Infantry Division artillery formations. Thus, the division's total strength was 11,000. This was severely reduced from the 16,000 men and 4,773 vehicles that had arrived in Korea at the beginning of the month. Very few vehicles were left and no tanks were available, all were en route. Dean knew he was in big trouble, but had to fight anyway.

1915 9 July 1950

His forces had captured Taejon and bagged over 1600 prisoners, with another 900-enemy killed, but it had been at great cost, casualties estimated to be in the region of 4,500 to 5,000 men. General Choe Yong-gon had promised his men a break from the relentless advance in the city if they took it, but the fierce hand to hand and building to building fighting had rendered it a poor place to stop. He had lost over 20 of the 50 or so tanks attached to his advance, although some could be repaired.

He would have to wait a couple of days before he resumed his advance, a dangerous thing when the enemy were getting stronger whereas his own forces were ever depleted, one of his divisions down to 50% nominal strength. Worse still, his air cover, initially dominant, was now on the defensive, the capitalist fighters dominating, their bombers starting to take effect.

0722 10 July 1950

Brigadier John Workman had been plucked from his home town in Napier to command the Australasian Korean Brigade. A combined arms formation, his final unit, 1st Heavy Tank Destroyer Company had arrived this morning. They were planned to be deployed on the front lines at the Pusan perimeter within five days maximum as the situation for the allies had become dire.
1557 26 July 1950

The 1st Heavy Tank Destroyer Company had been deployed separately on the high ground around Chinju in support of the 1st Provisional Marine Brigade, along with twelve M24 Chaffees. They had let the approximately 40 T34-85 come within range before all ten of the huge tank destroyers had opened up with their high velocity 32 pounder guns, tearing the lighter tanks apart. With ample air support and with the M24's adding their own weight of fire and using their height advantage, they had torn the North Korean armour apart. Attacks by North Korean infantry had been driven off by the well-entrenched marines and aerial recon would later confirm 33 knocked out T34-85's. Only two M24's had been lost, one to enemy artillery fire. One Tortoise had been immobilized.

2313 30 August 1950

General Walton Walker was happy with the progress of the battle. Over the last month, his forces had gradually ground the North Korean attackers against his defensive line around Pusan. President Truman had authorised an expenditure of 12 billion to fund the war in Korea and the effects of that were now being felt, with many air and naval units now finding their way to the conflict zone, as well as a number of newly reactivated units. As well as the units that he currently possessed, including troops from the U.S's two closest allies, the UK and Australasia, contributions from other countries were also now starting to roll in.

He had been mainly worried about the enemy taking Pusan "on the bound" early in the month. This had now not happened and with each passing day, his own forces were getting stronger, the enemies proportionally weaker.

The U.S. Army had withstood KPA attacks meant to capture Pusan at Naktong Bridge and Taegu. His air units had interrupted North Korean logistics with 45 daily ground support sorties that destroyed 35 bridges, halting most daytime road and rail traffic. North Korean forces were forced to hide in tunnels by day and move only at night. To deny matériel to the North Koreans, the air units destroyed logistics depots, petroleum refineries, and harbors, while the U.S. Navy air forces, along with newly arrived carriers from both the UK and Australasia had attacked transport hubs. Consequently, the over-extended North Koreans could not be supplied throughout the South.

Meanwhile, U.S. garrisons in Japan continually dispatched soldiers and matériel to reinforce the defenders in the Pusan Perimeter. Tank battalions deployed to Korea directly from the U.S. mainland to Pusan. He now had had some 500 medium tanks battle-ready, plus another 80 UK and Australasian units. Intelligence estimated, South Korean Army and UN Command forces outnumbered the KPA 190,000 to 100,000 soldiers. His operation at Inchon, slated for a 2nd September start, would be the precursor to a general breakout for the Pusan perimeter.

0456 6 September 1950

The news could scarcely be more dire. The Americans had landed at Inchon two days ago and had secured a strong bridgehead, capturing the town and nearby Kimpo airfield, where his forces had been forced to abandon over 20 aircraft to the US forces.

His campaign in the South had been built upon a successful conclusion within 4-5 weeks. With the degradation of his forces in the South, the emasculation of his air force and now the landing at Inchon, he knew full well his own forces were doomed without outside intervention.

He would have to appeal to Stalin for more equipment. But it was also men that would be required. That would require him supplicating himself to Zhu De, however, it would be necessary if he was to avail himself of the assistance of Manchuria's massive land army. With China still involved in a sideshow war between small land units in the Himalayas with India, perhaps he would receive the assistance he now so desperately needed.

1456 28 June 2014(flash forward)

Flying Officer Mark Viney was glad to finally bring in the He 166 Mammoth into Point Cook after the flypast. It was the last flight for this old girl and it was a bit of a struggle to bring her to a stop on the smaller airfield at Point Cook, Ernest Hencall Field. Even virtually empty the huge aircraft still weighed in excess of 100,000kg and was almost 200ft long and Point Cook's runway was not normally designed to handle the latest or largest aircraft any more. None the less, for a 24-year-old, it was a honour to co-pilot her on the last mission. She had been the main delivery system for Australasia (and Canada for that matter)'s nuclear bombs, the last of which was the Blue Devil. She would now be on display at Point Cook. Most of her 121 sisters had been scrapped, but some were still present at the

RAAF's inactivation facility and airfield at Oodnadatta, which acted as a halfway house, storage facility and boneyard for old aircraft, in some cases civilian as well as military. The towns extreme dryness, caused by heat which could reach 50 degree Celsius guarded against decay.

He had an undeserved reputation as a bit of a ladies man and had been dared to ask the Crown Princess for an autograph by his mates and proceeded to do so, much to his C.O's embarrassment. She was a great looking girl and did not seem to mind, not being at all phased at the little joke, laughing and taking his piece of paper before exchanging pleasantries about flying, time away from home and general loneliness. She indicated her father was a licensed pilot and that she had taken the controls with him. Finally, she moved on before seemingly looking back at him appraisingly.

What he had not expected when he finally received the paper back was not an autograph, but a mobile number. Struggling to keep his face straight, he felt he was now the victim of a practical joke as the girl smiled back knowingly, fully aware he could say no more in public.

Two days later, as he pulled his Hilux off the bustle of St Kilda Road onto Birdwood Avenue, through the roundabout and up to the guarded checkpoint, he was honestly able to say he was as nervous as he had ever been for anything to keep this arranged date. As he was to tell his mates later, "literally shitting bricks", in fact.

1014 16 September 1950

Marshall, First Chairman of the Communist Party of Manchuria and President Zhu De looked over the maps of the Korean Peninsula. The U.S and their allies had penetrated past the 38th Parallel, driving back Kim's pathetically broken forces, those that had not already surrendered like frightened dogs. With the Nationalist Chinese forces bogged down in a low intensity war with India over Northern Kashmir/Southern Tibet now was as good a time as any.

He felt he had been given enough provocation. U.S aircraft had already had the temerity to bomb Manchurian airfields. He even had evidence from one F-82 that had been shot down, its pilot captured. He claimed that it had been a mistake and they were meant to bomb North Korea instead. A little bit of "persuasion" would change his tune to what was required.

In any case, he could not afford a strong, unified, hostile capitalist power on his doorstep. They would need perhaps a month to prepare, but he intended to give the go ahead for an operation in Korea this afternoon to assist in its "liberation".

1415 18 September 1950

It had been a subdued opening, a small speech from Menzies and some rather scrummy tea cake. Phillip Baxter had been appointed head of the Australasian Atomic Energy Commission only 2 months before, quite a rapid advancement for someone who had only been in the country from the UK six months. He had been fully briefed on the requirements of his office and the government's desire to construct a functioning reactor to contribute further to the fissile material already on hand from Canada's Fall River and the U.K's Windscale reactors.

He had already been confidentially appraised of the U.K's desire to conduct their first test in Australasia, to which Menzies had acquiesced. It was now important to sped the country's involvement so that the maximum benefits could be obtained from possession of such weapons, especially since the U.S was not passing along any assistance after the McMahon Act and the USSR had already detonated a weapon.

Menzies had agreed with Louis St. Laurent and Queen Patricia's government that they would be pushing hard to gain full access to weapons technology themselves considering Canada was providing a fair percentage of the material components and Australasia the facilities for the test.

2356 18 September 1950

The Politburo meeting had gone late into the night, the subject the developing disaster in Korea. Stalin had dispatched Marshal Matvei Vasilevich Zakharov to assist but he had advised the current situation was untenable-that fool Kim's forces were clearly finished without intervention. He had "removed" the local Soviet advisors and would now have to request that Zhu De, a man he had never truly trusted, restore the situation. Too many incompetents and too much reliance on outside forces he could not truly trust.

Whilst on the subject of trust, he wondered when he would need to move again to protect his position. Zhukov had been isolated and moved away from his power base. Beria and his NKVD had put down incursions in the Ukraine. Now that things had stabilised, did he really need either him or his "appetites". He had a mountain of evidence already prepared, of course, in Beria's case almost all of it actually legitimate.

He scanned the 1948 letter from Lydia Timashuk in regards to Zhdanov again. There may be a more subtle way to approach the matter, a more subtle way that would eliminate the last of the subterranean opposition he knew still festered.

10 October 1950

General Walton Walker was more than happy with the speed of the advance. His forces had captured Pyongyang two days ago and a series of airborne assaults had blocked the Northern approaches to the city, hopefully blocking of any attempt at escape by Kim and his leadership.

His forces now had total control of the ground war and the front line was essentially fluid. When the pocket of North Korean Army troops was reduced at Pyongyang, he could resume his advance to the Yalu River, now in some cases less than 50 miles distant. His forces had done well, having secured control of both the air and the ground to complement their total control of the sea.

14 October 1950

Zhu De's Manchurian forces were already in North Korea and he was prepared to start offensive operation tomorrow, without a declaration of war. He had stockpiled a large force, including a great deal of armour which included both T34-85 and JS-3 tanks.

His air force was also prepared to launch offensive operation tomorrow morning at first light. He had committed a number of the latest fighters that he had been supplied by the USSR, including jet powered Sukhoi Su-9 fighter/bombers and Yak-17 fighters.

1316 20 October 1950

The CAC-15G's warmed up on deck of what was the largest ship of the "Commonwealth" task force, HMAS Sydney. She was part of a three carrier task forces with the RN Triumph and Theseus. The CAC-15G's were the fastest piston engine fighters in existence, but as Commander David McKeon had already discovered, they were not as fast as the Manchurian jets.

Thankfully the jets themselves were not common, the majority of the Manchurian aircraft still being piston engine types. The squadron, along with RN Seafires from Triumph, was to escort a heavy raid of He-2 jet bombers staging out of Butterworth air base in Malaya, targeting Manchurian airfields.

Over the last two days, as the fracture in the allied lines had appeared, virtually every air unit had been thrown in to try and stem the Manchurian advance, particularly that of their armoured spearheads.

1415 25 October 1950

President Rajendra Prasad of India had made the decision to agree to the Chinese proposals. India had not been in a military position to dislodge the Chinese in any case, so a formally signed agreement on the borders was in many ways a worthwhile exercise, since they had effectively been in dispute for almost a century. The Chinese had agreed to abide by the McMahon Line, even conceding some extra ground around Galou Shanko North of the line to fall into the original treaty requirements nominating the highest points of the Himalayas.

On the Aksai Chin front, whilst China had agreed to all previous borders to the South, the area North of Khurnak Fort, which was currently controlled by China anyway, would be ceded to China. Sikkim was to move from being an Indian Protectorate to a completely independent country under Chogyal Tashi Namgyal.

28 28 October 1950

Captain Tim Matthewson, a World War 2 vet, had been tapped to be the first to go to Korea with the new fighter. The appearance of Manchurian jets had come as a nasty surprise to the US and UN forces and losses among some of the older bomber types, particularly the B-29 had been heavy.

The North American F-86 Sabre would go on to establish itself as the dominant fighter of the Korean war, easily outstripping both the Yak -17 and the Sukhoi Su-9 in performance, as well as allied machines such as the Gloster Meteor and the Australasian He 280 when it finally arrived in 1951.

1706 16 November 1950

The situation in the land war had changed rapidly. Shocked by the rapidity of the Manchurian advance and the amount of armour they had available to support it, General Walker's UN troops were being pushed back on every front. Some his formations, like 1st Marine Division, had barely escaped encirclement and casualties had been high.

In the air war, his forces had gone a long way to wresting back the initiative, however, the initial attacks on UN airfields and the appearance of the Manchurian jets had been an unpleasant surprise. Hopefully the new fighters would prove themselves superior to the Manchurian jets, which, were so far thankfully in short supply. At this rate he would be back at the 38th Parallel by mid-December.

Thankfully, more forces were arriving from stateside, as well as smaller contributions from other countries, including a full Brigade from the U.K. The question, however, now remained. Should he sacrifice more troops than may be necessary, or should he consider the nuclear option?

0809 17 November 1950

President Truman mulled over General Walton Walker's request for the deployment of nuclear weapons, if required. U.N forces were continuing to retreat and although Walker was still confident that with increased manpower and more modern and numerous application of air power that he could stabilise the situation, he was also quick to point out that he could give no guarantees that this would be the case.

In truth, Truman was quite certain in his own mind that he had made the right decision in 1945. In fact, it seemed likely upon reflection that the application of nuclear weapon had saved lives, and not just allied lives either. Of course, the weapon's consequences were unfortunate, but so was war.

It was not as simple as in 1945. Stalin now had the bomb as well and although the USSR was not technically at war, the usage of nuclear weapons could result in them jumping into the conflict, possibly with a release of their own weapon. The other thing he had to consider was the fact that it was a UN sanctioned mission and the UN itself had not discussed the use of nuclear weapons, of which he was quite sure his allies that had put troops on the ground would expect to be consulted.

It was important politically that be seen to be a joint effort, with the U.S merely leading the way rather than setting policy. He would advise Walker that at this stage permission was refused, but if a cross back over of the 38th Parallel occurred he would review the situation. As it was, he had to deal with the consequences of a nuclear "attack" that had actually been delivered, with the Canadians complaining vehemently about the Air Force B-50 that had dropped a nuclear bomb as the aftermath of an inflight emergency over Quebec a week ago, sans it's plutonium core.

1615 24 November 1950

The demonstration had gone well in front of the two U.S Air Force Colonels, the CF-100 Canuck (already being known as the "Clunk" performing well. "Jack" Frost, the head designer of Avro Canada, would be delighted if the Americans were interested enough to order. From what he had seen, his kite did not match the latest US machine, the F-86 at all, but it offered one thing the US machine did not, all weather performance, which was a gap in the current U.S inventory. Any capital gained from sales to the U.S could be put towards the next aircraft he was envisaging, an aircraft that would take performance much past the sound barrier.

1620 8 December 1950

As of yesterday they were now an all jet air base. Osan air base was home to five squadrons, now consisting totally of jet aircraft, two squadrons of He 280's and three of the new US fighter, the F-86 Sabre.

"Cobber" Kain had loved the old CAC-15, but the squadron had been converted rapidly over the last two weeks to the new machine and there was no going back. He was an old man now, for a fighter pilot, 32 years old, with more than six years of combat flying.

They should now have the edge on the Manchurian jets for speed, making escorting the U.N bombers on mission much easier, their opponents not being able to slip away from an engagement as and when it suited them.

Truth is, they could do with all the help they could get, for the Manchurian advance, although slowed, had not stopped and Seoul was again in danger. The allied air forces had established superiority, using their piston engine machines for much ground attack and tank busting, but at some cost, the Manchurian Air Force proving a much more serious opponent than Kim's North Korean one.

He 280 line drawings

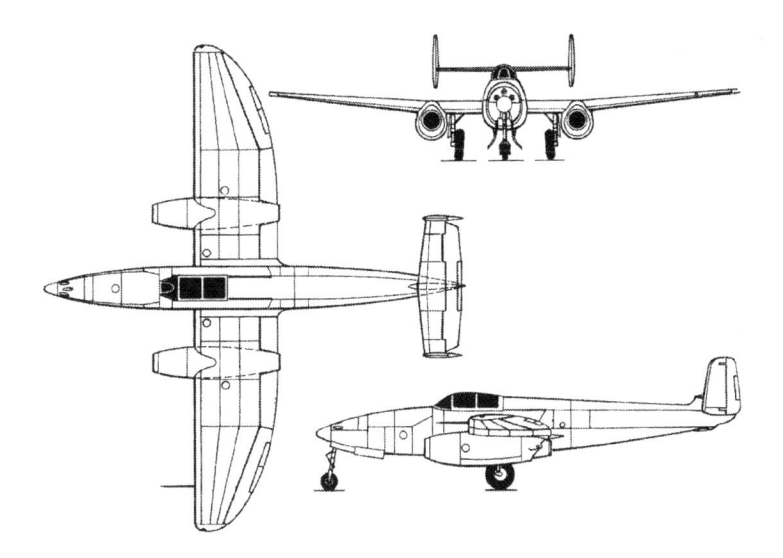

1237 23 December 1950

Walton Walker was late for his lunch dates with his son Samuel, who was on leave from his unit, which was fighting in Korea. Things were still looking decidedly dicey around Hungnam, where his forces were fighting hard to try and stabilize the front. Failure meant an amphibious evacuation would have to be attempted.

As the jeep sped through the streets of Uijeongbu he could at least content himself that the air forces of the allies had finally wrested total control of the air space above the battlefield at that his attack planes like the rocket equipped F4 Corsairs were staring to cause havoc with the Manchurian armour.

He noticed his driver's attention swing to the left as a party of what was later shown to be Danish nurses passed by on the street corner. The General turned and briefly glanced himself, not immune to a pretty woman and remembering his own youth. By the time both eyes were back on the road, the jeep had passed the intersection at high speed, completely missing the lumbering truck, full of fresh vegetables.

Even the presence of trained nurses and a female doctor on site was enough to save the General, who was killed instantly on impact. The U.N forces in Korea had lost their commander, just when things had started to stabilize militarily.

0809 25 January 1951

Lt General Matthew Bunker Ridgway had assumed command of the UN forces in Korea. It had been initially a chaotic period, as he struggled to familiarise himself with his new command, a command under crisis. It had taken a month of hard fighting, but the Manchurian forces attempting to take Seoul had been bled by intensive house to house fighting and finally, at the end of their logistical rope, had been forced to pull back out of the city.

Ridgway's forces had blooded them, now, come 31st January, it would be time to try and push them back. He had achieved overwhelming air superiority and would now be using his heavy bombers to blast a way through with area bombing before releasing the reserves of armour that had arrived in the last two months and remained uncommitted to battle. The enemy was not moving at all, except at night. If he could engage and defeat them in place, their units could be decimated by his aircraft in their retreat.

0706 1 March 1951

As the U.N forces pushed slowly Northwards, driving, the Manchurian and North Korean forces back out of artillery range of the battered capital, Seoul, their air forces continue to dominate the skies. The American Ridgeway had clearly asked them to concentrate on interdicting enemy supply and the difficulties for the communist armies became that much more palpable. On the 9th March Zhu De sent a cable to Stalin, in which he emphasized the difficulties faced by his forces and the urgent need for air cover, especially over supply lines.

Stalin finally agreed to supply the equipment for two anti-aircraft divisions, and seven thousand trucks. However, these would take time to arrive and, in many cases, would prove to be too little, too late. Manchurian and North Korean troops in Korea continued to suffer severe logistical problems throughout the war. What Manchurian soldiers feared, Zhu De said, was not the enemy, but that they had nothing to eat, no bullets to shoot, and no trucks to transport them to the rear when they were wounded.

1246 2 March 1951

Lt Afred Kimball's Republic F-84 Thunderjet rose as the weapon was released. 38 Thunderjets were attacking the Taksan dam and as he flew over the target, the F-84's protected by their F-86 escorts, he could clearly see the breach in the dam wall.

By the end of the day, Toksan and Chasan dams had both been breached by the Thunderjets, Kuwinga Dam by B29's and Sup'ung Dam by RAF Lincoln's in a specially conceived mission using huge "Grand Slam" bombs that had been flown out from the UK in January. Two other dam busting mission, one by the U.S Air Force and another by the RAAF, failed, but these four were success enough. It was to inundate three river basin and place large parts of the North Korean capital under three feet of water, eventually disrupting Zhu De's planned Spring Offensive.

2314 29 April 1951

Seven months ago they were in this situation, now they were right back there again. The UN Forces had given Zhu De's Manchurian fools the same sort of trouncing that the North Koreans had sustained. UN Forces had bridgeheads over the Ryesong River, on the West Bank. They had encircled 100,000 troops in a pocket centred on the city of Kaesong, their spring offensive forestalling the Manchurian and North Korean forces and trapping them in their forward locations. Strong on the East flank, the UN forces had broken through and captured large numbers of men and material.

It was time to bring this foolishness to a close. He had authorised the movement of Soviet troops into North Korea, the conducting of a nuclear test on Sakhalin for the 12th May and had instructed Andrey Vyshinsky to start negotiations with the US and their allies to achieve a peace. They had failed. All that now remained was to win the peace and retain some of the cake that was Korea.

0600 12 June 1951

As they tumbled out of the huts onto the road at Brighton Army Camp, Sergeant Major Harry Morris, a World War 1 and World War 2 vet, could scarcely say he was impressed. They were the first batch taken in under the new National Service legislation, brought forward to correct the dramatic slide in numbers in the defence forces and provide soldiers for the Korea War, soldiers that would likely now not be needed. Conscription had started in Australasia.

1845 5 September 1951

It had taken five months of back and forth demands and negotiation, but finally a peace treaty was to be signed. Harry Truman had a busy week, all of it in San Francisco. Firstly, on September 8th, the representatives of 51 nations were gathering to sign the Treaty of San Francisco to formally end the war against Japan. It would result in a gradual withdrawal of occupation forces between now and 30 June 1952. Only Okinawa, strategically important, would remain occupied for the foreseeable future.

On September 10th, Turkish and Greek representatives would attend a ceremony to formally sign themselves in as members of NATO. Naturally they had asked for separate ceremonies, which had been rejected.

Finally, on September 14th, an armistice agreement would be signed to end the Korean war. It was in many ways unsatisfactory, but would do for now as a means of ending the conflict. To push further would possibly result in a direct conflict with Soviet Russia and the risks were not worth the reward.

As it was, they had recovered a large swath of territory above the 38th Parallel, including the cities of Haeju, Kosong and Kaesong, freeing millions from Communism and strengthening their position in the South. Plus, they would recover lost US and allied servicemen via a prisoner exchange.

Certain things still stuck in his craw, but he would be forced to let them go. The North Koreans claimed they had captured 55,000 South Koreans, but now claimed that only 8,000 wanted to return. They had also abducted South Korean civilians, but claimed they held none. War crimes would go unpunished. Perhaps the later was just as well, as he was well aware of the excesses of South Korean President Syngman Rhee's and his government, with perhaps 100,000 suspected leftists "disappeared".

Of one thing he was sure, Korea would require garrisoning for many years, perhaps permanently, as Kim would never accept the loss of the territory that North Korea had been forced to endure.

Korea after the war, September 1951

1345 31 March 1952

Sir Winston Leonard Spencer-Churchill had regained the office of Prime Minister at the end of 1951. He had planned to make the trip earlier but George V's sudden death had caused it to be postponed. There was much to discuss on the trip to Australasia, not least of which was the use of Australasian soil to conduct the nuclear tests. Both Australasia and Canada were pushing hard to obtain the bomb after Britain, something that was firmly opposed by Harry Truman.

AS he stepped up the gangplank of *HMS Vanguard*, now the only operational battleship in the R.N, he hoped her bulk would assist in overawing the Australasians and Canadians at the Melbourne meeting, as he tended to agree with Truman's line, however, it would not be easy to fend of either government with platitudes. Both had done more than their share and Korea and he needed Australasia, in particular, to provide help with the developing issue of communist guerrillas in Malaya.

1406 8 April 1952

It was a series of mutually interlocking contracts that should assist both countries with their defence and aviation requirements. Firstly, the intervention of both the Australasian government and the ubiquitous American billionaire Howard Hughes had propelled the Avro C-102 Jetliner into production, with 50 to be license built by Commonwealth Aircraft

Corporation for both TAA and Qantas. Trans Canada airlines would purchase 50 as well, with 30 to be built by Hughes either in Canada or Australasia, whichever could produce the design the quickest.

Secondly, both governments committed themselves in principle to the purchase of the new designs, being an all-weather, supersonic fighter, to be produced mainly in Canada, with only aerodynamic testing in Melbourne, to be known as the CF-105 Arrow. At this stage the initial design had been completed. Similarly, Hencall had completed the design stage of what was hoped to be the new strategic all-weather bomber, the He-166 Mammoth. Both countries had committed in principle to the design, which would allow delivery of the nuclear capability that both hoped to have.

Lastly from an aviation point of view, de Havilland Australasia's new STOL design had been purchased by Canadian representatives. With a capacity to carry 20 passengers or up to 5000lb of cargo and land on and take off an airstrip less than 800ft in length made it suited to the many rural airstrips in Canada, as it was to the many dirt trips in Australasia.

In other agreements, Australasian yards would build one *Daring Class* destroyer Australasian variant for Canada, who would build three more themselves. Canada would also purchase a quantity of Australasian Uranium from the two operating mines, Radium Hill and Rum Jungle.

Hencall was now 64, however, he was happy to have the challenge of a brand-new project ahead of him. He was not far off retirement, but wanted to see this one through before he did so.

1310 22 April 1952

Queen Alice gave the royal assent to the treaty, commonly later known as the AUS Treaty. It bound the signatories to recognise that an armed attack in the Pacific area on any of them would endanger the peace and safety of the others. It stated 'The Parties will consult together whenever in the opinion of any of them the territorial integrity, political independence or security of any of the Parties is threatened in the Pacific'. The two nations also pledged to maintain and develop individual and collective capabilities to resist attack.

It seemed a fitting end to the close wartime cooperation that both countries had practiced and upon her urging the governments only stipulation had been that Krueger, still immensely popular in Australasia, had led the U.S delegation.

1235 26 April 1952

In the finish Churchill had acquiesced, after much backwards and forwards negotiations. The U.K needed a safe place to test, plus the rocket firing facilities at Woomera would also be required for further developments of potential delivery systems. The U.K also required access to an uninterrupted supply of fissile material and also ideally required Canada's Chalk River facilities to produce a quantity of weapons grade plutonium.

In the finish what had swayed the deal was that Churchill had negotiated the use of

Australasian, plus a lesser quantity of Canadian troops in Malaya to quell the communist insurgency. He had appealed to Churchill as to all three nations Anglo-Saxon backgrounds and their solidarity as members of the Commonwealth. He also thought that the chance to show his old compatriot Eisenhower, assumed to be the likely next U.S President, that he was not a complete pushover for US policy, was also an attraction.

Menzies was happy, as the timeline of the agreement committed the U.K to providing four devices in each year from 1956-60 to Australasia and Canada. It was assumed that by 1960 both nations would be able to produce their own material and manufacture their own weapons. It also committed all three nations to joint access to any research and development tested at Woomera in regards to delivery systems.

1315 1 November 1952

It was doubtful if any ships had ever been destroyed so thoroughly as the old *River Class* Frigate *HMS Plym*. Anchored in the lagoon at Trimouille Island in the Monte Bello Islands, some 80 miles off the West Australian Coast, the bomb exploded with the force of 25 kilotons of TNT.

As the two Drake-Brockman brothers watched, one in the capacity of Prince Consort, the other as a retired Major General and current Senator for Western Australia, it was brought home all too clearly that the nuclear age had arrived, rightly or wrongly.

2359 20 December 1952

Anastas Ivanovich Mikoyan, exiled onto the periphery since he had fallen into disfavour and conducting missions like this trade and propaganda mission to assist in propping up Kim's tottering North Korean regime, both economically and militarily.

He should never have found himself here, but in many ways it was a relief to find himself out of Moscow. Stalin was winding himself up for a new set of purges with the entirely fabricated "Doctor's Plot", indeed it had already commenced in Czechoslovakia. He was aware of a plan to bring an end to these activities when he heard the raised voice across the room.

Boris Merkulov, a man also lusting after former glory, a wedge driven between him and his mater, Beria, was well into his cups, a not unusual state of affairs lately. He strayed close enough to hear ""Sooner or later there will be a full-on clash between the Communist Bear and the Western Bulldog. There will be no mercy for our sugar-coated, honey-dripping, wheedling, grovelling former allies! We'll blow them to blazes with all their kings, with all their traditions, lords, castles, heralds, Orders of the Bath and Garter, and their white wigs. When the Bear's paw strikes, no-one will remain to nurse the hope that their gold can rule the world. Our healthy, socially strong young idea, the ideas of Lenin, will be the victor! (...) When we roar, they sit tight on their tails! I am told that there were Tsars who watered their horses in the [River] Oder. Well, the time will come when we will water Soviet horses in the Thames!".

And then it all came apart as Merkulov restarted, address a circle of North Koreans that included Foreign Minister Pak Hon-yong, among others "It's only Stalin and his crazy policies and paranoia holding us back, but don't worry, soon he will be gone as well".

Mikoyan, due to fly back to Vladivostok on the 22nd, knew he could not make the trip any more. Somehow, he was too sure exactly how, he needed to disappear. For those stuck inside the Soviet Union, escape became no longer a possibility.

2234 15 January 1953

On January 13, 1953, some of the most prestigious and prominent doctors in the USSR had been accused of taking part in a vast plot to poison members of the top Soviet political and military leadership. Pravda, reported the accusations under the headline "Vicious Spies and Killers under the Mask of Academic Physicians."
"Today the TASS news agency reported the arrest of a group of saboteur-doctors. This terrorist group, uncovered some time ago by organs of state security, had as their goal shortening the lives of leaders of the Soviet Union by means of medical sabotage.

Investigation established that participants in the terrorist group, exploiting their position as doctors and abusing the trust of their patients, deliberately and viciously undermined their patients' health by making incorrect diagnoses, and then killed them with bad and incorrect treatments. Covering themselves with the noble and merciful calling of physicians, men of science, these fiends and killers dishonoured the holy banner of science. Having taken the path of monstrous crimes, they defiled the honour of scientists.

Among the victims of this band of inhuman beasts were Comrades A. A. Zhdanov and A. S. Shcherbakov. The criminals confessed that, taking advantage of the illness of Comrade Zhdanov, they intentionally concealed a myocardial infarction, prescribed inadvisable treatments for this serious illness and thus killed Comrade Zhdanov. Killer doctors, by incorrect use of very powerful medicines and prescription of harmful regimens, shortened the life of Comrade Shcherbakov, leading to his death.
The majority of the participants of the terrorist group… were bought by American intelligence. They were recruited by a branch-office of American intelligence — the international Jewish organization called "Joint". The filthy face of this Zionist spy organization, covering up their vicious actions under the mask of charity, is now completely revealed…
Unmasking the gang of poisoner-doctors struck a blow against the international organization…. Now all can see what sort of philanthropists and "friends of peace" hid beneath the sign-board of "Joint." Sadly, it appears that they received assistance and access to high ranking officials through other high-ranking officials within the party.

Other participants in the terrorist group (Vinogradov, M. Kogan, Egorov) were discovered, as has been presently determined, to have been long-time agents of English intelligence, serving it for many years, carrying out its most criminal and sordid tasks. The bigwigs of the USA and their English junior partners know that to achieve domination over other nations by peaceful means is impossible. Feverishly preparing for a new world war, they energetically send spies inside the USSR and the people's democratic countries: they attempt to accomplish what the Hitlerites could not do — to create in the USSR their own subversive "fifth column. The Soviet people should not for a minute forget about the need to heighten their vigilance in all ways possible, to be alert for all schemes of warmongers and their agents, to constantly strengthen the Armed Forces and the intelligence organs of our government."

They had come for Beria on the night of the 14th and the man who had authorised so much torture upon other was so easily broken by it himself. The Doctors plot may have been set up as a fabrication, but Beria was not long in selling out his co-conspirators Malenkov and Molotov, as well as other such as Merkulov and Mikoyan, who had found no alternative to going back to Russia.

It was to touch off a series of purges reminiscent of those of 1937-38, 318,000 were to be shot in 1953-54, with another 900,000 going to the camps. The Soviet Jewish population, who had suffered so terribly under Hitler, suffered again as their numbers formed a much larger portion per capita than any other ethnic group, despite their involvement in any such plot being completely fabricated.

1708 6 February 1953

As the limousine turned into Victoria Street on its way back to St Kilda, Queen Alice reflected on the loss of yet another former Prime Minister. Since the start of World War 2 she had lost Michael Savage, John Curtin, Peter Fraser and now James Scullin. Scullin had very much been a fixture of her youth and she knew she would miss both his wise counsel and his dry wit.

He had been the driving force that had brought Australasia through the Depression, the architect of the economic policies that had buffered the country. In many ways the streamlined 4-6-2 express train that she had travelled back from Brisbane on, traveling at times over 60mph, were a true monument to the national infrastructure that he had done so much to create. Unusually, she had delivered one of the eulogies personally in the Catholic Cathedral, wanting to let people know how much she would miss her old friend.

1909 2 June 1953

They had been in London for some time but it was at the official state dinner that Queen Alice noticed the looks and moments spent together for the first as perhaps something more than an innocent flirtation. Her own sister, in London with the Greek Royal family, had confirmed her suspicions.

She had brought her youngest, Marie, to the Coronation of Elizabeth II in London and she had noticed the inordinate amount of time she had spent with her fellow 19 year old, the Rajah Muda, or Crown Prince, of Sarawak, Simon Brooke Mackay.

He was a pleasant young lad, to the best of her knowledge and it appeared she would be seeing more of him as her daughter informed her the following day that she had invited him to stay at the family Ski Lodge, at Kurow, near Otago, on New Zealand's South Island.

The family maintained a number of properties inside Australasia, aside from Domain Palace in Melbourne, namely a beach property, "Avon Dale" at Palm Beach in Queensland, "Green Point Cottage" in Sydney, "Cape Portland Estate", a farm in North Eastern

Tasmania, "Alberton" in Auckland and Kurow House. Of all of these locations, Kurow, along with Cape Portland, was by far the most private.

1934 1 September 1953

Admiral John Collins sat in his office and pondered the report he would be submitting to the government of the state of the armed forces. He strongly suspected that Menzies government already had its eye on the election that was due next year, probably a sensible proposition if you were a politician, which thankfully he was not.

The war in Korea had highlighted certain points, not least of which was the lack of effectiveness of piston engine aircraft, no matter how high the performance. Never the less, the CAC-15 had been very effective indeed in ground attack missions.

The RAN had been scarcely challenged, although he could see the evolution of missiles, currently in its infancy, would be a game changer. The navy's submarine force, the only arm not updated since World War 2, was also badly in need of an update. With the retirement of *HMAS Brisbane*, the navy lacked an amphibious carrier.

For the army, the priority was getting new, self-loading rifles, as well as updated artillery and ordinance. It's "big ticket items", such as armour, were well provided for. The L1 A1 had been selected to go into production at Lithgow in 1955 as the standard army rifle. The Owen gun still remained the standard sub machine gun, the Bren the standard light machine gun.

The RAAF had been held at 40 squadrons after the Korean scare and had been updated with more jet engine types and consisted of:

Bomber/Photo Recon/Maritime Patrol
He 2 jet bombers 226
He 200 maritime patrol 76
De Havilland Vampire fighter/bombers 78

Fighters
He 280 jet fighters 302
CAC 15 Cockatoo fighter/bombers 126

Transport
Douglas C47 164
De Havilland Duck 44

RAN
De Havilland Sea Vampire 82
CAC 15 Cockatoo 116

The navy's main combat strength still resided in its three main ships, the fleet carrier *Sydney*, light carrier *Wellington* and heavy cruiser *Melbourne*. With the completion of the last three *Daring Class* destroyers in 1954, the navy would have ten modern destroyers and the last of the old *Tribal Class* would be disposed of. The old Landing Ship carrier

Brisbane had also been sold. Currently the navy's strength was:

1 CV
1 CVL
1 CA
10 DD
8 SS
plus smaller ships and support vessels

The army had been set at a strength of 3 Divisions and two Brigades, the introduction of National service assisting numbers.

1435 7 April 1954

At the same time as new U.S President Dwight Eisenhower was making his well-known "dominoes of communism speech" in Washington, the CF-102 Jetliner was making its maiden operational flight on the Toronto to New York run, arriving to an enthusiastic reception in New York. The flight time of just under an hour cut the previous times in half.

It was to make an appearance later in 1954 and 1955 with TAA, Qantas, Kiwi Air and in the US with TWA, as well as in Canada. From 1955 to 1959 it dominated the aviation market, until the appearance of the Boeing 707 highlighted its shortcomings in relation to passenger numbers and payload.

However, in these early years its only real competitor was the Caravelle, the British Comet being dogged with safety issues. The money earned in exports went towards development of Avro Canada's military projects and hastened the development of their latest fighter, the Arrow.

2213 12 July 1954

Doc Evatt privately conceded to himself if not yet in public. He and the ALP had lost what was widely seen as an unlosable election, seemingly by as little as 4-6 seats. Menzies had campaigned the 1951 election on an anti-Soviet theme and he had personally gone on record to say there were no Soviet spies in Australasia. The revelations by the Soviet defector Petrov and his wife to the contrary had been a devastating blow to his electoral chances.

1909 26 February 1955

It was an outcome that was to be disastrous for the Australasian Labour Party, an outcome that consigned them to the political wilderness for the next 17 years. Evatt had, in late 1954, blamed his election loss on elements of the right wing, Catholic, Victorian State Branch of the ALP, the power base of Bob Santamaria and his supporters in the Victorian Labor Party, called "the Groupers". He had also taken aim at the former Communist Party leader, Don Ross, who had been elected as a Labor MP in Auckland and enjoyed wide spread support but still agitated for the restoration of the Communist party of Australasia, which was currently banned.

On 31 October 1954, a Sydney paper reported on a letter sent by the Victorian Minister for Lands, Robert Holt, to the federal secretary of the Australasian Labor Party, J. Schmella, which the paper described as 'probably as explosive, politically, as any document in Australasia'. Holt stated - "My charge is that the Victorian branch is controlled and directed in the main by one group or section through Mr. B. Santamaria ... my criticism is not personal. It is levelled against those ideas which are contrary to what I believe Labor policy to be. Moreover, I have been requested by my numerous and trusted friends, who happen to be Catholic, to fight against the influence of Mr. Santamaria and those he represents, when he seeks to implement his ideas through an abuse of a political movement, designed to serve a truly political purpose. He went on to say " we need to get rid of Don Ross and his kooky bunch of intellectuals based here in Sydney but more particularly Auckland. His sycophantic, fawning admiration for Stalin is to be despised"

It was to all come to a head at the party's 1955 conference in Hobart. In early 1955 the Labor Party's executive federally dissolved the Victorian state executive and appointed a new executive in its place. Both executives sent delegates to the 1955 National Conference, where the delegates from the old executive were excluded from the conference. The Victorian branch then split between pro-Evatt and pro-Santamaria factions, and in March the pro-Evatt state executive suspended 24 members of state Parliament suspected of being Santamaria supporters, including four ministers. Don Ross was also suspended from ALP membership and went to the cross benches.

Both parties acted quickly and by April 1955 Santamaria had formed the Democratic Anti Communist Labor Party (DACLP), its State members having crossed the floor and brought down the Victorian State Labor Government. Nationally, it was to result in the loss of 13 MP's. Ross had also acted quickly, establishing the Socialist Party of Australasia (SPA), crossing the floor with fellow MP Tim Whitfield, further weakening Labor.

1314 15 May 1955

Stalin had personally come for the laying down of the keel of the fifth ship of the class, to be named *Tiflis*. Her 82.9% complete sister *Moskva*, the second ship of the battlecruiser class lay fitting out across the bay. *Tiflis* was to be the last ship of the class.

The navy had expanded rapidly since the end of the 1940's. In addition, 13 *Sverdlov Class* light cruisers had already joined, with 12 more under construction, three of those launched. In regards to submarines six long range Project 611 boats had been completed, fully 116 medium range Project 613 and 18 Project 615 coastal boats. The navy's first nuclear powered submarine was also under construction. As Stalin stepped up to make a very brief speech, he felt a kick like a mule to his chest and felt himself rapidly falling, before blacking out. He was never to regain consciousness from the massive heart attack.

1843 28 January 1956

He had come for the summer and Alice had noted that he lost none of his famous bluntness as she met him aboard Brooke's yacht, the Vyner Brooke. "Well then, seems like your daughter wants to marry my Grandson" was his opening line. "or the other way around" she replied. "or that, yes" he said.

"Look, I've just about had it" said Brooke, "I'm 81 years old and I'm about buggered. It was bad enough that I was almost assassinated by my own nephew in 1953. I've taken steps to deal with that and now I am thinking about giving it away, probably a good a time as any would be early 1957, don't want a huge fuss about 40 years in power so thought I would go before then. That being the case we need to get these kids married before they have to get married. How does that sound?". Alice was used to his gruff manners so they settled down to make the details for what would be a February 1957 wedding and a coronation in April.

1816 29 June 1956

Sir Anthony Eden was happy with the result of the meeting. A final date for Malayan Independence had been set, 31 January 1957. He had committed U.K forces to continue quelling the communist insurgency alongside Australasian troops, which was dying out anyway.

The main regional concerns all revolved around communist countries or countries that had decided to align themselves with communist countries. In Vietnam, communist forces had used the overthrow of the Emperor Bao Dai in 1955 by Ngô Đình Diệm and the clearly fraudulent May 1956 referendum about the abolition of the dynasty as a cassis belli for a full scale Communist uprising. If it was a curious happening that the abolition of the monarchy had provoked a communist uprising, it made it no less alarming.

Perhaps more alarming from the point of view of Malaya, in particular, was the drift of Indonesia into the Soviet camp, confirmed by the sale a month ago of a Soviet cruiser to the Indonesian navy. Indonesian officials had recently made several provocative speeches about Borneo and East Indonesia and the fact that the populations thereof were 'part of the Indonesian sphere" and "ethnically Indonesian", worrying statements.

1818 8 December 1956

Hencall listened as the Queen made the closing speech of what had been spectacularly successful Olympics. He had received ten tickets so had taken his family and whilst he had enjoyed the day's events, particularly the marathon finish, he was more interested in what was to come. As the echoes of the Queen's speech died away three He 280 fighters flew across the stadium at subsonic speed until finally the plane he had laboured on for over five years, the giant He 166, crossed over the stadium, the pilot going to afterburners and creating a sonic boom over the stadium.

For him it was a culmination of 6 years of development and this machine, the second prototype, would be the first production aircraft with some minor tweaks. He planned to deliver it and a second machine to the RAAF on Australasia day, 1957. He could then work on the contract for 100 from the RAAF and 40 from the RCAF. In truth, he knew it would be his final design, he was nearing 69 years old and would be looking to retire soon and devote his attention to his grandchildren and the snapper of Port Phillip Bay. There was already an offer from the government on the table to merge with Commonwealth Aircraft Corporation-once the 166 was cleared for series production he would take it up.

He had enjoyed assisting with the Canadian kite as well, where Hencall Aviation had done much of the wind tunnelling and aerodynamic tests. He had not been directly involved since then but had advised Avro Canada to not worry about targeting radars and the like, just to get the plane in the air first. Armament and weapons targeting systems for missiles could follow. The aircraft had been unveiled to a large publicity splash on 28 September and was due to fly in January 1957.

It felt good to hear the ooh and aahs of the crowd. It was just as well she was so far along. Relations with Australasia's Northern neighbour were strained close to breaking as Sukarno's Indonesia was almost daily making inflaming comments about Malaya, claiming a "right" to all of Borneo and East Indonesia. Things could very well get ugly quickly.

1515 31 January 1957

On the same day that Malaysia was coming into existence, the aircraft was put through a full range of tests yet again, having first flown successfully on the 18 January. It showed both excellent manoeuvrability, rate of climb and speed, with Mach 1.9 exceeded. With the cancellation of the "Velvet Glove" missile system, the US Sparrow would be adopted, along with a potential to launch the AIR-2 Genie nuclear missile, although the US had not approved their sale to either Canada or any other country, as well as two Aden cannons.

"Jack" Frost was ecstatic. His design had finally passed the last hurdles and now simply needed to have a full weapons system fit. He expected series production to start late 1957 and had already two identical orders, each for 100 with an option for 20 more, from both Canada and Australasia. Neither were the only country showing interest.

1312 2 February 1957

Stalin's "big ship" program had been wound back by Gorshkov on Stalin being replaced by new General Secretary Nikolai Bulganin. Foremost among the casualties had been the Project 68bis and 68bis-ZIf light cruisers. Originally projected at 25 ships, it had been curtailed at 19 units, one of which had been sold to Indonesia. The Project 82 battlecruisers had also suffered, from an original five ships, only three had been completed, the last only two months hence. With the ex-Italian battleship *Roma*, it gave the Soviet Navy a heavy ship for each fleet, namely the Baltic, Black Sea, Pacific and Northern Fleet. In truth, Gorshkov was more concerned with other methods to cut down the U.S Navy's huge lead, such as submarines, the first nuclear one of which was currently under construction.

1908 25 February 1957

Queen Alice Drake-Brockman and her husband Karl were still holidaying and staying in Kuching at the Astana Palace after celebrating the marriage of her daughter Marie on the 20th to Simon Mackay-Brooke, Sarawak's heir. The young couple would be crowned as the new Rajah and Ranee of Sarawak on 2 March 1957. In truth it was a welcome break and she was here with her whole family, including her other daughter Adelaide and her son, Charles, now aged 28 and 25 respectively. Her sister was due to arrive from Greece via Aden and Singapore that night for the Coronation.

It was later that night, when she was catching up with her newly arrived sister that the news came through. Indonesian troops had crossed the frontier from Kalimantan (Indonesian Borneo) at 4.00pm that day. Within the hour she could also confirm Indonesian landings at Kupang in West Timor, part of East Indonesia. The following day Australasia would again be at war.

1945 26 February 1957

Captain Steven Saunderson recalled his earlier conversation with the Queen as his ship slipped out of Kuching harbour.

"Captain I don't give a damn what your instructions from Melbourne or Mr Menzies are. I'll be safe enough here in Kuching for the moment and will be able to get out via aircraft or even via Brooke's yacht. As you yourself so kindly pointed out they are running reinforcements into Permangkat. Use this vessel and *HMAS Kokoda* to disrupt those reinforcements, that was your secondary mission after you had ferried me. I would suggest that you get about it now. In fact, as your commander in chief, I more than suggest you get about it".

HMAS Melbourne, in Kuching as a virtual Royal yacht for the wedding, found herself sailing to war with her *Daring Class* destroyer companion. He could expect air cover in the morning, but had sailed at night when he should not need it, as the Indonesian air-force did not have any all-weather aircraft and was only day capable.

Much as he worried about leaving the Queen behind, especially since Kuching had already been targeted, however, this had been broken up by the single squadron of CAC-15's that comprised Sarawak's air force. It was a curious mixture of aircraft, 18 B25 Mitchells escorted by a variety of piston engine aircraft including 14 P51 Mustangs and even three ex Japanese A6M Zeros. Most of Indonesia's modern aircraft were kept for air defence against possible attack or committed to strikes on East Indonesia in support of landings.

Perhaps the Queen had known something, for at 2358, thirty-five nautical miles Southwest of Pemangkat, his surface search radar detected multiple contacts at a range of 23 miles out. It rapidly developed into six large and three small blips, traveling slowly at 12 knots. What was to be the last gun only battle between heavy ships was about to develop.

2216 26 February 1957

Captain Steven Saunderson's *HMAS Melbourne* had been badly battered by the encounter, taking 21 6 and 5.1 inch shell hits and having 57 casualties, however, he had achieved his objective.

He had initially achieved surprise and smothered the Indonesian cruiser *Sumatra* with 8 inch shells, leaving her aflame and in difficulties. The three Indonesian *Skoryy Class* destroyers had attempted to launch a torpedo counterattack, banging away with their 5.1-inch guns whilst the light cruiser hung back and used her 6-inch guns, finally gaining hits at 2021. The huge rate of fire of his heavy cruiser, 108 rounds per minute, quickly decided the matter, leaving one destroyer shattered and sinking and another badly damaged, which in itself was finished off by Melbourne's companion, *HMAS Kokoda*.

By the time he swung back to the Indonesians and fully engaged again at 2054, they had already lost two destroyers and their light cruiser *Sumatra* was crippled. They had ordered the five transports to scatter at about that time, however, the two Australasian ships had closed the range, *Melbourne* shrugging off hits from the *Sumatra* and crippling the last Indonesian destroyer, leaving her sinking. This freed *Kokoda* to pursue the lumbering transports whilst *Melbourne* pounded the Indonesian cruiser to death over the next 30 minutes, *Sumatra* finally sinking, swept by fires and listing badly to port, slipping beneath the waves at 2133, *Kokoda* had already caught and sunk one transport.

By the time that Steven Saunderson called off the pursuit of the remaining transports, only one had made it to Permangkat, another turning back. Three transports, one light cruiser and three destroyers had been sunk, almost half the tonnage of the Indonesian navy. In the water, more than 4,000 men would perish. It was a disaster for the Indonesians and represented the last encounter between traditional guns armed ships of any significant size.

1348 28 February 1957 Morotai Air Force Base, Indonesia

The three giant He 166's, the only three operational aircraft in the RAAF streaked over the airfield, scattering 60,000 kilograms of bomblets all over the runway. Accuracy at the speed flown was nothing to write home about, never the less they managed to comfortably outdistanced the 10 Yak-23's that had scrambled and assumed an easy interception.

However, the 923km/hr fighters were left in the wake of the bombers, which, after dropping their bombs, went to afterburner and rocketed to over 1,900 km/hr, making an assumed cutting the corner interception not possible. Only five aircraft were destroyed on the ground, with another seven damaged although three of those destroyed and two damaged represented half Indonesia's current fleet of Tu-16's long range bombers.

The real damage was caused by 12 CAC-15's which swept low over the base whilst the CAP was chasing the He-166, firing rockets and cannons and destroying 19 aircraft and damaging 12 others, losing only one aircraft to the Yak-23's as they made their retreat and another to anti-aircraft fire.

0616 2 March 1957, Garden Island Sydney

Rear Admiral Wilfred "Arch" Harrington had assembled his Task Force for the Indonesian operation. Its objective was simple enough, to interdict all Indonesian shipping in the Java Sea. He no longer had any real reason to fear the Indonesian Navy, it's only offensive vessels left after their disastrous encounter with *HMAS Melbourne* being three *Whiskey Class* submarines and five destroyers.

It was their land based air that would pose the most problem, however, the raid on the 28th February had destroyed the Indonesian fleet of Tu-16 bombers and it would be only the older types that need concern him. Firstly, his own flagship *HMAS Sydney* would be accompanied by the light carrier *HMAS Wellington* and six *Daring Class* destroyers. Two submarines had already departed from Fleet Base Perth, another two would follow from

Fleet Base Auckland within days. Finally, underway replenishment forces, escorted by older *Bathurst Class* ships and the old destroyer *Arunta* would also follow.

The two carriers had large air wings, consisting of:
Sydney: 32 de Havilland Venoms, 24 Fairey Gannets, 4 Westland Whirlwind Helicopters
Wellington: 16 CAC-15's, 8 Fairey Gannets, 4 Westland Whirlwind Helicopters

The air force was moving assets to RAAF Butterworth in Malaysia as well as Darwin to support operations, including He 280 fighters and Vampire fighter/bombers. Strategic Nuclear forces had gone to a higher state of alert, status Yellow, from a peacetime status of Blue.

The army plans involved deployment of two Brigades as soon as they could be fully assembled and equipped, possibly followed by four more, including one armoured. Rumours abounded that SAS troops had already been deployed to Timor.

1130 4 March 1957, Parliament House, Melbourne

One thing the Indonesian war, so soon after Korea, had made quite clear was that Australasia had drawn down its armed forces too much and that the current defence budgets would not do, either for now or the foreseeable future. The currently percentage of GDP the government was allocating to defence, 2.4% was simply not sufficient.

One of the major sufferers of the draw down had been the senior service, the navy. Keith Hollyoake, as Defence Minister, watched he jackals of the press corps gather for the conference. He announced the RAN would purchase *HMS Terrible* from the Royal Navy; the ship newly decommissioned. In addition, *HMS Perseus*, also newly decommissioned would be purchased as an amphibious transport and Australasia would construct three Type 41 frigates built locally.

Australasia's defence GDP was to rise from 2.4% to 4.3%, representing a substantial sum for a country now at 17 million people. Earlier procurement of the He-166 in greater numbers was also on the cards and the contract for 100 plus an option of 20 more Avro Arrows had been increased to 150 definitive orders with an option on 50 more. It was also specified that 20 be delivered by end July 1958.

6 March 1957, Sarikei, Kingdom of Sarawak

In response of appeals from the King, British forces, mainly consisting of Major General Richard Neville Anderson's 17th Gurkha Division had landed at Sarakei with the purpose of driving the Indonesians back and recapturing the capital, Kuching, which had fallen two weeks before. With the Indonesians shipping starting to be interdicted by RN and RAN vessels, as well as RAF and RAAF aircraft, they no longer had much capacity of resupply or reinforce.

The Indonesian air force had, in fact, largely melted like butter, their two largest bases, Morotai and Surabaya, being hit badly by RAAF and RAF raids, respectively, destroying many aircraft on the ground. Two battalions of troops had also been deployed to Sandakan to hold British North Borneo until further reinforcements arrived. It was common knowledge that Australasia had a Task Force aimed at Timor, aiming to reoccupy the island from Indonesian troops. The destruction of the greater part of the Indonesian army and air force had stymied their objectives and their advance was slow indeed, in many cases unsupported by supplies.

26 March 1957 Dili, East Timor

The Portuguese government agreeing on the 14th March to allow Australasian aircraft to use Dili in East Timor was to make the task of the RAAF and RAN just that much easier. With 38 He-280 fighters based at Dili, along with 10 CAC-15s as ground attack, the arrival of the RAN task force was to see almost 100 fighters able to cover shuttle raids of bombers from the air bases at Darwin.

The RAN Task force was able to invade and recapture the port of Kupang after a short but hard two day fight on the 26th March, losing one transport thankfully only after it had unloaded to an Indonesian submarine that was later itself sunk, driving the scattered Indonesian forces into the jungle. The Indonesians were now completely on the defensive, isolated in West Timor against a hostile local populace and in control of a large section of Borneo, but with substantial enemy forces in their line of advance and no way to resupply or reinforce.

It was an untenable solution that any military analyst could tell was no able to be sustained. The final catalyst for change was to be a controversial but certainly effective raid against Jakarta. It had been approved as Australasian intelligence sources were concerned that Soviet Russia was potentially readying itself to involve its Pacific Fleet in the war, a worry that was later to prove groundless.

68 older He-2, as well as 5 He 166 bombers, escorted by 26 He-280 fighters attacked the city on the 12 April, laying waste to a large part of the Gambir district of the city, particularly the Presidential Palace. One day later Indonesia offered to surrender all forces outside Indonesia and withdraw from all captured territory. Mohammad Hatta had been installed as the new President; Sukarno having survived the bombing of the Presidential Palace but having been "retired." It was an offer that was accepted and a peace conference was set for 16 April in Kupang.

17 April 1957, Kupang, East Indonesia

Mohammad Hatta duly signed the peace treaty of behalf of Indonesia. In truth, he had little choice. At least in the firestorm of international protest at the bombing of Jakarta, Indonesia had gotten way with no territorial losses and little in the way of reparations, only 12 million to East Indonesia and 8 million of Sarawak.

Sukarno had been a fool, overreaching himself spectacularly. It was almost too late in life for Hatta to be President, but he was stuck with the job now. It was certainly preferable to the other option, military government. It was a blow to the country's prestige and indeed economy that was to take until the early 1970's to recover.

12 August 1957, Domain Palace, Australasia

Sir Robert Menzies relaxed comfortably in the back of the limousine on the way to the palace. The aftermath of the Indonesian war and it's swift and decisive victory after the bloodbath of the Second World War and his government's policy of essentially thumbing their nose at international condemnation of the Jakarta bombing had paradoxically made his government immensely popular at home.

The country had accepted a large number of East Indonesian refugees in the few months of the conflict and he had made provisions for some that had no homes to go back to be able to stay as refugees. With a 57 seat majority and popular support he could increase defence budgets to ensure the countries security and embark on a new, ambitious set of capital work programs by a modest increase in taxation that would partly be offset by the countries burgeoning population, now at more than 17 million and growing rapidly.

With the Snowy Schemes underway and the Ord River scheme an election promise that he intended to implement, Menzies wanted a definitive Nation building project to stamp his prime ministership on. With his government's majority, he had virtually a six-year term. Investigating thermal power in New Zealand was certainly one, but the largest project, one that had come up many times in the past, was the Bradfield scheme. Estimated at 30 million pounds in 1937, it would be dearer but more feasible from an engineering point of view now. He had some ideas on how to fund it, not least of which was to release the brake on exports of both Iron Ore, of which vast deposits had been discovered in Western Australia and Uranium, present in both South Australia and the Northern Territory.

10 November 1958 RAAF Richmond

"Jack" Frost watched as the first eight Avro Arrows were delivered. They were the first eight of what was to be an eventual order of 120 machines, slightly less than had been asked for during the Indonesian Crisis in 1957, but the same as the original order. Avro Canada was booming and would have fulfilled delivery to the Royal Canadian Air Force by end 1960 and the RAAF by mid-1961.

Also present was Ernst Hencall. He had chatted to Hencall about the development and delivery of the He-166. Constructed now by Commonwealth Aircraft Corporation after Hencall had sold his own concern, Hencall had finally been retired in 1957 aged 69. Sadly, this was the last time Frost would see him, leukemia claiming him in early 1960 after a life that had revitalized the Australasian aircraft industry. The 166 would eventually be made for both Australasian (122 machines) and Canada (48). It was to see the He-280 pushed back to service in the air force reserve only by the end of 1961, still, ironically, alongside the CAC-15, which was deemed the better machine for ground attack.

11 January 1960 State Dockyard, Newcastle, New South Wales

The Queen conducted the official ceremony to bless the ships before her maiden voyage next week. *Princess of Oceana* was the second ship of her class and represented a dramatic change in the way Australasian National Line was running their passenger services. Like her sister *Princess of Tasmania*, now in service on the Melbourne-Launceston run, she was a smaller ship, 3,900 tons, but roll on roll off. Her regular run would be Cairns- Guadalcanal- Bougainville- Port Moresby-Darwin.

It was planned to revitalise the shipping line and retire the older, larger, less efficient vessels. Also, under construction at Cockatoo Island Dockyard were two larger, 12,000-ton ferries. These, to be completed later in 1960, would ply the Melbourne-Auckland and Melbourne-Wellington/Christchurch routes. A sister, *Queen of Fiji*, had started on the Brisbane-New Caledonia-Fiji route three months ago.

She had to get back to Melbourne to attend the funeral of Ernest Hencall on the 14th. It was to be a proper state funeral, as befitted a man who had made such a significant contribution to World War 2. She was also worried about her own son Charles. At 28 it seemed his main interests were racing cars, racy women and inappropriate music.
14 June 1960, Toorak, Melbourne, Australasia

Menzies had comfortably won the 1960 election, losing only six seats to the Labor Party. It was a crushing parliamentary majority of 105 to 54, with two independents. With Australasian riding the crest of an economic boom that showed no signs of slowing, courtesy of mining and mineral exploration and significant capital works that had resulted in virtually zero unemployment, he was now ready to start what he had campaigned on, the massive Bradfield hydroelectric and irrigation scheme that would hopefully result in a permanently flooded Lake Eyre and construction was to commence in October 1960, preliminary planning having already been done. It was not to be completed until 1977.

It would be the biggest civil engineering project ever attempted in Australasia and one of the bigger ones worldwide. He now had a mandate to do it, however, it being part of the election promises that he had made. With Labor in disarray, their leader Walter Nash almost 78 and infirm, their deputy Arthur Caldwell an uninspiring political figure, he could see himself in the prime ministership for some years yet.

22 November 1962, Marlborough, South New Zealand

For newly minted Admiral Peter Phillips, it had been a good day at home. Watching the start of the Commonwealth Games on TV, newly promoted to head of the Australasian navy and in addition, he had had his choice of the previous year, the A4 Skyhawk, confirmed as the new fleet fighter. It was to replace the Venom and, finally, the CAC-15 in 1963.

The whole navy was reequipping. The Skyhawk and the Sikorsky Sea King, the new choice of helicopter, would be made by Commonwealth Aircraft Corporation. In all, to equip all three carriers, 72 Skyhawks had been ordered.

There was also an article on the news about Australasia making a small contribution to quelling the ongoing activities of communist rebels in Vietnam, rebels that had been, for a time in control of the North of the country but were now running an ongoing insurgency. At the time, it seemed like nothing, however, it was to drag on to be a lengthy and controversial contribution.

25 April 1965, Domain Palace, Melbourne

As the Queen returned from ANZAC Day, as they said in the song, "times they were a changing." For things in Australasia that was also the case, Menzies had won the 1963 election comfortably, defeating Arthur Caldwell and he had announced to her last week that, after some though, he would contest the 1966 election as well, wanting to see his now well underway Lake Eyre project progress further. There had been increasing resistance to its huge fiscal cost, but Menzies had brushed that aside, having a solid grip on the leadership after 15 years as Prime Minister and 25 as party leader. He had also announced last week an increase in Australasia's commitment to the Vietnam insurgency, an insurgency that had already resulted in the deaths of two army advisers.

The Queen was now almost 68. The country was undergoing great change. Rock bands the Beatles and the Rolling Stones had both toured the country to huge crowds. Older ideas and institutions were being challenged by a newer generation. The end of pounds as the currency was set for 1 July 1967, to be replaced by dollars. There was increasing pressure for her, personally, to provide an opinion or even intervene in the debate about capital punishment. Increasing resistance was being brought to bear in opposition to a nuclear reactor proposed for Port Pirie. Hand backs of traditional tribal lands had been mooted, particularly in New Zealand.

There was also international pressure to prepare those areas still administered by Australasia as Territories, namely the Solomon Islands, Papua New Guinea, Nauru, New Caledonia, Bougainville and so on.

At this stage, if she was able to make it, she planned to abdicate within ten years in favour of her son. However, he was still, in her own mind, not behaving as she would desire. He had settled down to one woman, but her suitability was certainly in question. He had met Judith Durham, unsurprisingly, at a car racing meet in 1963. She had just started a band called "The Seekers", who were to garner fame earlier this year when their first record rocketed to number one in both Australasia and the U.K, the publicity of dating her son certainly adding to the mix. She worried she would be unsuited to the life and her son was 12 years the twenty-year old's senior, another concern.

25 December 1967, Domain Palace, Australasia

It was the sort of shock that any mother does not need. It had been a good Christmas celebration with her family, when, after lunch, her son had pulled her aside. It did not take long to come to the point "Judy's pregnant".

It had been a turbulent two years. Menzies had been re-elected again in 1966, a blow that had finished Arthur Caldwell's political career and saw him replaced by the new comer, Gough Whitlam. The debate about both the Vietnam insurgency and capital punishment had both reached a fever pitch after a helicopter crash had killed 15 troops in August and Ronald Ryan had been hung in February. The dreadful fires in Tasmania in February 1967.

Seeing some conscientious objectors pulled out of their homes for national service many feared would lead to Vietnam had cut deeply into the Menzies government's popularity and the capital punishment debate was not helping either, many pushing for the Commonwealth to exercise its power to abolish such punishments in Federal law. Both New Zealand's, Tasmania, Queensland and New South Wales had all abolished.

Well, thought Alice, now it looks like we have a shotgun royal wedding. Thankfully the girl was only nine weeks. If they could get it done quickly enough, she might not be showing.

22 November 1969, Domain Palace, Australasia

Alice had stumbled through the swearing in of the latest Menzies Ministry, more from memory than anything else. As the ruling Liberal/National coalition government had become steadily more electorally unpopular it had resulted in the closest election ever in Australasia, the Liberal Party's win in the seat of Corangamite by 52 votes being confirmed only more than a week after the 8th November poll.

It had in all senses for herself been a disastrous year. The death of her son Charles driving a Monaro in a massive pile up on the first lap of the Hardie-Ferodo 500 had been devastating, leaving as it did a one-year old girl and a five months pregnant wife. It had produced a massive state funeral of a size not seen since her own father so long ago where she had struggled to hold herself together and her daughter in law had been unable to attend.

It would be the last victory for Menzies, who had privately announced to her his intention to retire in 1970. The Labor party, rejuvenated by Gough Whitlam, had run a campaign that had almost brought it to government for the first time in 20 years. Vietnam had been a continuing noose around the government's head and the execution of a convicted multiple murderer in New Caledonia in 1969 had again reignited the capital punishment debate.

Party	Votes	Votes	Seats	
Australasian Labour Party		4,680,792	107	+29
Federal Liberal Party of Australasia		3,610,987	88	?26
National Party		585,232	21	?2
Democratic Labour Party		581,977	0	0
Australasia Party		97,646	0	0
Democratic Party		519,465	1	+1
Independents		191,090	0	?1
Communist Party		118,345	0	0
Other		62,394	0	0
Total		6,114,118	217	+2
Liberal/National coalition		WIN	109	?16
Australasian Labor Party			107	+29

3 May 1971, Sydney International Airport

It was his last official act as Prime Minister, opening the new Sydney Airport. He had held on until the opening of the first stage of the Lake Eyre project had resulted in the first release of water from the Thompson River into Lake Eyre. By the end of 1971 the Lake would be permanently flooded, although all work on the scheme would not be completed until 1978 at the enormous cost of 2.95 billion dollars. The scheme had prompted a large wave of immigration to Australasia of ethnic groups that had not appeared before, in particular Indians, but also numbers of immigrants had started to arrive from Vietnam, fleeing the fighting and instability there. With things in Vietnam quietening and there being feelers as to peace talks, now was the time to go, leaving his successor, Keith Holyoake, to fight the 1972 election against Whitlam.

20 May 1973 West Launceston, Tasmania, Australasia

Lance Barnard, Deputy Prime Minister and Minister for Defence, contemplated the last six months of the new Labor government. Whitlam's iconic election mantra, "It's Time", had resonated with the general public and Labor had secured a large swing to gain power on 9th December.

Many of their election promises were now in the wings. With talks in Vietnam still dragging in, the government had announced a withdrawal of Australasian troops in any case, to be completed by August. Hollyoake's Liberals government had decriminalized homosexual acts last years and the government was also pushing forward on allocating traditional tribal land back to aboriginal people in Northern Territory and Western Australia despite State government opposition. This had already occurred some years ago in New Zealand and many years ago in Fiji.

The main focus now was on Australasia's external territories and colonies. Commissions had been set up to arrange for a transition for Papua New Guinea, Bougainville, Solomon Islands, Nauru, New Caledonia, Cook Islands, Gilbert and Ellice Islands, Tonga, Samoa, Tokelau, Cocos Islands and Christmas Islands.

Options included statehood, which was also being considered for the Northern Territory, becoming an official overseas territory, independence or remaining a colony, although the government did not really want to pursue the last option. The government had set an official date of 1 July 1975 for these decisions to be actioned, the same date as the breakup of the PMG department into Telecom and Australasia Post had been set for and the target date for the sale of the Commonwealth Bank, which would go a long way to hopefully providing the remainder of the money required to finish the Lake Eyre and Snowy Mountains schemes.

He was also reviewing the armed services and in light of the draw down with Vietnam and the seeming absence of other current external threats would bring the defence budget back to 3.3% of GDP. At this stage, national service was still operational and there were several dissenting views as to its continuation. Personally, The armed services currently consisted of:

Air Force:
Bomber/Photo Recon/Maritime Patrol
He 166 jet bombers 114
Lockheed Orion 54
Lockheed Neptune 42

Fighters
Avro Arrow 145
He 280 38
RF111 8

Transport
De Havilland Caribou 92

Navy:
The navy had disposed of all of its light carriers and had purchased two U.S *Essex Class* carriers to supplement *HMAS Sydney*, it deeming the light carriers too small to operate modern aircraft in significant numbers. One such ship, ex *USS Bon Homme Richard*, had been renamed *HMAS Christchurch*. The second, ex *USS Kearsage*, would be moored and cannibalized for spares. The navy now consisted of:

2 *Essex Class* carriers, operating A4 Skyhawks, Grumman Trackers and Sea King helicopters
1 Heavy Cruiser, *HMAS Melbourne*
4 *Charles Adams Class* destroyers, 7 *Daring Class* destroyers
6 *River Class* frigates, 4 *Leander Class* Frigates

1 July 1975, Noumea, Australasia

At 77, the Queen had been using her unmarried daughter Adelaide more and more as her representative on trips that required extensive travel. Some events, such as today's, were simply to important and besides her daughter was in Darwin for a similar ceremony, her daughter in law in Arawa for another. It marked a day when Australasian states went from 9 to 12, with the admission of Northern Territory, New Caledonia and Bougainville, the later quite unexpected.

Referendums in the Cook Islands, Tokelau and the Ellice Islands had resulted in all four joining Australasia as external territories under a special arrangement that granted much local autonomy and included provisions where the islanders were classed as Australasian citizens, but the reverse was not true. i.e. Australasians were not citizens of the Ellice Islands external territory as so on.

Both the Gilbert Islands and Nauru had opted for independence, which was due to be granted on 4th September and 1st October, respectively, as had Samoa and Tonga. Papua New Guinea had been granted independence of 1 April and the Solomon Islands on 12th May. Christmas Island was kept as a dependency, as was Cocos, which was forcibly purchased by the government from the Clunes-Ross family after years of mismanagement and abuse of power.

The three new states would not have the same representation as the original nine states of Australasia, a reflection to some extent of their lower populations. Instead of 12 senators, they would have only two senators.

Bougainville had been offered independence as part of either the Solomon Islands or Papua New Guinea but had been steadfast in its refusal of both and in early 1975 Alexis Sarei had petitioned the Australasian government for statehood within Australasia or as an external territory. There was little doubt that the Bougainville people wish to be isolated from their neighbors was only part of the reason, the other being the enormous Panguna copper mine, but, in May 1975 this was agreed and voted upon, with the residents overwhelmingly in favour.

This left the Australasian States as:
State Population Capital
New South Wales 7.01 million Sydney
Victoria 5.78 million Melbourne(Nat Capital)
Queensland 3.11 million Brisbane
North New Zealand 2.31 million Auckland
South Australia 1.97 million Adelaide
Western Australia 1.86 million Perth
South New Zealand 1.01 million Christchurch
Tasmania 0.54 million Hobart
New Caledonia 0.22 million Noumea
Northern Territory 0.19 million Darwin
Bougainville 0.12 million Arawa

Total Population (including external territories) : 24.13 million

12 November 1975 Domain Palace, Melbourne

For Alice, it had been the most difficult thing politically that she had ever done. Gough Whitlam had finally, after a night to think, acquiesced to calling a federal election that had, in any case, shortly been due.

The government had lost control of the Senate and, in the aftermath of the Khemlani loans affair, topped by several government ministerial scandals, the Liberal/National coalition under Robert Muldoon, led in particular by his own deputy Malcolm Fraser, who had threatened Muldoon with a leadership spill if he would not do so, had stopped supply of money bills through the senate for Whitlam's government.

It had quickly developed into a crisis from which there was no retreating and it had required the Queen to indicate directly to Whitlam that if he did not called a double dissolution election immediately that she would be forced to dismiss him as Prime Minister and appoint Muldoon, which she did have the constitutional power to do. She had made this very clear indeed, asking "Do you wish to me the man that brings this countries constitutional structure crashing down and then go to an election asking for the public's vote or do you wish to call an election under your own steam and place your faith in the Australasian public?"

11 February 1980, Domain Palace, Melbourne

Muldoon's government had won a snap election called some nine months early and had gained a second term. It had been a troubling two years with unemployment rising and the 1975 world oil price crisis disrupting many world economies. The government had been returned with a much lower majority and the recent testing of nuclear weapons by Manchuria in late 1979 had made all democratic countries concerned about the level of tension in Asia.

The giant Lake Eyre irrigation scheme had finally been completed after some 15 years and had resulted in greatly increased agricultural possibilities in South East Queensland and Northern New South Wales and had resulted in two 20,000 plus person two towns springing up that had not existed before, Warburton and Emeros Point.

For Alice, now 82, it had been a much longer period than she had anticipated. She now had to wait for her Grandson, almost ten, to reach 18 to hopefully avoid the complications of a Regency.

16 June 1983 Domain Palace, Melbourne

Bob Hawke, was the new Prime Minister, the immensely popular former ACTU Trade Union Leader having swept to power in a landslide election on 2nd June. The Muldoon government, wracked by high unemployment and a series of drunken scandals by their own leader had delivered the coalition's worst ever electoral result, a result that had also witnessed a sharp increase in vote for the Democratic Party, trying to establish itself as the countries third party, that had returned it seven senate seats and a close result in the Melbourne seat of St Kilda. For Alice, both of her sisters had died within 8 months or each other in 1982, her second sister eventually resettling in Melbourne after Greece was to vote for a Republic in 1976.

25 July 1987 Domain Palace, Melbourne

The first few years of the Hawke government had brought many changes, floating the Australasian dollar, the final abolition of the death penalty in 1984, an end to National Service in 1984. Perhaps the biggest changes had been to levels of government at the State and local level. In a bitter battle at local level, the Federal Government, with the support of the mainly State Labor governments, had pushed through reforms to local government that had resulted in mass amalgamations of local government areas in Australasia, with a minimum mandated local government area requiring a population of at least 40,000, subject to certain clauses in regards to area and geography. It had been both revolutionary, controversial and bitterly fought in some areas. It had also been proposed and ratified in 1985 to create an office of Governor-General and to abolish the expense of individual state governors, instead using the Governor-General as the Queen's representative for selected ceremonial events at a state level and as an advisor to the Queen and as someone who would function as regent in the event of the accession of a minor. With modern communications it was seen as a cheaper and easier alternative to having the expense of a Governor in each state.

One movement that had grown greatly in support was the anti-nuclear movement, fuelled by the 3 Mile Island nuclear incident and then magnified by the Chernobyl disaster of 1986. It had resulted in the government announcing the closing of the Port Vincent Reactor and the plans to phase out nuclear weapons in the defence forces.

Australasia's nuclear bomb stocks would be the first to be looked out for disposal, followed by a review of the 66 Blue Streak MRBM sites in the Northern Territory and Western Australia.

For Alice, it was her 90th birthday. Thankfully she had retained her marbles long enough and her grandson was now only eight months away from turning 18 and being able to assume the role that she had been grooming him for the last year. She had seven grandchildren. In Sarawak, her son in law was still King and him and her daughter Maree had five children, James Brooke, Asia Alice, Joshua Alexander, Iona Heloise and Rebecca Alexandra. Here in Australasia her granddaughter Alexandra Alice was 19 and her grandson and heir John Christian was 17.

20 March 1990 Domain Palace, Melbourne

It was the biggest funeral ever seen in Australasia, more than one million people were estimated to line the streets to pay their last respects to the women who had been Queen for 52 years. She had died in her sleep aged 92 after a short illness in the 12 March. Eulogies had been given by all three living Prime Ministers, two past and one present. Bob Hawke, had, of course, cried profusely.

For the new King John I, aged 20 as of only two weeks ago, it was going to be a huge learning curve. He remembered not only her contribution to World War 2 and the changes of her reign, but his own memories, particularly the time spent during her Golden Jubilee in 1987 and during the bicentennial celebrations, which had also been held to celebrate Australasia's 30 millionth citizen.

12 March 2015 St Kilda, Melbourne (flash Forward)

For 27-year-old RAAF Flying Officer Mark Viney it had been a whirlwind few months and the idea of dating the girl who would be one day Queen was still a bit mind blowing. He was still a bit spun out every time he pulled up to Domain Palace. It had been a nice wedding they had both went to, for his sister, and the arrival of Maree, even though guests had been previously aware, had caused somewhat of talking point. It was still a weird feeling being the centre of attention wherever one went. He was now a little buzzed and thinking about the beach tomorrow.

Crown Princess Maree was thinking about the changes the country had gone through, the development. It came from her recently completed Political Science assignment and she had been unable to get it out of her head. Australasia was the world largest coal and iron ore exporter, the largest wool and meat, the second largest of gold, titanium, uranium, lead, copper and alumina, it's population now estimated at 42 million, Melbourne alone having 6.4 million and Sydney 5.6 million.

The country had a strong human rights record, and, in light of the external threats presented by countries such as North Korea and Manchuria, a strong military, it's main fighter the Hornet, which had finally replaced the Avro Arrow on 1998 and was due to be replaced in 2016 by the first F-35's, both within the RAAF and aboard the navy's only and soon to be replaced aircraft carrier, the *ex USS America*, now *HMAS Melbourne* and also the three smaller amphibious carriers of the *Adelaide Class* that were shortly due. She stopped herself from daydreaming. Looking across at Mark, like most 20 years old girls at a wedding, she started daydreaming again. Both her and Australasia would be alright.

RAAF equipment and bases as of 1.1.2016.

Queensland
RAAF Amberley
No 1 Squadron F/A 18-F fighter/bombers

No 6 Squadron F/A 18-F fighter/bombers
No 5 Squadron MQ-9 Reaper Drones
No 33 Squadron KC-30A tankers
No 36 Squadron C-17 Globemaster transport

RAAF Scherger
Bare Base

RAAF Townsville
No 27 Squadron Reserve unit
No 38 Squadron Beechcraft King Air 350 light transport/recon

New South Wales
RAAF Richmond
No 7 Squadron F-35 fighter/bomber
No 35 Squadron CJ37 Spartan light transport
No 22 Squadron Reserve unit
No 37 Squadron C130 Hercules

RAAF Williamstown
No 2 Squadron 737AEW AWACS
No 4 Squadron PC-9 trainer
No 76 Squadron BAE Hawk
No 26 Squadron Reserve unit

Northern Territory
RAAF Darwin
No 10 Squadron C3 Orion
No 8 Squadron F/A -18 fighter

RAAF Tindal
No 75 Squadron F-22 Raptor fighter
No 77 Squadron F-22 Raptor fighter
No 73 Squadron EA-18G Hornet

Western Australia
RAAF Pearce
No 2 Flying Training School
No 25 Squadron Reserve Unit
No 79 Squadron BAE Hawk
No 3 Squadron F/A-18 fighter

RAAF Learmouth
No 13 Squadron 1A1 Huron and M-Q 4C Drones
No 30 Squadron C-17 Globemaster transport
No 34 Squadron C3 Orion

RAAF Curtin
Bare Base

Victoria
RAAF East Sale
No 1 Flight Training School
No 32 Squadron Beechcraft King Air 350 light transport/recon
No 23 Squadron BAE Hawk

RAAF Point Cook
RAAF HQ
No 24 Squadron 737/Learjet VIP travel and RAAF historical flight
No 21 Squadron Reserve unit

South Australia
RAAF Edinburgh
No 10 Squadron C3 Orion
No 9 Squadron P-8 Poseidon

RAAF Woomera
Testing ground and live fire range

RAAF Oodnadatta
No 100 Squadron - Air Force boneyard

North New Zealand
RAAF Auckland
No 11 Squadron F/A-18 fighter
No 12 Squadron C3 Orion
No 19 Squadron C130 Hercules
No 28 Squadron BAE Hawk

RAAF Ohakea
No 3 Flying Training School
No 29 Squadron Reserve unit

South New Zealand
RAAF Wigram
No 20 Squadron FA/18 fighter
No 15 Squadron Beechcraft King Air 350 light transport/recon

Tasmania
Nil

Bougainville
Nil

New Caledonia
RAAF Magenta
No 14 Squadron Beechcraft King Air 350 light transport/recon
No 16 Squadron F/A 18 fighter

Fiji
RAAF Nandi
No 17 Squadron CJ37 Spartan light transport

C-35 to replace all F/A 18 squadrons by 2019

18 March 2015, RAAF Oodnadatta, South Australia

Warrant Officer 1 Brian Sparks was effectively in charge of the logistics of every new arrival at No 100 squadron. There were only five officers present at the whole base despite its size, the C.O Squadron Leader Tennant, a preservation officer, two taxiing officers and a security officer.

His grunts did most of the work, storing preserving and in some cases destroying archived aircraft and, since 1983, tanks and armoured vehicles for the army as well.

The base was spread over 8000 acres or 13 square miles, consisting of a series of interconnected runways, storage sheds and its own train station. The very dryness of the climate assisted in the preservation of the material stored within, which included numbers of out of service RAAF machines, including the huge and recently retired He 166. The current inventory was:

He 166D Tanker 18
He 166E Bomber 44
He 166G EW 5
RF 111 6
Lockheed Neptune 16
Avro Arrow A5 48
De Havilland Caribou 26
Historical: CAC-15 4

Army:
Bell Iroquois 30
Leopard1A5 Tank 55
Hammerhead Tank Destroyer(up armoured Leopard 1 with 120mm gun) 24
M113 APC 308

Navy:
Grumman Trackers 4
Sea King Helicopter 12

Many things came here to die, but generally only the large, big ticket items. Smaller equipment was stored in the respective service's own storage facilities.

Oodnadatta had, for a time, been the home of the Kingdom's nuclear warheads as they had been progressively been decommissioned, stored and then dismantled in that order. This work had finally been completed in 2004, although some of the Blue Streak missiles had been stored as a hedge against their being used for satellite launches.

The days were full of routine and heat and it was not a popular posting. It was, of course, a nonoperational squadron, the only one of its kind aside from Reserve Units. Its aircraft awaited the call to battle that mostly never came, cared for by his own skeleton staff.

Royal Australasian Army Deployments and Equipment 1.1.2016

1st Division(HQ Darwin)

1st Brigade and 12th Brigade, Robertson Barracks, Darwin consisting of one heavy mechanised Brigade and one mixed Brigade

3rd and 7th Brigade, Laverack Barracks, Townsville, Queensland, consisting of one light infantry and one motorised Brigade

15th Combat Support Brigade and 16th Aviation Brigade, Enoggera Barracks, Brisbane, Queensland

2nd Division(HQ Sydney)

4th Brigade and 5th Brigade, Holdsworthy Barracks, Sydney consisting of one heavy mechanised Brigade and one mixed Brigade

6rd and 9th Brigade, Simpson Barracks, Melbourne, Victoria, consisting of one light infantry and one motorised Brigade

10th Combat Support Brigade, Lone Pine Barracks, Singleton, New South Wales

18th Aviation Brigade, Freyburg Barracks, Auckland, North New Zealand

3rd Division(HQ Perth), Reserve aside from 2nd Brigade)

13th Brigade, Karrakatta Barracks, Western Australia
14th Brigade, mixed South Australia and Western Australian Brigade)
2nd Brigade, Karrakatta Barracks, Western Australia, a heavy mechanised Brigade
11th Brigade and 12th Brigade, Victorian and Victorian/Tasmanian Brigades

4th Division(HQ Auckland), Reserve formation

8th Brigade, Freyburg Barracks, Auckland, North New Zealand
17th Brigade, New South Wales
18th Brigade, New South Wales
19th Brigade, Queensland
20th Brigade, South New Zealand, Fiji, New Caledonia, Bougainville

Independent Units:
1st Special Forces Brigade, HQ, Swanbourne, Western Australia
2nd Special Forces Brigade, HQ, Tekapo, South New Zealand

Equipment:
128 M1A1 Abrams
64 Dingo Light Tanks
22 Hammerhead Tank Destroyers
554 AUSLAV's
812 Dingo APC's
2360 Bushmaster PMV's
126 MRH helicopters
114 Eurocopter Tiger helicopters
15 Chinook helicopters
33 PZ 2000 SP Artillery

There was, of course, the RAAF historical flight and museum based at Point Cook, near the active base. The army had co-located its own historical section on the same base. The navy had its own historical section on Garden Island, where the old cruiser *Melbourne*, victor in the Australasian/Indonesian conflict and the last surface conflict between gun only ships lay. Along with a *Snake Class* submarine and two *Bathurst Class* corvettes, she was the centrepiece of the navy's historical display. The *Des Moines Class* cruiser, which had commissioned into the RAN in 1949, was to remain in service until 1996 and in reserve until 2003, being upgraded in 1982 in an expansive refit similar to that of the *Iowa Class* battleships in the USN.

Royal Australasian Army Deployments and Equipment 1.1.2016

Fleet Base East, HMAS Kuttabul, Sydney, New South Wales

2 *Adelaide Class* assault carriers, any combination of up to 18 helicopters or 8 F-35's and 6 helicopters
2 *Auckland Class* destroyers
4 *ANZAC Class* frigates
2 *Perry Class* frigates
1 *Durance Class* tanker
4 *Launceston Class* corvettes
2 Patrol Boats

Fleet Base East, HMAS Stirling, Perth, Western Australia

1 *Adelaide Class* assault carrier, any combination of up to 18 helicopters or 8 F-35's and 6 helicopters
1 *Auckland Class* destroyer
4 *ANZAC Class* frigates
2 *Perry Class* frigates
1 *Durance Class* tanker
2 *Launceston Class* corvettes
4 *Upholder Class* submarines
2 Patrol Boats

Fleet Base Pacific, HMAS Devonport, Auckland, North New Zealand

1 *Adelaide Class* assault carrier, any combination of up to 18 helicopters or 8 F-35's and 6 helicopters
1 *Auckland Class* destroyer4 *ANZAC Class* frigates
6 *Collins Class* submarines
1 *Durance Class* tanker
4 *Launceston Class* corvettes
4 Minesweepers

HMAS Cairns, Cairns, Queensland
8 Patrol boats
2 Survey Vessels

HMAS Coonawarra, Darwin
8 Patrol Vessels
2 Minesweepers

HMAS Suva, Suva, Fiji
4 Patrol Boats
1 Survey Vessel

HMAS Williamstown, Williamstown, Victoria
Reserve Fleet:
Cruiser *HMAS Melbourne*(assigned to reserve fleet but actually opened for public inspection in Sydney)
1 tanker
1 LSD

Appendix 1 - Australasian Leaders

Australasia Monarchs:

1896-1901: Queen Victoria
1901-1910: King Edward VIII
1910-1936: King George V
1936-1937: King Christian
1937-1990: Queen Alice
1990-present: King John

Governors-General
1896-1903: David Boyle, 7th Earl of Glasgow
1903-1936: Prince Christian Victor

Prime Ministers:
1894-1895: Parkes
1895-1897: Barton
1897-1904: Seddon
1904-1904: Watson
1904-1905: Reid
1905-1907: Deakin

1907-1908?: Watson
1908?-1910: Deakin
1910-1915: Fisher
1915-1923: Hughes
1923-1929: Bruce
1929-1935: Scullin
1935-1939: Savage
1939-1945: Curtin
1945-1949: P.Fraser
1949-1971: Menzies
1971-1972: Holyoake
1972-1975: Whitlam
1975-1983: Muldoon
1983-1991 Hawke
1991-1996 Keating
1996-2007 Howard
2007-2013 Rudd
2013 - 2017 Key
2017- Ardern

Appendix 2 - Top 10 countries by total GDP

1) United States
2) China
3) Germany
4) UHE
5) Japan
6) United Kingdom
7) India
9) France
9) Canada
10) Australasia

Made in the USA
Monee, IL
18 December 2019